Advance Praise for *Two Rivers*

"From the moment the train derails in the town of Two Rivers, I was hooked. Who is this mysterious young stranger named Maggie, and what is she running from? In *Two Rivers*, T. Greenwood weaves a haunting story in which the sins of the past threaten to destroy the fragile equilibrium of the present. Ripe with surprising twists and heart-breakingly real characters, *Two Rivers* is a remarkable and complex look at race and forgiveness in small-town America."
—Michelle Richmond, *New York Times* bestselling author of *The Year of Fog* and *No One You Know*

"*Two Rivers* is a convergence of tales, a reminder that the past never washes away, and yet, in T. Greenwood's delicate handling of time gone and time to come, love and forgiveness wait on the other side of what life does to us and what we do to it. This novel is a sensitive and suspenseful portrayal of family and the ties that bind."
—Lee Martin, author of *The Bright Forever* and *River of Heaven*

"T. Greenwood's writing shimmers and sings as she braids together past, present, and the events of one desperate day. I ached for Harper in all of his longing, guilt, grief, and vast, abiding love, and I rejoiced at his final, hard-won shot at redemption."
— Marisa de los Santos, *New York Times* bestselling author of *Belong to Me* and *Love Walked In*

"*Two Rivers* is a stark, haunting story of redemption and salvation. T. Greenwood portrays a world of beauty and peace that, once disturbed, reverberates with searing pain and inescapable consequences; this is a story of a man who struggles with the deepest, darkest parts of his soul, and is able to fight his way to the surface to breathe again. But also—maybe more so—it is the story of a man who learns the true meaning of family: *When I am with you, I am home.* A memorable, powerful work."
—Garth Stein, *New York Times* bestselling author of *The Art of Racing in the Rain*

Turn the page for more outstanding
praise for *Two Rivers*.

"The premise of *Two Rivers* is alluring: the very morning a deadly train derailment upsets the balance of a sleepy Vermont town, a mysterious girl show up on Harper Montgomery's doorstep, forcing him to dredge up a lifetime of memories—from his blissful, indelible childhood to his lonely, contemporary existence. Most of all, he must look long and hard at that terrible night twelve years ago, when everything he held dear was taken from him, and he, in turn, took back. T. Greenwood's novel is full of love, betrayal, lost hopes, and a burning question: is it ever too late to find redemption?"

—Miranda Beverly-Whittemore, author of *The Effects of Light* and the Janet Heidinger Kafka Prize–winning *Set Me Free*

"In the tradition of *The Adventures of Huckleberry Finn* and *To Kill a Mockingbird*, T. Greenwood's *Two Rivers* is a wonderfully distinctive American novel, abounding with memorable characters, unusual lore and history, dark family secrets, and love of life. *Two Rivers* is the story that people want to read: the one they have never read before."

—Howard Frank Mosher, author of *Walking to Gatlinburg*

TWO RIVERS

T. Greenwood

KENSINGTON BOOKS
http://www.kensingtonbooks.com

KENSINGTON BOOKS are published by

Kensington Publishing Corp.
850 Third Avenue
New York, NY 10022

All Kensington titles, imprints and distributed lines are available at special quantity discounts for bulk purchases for sales promotion, premiums, fundraising, educational or institutional use.

Special book excerpts or customized printings can also be created to fit specific needs. For details, write or phone the office of the Kensington Special Sales Manager: Attn. Special Sales Department. Kensington Publishing Corp., 850 Third Avenue, New York, NY 10022. Phone: 1-800-221-2647.

Kensington and the K logo Reg. U.S. Pat. & TM Off.

ISBN-13: 978-0-7582-2877-2
ISBN-10: 0-7582-2877-5

First Printing: January 2009
10 9 8 7 6 5 4 3 2 1

Printed in the United States of America

For Patrick

ACKNOWLEDGMENTS

I would like to give thanks to the following people for their contributions both big and small:

First, to the National Endowment for the Arts and the Christopher Isherwood Foundation, whose generous financial support enabled me to find both the time and space to write this novel. To my family, whose unwavering support has been nothing short of heroic. To Nicole Norum, Ann Marie Houghtailing and Jim Kokoris who read early versions of the novel and said to keep writing. To Penny Patch, who shared with me her remarkable personal experience during Freedom Summer. To Karl Lindholm for all things Middlebury and to Matt Van Hattem and David Warner, who answered all of my questions about trains. To Denise Johnson for dancing on the hood of her car. To Beya Thayer, who told me who Maggie was and what she was doing in Two Rivers (and for everything else too). To my father, Paul Greenwood, who helped me get all the important details right. To the folks at Newbreak Coffee Co. in Ocean Beach, CA, for the good bagels, endless cups of coffee and ocean view. To my students and colleagues at The George Washington University and at The Writer's Center, who teach me something new about writing every day. For the readers of my Mermama blog, who continue to cheer me up and cheer me on. To my extraordinary agent, Henry Dunow, for holding my hand through every step of the revision process, and for believing in this story despite everything. And to Peter Senftleben, who made this all, finally, happen. Lastly, to Patrick for his enormous patience and gigantic heart, and to Kicky and Esmée, whom I love . . . to the bottom of the ocean and back to the top.

"All water has a perfect memory and is forever trying to get back to where it was."

—TONI MORRISON

PROLOGUE

1968: Fall

Blackberries. The man's skin reminds him of late summer black-berries. The color of not-quite midnight. The color of bruise. This is what Harper thinks as he looks at the man they have taken to the river, the one who is half-drowned now, pleading for his life: the mira-cle that human skin can have the same blue-black stillness as ripe fruit, as evening, as sorrow itself.

Of course he also thinks about what you might see (if you were here at the confluence of rivers). Three white boys. One black man, beg-ging to be saved. The harvest moon casting an orange haze over every-thing: just a sepia picture on a lynching postcard like the ones his mother had shown him once. He'd had to look away then, both be-cause the hanged man had no eyes, and because it was the only time he'd seen his mother cry. And he knows that if she were still alive she'd be weeping now too, but not only because of the black man about to die.

It was anger that brought him here. After he understood that Betsy was dead (not wounded, not hurt, but gone), everything else—the grief, the sadness, the horror—became distilled, watery sap boiled down into thick syrup. All that was left then was anger, in its purest form. It was rage that brought him here. But somehow, now, in the cool forest at the place where the two rivers meet, as the man looks straight into Harper's eyes and pleads, the anger is gone. Swallowed up by the night, by old sadness and new regret.

"Please," the man says, and Harper thinks only of black-berries.

He will see this color when he closes his eyes tonight and every night afterward and wonder what, if anything, it has to do with the most despicable thing he's ever done.

1980: Wreckage

People say we are defined by the choices that we make; some of them are easy, small, while others are more difficult. These are the decisions that keep us up at night, forcing us to weigh the pros and cons, to examine what is right and what is wrong. They require us to examine the options, scrutinize the possibilities and potential outcomes. But what about the split-second decision? What about the one made without the luxury of contemplation, the one made from the gut rather than the brain? Does this speak more loudly to who we *really* are? The Chinese philosopher Mencius believed that man is innately good. He argued that anyone who saw a child falling into a well would immediately feel shock and alarm, and that this impulse, this universal capacity for commiseration, was proof positive that man is inherently good. But what about the man who feels nothing? What about the man who stands at the edge of the well and *does* nothing? Who is he? Once, a long time ago, I made a split-second decision that has made me question who I am, what I am capable of, every day since. And this instant, this horrible moment, has haunted every other moment of my life. I don't think I am a bad man, but sometimes I just don't know.

What I *do* know is that, twelve years later, all I wanted was forgiveness. I just needed to make things right, to somehow make amends. Over the years, the sorrow of that night had settled into my bones. Deep inside my joints. In my shoulders. In my hands. I needed absolution. I needed a second chance. I imagined the guilt dissolving like salt in hot water. I imagined it lifting off me, taking flight like a strange and terrible bird. But what I didn't imagine was that my one chance at forgiveness would find its way to me in a train wreck and a pregnant girl with mismatched eyes. But opportunities are often disguised. I know that now.

The night before the wreck, I didn't sleep. After Shelly went to bed, I stayed up, making cupcakes for her to bring to school the next day for her birthday: sad chocolate cupcakes with pink frosting. My efforts at holidays always seemed to fall short of what Shelly really wanted, though she would certainly never say so (store bought Halloween costumes instead of homemade, *homemade* valentines instead of the glossy ones sold at the Rexall, and so many bad cupcakes). Hanna would have made a cake from scratch, inscribed Shelly's name in sweet calligraphy on top. Shelly's great-aunt had taken care of the first eleven birthdays; when my efforts invariably failed, she always quietly stepped in and saved me from whatever disaster I'd made. But now, I was on my own, frosting cupcakes whose middles were as soft as pudding, chocolate crumbs mixing with the pink frosting like gravel. In the morning Shelly would be twelve. *Twelve years.* And I still felt as incompetent as the day I brought her home from the hospital.

Our new apartment was above the bowling alley. We'd lived there since we left Paul and Hanna's house at the beginning of the summer. This too was a temporary situation; I had to keep telling myself that. I wouldn't let the years slip by here, not in a dingy apartment above a bowling alley. I wanted so much more for Shelly.

Moving in with Betsy's aunt and uncle was a decision I had made twelve years ago out of grief and desperation. Alone, with a brand new baby to take care of, I needed someone to keep me from shattering into a thousand pieces. None of us had planned on this lasting forever. But Shelly was happy there, and the years had just sort of passed by. It wasn't until she finished up the sixth grade earlier that summer that I knew it was time to move on. She was too old to be sharing a room with her daddy, and I couldn't help but feel like we'd overstayed our welcome. Our room was drafty and smelled like other people's things. In all the years we'd slept there, Paul and Hanna never managed to move out the broken bureau or the old clothes hanging in the closets, and I never felt right asking them. Of course they offered to let Shelly stay, *wanted* Shelly to stay, but the thought of giving her up too was more than I could bear.

When I found the apartment downtown, I raided my savings account and paid six months' rent in one fell swoop. This was mostly for Hanna. She doubted me, I knew this, and I wanted to prove that I was capable. That we would be fine on our own. And though she adored both Paul and Hanna, Shelly didn't seem to mind leaving much. She took only the clothes that would fit into a small suitcase. She even left some of her belongings behind: a pair of ratty old slippers, a magnifying glass she used to spy on things she found in the river, a piggy bank filled with coins. I guess a child who loses her mother the moment she's born learns not to grow too attached to things.

Besides, the new place had two bedrooms: one of them just for her. The first night there, Shelly stood on the mattress I'd put on the floor in her bedroom with her arms stretched out and spun around until she got too dizzy to stand. "I love it, love it, love it!" she said. And I felt for the first time in a long time that I'd done something right. She fell asleep before I even had a chance to put sheets on the mattress. Below us, the rolling balls and the crashing pins were an odd lullaby.

Tonight, I knew that between the heat of Indian summer and the sounds of the bowling alley below, sleep would once again pass me by. And so I resigned myself to wakefulness, figured I'd spend the night as I spent most every night lately: sitting on the roof looking at the cool shimmering green of the public pool across the street, closed for the summer now, while Shelly slept in the other room.

I poked my head in to check on her. A few weeks earlier, when summer came back, I'd put our only fan in her room. It whirred in the window, making the curtains billow out like ghosts. She was flat on her back and fast asleep, wearing one of my old Middlebury T-shirts and the gum wrapper necklace she never took off.

I quietly closed her door and went down the hall to the window, which led to my rooftop refuge. Even at almost midnight, the tar paper still held some of the sun's warmth, and the air was thick. Across the street, the water in the pool was still. Shelly's birthday again, and here it was: another batch of sad cupcakes. Another week of restless nights. I was kidding myself blaming my unease on the heat. It wasn't the heat at all but rather the passing of another year. It was that Shelly had outgrown another pair of sneakers, another winter coat. It was that she didn't need me to tie her shoes or brush her hair: each small milestone a cruel reminder that life was going on. Moving forward. She was growing up. And each year she grew older, Betsy was that much further away. A child's birthday should never be the anniversary of her mother's death.

Betsy. Before this, before I knew the color of the sky at three A.M., before I knew the sound of a child sleeping—before I knew the fear of being entirely alone as the world slept—there was Betsy. Her name found its way to my lips on those waking nights, and I practiced their syllables as if I were reciting a poem or a prayer. She was always there. Before this, I had not known the world without her in it.

I looked for Betsy in Shelly. And sometimes I found her there: in the lazy blinking of her eyes, in a sigh, in a blush. But more often than not, in searching for Betsy, I only found myself. Shelly had my awkward long limbs, my pale skin, the same squinty blue eyes. She was almost *twelve* now—the same age that Betsy was when I first fell in love with her. But no matter how hard I looked at Shelly's face, Betsy simply wasn't hiding there.

Twelve years.

My rooftop reveries inevitably ended with thoughts of Betsy. It didn't matter if I tried to concentrate on other things (the house for sale on Finney Ridge, the Sox's recent loss to the Yankees, the John Fowles novel I was reading), my mind always found its way—no matter how circuitous the route—back to her. And as Shelly's birthday approached, the journey back to Betsy Parker became less and less oblique. I'd start out considering what the mortgage might be on that three-bedroom Cape and wind up thinking about something Betsy once said about wanting to own a home that had an orange tree out front. (I hadn't had the heart to tell her that oranges almost never grow in northeastern Vermont.) If I started out with baseball, I saw Betsy yanking Ray's old Sox cap off his head and putting it on her own. It had covered her eyes, and we all laughed. And when I thought about that novel, the one where a collector of butterflies falls in love with a stranger and decides to first kidnap and then keep her, I began to wonder if Betsy ever felt like that: like a captured butterfly.

And here she was again tonight, curling up next to me on the roof. Waiting with me until the sun rose, insistent, over Depot Street. I left her only when I sensed that Shelly was stirring, that the day I'd been dreading had arrived.

Shelly came out of her room as I was making coffee. She rubbed her eyes and then spied the cupcakes sitting on the counter.

"I hope they're okay," I said. "The middles might be kind of soft."

She smiled at me in that sad way she had and picked one of

them up. She licked the frosting off the top and said gently, "Thanks, Daddy, but I'm kinda too old to bring cupcakes to school now." And then, because she probably thought she'd hurt my feelings, she peeled the paper cup off the cupcake and popped half of it in her mouth. "Mmm. It's really, really good, Dad."

In my pocket was the gift I'd bought for her: a pair of glittery barrettes. I had planned to give them to her at breakfast, but decided then to wait, suddenly certain that the gift was all wrong. I didn't want to let her down again. I'd have to stop at Kinsey's after work. Maybe a charm bracelet would be better. A pair of earrings. A watch.

I was grateful for the morning's rituals (making coffee, getting myself dressed and Shelly fed, packing our lunches) as well as for the morning's unexpected events (a lack of hot water, milk gone sour in the fridge and a missing sock). Sometimes I felt like the mundane details of our lives were the only things tethering me to the world. I could hold onto them—distractions necessitating action. They gave me a sense of purpose. If not for the leaky faucet, the sandwiches, the bills, I might not know what to do with my hands.

Shelly kissed my cheek and then walked down the hallway to our neighbor's apartment as I watched her from our doorway. Mrs. Marigold, an elderly widow, took care of Shelly before and after school, while I was at work. Shelly insisted that I not use the word "sitter," and especially not "*baby*sitter" when referring to Mrs. Marigold. But, whatever her job title, she made sure Shelly got to the bus stop. That she had a place to go after school. In exchange, I ran errands for her: buying groceries, depositing her husband's pension checks at the bank, that kind of thing. She used to be a nurse, probably a hundred years ago, but this made me feel somehow safe.

"Happy birthday!" I called after her.

"Thanks, Daddy," she said over her shoulder, and skipped down the hall.

I had to leave for work earlier than I would have if I were driving, but as long as the weather permitted, I preferred to ride my bike. Most of the time, I left my car parked in the alley behind our building; I didn't drive unless I had to anymore. After Betsy died, the world started to seem like a dangerous place. Every time I got behind the wheel, especially with Shelly in the car, I couldn't help but envision every horrible thing that might happen. Every catastrophe. And so I'd opted instead for a bicycle, a J.C. Higgins three speed, which I knew had seen better days. I bought it at the Methodist Church rummage sale for five dollars and fifty cents. The spokes were rusted, and the seat was stuck at an elevation reserved for a taller man than I; even at 6 feet 4 inches, I had to stand on the pedals as I rode to avoid the unfortunate angle of the seat. But despite the inadequacy of the bike, there was something perfect about the two-mile journey to the railroad station each morning. In a month or so, when snow came and I had to negotiate my old VW Bug through the snow, I'd miss these mornings: the rushing air, the burning in my calves as I pedaled up the winding hill. The ride usually cleared my head, invigorated me, but today nothing could dispel the awful disquiet I was feeling.

By the time I got to work, I was antsy, like I'd had too much coffee. Too little sleep. I tried to look forward to the daily tasks, to losing myself in a stack of invoices, the bills of lading. I had been working at the freight office at the railroad station since I was twenty-two years old. I'd worked my way up, as much as you can in a place like this, and was now the freight traffic manager. It was hardly the job I'd thought I'd wind up with, but my ambition, like everything else, sort of flew out the window when Betsy died. I had never planned to make this job my career, but here I was. And I have to admit, there was a small but certain satisfaction when the numbers balanced out at the end of the day, the week, the month. At least there was order here. Predictability.

While I waited for the night shift to end, I sat at the grimy table in the break room thumbing through the previous Sunday's *Free Press* and grabbed a doughnut from a box that somebody's wife must have dropped off. *It's just another day*, I thought. But just as I was about to take a bite of the doughnut and look in the sports section to see whether or not Boston had won Saturday's game, Rene LaFevre, one of the French Canadian car knockers, came rushing through the door.

"Down by da river," he said, breathless. "Dere's people everywhere. Some's drowned. And the ones that ain't drowned are bleeding half to death. You gotta come wid me."

Though it was almost October, the air was muggy and thick, not the normal crisp prelude to autumn. I could feel the hot, wet air in my lungs as I rode behind Rene on my bike, following the tracks out of the train yard toward the river. In the woods, the scent of apples was thick, nauseating. Apples had ripened with the first signs of fall and then rotted in the heat, their small suicides leaving only sad remains, pulp and empty brown skin littering the ground beneath our feet. I dodged them like land mines while Rene plodded and plundered through the rotten mess. Rene, who had to have weighed close to two hundred fifty pounds, had to stop several times to catch his breath. I waited as he bent at the waist, clutching his chest.

"You okay?" I asked.

Too winded to speak, he nodded. But despite Rene's obvious exhaustion, we kept traveling further along the river's edge, early morning sunlight struggling through the thick foliage.

Teacups. The first thing that I saw were about a dozen perfect china teacups floating along in the current, bobbing and dipping downstream: some with rims lipstick-kissed, some still filled with tea now mixing with river water, *all* of them disengaged from their saucers. In the hazy sun, it was almost beautiful, only a floating tea party. Before I saw the wreckage, I saw this.

Then, with a gesture that struck me as almost grand, Rene motioned toward the place where the woods opened up, where the train had jumped the tracks. It had derailed just after the bridge, and one of the rear cars had fallen into the river. The early morning sun glinted in the silver metal of the train, in the broken glass, and in the water. The other cars were tipped on their sides, bloodied people crawling out of the broken windows and doors. Some passengers sat stunned and silent on the bank of the river, while others screamed.

"My baby," a woman wailed, futile in her attempt to climb the embankment where a child lay motionless on the grass. Her feet kept slipping, her fingers clawing at the earth. She looked up at us and screamed, *"Why?"* Rene reached for her hand and, bracing himself, helped her up the hill. She staggered across the grass and then collapsed on top of her child, her whole body shaking.

I turned toward the river, paralyzed. I could feel my pulse beating in my neck, in my temples. I willed the other thoughts out of my head, the other disasters.

"Dere's people stuck inside," Rene said to me, grabbing hold of my arm, as if to wake me from sleep. "You got to go in dere."

Rene went to a woman who was beating her fists on the window of a wrecked car, and I rushed blindly down the riverbank to the car that had tumbled into the river. The water was cold and smelled swampy. It soaked my work clothes, the weight of water like the weight of deep sleep. Remarkably, the car was still upright. I shielded my eyes against the sun and scanned the row of windows looking to see if anyone was trying to get out. I fought against the current, holding on to a fallen tree so as not to get swept away. There were several shattered windows; I made my way to the closest one and hoisted myself up into it. I swung my leg over the edge and lowered myself into the car, where I was waist-deep in the water again. Inside, I saw more teacups as well as white tablecloths floating in the water. Plates and soup bowls, water and wineglasses. I pushed through the water using the dining tables for leverage.

"Hello?" I hollered, but my ears were filled with the sound of the river. "Is anybody in here?" I made my way from one end of the dinette car to the next, my legs shaking with the effort and the cold. I could see the narrow serving area and the entrance to Le Pub, the lounge car. "Hello?" I said again, louder this time.

I fought my way to the far end of the car and looked for another open window. My hand throbbed with the beat of my heart. There was no one here. But just as I was about to hoist myself out of the water, I saw something through the window into the next car. I pried the doors open and stepped through into the lounge. An upright piano was floating in the water, bobbing and dipping in the current as the river rushed through the windows. Relieved, I turned to go back. And then out of the corner of my eye, I saw something else.

The porter's black and white uniform was fanned out like a nun's habit; his head was immersed in water, his arms outstretched. The dead man's float. Shelly had learned how to play dead at the public pool that summer. I'd watched all of the children in her swim class floating like toys in the water. It had given me a sick feeling in my stomach then. Now, my stomach turned again. I was shaking badly. It felt like the river was inside me, cold and wet. Unforgiving. I went to the man as quickly as the river would allow, and gently rolled him over.

His face was bloated, pale blue and swollen. At the sight of his face, I turned away, feeling bile rising in my throat, and I vomited into the river water. I turned back to the man and felt the shivering turning into something more like a small convulsion. I had the momentary impulse to give in to the current. I was so full of the river by then I could have just let it carry me away. But something inside of me pulled me out of the wreckage, back into the water, and slowly, slowly, up onto the muddy shore, where I could barely feel my legs.

The police and the town's only ambulance had finally arrived. The emergency vehicles were parked cockeyed and tilted on the grassy shore. The red and blue lights swirling and humming reminded me of a carnival. Of a midway. Of some terrible ride.

There were other drowned people. Their bodies lay along the river's edge, a morbid picnic. There was so much blood; the grass beneath my feet was slick with it. Children cried in their parents' and strangers' arms; the air was loud with the sound of sirens and screaming. I recognized faces but could not connect the faces with names. I concentrated instead on teacups, a hundred bobbing teacups, and I made my way out of the river. I climbed the bank, my boots and eyes filled with water, walking and walking until I couldn't hear the sirens or see the train. About a hundred yards from the accident, I sat down under a great willow tree, exhausted, and put my face in my hands. I was fatigued, delirious. I blinked hard against the exhaustion and all of the pictures on the backs of my palms and on the backs of my eyes. But no matter how hard I tried, all I saw was the dead man's face, and every breath reminded me of the other man I'd left for dead in this river.

I could have been there minutes or hours. The lack of sleep seemed to make time mutable. I could barely keep track of it anymore. Entire days went by sometimes without my noticing. Months could have passed while I sat at the river's edge. Seasons changed.

I lifted my head only when I sensed someone standing in front of me. The sun was bright behind her, but I could make out the silhouette of a young girl, maybe sixteen, seventeen years old, her belly swollen like an egg. An apparition. A cruel trick of my mind, intent on its return, as always, to Betsy. Her name found its way to my throat but not through my lips. I squinted against the sun and quickly realized that this was not a ghost, *not Betsy*, but a real girl. A girl with skin the color of blackberries, holding a suitcase, her hair dripping river water onto my legs.

"What's your name?" she asked, her accent jarring me, clearly placing her far away from home.

"Harper," I answered, standing up awkwardly, as if I were only going to shake her hand.

"Harper," she said. And then she pressed her tiny hand against her swollen stomach, a gesture I could never forget. "Please," she said. "You gotta help me, sir. My mama's dead. I got nowhere to go."

What happened after this (the moments that followed, the months that followed) I can only explain as the acts of a man so full of sorrow he'd do just about anything to get free of it. Here I was at the river again, with only a moment to decide. *Forgiveness.* For twelve years, I'd only wanted to say I was sorry, but before this there was no one left alive to offer my apologies to.

"Please," she said again.

And this time, I didn't turn away.

ONE

Two Rivers

There aren't *really* two rivers in Two Rivers, Vermont. There's the Connecticut, of course (single-minded with its rushing blue-gray water), but the other river is really just a wide and quiet creek. Where they intersect, now that's the real thing. Because the place where the creek meets the Connecticut, where the two strangely different moving bodies of water join, is the stillest place I've ever seen. And in that stillness, it almost seems possible that the creek could keep on going, minding its own business, that it might emerge on the other side and keep on traveling away from town. But nature doesn't work that way, doesn't allow for this kind of deviation. What must (and does) happen is that the small creek gets caught up in the big river's arms, convinced or coerced to join it on its more important journey.

The girl was shivering, her arms wrapped around her waist, her hands clutching her sides. Her teeth were chattering. They were small teeth in a tidy row, like a child's.

I peeled off my flannel shirt, which was the driest thing I had on me, and offered it to her. She accepted the shirt, awkwardly pulling it on. The sleeves hung over her hands; she almost disappeared inside it when she sat down.

"What's your name?" I asked softly. She was like a wounded animal, knees curled to her chest and trembling.

"Marguerite," she said, shaking her head.

"Your mother's dead?" I asked.

The girl looked down at her hands and nodded.

"Was she on the train?"

She kept looking at the ground.

"Where were you going?" I asked.

"Up north," she said.

"Canada?"

She looked up at me then, water beaded up and glistening on her eyelashes. She nodded. "Canada."

"Do you know somebody up there?"

She looked toward the woods, chattering. "I got an aunt," she said.

"Well, let's get back to my house and you can give her a call. Let her know you're okay," I offered.

"It ain't like that," she said, shaking her head.

"What do you mean?"

"I mean, she don't know I'm coming. My daddy . . ." Her voice trailed off.

"Can we call *him*?"

"No!" she said loudly, shaking her head. And then she reached for my hand. "He sent me away. My mama's dead. I ain't got nobody."

"Okay, okay," I said, trying to sort everything out in my mind.

"We need to go to the station, let them know you're alive. Then they can get in touch with your aunt and we'll get you on the next train. And if she can't take you, we'll go to the police. They'll talk to your daddy. He's your father. He has obligations."

"No!" she cried again, squeezing my hand hard. "*Please.* Maybe I can just stay a little while. I can't go back there. I can't." Her eyes were wild and scared. One was the same color as river water, blue-gray and moving. The other was almost black. Determined. Like stone. "Let them think I drowned."

"You can't just pretend you're dead."

"Why not?" she asked, both of her eyes growing dark.

I flinched. "Two Rivers is a small town. People are going to wonder where you came from."

"Maybe I'm your cousin," she said, her eyes brightening. She wiped her tears with the back of her hand. "Your cousin from Louisiana."

I raised my eyebrow. "I don't have any cousins from Louisiana."

"From Alabama then. I don't know. Mississippi," she persisted, clearly irritated.

"Listen," I said. "I'm not sure folks are going to buy the idea that you and I are *family*."

The girl looked square at me, studying my face, as if contemplating the possibility herself.

"I've got a little girl," I said. "I can't just bring a stranger into my house."

At the mention of Shelly, the girl reached out and grabbed my wrist, pressed my hand hard against her pregnant belly. When I pulled my hand back, she held onto my wrist, and she moved toward me. She was so close to my face I could smell the bubble gum smell of her breath. Her eyes were frantic, and she quickly pressed her lips against my forehead. It was such a tender gesture, it made me suck in my breath.

"I won't be any trouble. I promise," she said.

She looked at me again, and I willed myself to look into those disconcerting eyes. I concentrated on the blue one, the one the color of the river, waiting for her to speak. But she didn't say anything else; she simply took my hand and waited for me to take her home.

"You can stay for a little while, just until we get everything straightened out." And then, because she looked as if she might cry, "I promise, everything will be okay."

★   ★   ★

"Thank you," the girl whispered, though it could have just been the wind rushing in my ears. She was riding on the back of my bicycle as I pedaled away from the accident at the river, through the woods, and back toward town. She held on to my waist tightly, her heartbeat hard and steady against my back. I was careful to avoid anything that might jar her or send us tumbling. We didn't speak; the only sound was of bicycle tires crushing leaves. I worried about what would happen when I stopped pedaling, when the journey out of the woods inevitably ended, and so I concentrated on finding a clear and unobstructed path through the forest, taking great care to slow down when the terrain grew rough. Too quickly, the woods opened up to the high school parking lot.

I stopped. "If it's okay with you, I should probably leave you here and have you meet me at the apartment," I said. "Not the best idea for people to see us riding through town together."

She climbed carefully down from the seat. She set the small suitcase she had with her onto the pavement, straightened her skirt, and touched her wet hair self-consciously. When she took off my shirt and handed it to me, I thought for a moment that she was going to let me go. I imagined pedaling away as fast as I could. I imagined forgetting all about her, about the wreck, about the river. But instead, I stayed on the bicycle, unsure of what to do next. I gripped the handlebars tightly, ready to go, but immobilized.

The lot was full of cars but empty of students and teachers. We were bound to be discovered by some kid ditching class or sneaking a smoke.

"This a high school?" she asked, looking at the low brick building in front of us. At the football field in the distance.

"Yeah," I said. It was *my* high school, unchanged in all the years since I'd graduated. I knew every brick in this building's walls. Every vine of ivy clinging to them. I knew the smell of the cafeteria vent on a cold autumn afternoon, the sound of the bell announcing the beginning of the day.

"No one will think nothin' of it if they see me here then?" she asked.

I shook my head, though I wasn't sure what someone would make of this girl, this dark-skinned girl, dripping wet and pregnant in the high school parking lot. While it had its share of matriculated expectant mothers, Two Rivers High had seen all of two black students in the last two decades.

"Walk that way," I said, motioning toward the road that would wind behind the school and ultimately down into the village where I lived. "I live on Depot Street. Upstairs, above Sunset Lanes Bowling Alley. Number two. I'll be waiting. I'll make you some soup or something. Then we'll figure out what to do."

I stood up on the pedals and pushed off, looking over my shoulder at her briefly, and then rode away as fast as my tired legs would allow. I should have gone home. It wouldn't take her long to walk from the high school into the village. I knew the apartment was in no condition for company, and that the folks at work were probably wondering where I'd gone. But my bike seemed to have a will of its own, carrying me away from the high school, down the winding road toward town, and then onto the little dead-end street I hadn't visited in more than twelve years. As if Betsy would simply be waiting there, ready to help me figure out what to do next.

Betsy

The neighborhood in Two Rivers where Betsy and I grew up was made up of row after row of crooked Victorians—crumbling monstrosities sinking in upon themselves. Each house on Charles Street had its own peculiar tendencies. The one next-door to ours had a widow's walk whose railing had, unprovoked by either natural or unnatural disaster, collapsed into a pile of pick-up sticks on the lawn below one afternoon. The family who lived at the end of the street had the misfortune of owning a house that wouldn't stay painted. No matter what pastel color they chose each summer, by the following spring it would have shrugged off the pink or yellow or lavender, the paint peeling and curling like old skin. My own family's house was tilted at a noticeable angle; if you put a ball on the kitchen floor and let go, it would roll straight into the dining room (through the legs of the heavy wooden table), past my mother's study, and finally into the living room where the pile of my father's failed inventions inevitably stopped the ball's trajectory. Most of the homeowners in our neighborhood had at some point given up, resigning themselves to sinking foundations and roofs. To the inevitable decay. There simply wasn't the time or the money or the love required to keep the places up. This was a street of sad houses. Except for the Parkers' place.

Though it was one of the oldest homes in the neighborhood, the Parkers' house was meticulously maintained. Its paint was fresh: white with green shutters and trim. Its chimney was straight. The cupola sat like an elaborate cake decoration on top of the house. A clean white fence enclosed the front yard, which looked exactly as the town barber's yard should. Rosebushes bordered the uncracked walkway, and other flowers littered the periphery of the yard in meditated disarray. A swing hung still and straight on the front porch, and the porch light came on without fail or flicker each night at dusk. On a street of forlorn houses, the Parkers' made the other houses look like neglected children.

Of course, I knew Betsy Parker long before I loved her. We had lived on the same street since we were born. Our fathers nodded at each other as they went off to work each morning. Our mothers made polite small talk when they saw each other at the market. Betsy and I had knocked heads once during a game of street hockey, the result of which were two identical blue goose eggs on our respective foreheads. In the sixth grade, we had been the last two standing in a spelling bee (though I'd ultimately won with the word *lucid*). But in the summer of 1958, when we were twelve, our relationship changed from one necessitated by mere proximity into a full-blown crush— on my part anyway; she didn't love me then. In fact, she didn't love me for a long, long time. But that summer the seed was planted, and my unrequited passion, like all the other untamed weeds in our yard, grew to epic and tangled proportions by summer's end.

When school let out in June, I'd taken up fishing, drawn by a local legend that, on a good day, the spot where the two rivers meet was teaming with rainbow trout. But by July I'd spent entire days with my line in the water, and I still had yet to catch a single trout (or any other kind of fish for that matter). The day I found myself smitten by Betsy, I'd also spent fishing, and, once again, I hadn't caught anything but a cold. I'd meant to go home. I thought I might take a snooze in the hammock in our backyard. But instead of walking down the shady side of Depot Street to the tracks and then heading up the hill toward home, I crossed the street, into the sun. Once there, I stood in front of her, rendered mute.

Orange Crush and skinned knees. This was Betsy at twelve. I'd walked past Betsy Parker a thousand times before. A thousand bottles of Orange Crush. A thousand Band-aids. But that day, as I strolled past her daddy's barbershop, there she was, with fresh scabs on both golden knees, and it felt like I was seeing her for the very first time. I'm not sure which made me dizzier–the twirling red, white and blue barber pole or Betsy. Can I remember the way I saw her then? You'd think it would be hard after all these years, but it isn't. Perhaps I was memorizing her before I even knew I should. Here's the way she looked to me in June when we were twelve: her fingers were long, her legs longer, stretched out on the steps of her daddy's shop where she sipped her soda through a straw. Her tongue was stained orange, and her hair was like syrup running down her back. (I remember touching my tongue to my lips when I saw her.)

Betsy sipped long and thoughtfully. Then she leaned toward me and looked into my empty bucket. "Whadja catch?"

I felt heat rising to my ears. "Not much today."

"Yesterday?"

"Not much yesterday either."

"Why do you bother?" she asked. "If you don't ever catch anything?"

I shrugged.

"You're probably the kind who sees the glass half full." She sighed and sipped the last of her soda pop loudly. "Not me, I'm a half-empty kind of girl."

I didn't know what she meant, only that she thought we were somehow fundamentally different, and this made my heart ache.

"You live on my street," I said stupidly.

"You live on *my* street." She smiled, setting the amber-colored bottle on the pavement between us. She stuck one bare foot out in front of her and spun the bottle with her toe. It clanked and spun and stopped, its neck pointing right at me.

I didn't know what to say, so I bent over and picked the bottle up. The glass was still cold. I dropped it into my empty bucket, as if that could make up somehow for my failure as a fisherman. "That's worth two cents."

"Coulda been worth a lot more than that," she said, smiling.

I walked home that day with Betsy Parker's Orange Crush bottle clanging against the inside of my bucket. From my bedroom window I could see the pristine facade of the Parkers' house, their immaculate lawn. I felt like an idiot. First, because I'd missed what I quickly realized was a chance at kissing Betsy. And second, because twelve whole years had already passed before I realized that she'd been there all along. Right across the street. I took the bottle out and held it to my lips. The glass was sticky, sweet. I tipped the empty bottle, leaning my head back, waiting for the last sweet drops to fall into my throat.

After that day, I gave up my fishing trips in favor of a *new* futile endeavor, one that would last longer than most boys my age would have had patience for. But Betsy was right, I was a "half-full" kind of person, and I had high hopes. I knew I'd get a second chance; it was just a matter of time.

The Girl

I only stood in front of the Parkers' house long enough to know I shouldn't be there. The house had recently been painted, and the lawn was trimmed, the hedges clipped. There was a new family living here. A child was peering out at me through the bay window. Soon, the child's mother opened the curtains and, seeing me, quickly drew the curtains shut. I got back on the bike and pedaled quickly home.

By the time I'd climbed the stairs to my apartment, I wondered if I'd only dreamed the girl at the river, a hallucination brought on by too many nights without sleep. I changed out of my wet clothes, made a pot of coffee, and called the freight office to say I'd been at the wreck all morning—that I'd come by the office in a few hours. Only Lenny Herman, the station agent, was there. Everyone else was still down by the river. When almost an hour had passed and she still hadn't appeared, I was fairly certain that I'd only imagined her. I started to gather my things to head back to work, when there was a weak knock on my door.

She stood in the kitchen holding her wet shoes in one hand and the dripping suitcase in the other. I motioned for her to sit down at the kitchen table, but she shook her head.

"Oh, I'm sorry, would you like to dry off?" I asked. "There are some clean towels in the bathroom. I can get some dry clothes."

She nodded and set her wet shoes down by the door. I figured I could find something of Shelly's that would fit her. She followed behind me slowly down the short hallway, stopping to look at the pictures hanging on the wall. Shelly's class pictures. Our wedding photo. She touched the top of the frame, gently straightening it. I grabbed a pair of sweatpants and a T-shirt from Shelly's drawer and handed them to her. She took them and disappeared into the bathroom.

I quickly assessed the state of my house, untidy still from the morning's chaos. There were dirty dishes on the table (cereal bowls with colored milk, glasses rimmed with orange pulp). Shelly's shoes were scattered all over the floor, which needed to be swept. I'd splattered chocolate batter on the backsplash when I made Shelly's cupcakes, but I hadn't noticed until now. I grabbed a dishrag and wiped at the mess in a useless attempt to make the kitchen less of a disaster. I was wringing it out in the sink when she came out of the bathroom.

"You're out of toilet tissue," she said.

"I am?" I asked, embarrassed. "I'm sorry. Let me see if I can find some." Though I knew there was no toilet paper, that the last time Shelly went to the bathroom I'd given her a paper coffee filter to use, I went to the bathroom, searched through the linen closet, under the sink. Nothing. "I'm out," I said, returning to the kitchen. "I can get you something, if you still need . . ."

"Nah. I'm okay. But I'm in the bathroom every ten minutes or so, so I might need something soon." She was sitting at the kitchen table drinking from my cup of coffee.

"I'll just run down the street," I said, checking my pocket for change. "I won't be more than a minute."

She sipped on the coffee and closed her eyes.

I charged down the stairs, two at a time, not considering, until I reached the drugstore, the ramifications of leaving a total stranger sitting at my kitchen table.

"You been down to the wreck?" the clerk asked. "They're saying a hundred people are dead."

"It's a pretty bad accident."

"Some folks," he whispered conspiratorially, "are saying it ain't an accident at all. My uncle's got a scanner. Picks up *everything*."

"How much do I owe you?" I asked, eager to get back to my apartment.

"Fifty cents," he said, reaching under the counter for a bag. "I'm going down there as soon as my shift lets out."

"Thanks," I said, grabbing the toilet paper, and rushed back to my apartment.

When she wasn't in the kitchen, I felt something sink inside me, and a sort of panic set in. I set the toilet paper on the kitchen table and peered down the dark hallway. I opened the door to my bedroom and to Shelly's room. Nothing. I returned to the kitchen and went into the living room, my heart racing.

I'd been too out of it that morning to even pull the blinds; the room was completely dark except for the dusty rays of light shining through the cracks in the shades. I flicked on the overhead lamp worried that this room too would be empty. And so I was startled when I looked down to see the girl curled up on the couch, clutching the green afghan Hanna had made for Shelly's last birthday. I felt my body sigh, my limbs relax.

In sleep, she looked even younger than she had at the river. Sixteen at the oldest, I imagined. She was holding the edge of the afghan against her cheek with one hand like a child would. Her other hand was cradling her rounded stomach, which poked out from under Shelly's T-shirt.

I looked at my watch. It was nearly eleven o'clock already. Only four hours until Shelly would be home from school. I worried that if she saw my bicycle out front she'd come straight to our apartment rather than going to Mrs. Marigold's next-door. And there still was the matter of work. I paced around the living room, trying to figure out what to do about the girl sleeping on my couch, until she stirred.

"You can go back to work," she said softly. "I ain't going to steal nothin'."

"I *know* that," I said, stung.

As she slept, I went next-door to Mrs. Marigold's and told her that my third cousin, a relative of my mother's, by marriage, my *adopted* cousin from Louisiana, had just come visiting, that she was sleeping on my couch. Mrs. Marigold stood with her hands on her hips, scowling at me as she abandoned a pile of half-peeled potatoes. I told her about the train wreck, that my cousin had gotten off the train unharmed, but that she was exhausted from the trauma of it, and that I was headed back to work and maybe back to the river to help out with the accident if they needed me. And finally, when she looked at me, confused not only by my convoluted story but by why I was telling it to her at all, I asked her if she could make sure Shelly got a good dinner tonight. That she did her homework. That I might be later than usual but that I would be by to pick her up after supper. Mrs. Marigold smiled and picked up the potato peeler. "Honey, don't you worry yourself about Shelly. You come by to get her whenever you want."

I checked on the girl one more time, and she was still asleep. I pulled the afghan gently up over her and turned off the light again. I found her pile of wet clothes on the bathroom floor and put them in the dryer. The wet fabric slapped around the inside of the machine, thumping rhythmically as I locked her inside the apartment and bounded down the stairs. I would figure out what to do after I got home. Maybe by then the girl would be having second thoughts and would call her father. She was probably still in shock about the accident. A good rest was probably all she needed. Some dinner. Some nice warm, dry clothes.

The Folding Machine

In the summer of 1958, my father set out to invent a machine that would automatically fold freshly laundered clothes. Most of his inventions were aimed at making my mother's life easier. She was an accidental housewife, a college graduate and once-aspiring musician whose life took a turn for the ordinary, as many extraordinary women's lives did, when she fell in love. My father's efforts at easing the burden of laundering and dishwashing and floor scrubbing were like small apologies for something understood but unspoken between them.

My mother, Helen Wilder, met Charlie Montgomery at Middlebury College, where Charlie, my father, was studying engineering, and she, music. They married not long after they graduated and, despite more grandiose plans, moved to Two Rivers when my grandmother died, leaving them the house that my father had grown up in. Convinced that they might be able to save some money before moving on, my mother agreed to spend the first few years of their married life in Two Rivers. My father accepted a job at the Two Rivers Paper Company, and my mother taught piano. But when she became pregnant with me, she must have known that her tenure in Two Rivers would last more than a few years. And before she knew it, I figure, she had probably resigned herself to bake sales instead of classical performances—to the quotidian life of a New England housewife instead of the glamour of a concert pianist's.

The truth was, though I adored my mother, I was also embarrassed by her. She wasn't like anybody else's mother. Not my best friend, Ray's, not Betsy's either. She was fluent in French (*Parisian* French, she emphasized, not the *bastardized* French of Two Rivers's French Canadian population), and she had even been to France as a foreign exchange student while in college. She was constantly using French vocabulary when English, in her opinion, would not suffice. This, like much about my mother, was upsetting to the regular people in Two Rivers. First of all, she hadn't taken my father's name when she got married, convincing many people that they weren't married at all but simply living in sin. She didn't cook and she didn't know how to sew. She wrote angry letters to the editor of the local paper and she refused to wear skirts. And, perhaps worst of all, instead of reading *Redbook* or *Ladies' Home Journal*, she had the Rexall order one issue of *The New York Times* every week. This would have been fine, except that she insisted on picking it up each Sunday morning when everyone else was just getting out of church and stopping at the drugstore for their Sunday sundries. Thanks to *The New York Times*, everyone in Two Rivers knew that Helen Wilder did not believe in God.

Betsy's mother, on the other hand, had learned everything she *knew* from magazines: glorious glossy magazines that were spread out in full-colored fans on every end table in the house. She made cupcakes that looked like witches at Halloween and robin's nests at Easter. Mrs. Parker believed wholeheartedly in God and went to church every Sunday in dresses she made herself from crinkly patterns that smelled like dust. Later, Betsy would let me hold the fragile parchment only after I'd washed my hands.

The summer that we were twelve, I fell in love twice. First with Betsy Parker, and then with her mother.

For a whole week after I'd spoken to Betsy outside her father's barbershop, I'd been trying to come up with an excuse to go see her again. I didn't need a haircut, or else I would have just returned to the barbershop. My father considered himself a competent lay barber and methodically cut my hair on the last day of every month (outside so as to avoid getting any hair on the floors, which already generated near tumbleweed-sized dust balls). Finally, after much rumination, I concocted a story about needing to borrow sugar.

It was a typical Saturday; my mother was curled up on the overstuffed chair in our living room lost inside a book, and my father was in the basement working on his folding machine. It had to have been eighty degrees outside, but my parents were *inside* people. Especially in the summer. My mother abhorred the sun, and my father preferred his basement workshop to the outdoors. As soon as I was allowed to operate the lawn mower, I took it upon myself to tend to the overgrown and unruly chaos that was our yard, but then, when I was only twelve and not allowed to touch anything with a motor, I made my way through the shin-high grass to the sidewalk and across the street to the Parkers' tidy plot.

When Mrs. Parker opened the door, she could have been Elizabeth Taylor. Her hair was jet black, even darker than Betsy's, and she was wearing a slinky sort of dress, looking more like she was at a cocktail party than simply puttering around that giant house. My ears were hot.

"I live across the street," I said, gesturing vaguely behind me.

Mrs. Parker looked at me, her eyes the stunned eyes of a doe.

"Do you have some sugar?" I asked, relieved to have re-membered my excuse.

She smiled then. "Sure, honey. How much do you need?"

I had no idea how much sugar one might need if one truly needed sugar. I was also suddenly aware that I had no way of getting the sugar home. "This much?" I suggested, making a bowl with my hands, seemingly solving both the quantity and container problem.

"About a cup? Sure thing, come on in."

The inside of Betsy Parker's house was as tidy as the outside. Fresh flowers stood erect in thin glass vases, catching light from any number of the windows. The floors were completely covered in carpeting. I'd never seen, or felt, anything like it before.

I followed her down a long hallway to the kitchen, where she motioned for me to sit at the clean white dinette set. Mrs. Parker opened up a tin marked "Sugar" in fancy red script and pulled out a scoop. She poured the sugar into a teacup and handed it to me.

"Here you go, exactly one level cup. What's your momma making?"

I hoped my ears weren't as red as they felt.

"Doughnuts," I answered, saying the first sweet thing that popped into my head.

Mrs. Parker's forehead wrinkled a little, and I was pretty certain I'd been figured out. "Can you be a sweetheart and get the recipe from her? You can bring it over when you return the teacup." Mrs. Parker smiled. "I can't find a decent doughnut recipe anywhere."

I nodded, and was backing down the hall, balancing the teacup by its delicate handle when I remembered why I had really come.

"Oh," I said. "Is Betsy home?"

"Sure, honey. She's in her room. Would you like me to go get her?"

I thought about it for a minute, even pictured Betsy Parker in her room, maybe lying on her stomach on her bed, thumbing through a magazine, but the idea of actually talking to her suddenly seemed ludicrous.

"Nah," I said. "Just tell her I stopped by."

Mrs. Parker raised one perfect black eyebrow and then winked at me. "Sure thing, sugar."

The next time I went back, I pretended my mother was making beef stew. I pulled a dusty cookbook down off the highest shelf in our kitchen and scanned the list of ingredients. *Bouillon* . . . I couldn't pronounce it. *An onion.* My mother didn't even hear me go.

This time, Betsy answered the door, breathing hard as if she'd been running.

"Hi," I said, my heart thumping in my chest so hard I was fairly certain you could see it pounding through my shirt.

She grabbed me by the hand and pulled me into the house. "Follow me," she said, leading me down the long hallway to the kitchen and then out the back door. Her hand was soft. She had a Band-aid on her thumb. Outside, she took off across the shady backyard, climbing nimbly up a giant maple. Once perched in the crook of two large branches, she whispered, *"Come up."*

Though the maple was unfamiliar, I'd climbed my share of trees and quickly ascended up into the tree's depths. To my dismay, Betsy seemed unimpressed by my tree-climbing skills; she was fixated on something in the distance.

The Parkers lived next door to Mr. Lowe, a widower with throat cancer and a reputation for losing his temper in public. He'd been seen screaming at waitresses and gas station attendants and store clerks all over town. Some people said the terrible sounds that came out of his throat were punishment for his temper. He'd even yelled at me once when I lost my baseball in his hedges. Through the trees, I could barely see the shadow of a figure moving in the yard below.

"What is it?" I asked.

"Shhh," Betsy whispered, pushing the back of my neck down so that my head lowered and revealed a better view.

He was standing in the middle of his backyard in a sleeveless white undershirt, a pair of shorts held up by suspenders. When he bent over to pick up the hula hoop at his feet, Betsy let go of the tree branch and smacked me in the arm. Hard. Below us, Mr. Lowe held the hula hoop tightly around his waist before he set it spinning, released it, and let his hips do the work. Betsy covered her mouth to keep from laughing, and I smiled. He was diligent in this task. Ridiculous. When we finally couldn't stand it anymore and Betsy started to giggle, the hula hoop dropped to the ground, and Mr. Lowe looked up. When he started to holler with that awful damaged voice of his and shake his fist at the sky, we scurried down the tree. By the time we got to the bottom, we were shaking with laughter.

"I saw him naked once," Betsy said.

"Nu-*uh*," I said.

"In one of those kiddy pools," she said, nodding. "He was wacking off."

"Shut up," I said, punching her arm. She didn't flinch.

"I know where there are some dirty magazines," she said.

"Really?" I asked. Earlier that summer Ray had stolen a copy of *Modern Man* from his dad's collection. He'd even let me tear out a page with Bettie Page and Tempest Storm, both nearly naked, which I'd studied like a treasure map. As I traced breasts and teensy panties with my finger, I imagined myself an explorer, the topography both treacherous and thrilling.

She nodded. "I'll show you tomorrow."

Now I didn't need another excuse to come back. I had a real, live invitation. And there was something pretty damn exciting about the prospect of looking at naked pictures with Betsy.

I went back. Between June and August, I must have followed Mrs. Parker down that softly carpeted hallway a hundred times. Mrs. Parker was always wearing something none of the other neighborhood mothers (certainly not my mother anyway) could have pulled off. There was always something bubbling on the stove top, and she always had a frosted glass of lemonade or a Cherry Coke to offer. Betsy and I would gorge ourselves on homemade German chocolate cake or Lorna Doones until our stomachs ached, and then we'd take off on one adventure or another, usually spying on someone in the neighborhood. Betsy taught me the scientific names for genitalia both male and female that summer. And once, she even showed me a picture of Mrs. Parker wearing what looked like a skimpy caveman's outfit, a giant bone in her hand. "A famous photographer took this of her. Before she married Daddy," she told me. "She was going to be a model." I beamed. I figured now that Betsy Parker trusted me, it wouldn't be long until she loved me too.

But about a week before school started again, I went to Betsy's house and she said that she wasn't allowed to have company and closed the door in my face. Stunned, I walked home and found my father unpacking a brand new Kenmore clothes dryer from a cardboard box. The folding machine hadn't worked, and it seemed to me that my father's reluctant concession was an admission of failure. But being the half-full kind of person I was, my own failure did not deter me. I went back to the Parkers' house the next day. And the next. But each time, Betsy said simply that she wasn't allowed to have guests and closed the door. By the end of the week, I began to worry. It was as if our friendship, like summer, had only been seasonal. As ephemeral and fleeting as Vermont sunshine.

At school, Betsy was careful to avoid me. She wasn't unkind, but she did make sure to sit across the room from me in homeroom, and she only spoke to me when necessary. By November, I'd forced myself to accept her indifference. I started to hang out with Brooder and Ray again, chucking dirt clods at first graders and chewing tobacco behind the school. In a way, it was as if Betsy had only been a dream.

But just before Thanksgiving, when an early snowstorm brought our first snow day of the year, I felt optimistic. And I missed her. After going back to bed for another hour, I decided to give Betsy one more chance. I thought that the prospect of pristine snow, just wet enough to make snowballs, might bring her back to me.

What I noticed first was the loose board on the front steps. It surprised me. Then I saw that the paint on the porch was peeling, that the roses, blooms long gone, had not been tended to. The bushes were skeletal, snarled.

Mrs. Parker answered the door wearing her slip, and I felt myself blushing. She looked exactly like Elizabeth Taylor now—in *Cat on a Hot Tin Roof* (which Brooder and I had snuck into the theater to see). Her hair was messy, and she was barefoot. She stepped out onto the porch and looked past me down the street.

"Is Betsy home?" I asked.

She stood shivering on the porch for what seemed like forever.

"Mrs. Parker," I said. "We should go inside. You'll catch a cold." She came back to me then and nodded.

Inside, the house was unfamiliar. There were stacks of old newspapers all over the floor. The sink was full of dirty dishes. Mrs. Parker had to rummage through them to find a pot, which she rinsed and then filled with milk to warm for hot chocolate. Betsy came out of her room, and while she and I sat silently at the table dunking marshmallows in our mugs of cocoa, Mrs. Parker disappeared. When she came back, she was carrying a child's sand bucket filled with snow. She set it down on the kitchen floor and smiled. "Let's build ourselves a snowman," she said. Betsy sank lower into her seat.

I sat quietly and watched. Mrs. Parker opened the back door when the bucket was empty and stepped out into the snow, still without any shoes on. She brought in more and more snow, until there was a huge pile of it on the linoleum. The kitchen was warm; the snow was melting all over the floor.

Betsy's eyes were wide and wet.

"Here," I said. "I'll help." I ran outside to the backyard and made a snowball. I set it down in a good patch of snow and rolled it back and forth across the lawn until it was the size of a large medicine ball. I went back into the kitchen to get them, to show them what I'd made, but by the time I got there Mrs. Parker had disappeared and Betsy was sitting on the floor next to the puddle.

She reached for my hand, pulling me down next to her. She looked at me as if she were trying to figure something out. Then she framed my face with her hands and kissed me so hard on the mouth that my front tooth bit into my bottom lip. I was a little puzzled but mostly excited. I started to kiss her back, but she pulled away. She looked hard into my eyes and said quietly, "I'll never marry you, Harper Montgomery. It's best that you know that now."

I felt heat rising into my face, despite the chill I'd carried in from outside. "I don't want to *marry* you," I offered, like some god-awful gift. "Why would I want to marry you anyway?"

She softened then, and looked at me with something close to sympathy.

"*What?*" I asked, still offended. I could taste my own blood.

Betsy's shoulders slumped. "My daddy's sending her away. To the state mental hospital in Waterbury. She's crazy, you know."

By Christmas, Mrs. Parker was gone and the Parkers' house was no different from the other crumbling monstrosities on our street. Even the Christmas lights strung around the porch railings seemed haphazard and half-hearted. By the following summer their yard had grown into a sort of jungle. And even though Betsy had sworn she'd never marry me, I was pretty certain there was still a chance she might one day love me.

News

"Where the hell you been, Montgomery?" Lenny asked. He was standing outside the train station, smoking a cigarette.

"I told you. I was at the wreck. I went home to dry off. Change my clothes," I said.

"Well, get in here," he said, snubbing out his cigarette under his boot and blowing three perfect smoke rings into the air. He held his finger up and put it through one of the rings, letting it circle his finger, smiling stupidly like he'd exhibited a new and remarkable talent.

The station was eerily empty. All trains coming through Two Rivers had been delayed or diverted. Normally, there was a bustle of activity at the station at any given time of the day. Today there was no motion but the whirring of the ceiling fans. I shut the door to the freight office and tried to concentrate on the pile of paperwork that had accumulated in my in-box. As luck would have it, the ceiling fan in my office was broken. It was hot, especially with the door closed, but I didn't want to be bothered. Within minutes Lenny was knocking.

Lenny had been a thorn in my side since he transferred up from Brattleboro five years before. He was the station agent, in charge of overseeing all of the operations at the station. His interpretation of this job description was poking his nose into my office, and generally impeding *all* operations at the station with his incessant drivel.

"The news wants to interview me," he said. "Burlington. NBC." He was examining his cuticles, trying to be blasé about it, I suppose.

"What for?" I asked.

"Duh," he offered by way of explanation, opening his buggy eyes wider. "*Earth to Montgomery.* A train wrecked in the river today."

"I mean, why do they want to interview you? You haven't even been down there yet, have you?"

"I've been waiting for *you* to show up all morning. I couldn't exactly leave, could I?"

"Why don't you go down there now?" I asked, hopeful.

"Maybe I *will.*"

"Great. Can you close the door on the way out?"

Since Lenny's arrival in Two Rivers I had found myself in more than a hundred such inane conversations. Every single exchange we had had a certain prepubescent quality to it. I worried sometimes that I might actually wind up in a school yard brawl with him one afternoon. I didn't know how much longer I could stand this job.

After Lenny was gone, I trudged through some bills of lading. I wanted to get through the mountain of paperwork so that I could get back to the apartment, to Marguerite, before Shelly got home from school. I was working on deciphering handwriting on an order when the phone on my desk rang, startling me so badly I felt like I'd been sucker-punched.

"My daughter!" the voice cried. "Please tell where my daughter is!"

Sweat broke out onto my forehead in cold drops. I thought about Marguerite at the river's edge, the sunlight behind her. *My mama's dead.*

"Excuse me?" I managed.

"Oh God, is she dead?" Her accent was thick. Southern.

I closed my eyes, thought of Marguerite reaching for my hand.

"Ma'am, please slow down. The connection's not so good. How can I help you?" Sweat ran down my sides; I could smell myself, the dank scent of the river and my own wet fear.

"My daughter was on the train. At least I think she was on that train. Dammit, we haven't heard nothin' from nobody. Who's in charge up there?"

"I'm sorry, ma'am. I understand you're upset. Please, let me see what I can do to help." I wiped my wrist across my forehead, blinked hard to squeeze the sweat out of my eyes.

"Her name's Sara. Sara Phillips. She got on in Virginia, headed to Montreal. Was she on this train? *Where* is my daughter?"

"Sara," I said, my skin tingling with sudden relief. Release. But my body felt like it had just woken from a nightmare; everything was still buzzing. I breathed deeply. "This is the freight office. Let me give you the number for the railroad. They should have a passenger list."

The woman was sobbing on the other end of the line.

"Ma'am?" I said, softly.

"Yes?"

"A lot of people made it out of the wreck just fine. I was there. I saw a lot of people who walked away without even a scratch."

"Thank you," she said. "This is the third number I've called, and you're the first person who's listened to me."

"Call that number," I said. "They can help you. If they can't, call me back."

When I hung up the phone, my neck was bristling. I closed up the file I'd been struggling with and stood up. If I'd smoked I would have gone outside for a cigarette. Instead I went out into the station and got a Coke from the vending machine. I drank the whole can in three gulps; it burned my throat but seemed to quench my thirst.

I needed to get the passenger list. At least then I could get Marguerite's mother's name. Marguerite's last name. For Christ's sake, I didn't even know her last name. Where exactly it was that she'd been coming from. Then I'd just make the phone call. She was a minor, a *child*. Her father, no matter what he'd done, had a right to know where she was. Where his wife was.

But just as I was about to make my way to the ticket office, one man carrying a camera and another carrying a microphone came through the front doors.

"Do you work here?" the one with the microphone asked. He was well-dressed, drenched in spicy cologne.

I nodded.

"Name?" he asked.

"Montgomery," I said. "Harper Montgomery."

"Have you been down to the scene of the accident?"

I nodded again.

The camera guy suddenly shined a bright light on the cologne guy and he started talking into the mic. "At the junction in Two Rivers, a passenger train carrying ninety-four people derailed early this morning on its way to Montreal. The number of casualties is not known yet as many passengers are still missing. We are here with Harper Montgomery, an employee at the Two Rivers station. Sir, can you tell us what you saw today?"

I don't remember what I said, I only remember the smell of cologne, the stifling heat, and the blinding white light in my eyes as I tried to articulate the wreckage.

April Fools

I was the only one outside Betsy's family who knew what really happened to Mrs. Parker. The official explanation for her absence was that she was suffering from a mysterious respiratory ailment and had been sent to see specialists somewhere in the Midwest. But everyone had their speculations, the most popular being that Mrs. Parker had run off with another man. *A photographer*, some said. *From New York City*. My mother, who was nobody's fool, said, "Phooey. That poor woman is probably frosting cupcakes in the sanitarium as we speak." My mother, who was also a self-proclaimed champion of all women (both meek and strong), offered, "I'd lose my marbles too, what with nothing to do all day but dust my husband's bowling trophies." (Mr. Parker was a local bowling phenom, having rolled a half-dozen 300 games in his lifetime.) Of course, I didn't tell her that she was right. I only shrugged and said I bet Betsy missed her. Betsy and I never spoke about what happened that snowy day on her kitchen floor. But there was an understanding between us afterward. We shared a secret both terrible and sacred.

At Two Rivers Graded School, there were rules for boys and girls. Rules that were handed down from the older kids to the younger ones like commandments. Only these statutes were not etched in stone but whispered conspiratorially on the playground. If you had a mentor, an older sibling or friend, you might be privy to the secret order of things. But most of us learned the rules the hard way: by breaking them. The rules for boys were different than the rules for girls (much as they are for men and women). Boys should *like* girls or else they were pansies. Boys should not, however, let said girls know they liked them. In fact, the more ambivalent and cold you were to the object of your affection, the better. As a boy who carried his heart on his sleeve, I learned this one early on. It only took one longing glance in Betsy's direction during lunch to earn me a cuff on the ear from Brooder. A conversation during recess resulted in a stern admonishment behind the gym after school.

"What the hell's the matter with you, Montgomery?" Brooder asked. He had a wad of tobacco tucked in his cheek, making him look remotely like a chipmunk. He'd been stealing his father's chewing tobacco since the fourth grade.

"Nothin'," I said, though I could feel my ears red-hot still from the brief encounter with Betsy.

"You look like you got goddamned beets on the side of your head," he said. "Over Betsy Parker?"

Just hearing her name made my stomach flutter. "Shut up," I argued meakly.

Brooder smacked my back and spit a long black stream of tobacco on the ground next to my feet. "Don't be such a pussy."

And so, I kept my feelings for Betsy as quiet as I could bear. The rules for girls (and women I suppose) remained (and continue to remain) a mystery to me. There were intricacies to the girls' rules. Nuances that escaped me. All I knew was that even after Betsy kissed me on the Parkers' kitchen floor, she still pretended that she and I weren't friends when we were at school. This was a charade I was willing to act out, however, because as soon as school let out, the world started spinning in the right direction again. When the last bell had rung for the day, and we made our way across the playing fields toward home, Betsy's affectations of cool ambivalence toward me disappeared, our friendship restored in an instant.

It was fun breaking the rules. As far as we knew, we were the only boy and girl in our grade who were carrying on such an illicit relationship. If I'd been older, I might have compared our after-school trysts to the kinds kept by married men and their mistresses. But I was thirteen, and it just felt like we were doing something dangerous. Every cold shoulder in gym class, every snide remark, every snub was simply part of a necessary performance. It was okay, because I knew that it was just pretend and that out of sight of the school, as we ran across the expanse of wet green grass, she would reach out for my hand, dragging me behind her terrific strides. Home again. Where Betsy and I were best friends.

And then in the spring of 1959, Mindy Wheeler moved to town, and all of the rules (for both boys and girls) flew out the proverbial window. Mindy Wheeler was fourteen; rumor had it she'd been kept back at her old school, which was either in North Carolina or North Dakota—no one knew for sure. She had hair the color of hay, and boobs. Big ones. She was also almost six feet tall, a better basketball player than anyone in our whole school. Mindy Wheeler had the mouth of a sailor and the body of a goddess. She was the source of great confusion for all of us (boys *and* girls). What was one to do with someone like Mindy Wheeler?

It started when Howie Burke invited her to play a game of three-on-three during recess. *Invited* probably isn't the right word; *allowed* might be better. When she grabbed the ball off the court midgame, dribbled it down to the rusty hoop, and made an easy layup, of the six boys, myself included, who had been arguing over whether or not a noogie constituted a foul, no one made a move to stop her. And Howie, perpetrator of the aforementioned noogie, said, "Okay, sub-in The Girl. Gauthier, you're out." And with that, everything I had come to accept as proper behavior became meaningless.

Boys openly fawned over Mindy Wheeler. She rendered

poor Ray speechless. Even Brooder softened around her. On any given day, any one of my peers could be found stumbling and stuttering before her. We both feared her and worshipped her. And the girls, surprisingly, adored her. You'd have thought that a girl of Mindy's stature, of her power to subvert an entire set of established social mores and, if nothing else, of her mere pectoral endowment, would have been more intimidating to the girls of Two Rivers Graded School. But instead, they fawned over her as well. They stumbled and stuttered. They feared and worshipped. Betsy Parker included.

Still, I didn't see it coming.

I lived for the last bell. Usually after school, Betsy was mine again. After school, we could give up the pretense. Feigning indifference for six straight hours was a certain kind of torture for me. After school, at Betsy's house, we spent hours going through her mother and father's drawers, looking for forbidden things. We looked at her father's dirty magazines, filled condoms with water and threw them over the fence into Mr. Lowe's yard. We studied the complicated lingerie her mother left behind and her father's jock straps. We once found a douche bag on the top shelf of a closet, and when Betsy explained what it was used for, I found myself so flustered I could barely speak. On less mischievous days, we mostly hunkered down in Betsy's room listening to records, eating peanut butter straight out of the jar, and planning the next adventure. But after Mindy's arrival, I couldn't count on anything. Sometimes instead of racing home with me, Betsy would linger after school with Mindy, doing penny drops on the monkey bars or playing H-O-R-S-E. On those days I'd shove my hands in my pockets and kick dirt all the way home. Resign myself to another afternoon spent watching Brooder terrorize the little kids who were just trying to get home too. Betsy would always catch up with me later, but by then I was sunk so deep in self-pity even Betsy couldn't pull me out.

It was spring then, and Betsy's latest scheme was a complex one aimed at framing Howie Burke in an April Fool's prank. Howie was notorious for his own annual April Fool's high jinx. He bragged endlessly about the rotten eggs he had thrown, the houses he had toilet-papered, the tires he had flattened. His crowning achievement (and the source of Betsy's greatest fury) being the shaving cream fiasco of 1957, when he broke into Betsy's father's barbershop and stole a case of Barbasol, which (to add insult to injury) he used to write "Besty Praker Eats Boogers" (Howie was likely dyslexic, though back then we just thought he was stupid) in the windows of Two Rivers Graded School. Betsy and Howie had been sparring since the second grade, when Betsy started the war by beating Howie in a recess footrace. Sometimes her passion for getting back at Howie verged on the manic, and I found myself feeling jealous. I never seemed to incite much of anything in Betsy; even when she and I were pretending to dislike each other at school, I got little more than a tongue stuck out. Eyes crossed.

Howie had a crush on our English teacher, Miss Bean. (The rules were different when it came to boys and pretty teachers too. We *all* loved Miss Bean. We all openly adored her.) However, of all of us, Howie's infatuation was the most intense, and Betsy Parker knew it.

"I've *got* it," Betsy said one Friday afternoon when Mindy was occupied with something, or someone, else and I was contentedly playing second fiddle. We were sitting on Betsy's bedroom floor drinking our third and fourth Cokes respectively. (Betsy's dad had a refrigerator in the basement, which was always stocked with extra sodas.)

"Got what?" I asked.

"We're going to TP Miss Bean's house," she said.

"Why?" I asked. Though my heart sang every time Betsy spoke in the plural, the thought of doing anything like this to Miss Bean seemed like sacrilege.

"We're going to TP the house, put eggs in the mailbox, AND shaving cream her car."

I shook my head. "We can't."

"Yes, *we* can," she said. "If you wear this Superman mask," she said, raising a lone eyebrow and reaching under her bed. She pulled out a plastic mask identical to the one that Howie Burke had worn for the last three consecutive pranks. (He was known to work in disguise.)

"And *you*?" I asked.

"Lois Lane?" she said, smiling in the way that made my knees feel like oatmeal. The idea of sneaking around in the dark with Betsy was almost more than I could stand.

"We can't," I said then, laughing and shaking my head. "Miss Bean didn't do anything. That's just mean."

"*You* like her *too*?" Betsy asked, accusingly.

"*No,*" I said, reaching for the mask, wondering if Betsy was jealous. Hoping Betsy was jealous. But I *did* like Miss Bean. I liked Miss Bean in her sweater sets and pastel pumps that matched. I liked the way she smelled like toothpaste and patted the top of my head when I said something insightful in class.

"She'll know it's not Howie," I said.

"How?"

"Because Howie's like six feet tall," I said. (I was a late bloomer. I wouldn't see six feet until I was sixteen. And then, as if my bones were making up for lost time, I would grow another four inches between my junior and senior years in high school.)

"True," she said sadly, and hung the mask on her bedpost.

Relieved, I picked up my Coke and drained the last few sweet drops. "We'll get him back someday," I offered, closing my lips tightly around *we*.

I figured out what happened during English class when Miss Bean slammed her books down on her desk and said, "Well, I hope you enjoyed your little prank. Very funny."

I heard giggles. Girl giggles.

I turned around and saw that Betsy was sitting next to Mindy, who was whispering something in her ear. Betsy was smiling. My heart dropped with the realization of what happened. Of course, *Mindy*. Mindy who was almost six feet tall. I felt like I was melting into my seat.

Howie sat in the front row as he always did, eyes wide and full of love.

"*Very* funny," Miss Bean said again, her voice shaking now. She looked out over us and frowned, her eyes teary. Then she opened her desk drawer and pulled out a shoe box. She took the lid off, and the smell of rotten eggs filled the room. She went to Howie's desk and set the box down. "I just got a letter from my fiancé," she said. "He's in the service. He's stationed in Germany. I haven't seen him in almost six months."

Howie looked confused as he peered into the box. When he reached in and pulled out the dripping wet letter, I heard Betsy gasp.

"*April Fools,*" Miss Bean said, crying now, and then she rushed out of the room.

Howie sat there, dumb. We all sat there, dumb.

After school, Betsy came running up to me as I made my way across the soccer field. "I should have listened to you," she said, reaching for my hand.

I nodded my head. "Yeah."

"I'm sorry," she said. "I didn't tell you, because I know how much you like Miss Bean. We didn't know there was a letter from her boyfriend in there," she said, running after me as I quickened my pace. "We did it because of Howie."

I kept walking as fast as I could.

"I'm sorry, Harper," she said. "We didn't do it to be mean to Miss Bean."

I stopped and looked at her. She had two braids and both of them were coming undone.

"It was stupid," she said. "Really stupid."

And she had no idea that though I felt bad for Miss Bean and her stinky, soggy letter, I felt worse for me. Because Betsy had picked Mindy Wheeler as her coconspirator. Because she and Mindy had their *own* secret, and that it had nothing to do with me. I went home sulking and mad. I didn't answer the phone when she called, and didn't answer the door when she came over.

But the next day when we got to school, Betsy was sitting at her desk, crying into her hands, and my heart sank. "Mrs. Praker's in a nuthouse," was scrawled across the chalkboard in Howie's backward script.

And even though we were at school and everybody was watching, I went to her. I put my arm over her shoulder and hugged her. In front of the entire eighth-grade class, I held her. And in the crook of my arm, she shook with a sadness I knew I would never be able to understand or share.

"I told Mindy not to tell anybody," she cried, wiping furiously at her tears. "She was supposed to be my friend. She *promised*. Why would she tell him?"

Mindy's motives became clear that afternoon when instead of playing basketball, she and Howie disappeared behind the school and came back five minutes later with leaves in their hair, looking both guilty and proud. (Howie said later that her boobs felt like peaches, an observation we all believed since none of us yet had evidence to the contrary.)

Mindy Wheeler moved away before school let out for the summer, and everyone in the whole school seemed to mourn her passing except for me. I was glad she was gone. But thanks to Mindy, at least I'd found my purpose. I had been put on this earth to protect Betsy. To keep her secrets and to keep her safe.

Jumbo Liar

After my bumbled TV interview at the station, I left work and went home, quietly unlocking the door just in case the girl was still sleeping. When I entered the kitchen, Shelly was sitting at the kitchen table, her schoolbooks spread out in front of her, and Marguerite was standing at the stove. My spine went stiff as a rod.

"Daddy!" Shelly cried when I stepped into the kitchen.

I took off my hat. "Hi, baby girl," I said, squeezing her, trying not to let on that anything was out of the ordinary. Normally, I would have thrown her over my shoulder like a potato sack and marched around the house until she pleaded to be released, but lately she'd gotten too heavy, too tall, and tonight there was a stranger standing at my stove.

"*Let go*," she giggled, and wriggled free.

The whole kitchen smelled like something I'd never smelled before.

"I thought you would be at Mrs. Marigold's," I said to Shelly, part question, part reprimand.

"I *was*," Shelly said. "But she said we had company. That our *cousin* was taking a nap on the couch."

"I see," I said.

"Did a train really wreck in the river?" she asked excitedly. "Jason Pittman in my class said a hundred people drowned."

"It derailed into the river. A lot of people got hurt. Not a hundred, but a lot."

"Were you there?" she asked.

I nodded.

"Did you *see* it?" Shelly was jumping from one foot to the other. She was always such a ball of nervous energy.

"I didn't see the accident happen. I got there afterward."

"Did you see anybody, you know, drowned?"

I looked at Marguerite, but she was busy peering into my cupboard.

"This isn't great dinner conversation," I said softly.

"We're not even eating yet," Shelly argued. "Did you?"

I turned to Marguerite, forcing myself to sound bright, cheerful. "So, what's for supper?"

"Maggie's making jumbo liar," Shelly said, climbing back up into her chair and reaching for her pencil box. "It's got sausage in it. And rice. It's spicy."

"That sounds great," I said, *"Maggie."*

"That's my nickname," she said, winking at Shelly. Then she looked at me, as if daring me to challenge her again. "With my *girlfriends.*"

"We're going bowling tonight!" Shelly said.

"No," I started. "Not tonight."

"Daddy," Shelly said dramatically. "It's Friday. It's *Ladies Night.*"

On most Friday nights since we moved into the apartment, Shelly and I would eat dinner (corn dogs for her, chili for me) at the bowling alley and then, before the ladies' leagues showed up, we'd bowl a few strings. Because it was Ladies Night, she could order whatever she wanted from the laminated menu, and she could also pick whatever songs she wanted on the jukebox.

"Ladies Night means ladies' choice," Shelly explained to

the girl, *Maggie*, who was tasting something from one of my wooden spoons. She scrunched her nose and shook in a few drops of hot pepper sauce she had excavated from the depths of my cupboards. She tested the concoction again and smiled.

I knew a lot of the women in the ladies' leagues: a lot of the girls we went to high school with, some of the wives of my coworkers down at the station. Hanna's sister, Lisa, bowled. Word would get back to Hanna one way or another about the girl. She knew I didn't have any family from anywhere but here; even my own mother's family tree's branches did not extend out of New England. We couldn't go. Anywhere. Two Rivers was too small for a stranger, especially a stranger of Marguerite's caliber, to get lost in the crowd. She could spend the night, but then she'd have to be on her way. And no Ladies Night.

"Y'all sit down," Marguerite said. "Dinner's ready."

Shelly sat obediently in her chair, moving aside her schoolbooks. I sat down too, exhausted and starving. The smells coming from that one pot were more intense than anything I'd managed to put together since we'd moved into this apartment. Sweet tomatoes, spices. I'd never really learned to cook; I hadn't felt comfortable trying to do more than make myself a cup of coffee in Hanna's kitchen.

Marguerite grabbed three plates and set them down on the table. She scooped a heaping pile of the stuff onto my plate and an only slightly less generous pile onto Shelly's. On the plate she'd set for herself, she plopped down some plain rice from another pot.

"*What* is it called again?" I asked, shoveling a heaping spoonful into my mouth.

"It's called jambalaya, Mr. Manners. Didn't nobody ever teach you it ain't polite to start eating without saying grace?" Marguerite asked.

Shelly set her utensils down, pressed her palms together, and closed her eyes. "Father, bless the food we take, and bless us all for Jesus' sake. Amen."

"Who taught you that?" I asked.

"Mrs. Marigold."

"Oh, did she?" I asked. I would have to remember to say something to Mrs. Marigold on Monday.

Shelly scowled at me. Marguerite leaned over to her and said, "At my house we say, 'For bacon, eggs and buttered toast, praise Father, Son and Holy Ghost.'"

Shelly giggled.

Marguerite pushed the rice around her plate as I finished first one, and then two more helpings. Shelly ate a whole plateful as well and asked Marguerite for more when she was done.

"Ladies Night," Shelly said, tugging at my sleeve.

I shook my head, and she looked at me sadly. "Please? It's my *birthday*."

Her birthday. With all of the confusion and excitement of the train wreck and Marguerite, I'd forgotten to pick up another birthday present. Feeling awful, I reached into my pocket and pulled out the pair of barrettes and handed them to her.

"Thanks, Daddy," she said, but her eyes were welling up with tears.

"It's your *birthday*?" Marguerite said, putting her hands on her hips. "Well, it's a good thing I made a cake. Not quite a birthday cake, but if your daddy's got a candle, you could still make a wish on it." She opened up the fridge and pulled out a pineapple upside-down cake.

Shelly beamed.

I agreed to Ladies Night against my better judgment, because of Shelly. It was the poor kid's birthday, and once again I'd failed miserably. So Ladies Night it was, and the three of us descended the stairs leading to Sunset Lanes. And luckily, when we got to the door, there was a sign posted that all league games were canceled due to the train wreck. Inside, the bowling alley was deserted save for a few regulars drinking coffee and a couple of kids shooting pool in the arcade.

"Where is everybody?" Shelly asked, clearly disappointed. Shelly was a mascot of sorts on Ladies Night. The women of Sunset Lanes fawned over her as if she were a small animal instead of a girl. Part of the reason I kept bringing her back on Friday nights was because all of those women made everything seem okay. Since we'd left Hanna's, the absence of a mother in Shelly's life seemed even more pronounced.

If I had been like most of Two Rivers's other widowers I would have simply found myself someone new, someone to fill the empty spaces Betsy left behind. But most of the widowers in this town were well into their seventies when their wives passed away. Remarrying was what kept them alive for another ten, fifteen years. I was twenty-two years old when Betsy died. I wasn't even sure then that I *wanted* to survive.

I suppose I could have found someone if I'd really wanted to. It was almost alarming how many women came out of the woodwork after Betsy passed away. Almost right away, girls we knew from high school, ones who never talked to me, were suddenly very concerned about my grief. Their casseroles arrived at Hanna's doorstep, with perfumed notes expressing their most sincere condolences. As time went on the casseroles stopped, and they started to bring things by for the baby. Tiny clothes and handmade blankets. I would have thought these gestures to be only our community's genuine efforts to take care of its wounded. But Hanna, who was always wiser than I, noticed that the gifts often came along with invitations—to go catch a movie at the Star Theatre, to join one of them or another at the Two Rivers Inn for supper, to attend the Christmas party at the Paper Company. "Those women are despicable," Hanna snorted. "Betsy's barely even cold yet." So I accepted their casseroles and baby sweaters but not their invitations, and after a while most of them gave up.

Of course, after a while I did start to date again. Over the years, there were probably a half dozen or so women I spent time with. But as nice as they were, as smart as they were, as pretty as some of them were (and some of them were very, very pretty), nothing ever got too serious. They probably knew that as hard as I tried not to, I was always comparing them to Betsy, holding them up against her. A few years ago when I met Lucy, an English teacher from Bennington whose brother lived in Two Rivers, I thought maybe I'd found someone I could share my life with. Lucy was beautiful, quiet. She loved books. But when I asked her to move to Two Rivers, told her I loved her, she just shook her head.

"You're in love with a shadow," she said. "A shadow that covers your whole world. I can't live in that kind of darkness, Harper. I'm sorry."

After Lucy, I figured it was likely I'd have to finish raising Shelly by myself. Lucy was right. Betsy's shadow loomed large. And as far as finding a new mom for Shelly, it wasn't like she didn't have women in her life. Hanna was like a mother to her. And now that we were on our own, we had Mrs. Marigold and the bowling league ladies.

At the bowling alley, Shelly played "Ladies Night" on the jukebox until a couple of guys groaned audibly, and I stopped giving her quarters. Marguerite was quite good. She said she and her girlfriends liked to bowl too. We bowled until Shelly slumped over in a booth, exhausted, and Marguerite said her feet hurt.

When we turned in the rental shoes, Kip Kilroy, the counter manager, said, "Hey, Harper, I saw you on the news. Man, what a disaster."

I was worried he would ask about Marguerite, but he only said, "Those size sixes work out for you okay, miss?"

She winked and said, "A five and a half woulda been better, but I still rolled a two-twenty."

Back upstairs in the apartment, I offered Marguerite my room for the night, put some clean sheets on the bed. I told her I'd sleep on the couch, though I doubted sleep would likely come tonight either.

"Tomorrow we need to get in touch with your family," I said as I handed her a clean towel and washcloth. She didn't say anything, but she accepted the towels.

"Thanks again," she said. "This is really nice of y'all."

In the morning I would call over to the train station, talk to the weekend crew, have them check their roster for a girl named Marguerite, for her mother. But for tonight, I let her rest. The kitchen still smelled like jambalaya, and when I opened the window it seemed the heat had finally broken. And, if I wasn't mistaken, the air smelled like rain.

The Road Less Traveled

When Betsy said she was running away, I knew I had no choice but to go with her. She needed me. Besides which, I would have followed Betsy Parker anywhere.

On the last day of eighth grade, as Miss Bean said her tearful farewells to us, Betsy leaned over across the aisle that separated us and whispered, "Today." I ignored her, staring straight ahead as Miss Bean wiped at her nose with a tissue she plucked from a box on her desk. Truth be told, I was moved by Miss Bean's heartfelt speech. I even felt a small lump swell in my throat as she spoke. She was the youngest teacher that Two Rivers Graded School had ever had—fresh out of college and still in love with the idea of teaching. Miss Bean, unlike our other teachers, believed in us; she believed that we would not only go on to graduate from Two Rivers High, but that we might even eventually find a way to change the world in some significant way. And perhaps it was Miss Bean's enthusiasm, her thrilling naiveté that got into my gut that early June afternoon as flies slapped sluggishly at the windowpanes in our basement classroom. It was Miss Bean, wearing a soft pink sweater and a matching scarf knotted at her throat, and her promises that the road less traveled would, indeed, make all the difference that made me consent to Betsy's wildest scheme yet.

Betsy and I had had endless conversations about leaving Two Rivers. I participated in these discussions mainly because

I loved Betsy Parker. It had everything to do with the way she smelled like lilacs, even in the winter, and nothing to do with actually wanting to leave our hometown. I loved Two Rivers. The way I figured it, I was probably about the only person who wasn't trying to get away. But I cherished this nothing place. I treasured it: the way the woods smelled after rain, the thunderous sound of the train, that still place where the two rivers meet. Betsy's machinations to flee contradicted every instinct I had. But Betsy Parker, like the giant maples that grew inexplicably in a perfect circle around the town's library, had also grown out of Two Rivers. And I loved her more than water, so I listened as she devised her plan. And agreed when she asked me to go. I didn't expect it to happen so soon. But now, Miss Bean was hugging me so hard I could feel the gentle cage of her ribs pressing into my cheeks, her *breasts* pressing into my cheeks, and Betsy Parker was giving me the signal that the time had come. Suddenly, I was thirteen years old, a graded school graduate, and the whole wide world lay before me like some sort of open road. That's the way I saw it; I pictured the dirt road that led from the river eastward, the one that would wind and twist and branch onto other dirt roads, leading, finally, to Maine, where Betsy had deigned we might finally settle.

Most other girls at thirteen might have pointed their starry eyes westward, fueled by too many winter nights spent curled up under covers reading about all of Laura Ingalls Wilder's frontier adventures. Not Betsy though. Betsy Parker was an adventurer of the truest sort. She knew her limitations, could differentiate between fantasy and potentiality. When she set out to do something, she did it. This was what made me both adore Betsy and fear her. She never made idle threats, and she never made idle plans.

Betsy chose Maine as a destination because of a photo of her mother that she had found in a box in her basement. In the picture, Mrs. Parker was perched on top of a large rock, the wind blowing her hair across her face, the ocean crashing against the shore below. It was taken on the coast of Maine, back when Mrs. Parker was an aspiring model, long before she married Mr. Parker. Betsy told me that one time her mother grabbed her arm tightly and said, "I died the day I met your father. You are looking at a corpse." She said her mother's fingernails left four bloody half moons in the soft skin of her upper arm; she even showed me the four faint scars, which I wanted, but didn't dare, to touch. It was hard for me to imagine Mrs. Parker with her oven mitts and patent leather pumps saying this about Mr. Parker *or* to imagine her hurting Betsy. But it wasn't hard for me to envision Mrs. Parker sitting on a rock with waves crashing below her, a photographer clicking away. Betsy wouldn't let me see *this* picture, but I imagined her looking like Annette Funicello, wearing nothing but a smile. I think Betsy envisioned herself perched above a rocky beach. When she fantasized about running away it wasn't about riding in a horse-drawn wagon but about walking barefoot in the sand, ankles numb in the cold Atlantic. "Besides which," she offered when I gave her my typically dubious smile, "you can fish. That's how we'll make our money."

As we left school that afternoon, Betsy didn't give in to my usual diversions. No stop for Red Hots at the drugstore, where Brooder and Ray would be parked at the counter, digging around in their pockets for loose change. No detours to the cemetery, where I liked to see how many angels I could hit with my slingshot. She was all business, pulling me by the hand until we were in her backyard. She left me standing by the oak tree and went into her father's shed, where he kept his tools and lawn mower and the stash of dirty magazines, and came out with a small shovel. I followed her to the far corner of her yard, where she looked up at the sky, crossed herself as if she were in church, and then started to dig.

"What are you doing?" I asked.

She didn't answer me. And after she had dug about a foot down into the earth, she silently dropped the shovel and knelt down next to the hole she had made. She continued to dig with her hands, her expression serious, intent. When she pulled out the soggy cardboard box, I thought it might be some sort of hidden treasure. There was a part of me, even then, that resided in the stories my mother read to me at night. *Treasure Island. The Swiss Family Robinson.* "What is it?" I asked.

When she looked up at me, her eyes were wet. She blinked hard and lifted the lid of the box. "When I was six," she said, quiet, like a question, "a bird smashed into our front window. A robin. My mom had just washed the windows, and the stupid bird must not have been able to tell there was glass there. I was playing jacks on the front porch, and I didn't see it, but I heard it. It sounded like a gun or something. And then the bird was just lying there in the rosebush. There wasn't any blood or anything, but its neck was all twisted. Its wing was crushed. Mom came running out of the house to see what happened, and when I showed her the bird, she covered my eyes with her hands. They smelled like ammonia. I remember they smelled so clean it could make you sick. She made me go inside, told me to go to my room and not come out until she said. After a long time, she finally came and got me. She told me that the bird was really hurt, but that she fixed its wing. She said that it flew away." Betsy's hands were trembling, the box was trembling in her hands. "So I forgot about the bird. And then a few days later I was out here and I saw this pile of dirt. I didn't know what it was, so I decided to dig it up. And I found this." She motioned to the box, to the bones inside the box. "Course it wasn't just bones then. It still had its feathers and everything. Its wing was still broken. Its neck was still broken."

I knelt down next to Betsy and looked into the box. Inside were yellowed bones, impossibly small and collapsed. The miniature skull with its empty eye sockets was looking up at me.

"She probably just didn't want you to feel bad," I said.

"Well I *did*," Betsy said, and she seemed almost angry.

"Are you going to bury it again?" I asked. There was something disconcerting about the skeleton. About Betsy right then.

She nodded and lowered the box back into the ground. "Dumb bird. Flying around, just being a bird, and then *bam*, it's over." She looked at me and frowned. "Nobody bothered to tell him about the glass. You'd have told me, right? If I were that bird? And you were my bird friend?"

I nodded. I would have.

She'd packed for both of us—everything we needed except for my clothes. She'd been stealing food from the pantry for nearly two months. She'd also been pilfering from the pickle jar where Mr. Parker threw his spare change. She had almost forty dollars, which she'd had Nancy Butler's older sister, who worked at the Two Rivers Savings and Loan, turn into bills so as not to raise any eyebrows. She had toiletries she'd shoplifted from the drugstore and even a pair of men's hiking boots she'd found at the Goodwill, which she offered to me like a gift. "We've got many miles ahead of us," she said. "I don't need you going home when your sole blows out." The way she said it made me think of my soul exploding. My mother did not believe in God, but I had my suspicions.

"Where will we sleep?" I asked.

"I've got a tent," she said. "I *was* a Brownie, before I got kicked out, you know."

I didn't ask any more questions.

I dawdled. I stood in my bedroom, looking for a way out. It was futile. I didn't even have a proper closet in which I could hide. My closet was full of more of my father's inventions; no one had dared open that door in years. Downstairs my mother was playing the piano, angry music. Last day of school music. She had a summer of daily piano lessons ahead of her. Never mind a thirteen-year-old boy puttering around the house. My father was at work. By the time he got home, I would be gone. It made me sad. Though Betsy had forbidden me to do so, I got out a piece of paper from my school notebook and scribbled down a quick note: "I'm okay. Don't worry. I'll call when I get a chance. Your loving son, Harper Montgomery." I wasn't sure why I bothered to sign my last name except that it made the whole thing seem somehow more official. I muttered "Good-bye" to my mother, kissed the top of her head, and she nodded her farewell as she continued to abuse the piano keys.

I met Betsy at the drugstore, as planned, for a final soda pop. I ordered a Vanilla Coke, and she got her usual Orange Crush. Luckily, Brooder and Ray weren't there or else I might have chickened out. We sat at the counter, both of us making those drinks last as long as they possibly could, until finally Betsy said, "Let's go."

By the time the sun was starting to set, I had lost my bearings. Betsy insisted that we travel through the woods until we were out of Two Rivers, lest anyone driving by might wonder what we were up to. She had calculated even the most minute details of our escape. She carried elaborate maps, which she had traced from her father's road atlas. A compass. A pocketful of stones to make a trail, even, I figured. But after the sound of the river faded into the sound of wind in the trees, I couldn't tell which way we were headed anymore and I was starting to wonder when one of us would finally say, "Uncle."

As the sun burned red and orange through the thick foliage all around us, Betsy stopped. "Let's camp here for the night." As she pitched the tent and unrolled the sleeping bags, I waited for her to stop what she was doing, to turn to me, punch me in the shoulder and say something like, "All right, let's head back." But she didn't. "Why don't you go find some wood for a fire?" she asked.

I agreed and set out in the waning light to look for kindling and firewood. Though I didn't have a watch on, I figured it to be about eight o'clock. If I were at home, my father would be climbing the stairs from his basement laboratory, stretching and calling out to my mother, "Helen, come watch *Wyatt Earp* with me." She would mutter something from the other room, and my father would fix himself a peanut butter sandwich as he waited for her. When she emerged from her study, bleary-eyed and yawning, he would motion for her to join him in the living room. They would settle onto the couch then, and my mother would lay her head in my father's lap so that he could stroke her hair. I would sit Indian-style on the floor in front of them, in front of the TV close enough to reach over and change the channel during the commercials. If someone were to ask me what the word *family* meant then, this is the image that would have come to mind. We did not eat together, but we did meet religiously for prime-time television. For this, I would abandon games of kick-the-can and hide-n-seek as soon as the streetlights hummed. Now, in the woods, I thought of my father walking up the basement steps, my mother devouring one more paragraph. I wondered at what moment they would realize that I was gone.

I bent over, selecting twigs and fallen branches haphazardly, without any real expertise. I hadn't joined the Boy Scouts because my mother considered them an organization of Christian zealots. She did think their survival tips were important however, considering the amount of time I spent outside. She found a used copy of the *Cub Scout Leader Book* as well as the *Wilderness Survival Guide* at a library sale, and taught me how to make a tourniquet, how to identify edible mushrooms, and how to track a badger. None of this seemed pertinent right now.

I brought the pile of sticks to Betsy, eager for her approval.

"Over there," she said, motioning to a circle of rocks she had created not far from the opening of the tent.

I dropped the branches on the ground and sat down next to them. I thought of my mother, unwinding her hair from the two frayed braids she wore pinned to the top of her head.

Betsy made a pyramid of twigs, crumpled a piece of newspaper, which materialized from the pack she'd been carrying on her back. She lit a match just as the last embers of sunlight burned beyond the forest, and started the fire. We ate creamed corn and hot dogs, charred from the open flame. I sat next to Betsy, eating quietly, and knew that my parents had probably realized by now that I was missing. I tried to remember if I'd ever seen my mother look afraid.

We talked about school, about the new Everly Brothers album, about Jack Kerouac and whether or not anyone would ever travel to outer space. We even talked about what we would miss. "Double Delights," Betsy said. (You could only get them from the ice-cream truck that drove through our neighborhood at dusk on summer evenings.)

"Chicken croquettes." I nodded. My father made them, with thick creamy gravy.

"Smoking candy cigarettes on the train tracks."

"Sugar on snow," I said. (Sugar on snow is hot maple syrup on clean white snow. It makes a sort of sticky candy. You eat it followed by a dill pickle and then a plain doughnut. It's one of the best things about spring in Vermont.)

"They've got that in Maine."

"Oh," I said. I'd forgotten for a minute about Maine.

"Spying on Mr. Lowe," she said. She smiled a little wistfully. "My tree."

The fire was burning low. I followed Betsy into the tent and accepted when she offered me half of her unzipped sleeping bag. We lay on our backs staring up at the roof of the tent, the edges of our bodies just touching: the sides of our hands, our hips, our ankles. The sleeping bag was heavy and warm. My skin, where it touched hers, felt electric.

"I'll miss my dad, " she said softly.

"Um-hm," I said, nodding in the darkness. I wanted to squeeze her hand, let her know that I was having second thoughts too, but I worried it would break the spell.

We lay there for a long time, and I waited for her to sit up, laugh, say, "It's too cold. Let's go home." But it only got darker and quieter, and soon the cadence of her breathing changed. She was asleep. And I knew that we *weren't* going home. We were running away. For real. I must have laid there for hours, listening to her breathe, trying to discern any restlessness, any fear. But remarkably, Betsy kept sleeping.

Soon I was cold, freezing cold, and I imagined Betsy (had she been awake) would have been cold too. My mother had also taught me the dangers of hypothermia, and so, in all my imagined chivalry, I crawled out of the tent into the almost absolute darkness and added another log to the fire. It took a while for it to catch, and I nearly hollered with joy when it finally did. I was thinking mostly about warmth, and maybe just a little about my mother's instructions on how to make a signal with smoke.

I must have finally fallen asleep out there, because in the misty half-light of dawn, when I awoke to the distant sound of voices and crashing of branches, my face was pressed against the dirt. I was still brushing dried leaves out of my hair when my father and Mr. Parker emerged from behind a thick grove of trees and arrived at our clearing.

Nancy Butler (whose sister worked at the bank) had apparently come forward as soon as word got out that we were missing. She gave elaborate details as to how much money Betsy had stolen from her father's pickle jar as well as her own suppositions as to where Betsy and I were headed. One theory was that we were headed to California, you know, like the pioneers. Our fathers set out to find us, and my little midnight campfire, just five miles outside of town, had been a virtual beacon.

Betsy never found out how it was that our fathers happened upon us in the woods. I never confessed. That would have been admitting that I had *wanted* to be found, and I could never admit that. I guess I knew that if it hadn't been for that fire, we might have wound up in Maine after all. That even if it was uncertainty I had heard in the quiet conversation we had inside that tent, Betsy had made up her mind, and once she set out to do something, there was no turning back. The reality was that if she *had* been a bird, she would have flown right into that window, even if I told her it was glass instead of air.

Rain

I must have fallen asleep, because the screaming invaded my dreams. First it was the wind of a vicious storm, and then the howling of a wounded animal. By the time it woke me, it had become the cries of an infant. I sprung off the couch and raced to Shelly's room, my heart beating so hard my chest ached. I turned on the light before I realized that the screaming was not coming from Shelly, who sat up in bed, startled and groggy.

"What's the matter, Daddy?" she asked, her voice raspy.

"Nothing," I said. "Go back to sleep." I hurriedly tucked in her covers and turned out the light.

Another scream.

"That's Maggie!" Shelly said, sitting up again.

"It's okay, honey. I'll go check on her. Stay here."

I walked quickly down the short hallway to my own room and knocked before I pushed the door open.

The curtains were open. Outside, the streetlights reflected off the cool green of the swimming pool and illuminated the room, making it look like an aquarium. It was raining; water streamed down the windows in slow sheets. I could see only the suggestion of Marguerite's body under the covers. Convinced that perhaps it had indeed only been the wind, or an animal, I turned and headed out the door, but just as I was pulling the door shut behind me, she screamed again. I opened the door and turned toward the bed.

Marguerite was sitting up, her arms thrashing as if she were fighting someone off. Her wild punches struck the air, and she wailed, "Noooo!"

"Marguerite," I said softly.

"Nooo!" she wailed again. She was kneeling on the bed now, her eyes half open and staring out the window.

The shimmering green made the whole scene subaquatic, a watery dream, and Marguerite a wailing siren.

"Maggie!" I said, loudly this time, trying her nickname instead.

She turned to look at me. Her face was streaked with tears, her hair wet with sweat. She was trying to catch her breath, panting with exhaustion. She stared at me, still stunned, for several moments until sleep left her. Her breathing slowly returned to normal, and a look of recognition came across her face. "It's raining," she said.

I nodded. "Are you okay?"

I could hear Shelly's feet padding softly down the hallway. I didn't have to turn around to know she was standing in the doorway.

Marguerite pulled the sheets around herself as if suddenly embarrassed, and nodded quickly. "I'm fine. The thunder scared me."

"Okay," I said, deciding not to argue. There was no thunder. No lightning. Only the softest rain outside. "Let me know if you need anything."

As I left the room, I put my arm around Shelly's shoulders and steered her back to her own room. She climbed up into her bed and pulled the covers under her chin; she would likely not even remember all of this in the morning.

"Love you to the bottom of the ocean," she whispered, our ritual.

"And back to the top," I whispered, kissing her head.

For the rest of the night, I sat up reading in the living

room, waiting. But there was only the tapping of rain, the ticking of the clock, and the sound of my own exasperated breaths when sleep would not come.

The next morning the rain had stopped, and the air was cooler. It was Saturday, so I went to the bakery for doughnuts and then to the drugstore to pick up a copy of the *Free Press*. The train wreck was on the front page. TRAIN DERAILS: 29 DEAD, 11 MISSING, PRESUMED DEAD. I read the paper as I walked back to my building, narrowly missing the fire hydrant, the broken sidewalk, and another pedestrian. The roster read like those published in the paper during the war. I pored over the names, searching for some sort of clue. And finally, I found among the missing, now presumed dead, *Margaret Jones,* 15, of Tuscaloosa, Alabama. A single ticket. No Mrs. Jones anywhere.

Inside my house, Marguerite, aka Maggie, née Margaret, was making pancakes. She was wearing a dress that was too young for her, and with her swollen belly looked even more so. The collar looked like a little girl's dress. Her knees were exposed and bony.

Shelly was standing at the stove with a spatula, helping Marguerite flip the pancakes.

"I don't like her playing with the stove," I said, angry at the girl, whatever her name was.

"We're *cooking*, Daddy. I'm not a little kid."

"Do what your daddy says," she said, swatting Shelly's behind, and Shelly backed away from the stove obediently.

"Can I talk to you for a minute?" I asked.

"Sure," she said, smiling. "Just as soon as I flip this here flapjack. I don't need no burned hot cakes."

"In the other room, please," I said, rolling my eyes toward Shelly, who was pretending to be absorbed in a hangnail.

In the living room, the girl sat down on the couch and looked up at me, those disconcerting eyes wide and attentive.

"Listen, *Margaret Jones*, or whatever the *hell* your real name is. I don't know who you are, but I do know you didn't get on that train in Louisiana. And your mother wasn't on the train either. And now everybody in the world thinks you're dead." I had no idea where I was headed; I only knew that I was pissed that she'd lied to me.

She reached up then, desperate, and grabbed my hands. I was surprised by how warm they were, like two small birds, shuddering. Even though her eyes disturbed me, I couldn't look away.

"Please," she said. "I never *said* I got on the train in Louisiana. I come from Tuscaloosa. And I just lied about my name because I was scared. Marguerite is my cousin's name."

"You told me your mother was dead. That she was on the train. You *lied* to me."

"She *is* dead. I ain't got no mama. That's the damned truth." Her lip was trembling but her gaze was steady.

"And what about this aunt of yours? The one in Canada?"

"Daddy sent me away," she said; she was crying now. I glanced quickly to the doorway to make sure that Shelly wasn't eavesdropping.

"To your aunt?"

"He wants me to take care of this," she said. "But I ain't giving this baby to no stranger."

"Your aunt is arranging for an adoption?"

She was silent.

"Your father will be looking for you. I'm sure he's heard about the accident by now. I'm sure they're both worried sick."

"I promise, ain't *nobody* looking for me. And I *ain't* going back there," she said angrily. Then she took a deep breath and wiped her nose with the back of her hand. "Please. Just let me stay until I figure out where else I can go. I'll help you with Shelly. You don't have to pay me or nothin'. I'll keep your house. I'll do the wash. . . ." She squeezed my hands tightly as she spoke, and I thought then about her fighting ghosts with these tiny fists. I thought about the sound of her screams. About the cool green of that room and the terror in her eyes. There were a whole lot of things she wasn't telling me, but there was one thing I knew for certain. She was terrified of something, and for some reason, she was trusting *me* to keep her safe.

"Maggie," I said, shaking my head.

And she muttered, like a prayer, *"Please, please, please."*

1968: Fall

Headlights flick on and then off, fireflies signaling each other in the darkness. The dirt parking lot is empty, except for the carnies' trailers and these two vehicles, speaking to each other in flashes of light. Beyond this, the electric glow of the midway has been extinguished for the night; the only light now comes from a harvest moon. When the man opens his trailer door and peers outside, his face is illuminated by this eerie orange glow. It is quiet. He has no idea that they are waiting for him.

The air still smells of the midway: sweet fried dough, greasy French fries, lemon ice. This is the smell of childhood. Of sweetness. Of everything good in the world. But tonight, as Harper waits for this man whose name he doesn't even know, as his own childhood becomes more distant than God, Harper feels nothing but rage.

When the man ducks back into the tiny trailer, Harper feels his pulse quicken. He looks through the windshield at the truck across the lot. Soon, the truck door opens, and Brooder's hulking figure emerges. His stride is fast and certain as he makes his way to the trailer. Ray, who has been silent until now, looks at Harper then, asking the question whose answer will change Harper's life forever.

"You sure?"

And because everything is gone, leaving only this perfect rage, there is only one answer. He nods, and Ray puts the key in the ignition.

TWO

Lightning

I saved Betsy's life once. I'd like to be able to say it was an act of courage, a selfless and fearless moment of sheer heroism, but the reality of that moment is that it was preceded by panic, and I acted too slowly. She almost slipped through my fingers. I got lucky, really.

After Betsy's mother was sent away, Mr. Parker entrusted her to our family. He must have thought that because my mother was home all day that she had some sort of tether on me. What he didn't know was that my mother lived inside a world of books; it would have taken a natural disaster to pull her out of that world, and even then she would have come out kicking and screaming. My mother, stuck in Two Rivers with a head full of unfulfilled dreams, escaped every chance she got via the Two Rivers Free Library—her library card both passport and necessary currency for her travels. And with my mother's freedom came my own. If I felt like fishing from sunrise to moonrise at the river, if I wanted to walk the train tracks from Two Rivers to New York City, as long as I was home for dinner, I could have. Betsy and I were left to our own devices—at least until the sun went down.

There was a kid's fort in the woods beyond the elementary school. We never saw anybody playing in it, but sometimes we would discover things inside that we swore hadn't been there before: a Strato-Space cap gun, a moth-eaten coonskin cap, some plastic submarines. The first few times we closed ourselves inside the garrison made of plywood and corrugated tin, we half expected to be ambushed. After a while, though, it was clear that whoever had built the fort had probably grown too old for it and abandoned it. Betsy and I, on the other hand, kept going to our borrowed fortress long after we'd outgrown the games of our childhood. When pure imagination would no longer suffice as entertainment, we still returned to this rusty place. Inside the tin walls, during storms, it sounded like music. We'd sit there for hours sometimes, smoking stolen cigarettes or fabricating elaborate plans for one project or another. It was our respite. Our escape.

The day I saved Betsy's life, we had plans to remodel the fort. Betsy wanted to repair the leaky roof, and I planned to build a secret hiding space beneath the dirt floor. In my father's junkyard basement, I'd found an old safe, complete with a key. I pulled it all the way to the woods in my old Radio Flyer wagon. The safe was small in size (not much bigger than a shoe box) but it had to have weighed fifty pounds. It was a struggle, but I'd gotten it there, and as Betsy fought with some discarded shingles, I dug a hole. I had also absconded with my father's only shovel, all metal and much too large for this job. I would have probably done better with a trowel.

It was overcast, cold in the woods. Betsy was wearing one of her mother's old sweaters. It was unraveling at the cuffs, some forgotten thing left to the moths and salvaged by Betsy. It was the color of a green olive, but cashmere, and soft. Betsy rarely took it off on days like these. I liked the way she looked in that sweater. It hugged her shoulders, her small breasts. It was so soft, sometimes I had to resist the urge to reach out and stroke her.

I was so engaged in my task, in the efforts of removing both soil and rock from the ground, that I barely noticed when it started to rain. The fort was at least partially covered; the first few drops could have just been cold sweat dripping from my brow.

"It's raining," Betsy said, standing with her hands on her hips, looking down at me, squatting next to my hole. My legs were cramped, my back stiff.

"Come in then," I said, and she crawled in next to me, gazing up at the half-finished roof above us. The rain tapped at the tin, sporadic. "It won't last," I said. My father had built a machine once that could predict the weather. It was part barometer, part wishful thinking. I trusted my senses more than I trusted that contraption. And today I sensed that the heavy clouds that had made the woods grow suddenly dark were transitory.

Betsy sat down next to me and inspected my work. "That's a good hole," she said.

I nodded, pleased. "Help me put the safe in?"

"Sure." Betsy was pretty strong for a girl, but I still took on most of the weight as we positioned the safe over the hole.

"Now let go," I said, and as we did, the safe dropped perfectly into the ground, and only the door was exposed.

"It's a good hiding place," Betsy said. The air rumbled, low and deep.

My father's machine measured sound waves, their depth and distance. Predicted the approach of thunder.

"We could keep money in there," Betsy said, as the rain grew stronger.

"Cigarettes," I said.

"I'm going to put my diary in there."

The idea of Betsy's private journal, her innermost thoughts, residing next to a pack of my mother's Kools was almost more than I could bear.

Thunder cracked again, followed shortly after by a flash of light. The whole forest was illuminated for a moment. Betsy grabbed my arm and my heart flew.

"My father takes sleeping pills," she said. Bravely. "I could get some of those."

Suddenly the safe was starting to feel dangerous.

"I've got to figure out something to put over it to hide it. Maybe bricks or something."

"Nah, you should just cover it with dirt. Better camouflage." Betsy stuck her hand out through a makeshift window and pulled it back in. "It's pouring."

We sat inside the shack, shoulder to shoulder, trying to light one soggy cigarette from the pack I'd left outside with an equally soggy pack of matches, and the rain did not subside. It was nice in there. She linked her arm in mine, and I couldn't tell which was softer—the sweater or her skin.

"What time is it?" Betsy asked.

I checked my watch, a brand new Elgin railroad wristwatch, a gift from my father for my fourteenth birthday. It cost him an arm and a leg as well as three separate arguments with my mother, but it had been designed by engineers to be accurate to the second, which was something important apparently only to railroad workers and my father. "Almost four-thirty," I said.

"Shit," Betsy said. "Aunt Hanna and Uncle Paul are coming over for dinner. I was supposed to put the roast in at three-thirty."

"We can make a run for it," I said, peering out the window at the glistening trees.

Thunder rolled under us, making the fort shudder.

"Let's go," Betsy said, grabbing me by the hand and pulling me to my feet. My back was aching from the dig. I put the shovel in the wagon, and I pulled it behind me as we dashed from the fort to the nearest tree, which provided little by way of cover. Rain pelted our skin and lightning flashed again. Every branch on the tree became a dark silhouette against the white sky. When the rain lessened for a moment, we ran again,

this time toward the edge of the woods near the school parking lot. We stood underneath a tree, waiting for the rain to stop
beating the leaf-covered ground, but it would not abate.

One thing my father's storm machine had taught me was that
thunder and lightning went hand in hand: that there was rarely
one without the other. I would never have admitted this to
Betsy, but I was afraid of lightning. My mother knew a boy
who was struck dead by lightning on a baseball field. So when
thunder roared again, incessant and angry, I held on to Betsy,
whose hair was drenched. "Wait."

"I *can't*," she said, clearly irritated and cold now. She was
shivering. "I told my dad I'd have dinner ready by six. I've got
to *go*." And with that, she pulled away, and I'd be a liar if I didn't
say it hurt my feelings to have her wriggle away from me.

She ran toward the parking lot, and I watched her navigate
rocks and trees, her long braid swinging behind her. I stayed
under the tree, waiting for the inevitable flash of lightning. I
kept my eyes on Betsy, watching from afar as she first ran and
then slipped on the wet leaves and fell. Before I had time to
think, I found myself repeating her haphazard path toward the
edge of the woods. The sky burst into a kind of white fire, and
I shielded my eyes as if from the sun. I was blinded, and suddenly deafened by a loud crack. It sounded like the very earth
was splitting open. When my eyes regained their focus, my ears
still struggled to make sense of the dissonance. By the time I
realized that the sound was of a tree first being ruptured and
then crashing to the ground, my senses were so confused, I
could barely discern where I was relative to the parking lot.
Relative to Betsy. And when the tree came down, its descent
both slow and adamant, I didn't realize that Betsy, still sitting
on the ground, likely with a twisted ankle or banged-up knee,
was in its path.

I made my way to her as if I were skating, the ground was
so slick. By the time I got to her, the tree had already landed

and was laying across her lower stomach. It wasn't a huge tree, just a skinny birch, but it had pinned her to the ground. On one side of the trunk were Betsy's legs, and on the other side was the rest of her. Her eyes were closed. I fell to my knees and touched her hair. It was my first impulse. My second was to run. I thought that maybe if I ran quickly enough I could get to one of the houses near the school. I could call someone, an ambulance, her father. I even started to run when I realized how ludicrous my plan was. What I needed to do was lift the tree off her.

I looked at Betsy, still unconscious, and at the tree. "I'll get it off you," I promised. I knelt down next to her and tried to lift the tree. It wasn't a big tree, but it was heavy. The pain in my back intensified with the effort. I would need to use something to act as a lever underneath the trunk. I remembered my father's shovel. I located the wagon underneath the tree where I'd left it. "I'll be right back," I said to Betsy, who could have only been sleeping.

I studied the shovel, frantically trying to devise a scheme. I conjured all the physics and geometry lessons that might help. If I were to wedge the shovel part under the tree and step on the handle, the tree might come up, but who would pull Betsy out? If she didn't wake up, or if she couldn't move, this idea would be futile. And, if I were to release my weight from the shovel's handle, then the tree would crush her. I got an idea then. If I were to put the handle under the trunk, and load the shovel with something heavy enough to lift the tree, then I could pull her out. Relieved and terrified, I shoved the metal handle well under the trunk, right near Betsy's body, and looked around for something heavy enough to do the trick. The rocks that I found were either too big and awkward to lift, or too light to make any difference. I filled the shovel with armloads of pebbles, and stared at the tree, which remained. Rain was in my eyes and ears, blurring everything when I remembered. *The safe.*

I ran as fast as I could back to the fort, dragging the wagon and shovel behind me. The dirt floor of the fort was muddy from the storm. It took every ounce of my strength and every last bit of my energy to dig the safe out of the ground. But somehow, I managed to lift it out of the muddy well and load it into the wagon. My legs shook with exhaustion as I pulled the safe to where Betsy and the tree had fallen.

Betsy's eyes were open when I found her. "I thought you left," she said, her voice small and afraid.

Ashamed, I shook my head.

The rest happened so quickly I can barely remember rigging up the contraption that would lift the tree off Betsy. What I do remember is this: the next flash of lightning made Betsy squeeze her eyes shut, but I willed mine to stay open. I remember the muddy trails her hair made on my arms as I pulled her out from underneath the tree. And I remember that she felt small in my arms when I cradled her.

"Wow. You saved my life," she said, looking up at me, wide-eyed and grateful.

"Shut up," I said, feeling just a little heroic but mostly relieved. We were sitting on the ground, and I was still holding her. I watched my fingers move the hair out of her eyes. I wanted to kiss her. To hold her and kiss her and kiss her. I even closed my eyes for a minute, leaned toward her.

But then she sat up, brushed her hands off, and threw her shoulders back, wincing a little. "You saved my life, now I owe you mine." She was all business. As if we'd just made a simple transaction.

"Nah," I said, disappointed. "You don't owe me anything."

She nodded. "That's what happens when someone saves your life. You owe them yours. It's the truth." She was dead serious, and it scared me.

"Okay then." I laughed. "But I don't plan on collecting anytime soon."

Betsy broke three ribs that day, as well as her wrist. For the ribs she had to stay in bed for a whole week, but for the wrist she got a thick white plaster cast. And instead of being mad about it, Mr. Parker took me aside and shook my hand: thanked me for taking such good care of his little girl. I didn't tell Betsy what he said, or that this whole incident was further evidence of my greater purpose in her life. Instead, I just asked to sign her cast. By the end of the summer, it was covered in Magic Marker drawings and signatures, but I knew mine was under there. The first.

Stations of the Cross

"Y'all coming with me to church?" Maggie asked on Sunday morning. She was standing in the kitchen in a yellow dress that was freshly pressed: no evidence whatsoever of train wreck or foray into the river. There was a pale yellow ribbon tying her hair back in a puffy ponytail, and she was wearing stockings but not her shoes, which were sitting neatly by the front door.

"Daddy doesn't believe in God," Shelly explained, though I had certainly never articulated my lack of faith to her in those terms. "He's an *atheist*."

"Where did you hear that word?" I asked.

"Mrs. Marigold," she said. Mrs. Marigold, the expert on all things sacred and profane.

Maggie looked baffled and then a little hurt. "You *have* to believe in God," she said, slipping on first one shoe and then the next. Her feet were tiny little things. Like a doll's feet. "Who do you think made all the birds and flowers and stuff? Who put the blue in the sky?"

"I want to go to church too," Shelly said defiantly.

"You do?" I asked. She had never expressed any interest in religion. Normally, we spent Sunday mornings watching reruns of *The Jetsons* together, eating frozen waffles and scrambled eggs. But before I could say no, Shelly was putting her own shoes on, making two loops and then tying them together. The way a child does.

I didn't know how to explain to Shelly that it was probably not wise to be seen in public with Maggie. I'd given myself the weekend to make up my mind about what to do with her. To either try to find this aunt in Canada or call her father. In the meantime, I figured it would be best to act as if all of this was normal. For Shelly's sake as well as my own.

"I'll go with you then," I said, thinking that my tagging along might make the whole trip less desirable.

Shelly raised one dark eyebrow, one of those few expressions that belonged to Betsy, one of those mannerisms that made a lump in my throat each and every time. "Okay," she said, shrugging.

"You got a Baptist church here?" Maggie asked.

"Everything but," I said.

"You got any place with singing?"

"I don't think so. The only church I've ever been to is the Catholic one."

"Good enough. One house of God is as good as any I suppose," she said. "That's what my daddy says. He's a preacher, you know."

Well, that explained things.

St. Elizabeth's was just down the street, so we walked. Right through town. My mind was racing regarding how I would explain who this girl was when we inevitably ran into someone I knew. Shelly acted as tour guide, pointing out all of Two Rivers's landmarks along the way as Maggie asked questions and stopped to ponder what she found. Laundromat. Bronze statue of Ethan Allen. The place I'd helped Shelly write her name with a stick in wet cement. Luckily, by the time my friend Stan, from the freight office, and his wife pulled up next to us and rolled down the window, I had it all figured out.

"Hey, Stan. Ginny," I said, nodding.

"Hey, Harper. Saw you down to the river Friday. Helluva mess. I'm goin' to work soon as I drop Ginny off."

I nodded.

"Who's this?" he asked then, leaning across Ginny and reaching out the window to shake Maggie's hand.

I spoke before Maggie got a chance to. "This is Maggie— my mother's college roommate's youngest girl. She's staying with us for a while." I didn't have any more to offer than that. I figured I'd let them come to whatever conclusions they wanted to.

"I'm here to help Harper take care of Shelly," she said. "Till my own baby comes, of course." Her smile was so broad and white, the rest of her almost disappeared behind it. The Cheshire cat.

"Pleasure to meet you," Stan said.

Shelly tugged at me, visibly thrilled. "She's staying? For real?"

As Stan and Ginny pulled away, waving, I squeezed Shelly's hand. I never made a promise I couldn't keep, not anymore, so I thought long and hard before I answered her. "She can stay for *a while*."

"But what about Mrs. Marigold?" Shelly asked. Shelly was one of those rare children who almost always thought about other people before herself. "I mean, I'm pretty much too old for a sitter, but she thinks I still need her. She thinks without her I'd be eating corn dogs every night, that I'd be *malnourished*."

My pride hurt; my knee jerked. "She *said* that? Christ. Yes, Maggie can keep an eye out for you. But just until we talk to her family."

Shelly smiled the rest of the way to church. She grabbed Maggie's hand, and they skipped ahead, swinging their arms like little girls. It was an odd sight; Shelly had gotten so tall over the summer, and in this dress Maggie's predicament was obvious. Regardless, they skipped all the way up the forty-four steps to the doors of the church, and then Maggie straightened her skirt, whispered something in Shelly's ear, and they proceeded quietly through the doors.

Inside, sunlight was streaming through the stained glass windows, which depicted Jesus' demise—each window showing one step in His journey to crucifixion. We sat in a pew next to the image of Him carrying His cross. It struck me as ironic, and a little sad, this picture in glass of a man carrying the very instrument that would kill him. Shelly wriggled next to me on the uncomfortable wooden pew. Maggie stared straight ahead, her hands folded neatly on her lap.

I watched as families entered the church and found their seats, whispering hello to people to the left and right of us. I saw a few people look slightly startled to see us, though we weren't the only strangers to the service. There were a lot of faces I didn't recognize. Families of the passengers from the accident, I assumed. At least it made Maggie a little less conspicuous.

We all fumbled our way through the Mass, sitting and standing when the people in front of us did, searching through the thick hymnal for the words to the songs. Shelly seemed mesmerized by it all, the incense and colored lights shining through Jesus onto our laps. When the other parishioners started to form a line, Shelly followed behind Maggie, who turned to her and shook her head. "You can't come if you ain't baptized."

"What are they doing?" Shelly whispered.

"Eating communion," she said. "The Catholics call it the Body of Christ."

Shelly looked mortified. She sat down next to me again and watched Maggie as the line moved slowly toward the front of the church. When Maggie, her mouth closed over the Eucharist, returned to our pew and knelt slowly down to pray,

Shelly whispered loudly in my ear, "She didn't really just eat Jesus, did she, Daddy?"

"No," I whispered back, loud enough for Maggie to hear. "It's just bread."

Maggie kept her eyes closed and her hands pressed together in prayer.

"Mrs. Marigold said that sometimes people eat other people, and that it's a sin. But only people from Africa. *Cannibals*, that's what they're called."

"Shhh," I said.

We made it through the Mass without further incident. Even when the elderly priest asked the Lord to hear our prayers regarding all the people who'd been on the train that spilled into Two Rivers, Maggie didn't flinch.

Still, I was grateful to get outside the church after Mass was over. The day was cool and crisp, the sort of early fall day that normally made me feel glad to be alive. As we made our way back home, I hung back as Shelly and Maggie skipped ahead. And then just as we were about to round the corner to our apartment building, Paul and Hanna rounded the corner too.

"Hi," I said, smiling dumbly.

"Harper," Paul said. "We heard about the wreck. Are you okay? Someone said you were there, that you went in, looking for folks."

"You must be . . . from the train?" Hanna said to Maggie, and then to me, "you know, Lisa and Steve have taken in two little girls whose parents were . . . oh, this is just so tragic. I'm sorry, what was your name, sweetheart?" she asked, reaching out for Maggie's hand.

Maggie accepted her hand and shook it up and down vigorously. "I'm Marguerite DuFresne. I wasn't in the wreck. My mother went to college with Harper's mother. I'm here to help out with Shelly. I'm like family, really. See, when my mother found out that Harper was raising Shelly all by himself, she sent me straightaway. Besides, it's good practice for me, what with the baby coming and all."

Hanna was speechless.

Paul, who never liked anyone to feel uncomfortable, smiled and said, "Pleased to meet you, Marguerite."

"Call me Maggie." She smiled.

"Then let's have supper," Hanna said, forcing a smile. "It's been over a month since you came by for Sunday supper."

Before I could apologize, explain, and decline, Maggie was talking. Again.

"I make a mean Bananas Foster, I mean, if you don't mind a little liquor in your dessert on a Sunday." She smiled at Paul, and then she and Shelly were off skipping again, hand in hand down Depot Street toward Sunset Lanes.

The Heights

After the lightning and the tree, the only place Betsy felt safe during a storm now was inside a car. She'd heard somewhere that the best place to be if lightning were to strike was inside a vehicle. So on the days when the skies turned gray and thunder trembled in the air, I knew that Betsy would arrive at my house shortly, looking for shelter. Sometimes, if the rain had already started by the time she got to my house, she wouldn't even bother to knock, going straight to my father's '51 DeSoto, which I inherited on my sixteenth birthday. She would wait inside that great beast until I discovered her there, where her anxiety dissipated into a sort of cool excitement. When I found her waiting in the passenger's seat, she'd smile at me through the glass, motion for me to get inside the car, mouthing, "Hurry!" Then she'd grab my arm, a gesture that was simultaneously desperate and relieved, and say, "Let's go watch the storm."

Two Rivers is located in a valley, surrounded on most sides by hills. The Heights, just about eight miles outside of town, is the best place to watch a storm. You have to climb about two thousand feet to reach the Heights; my father's old car was a weary soldier on these missions, but the journey was worth it when we got to the top. From up there, you can see all of Two Rivers: the paper mill with its sulfurous smoke hovering over the river, the train tracks, almost serpentine below. The churches, all three of them, steeples each jutting into the air with purpose and escalating grandeur (*Methodist*, *Episcopalian*, *Catholic*). Depot Street, the hub of our world, and all the tiny houses with their inhabitants' tiny lives inside. During a thunderstorm, with the headlights out, it was better than the Fourth of July.

In the fall of 1963, not long after my senior year started, we had a week of storms. I remember this week as vividly as anything else that year. It was the same year that Martin Luther King Jr. spoke before a crowd of two hundred thousand people in Washington, D.C., and the Celtics beat the Lakers in the NBA Finals, but all that I remember was the incessant rain, the long slow drive up to the top of the Heights, with Betsy sitting next to me. The storm came in on a Sunday and did not leave until the following Saturday. Seven days and seven nights. Two Rivers had one of the worst floods in its 250-year history, a flood that killed livestock, destroyed homes, closed every school and almost every shop for a whole week. The playing fields by the school turned into ponds, causing Homecoming weekend and all of its ancillary activities to be cancelled, including the Two Rivers/Westport football game (a rivalry that reached epic proportions this time of year), much to the dismay of everyone, it seemed, but me. I welcomed the deluge, could have danced in the puddles, because each crack of thunder, each streak of lightning sent Betsy Parker into the front seat of my father's car. In the late fall of 1963, President Kennedy was shot and killed, but all that I remember is the static on the radio, the giant sweep of my windshield wipers, and Betsy's long legs stretched out in the front seat.

Though it had been nearly five years since Mrs. Parker was sent away, the family stuck to their story that she was simply ill, convalescing somewhere in the Midwest, though most people in town still believed otherwise. Only I knew that once a week

Betsy and her father drove to Waterbury to visit Betsy's mother. Every Sunday morning, they descended the crooked steps of their house, Betsy wearing a dress and pumps, her father in a good shirt and pressed pants. His hair was always shiny with pomade, but on these days it looked like he'd spent an extra minute in front of the mirror. There was no reason for anyone to suspect that they were headed anywhere but to St. Elizabeth's. My parents certainly never did. For one thing, they never went to church, despite the fact that they were both baptized Catholics. My mother hadn't been to Mass in more than thirty-five years, not since she cussed at a priest and stormed out of a confessional after her first stab at this holy sacrament. In her version of the story, the priest had it coming; she said he'd told her that if she didn't say a hundred Hail Marys that she was bound straight for hell. Her sin? Coveting her cousin Bobby's bicycle. Not for the coveting, but because girls shouldn't want to ride bicycles. She made it a point to ride her bicycle in front of the rectory every day after school after that. My father had lapsed not long after marrying my mother, and I wasn't even baptized. (I didn't tell my mother that sometimes I went to Mass with Ray and his family if I spent the night at his house on a Saturday. And I certainly didn't tell her that I sort of liked the sounds of the organ, the smell of incense. The promise of prayers.)

But on the Sunday that the flood of 1963 started, Betsy and her father didn't make their weekly trip. I was at home, helping my father build a device that would allow my mother to clean behind the toilet without getting on her hands and knees. It was really just a modified mop, with a swivel added on. My mother was in the kitchen, reading an article in *The New York Times* about four little girls in Alabama who were killed when a bomb went off in a church. She was talking to herself really, as my father was so engaged in the task of converting the mop, and I was busy checking the window, wondering why Betsy's father's car was still in the driveway.

"Children," she said. *Little girls.*"

I held one end of the mop as my father fastened the swivel to the other end.

Her voice grew louder and louder as she paced the kitchen floor. "Children who are kept ignorant so they can't fight back. That's the real reason all those bigots don't want integration. Knowledge is power. And giving power to a Negro is just too scary."

The whole idea of integration was as relevant to me and my life as a discussion about what to eat on the moon. There were no Negroes in Two Rivers. I'd seen one black person in my entire life when we went to visit my grandparents in Boston. He was standing at a bus stop, eating a hot dog. I didn't really see what the fuss was about.

"And so they kill these children before they even get a chance. It makes me nauseated. Doesn't it make you nauseated?" she asked us.

"Helen," my father said, clearly excited about his latest contribution to her homemaking endeavors. "Look!" He held up the ridiculous gadget, smiling stupidly at her.

Her expression grew from one of abstract frustration to one of pure anger. I'd never seen her look so furious.

"Jesus Christ!" she said, grabbing the mop from my father. She held it horizontally, like a barbell without any weights on the ends. Motionless. And then, with one turn of her wrist, it became a javelin, and she threw it toward the kitchen sink. For a second I was sure it was going to smash through the window over the sink and land in our front yard. It did crack the glass but, surprisingly, did not exit our house. Instead, it ricocheted, shooting back toward us, making both my father and I jump out of the way. It landed on the floor, and (because of the unfortunate incline of our house) it began to roll. It rolled clear through the dining room and stopped only when a chair leg obstructed its path. All three of us stood staring toward the dining room, bewildered.

"I'll be in my study," my mother said, gathered the newspaper under her arm, and left us.

Outside the air was tight. The rain was deceptively soft. If it hadn't been for the crack of thunder that was louder than shattered glass, you might think it was only a little sprinkle. My father and I didn't speak as he retrieved his invention. I waited for Betsy to rescue me from this awful silence, and thankfully, within moments after the first flash of lightning, I heard the door of the DeSoto slam shut.

"That's Betsy," I said to my father, and he nodded.

I ran outside; the rain was coming down harder.

"Please," she said. "Let's drive."

It was cold. One thing about that old DeSoto—the heater worked like a champion. Within a few minutes we were on the road, and hot gusts were blowing out of the vents. Betsy was wearing her mother's ratty green sweater and jeans, the same thing she'd had on the day before.

"You didn't go to the hospital today?" I asked. I always called it a hospital because in my imagination it looked just like the North Country Regional Hospital, where I had my tonsils taken out in the second grade. Only filled with crazy people. I tried to picture Mrs. Parker there, but my imaginings almost always involved her wearing a nurse's uniform. Clean and white and pretty. Sometimes, in my fantasies, she was feeding me ice cream. If I *had* been religious, thinking about Mrs. Parker like that probably would have been a sin. Sometimes it was best to be godless.

Betsy stared ahead, silent.

The DeSoto sluggishly made its way up the road toward the Heights.

"She was supposed to come home," Betsy said.

"What?"

"The doctors said she was *rehabilitated*. She just needed some rest."

"It's been *five years*," I said in utter disbelief.

Betsy was staring at the window. "There's medication, you know, to take care of the depression. It helps people, people like her, to *function in society*."

I thought of my own mother, hurling the mop, screaming about racism and bigotry. I remembered Mrs. Parker's lemon bars. The sway of her hips as she led me time and time again into that kitchen.

"That's great!" I said. "When is she coming then?"

Betsy's eyes filled, but she didn't blink. A sob snarled in her throat. "She's not."

"Hey, you okay?" I asked, reaching for her hand. It was soft. Warm.

"They found her this morning. She took pills, her pills and a whole bunch of pills she must have stolen from the other patients." She blinked hard, and wiped hastily at her wet cheeks. She laughed then, grimly. "I guess the idea of coming home was worse than staying in the hospital."

We drove in silence the rest of the way, as the rain picked up momentum outside. When we pulled over at the overlook, it beat against the windows. I left the car running, the heat blowing. Streaks of lightning split the sky, and Betsy pulled the sleeves of her mother's sweater over her hands. She looked straight ahead. She didn't ask me to turn on the radio like she usually did. I wanted to touch her, but I didn't know how.

When she turned to me, I thought for one terrible but thrilling moment that she was going to kiss me. I anticipated the way her lips would feel pressed against mine. This wasn't the first time I'd dreamed this. I'd been rehearsing this moment ever since she first kissed me. And then the reality of the moment crested: *Mrs. Parker was dead*. Guilt washed over me in one, big wave.

But before I had time to speak, she grabbed my wrist, hard, and pulled my hand toward her. Then she was lifting her shirt with her free hand, and my knuckles were grazing the soft skin of her stomach. I could feel her ribs, the fabric of her bra, and the soft swell of her breast underneath. I caught my breath. She was still holding my hand, but she was forcing my fingers open, spreading my palm flat against her skin.

"Sometimes," she said, "my heart stops. Sometimes I can't feel it beating at all."

She was pressing my hand so hard into the center of her chest I could feel the resistance of bone. I wondered if she pressed hard enough, if it might just crumble.

"Do you *feel* it?" she asked. There was an urgency in her voice, a tremble I'd never heard before.

I pressed my hand harder. I could feel the rhythmic beating of her heart in my palm. Its cadence pounding through my whole body.

"*Do you?*" she asked again. Frantic.

I nodded. "Yes."

We stayed like this for a long time, me feeling her heart in my fingers, in my shoulders, in my *whole body*, and then she moved my hand. To her breast, slowly, and I looked at her (for some sort of explanation, for permission, *something*), but her eyes were closed. She leaned her head back then, and let go of my hand. Tentatively, I moved my palm back down to her rib cage, pushing my thumb underneath the bottom edge of her bra, holding my breath as I touched her. Her skin was so hot and soft, it hardly seemed real. I had to force myself to breathe as I reached further, holding her whole breast in my hand, cradling her in my hand, my thumb stroking the surprisingly hard nipple at the center of all of this soft warmth.

Betsy moaned softly, arching her back, her head thrown back and her throat exposed.

"God," I whispered, my whole body aching.

Betsy reached up then and held my hand again, guided my fingers in slow circles. Under my fingertips, her heart beat hard and fast, but her breath was faster. And then her whole body trembled, electric. Blood pounded in my temples, between my legs. Outside, thunder cracked and she lowered her head, burying it in my neck. I stroked her hair, her face, her shoulders.

"I'm going to go to college," she whispered. "Next fall."

I couldn't make sense of a single thing she'd said. I could still feel her skin, hot and tingling in my hand. I heard my mother's voice, *Knowledge is power. Little girls.* I thought of Mrs. Parker building a snowman inside that winter kitchen, swallowing pills. All of this was jumbled inside my head, which was throbbing.

"College?" I repeated.

She sat up and looked out the window at the blue-black sky.

"Just the state college, in Castleton. It's not so far away. I'll be home every weekend." She was talking quickly, almost manic, tugging at a loose thread in the cuff of her mother's sweater. Thunder roared as she went on and on. "I've been thinking about studying art. Photography. Music, I don't know." She shook her head.

When lightning split the sky, I felt it rip through me.

Betsy pulled the thread slowly, carefully and meticulously unraveling.

"You *can't*," I said.

She stopped talking and looked at me, her face blank.

"My mother is dead," she said, loudly. Angrily. It was the first time she had ever yelled at me, and I felt like I'd been punched.

"I don't want to wind up like her. I don't want to be some housewife making potpies and pitchers of Kool-Aid. It *killed* her. Can you try to understand that?"

"Betsy," I said, already sorry.

"Please," she said, exasperated. "Turn out the headlights. Let's just watch the storm."

Sunday Supper

Paul and Hanna have known me for ages. When we were kids, I went with Betsy to their house for dozens of Sunday suppers. We continued this Sunday ritual all through high school and even later whenever we were both home from college. By the time Betsy died and Shelly and I moved into their little house by the river, the smell of a New England boiled dinner, mixed with Paul's sweet cigar smoke, already felt like home. Even now, when Hanna ushered us into the foyer, the smell of turnips and tobacco was pacifying. It even made me feel a little homesick.

"I hope you brought your appetites," Hanna said, smiling. She was wearing lipstick in a color I didn't recognize, an orange-y hue. Her lips were cracked, and the color bled garishly around her mouth, making her look clownish. She couldn't look me in the eye, even as she took my hand and led me into our old room to show me what she'd done.

"That was my mother's machine," she said, gesturing toward a treadle sewing machine. It was in the window where my bed used to be. There were baskets brimming with fabrics and yarn all over the room. A chair that used to be out on the porch was in the corner where my dresser had been. There were bright new curtains, yellow with white polka dots, and I realized that this was probably what she'd been wanting to do with this room for twelve years.

"It looks great, Hanna," I said.

She nodded. I had left Shelly and Maggie in the kitchen with Paul. I had one ear listening to Hanna, and one straining to hear what might be going on in the other room.

Hanna looked toward the door, checking to make sure we were still alone. "Your *mother's friend's daughter?*" she said.

"Yes."

"Come to help out with Shelly?"

I nodded. I tried to remember if I'd ever met my mother's college roommate. I had a vague recollection of a woman with long blond hair. I'd met her only once, and at the time I don't think she had any children. Certainly not a girl like Marguerite. *Margaret.*

"You could have asked *us* for help, you know."

I realized then that Hanna was less concerned with Maggie's sudden appearance and more hurt that I'd somehow sought help from outside the family. She thought that I hadn't been able to do things on my own, that I was already failing in my efforts to parent Shelly myself.

"You could've always come back here—if it wasn't working out for you. If it was too much. You didn't need to get somebody, a stranger . . ." she started, her voice trembling.

"I know, Hanna," I said. "But with Shelly starting seventh grade, and everything, it was time for us to get our own place. We all know that. And Maggie's just going to be with us for a little while."

Hanna dabbed at her nose with a tissue she had pulled like a magician from the cuff of her sweater.

"Besides, where would you have set up shop?" I tried to make light of what was becoming an uncomfortable situation.

The smell of turnips was suddenly almost unbearable.

"I only hope she's not a bad influence on Shelly," she whispered then, leaning into me. "I mean, what with a baby comin', and her not even being married. . . ."

I scowled at her.

Hanna's gasp was audible. "Oh, honey, I didn't mean nothin' by it. You and Betsy, your wedding came long before . . ." Tears welled up in Hanna's eyes, and it made me feel terrible watching her try to back out of this one.

"I know," I said, squeezing her hand. "I'm just trying to help out one of my mother's friends. That's all. And this will be good for Shelly." As I spoke, I tried to convince myself of it as well. I hadn't even considered how to explain the mystery of Maggie's baby's father to Shelly. I'd have to think of something before Maggie took the explaining upon herself.

"How far along is she?" Hanna whispered again.

"I don't know." I shrugged. "Maybe four, five months?"

"Is she going to keep the baby?"

I thought about Maggie in the woods then, the river and the accident, muffled cries in the distance. I thought about the aunt in Canada, about what her father had planned for Maggie's baby.

"I don't think she's gotten that far," I said.

"Okay, okay," Hanna said, shaking her head. She straightened a basket brimming with fabric. "None of my beeswax. Let's go have a nice supper. I made popovers."

Maggie laughed at something Paul said as she spread butter on one of Hanna's famous popovers: golden and crisp on the outside, filled with sweet hot air inside. I must have eaten five or six of them without realizing it. I missed Hanna's cooking. Shelly must have too; she was shoveling beef and potatoes into her mouth as if she were starving.

"Hey, Harper, real sorry to hear about Tony," Paul said, as Hanna was serving up hot spoonfuls of apple crisp for dessert. (She'd passed on Maggie's unholy Bananas Foster.)

"What's that?" I asked.

"Here, honey. Have some ice cream on it. It'll cool it down

a little," Hanna said to Shelly, who was blowing into the hot apple steam.

"Your friend, Tony Kinsella. Didn't you pal around with him in high school?"

"Brooder." I nodded. "We called him *Brooder*." My throat felt thick as I said his name. I hadn't uttered it in nearly twelve years. "Why, what happened?"

Hanna shot Paul a look that was both a reprimand and a plea for him to stop talking.

"What?" I asked.

Hanna set down the casserole dish and reached for my hand. It was the first time she'd looked me in the eyes since we got there.

"He's *passed away*," she said.

I felt like someone had hit me in the gut.

"Passed away?" Those were words you used for someone who dies in his sleep. Who simply closes his eyes. I knew that nothing about this could be peaceful.

Hanna clenched her jaw tight, pointed her chin toward Shelly, and raised her eyebrow.

"What *happened*?" I asked again.

"Shelly girl, come see the birdhouse I'm building," Paul said, rescuing us all.

"Can I come too?" Maggie asked, gobbling a giant spoonful of apple crisp and ice cream.

"Sure, honey. Come along."

When the screen door slammed shut behind them, Hanna said, "It was his wife that found him. He used his grampa's shotgun."

"Jesus Christ," I said, more invocation than curse.

Sliding

Ray Gauthier and Brooder were buddies of mine from first grade on. When I wasn't with Betsy, I was with them. Ray came from a big French Canadian family (six older sisters) and Brooder lived alone with his grandparents in a farmhouse out in the sticks. The story was that when Brooder was just a couple of years old, his mother left him and moved down south to Florida, where she worked as a mermaid at Weeki Wachee Springs, a roadside attraction where women dressed as mermaids and performed, seemingly breathless, in an underwater theater. He had a black and white photo postcard to prove it; a dark-haired girl brushing her hair under water, a shimmering tail curled underneath her. He kept the picture over his bed like any other pin-up.

Brooder's grandparents were good people; very old and mostly oblivious, which was probably a good thing to be with Brooder living under their roof. Italian immigrants, neither one of them spoke much English. Between the two of them, they were pretty useless when it came to keeping Brooder out of trouble. Brooder was behind almost every stupid thing I did as a kid. He initiated every fight, every drunken escapade, every misdemeanor. He was hardly the kind of friend my mother envisioned for me. She wouldn't even acknowledge him when I brought him by the house. He was unswayed by her treatment of him, bringing her more than one straggly bouquet of roadside wildflowers, paying her more than a hundred compliments on everything from her hair to her miserable cooking. "He's like a wild animal, Harper," she said to me once after he dropped me off after school. "A wild, rabid animal."

Indeed, Brooder was an instinctual creature, acting almost always in response to either some base need or desire without regard for consequences. By our senior year in high school, he'd even started to look the part: his curly hair growing outward like an untrimmed hedge, a mustache and beard growing in thick and wolflike. His permanent scowl, which had engendered his nickname when he was only a baby, was now topped by a row of bushy eyebrows, which intensified the brooding quality of his expression. Girls liked him because they thought he was deep. Plus, he could play the guitar, and his voice was pure and sweet, like thick maple syrup. Betsy was unimpressed. "He's going to get you in a lot of trouble some day," she said.

Ray, like me, was a follower. With six older sisters, he'd learned early on to just give in. He'd been dressed up in doll clothes, pushed in strollers, and generally humiliated his whole life. Rather than fight what would certainly prove to be a futile battle, he submitted to their whims. Becoming one of Brooder's sidekicks was probably a relief; at least Brooder didn't make him wear makeup. What Brooder did do, however, was set into motion all sorts of regrettable situations. I can blame every episode that caused me either embarrassment or shame on Brooder. But there was something about him that made it virtually impossible to say no. He was as cunning as a medicine show doctor, but loyal. He might get you into a world of trouble, but he'd never stab you in the back. He wouldn't so much as utter an unkind word about you. He was loyal to a fault. I have to remind myself of that now.

After Betsy's mother died, I started to spend more time with Ray and Brooder. I was uncomfortable at the Parkers' house now. It felt haunted somehow, now that she was truly

gone. I was also hurt that Betsy had decided to leave me in
Two Rivers to go to college. That winter of my senior year I
spent a lot of time with the guys, preparing myself, I suppose,
for when Betsy was gone. Punishing her for leaving me.

The winter of '63–'64 was a bitter one. I've never been
one to complain about the weather, but there was more than
one time that winter that I wished I had the common sense
that both the birds and Brooder's mother had had to go south.
One particularly frigid afternoon, Brooder got a wild hair up
his ass and wanted to go sledding. In the middle of the day. In
the middle of the week. In the middle of Old Man Keller's
pasture. Keller was a notorious asshole, shooting at kids who
snuck onto his acres and acres of land to steal apples or at cou-
ples who wandered there accidentally looking for a place to
make out. He had three dairy cows and a new pig each year.
He always won the blue ribbon for his swine at the county fair
and, to me, had more than a few porcine qualities himself. He
lived alone in a big old stone farmhouse at the base of a beautiful rolling hill. This was what Brooder had in mind.

Keller owned and ran the feed store in town, which was
open late on weeknights, so we figured we'd be pretty safe
until nightfall. We parked the truck out at the Catholic cemetery and trudged through about three feet of snow to Keller's
clearly marked property, Brooder spitting his mouthful of
chew at the NO TRESPASSING sign, which was nailed to a tree.

It had to have been near zero, and I wasn't dressed for sliding. (In Vermont it's called "sliding," probably because icy hills
lend themselves more to sliding than sledding.) Brooder had
pulled me out of the cafeteria during lunch, giving me little
time to grab more than my jacket and a hat from my locker. I
had boots on, but no mittens and no long underwear. Ray didn't
even have a hat, and his ears, which already stuck out from the
sides of his head like wings, were beet red by the time we got
to the top of the hill with the dented metal flying saucer

Brooder had stolen from some kid's backyard. It was overcast out, not a ray of sunshine penetrating the gray.

"Have some of this," Brooder said, pulling a metal flask from his pocket. "That'll warm you pussies up."

I took a sip (bourbon, which was sweet in my throat and warm in my chest) and then passed it to Ray, whose nose hairs were starting to crystallize. He took a swallow too, even though his daddy was a raging alcoholic, and normally he never touched the stuff.

Brooder was the first one down, of course. He had to demonstrate. There was, actually, a bit of a trick to it. Keller's house was right at the foot of the hill. To the left was a giant elm, and to the right was a small duck pond. It was more than likely frozen over, but you didn't want to take a chance like that. And so we aimed, instead, for his back steps. Brooder hurled feet first toward the stone steps, stopping himself just before he flew into Keller's back door. I was the next to make the trip, actually flying up two steps. By the time Ray went, he almost smashed into Old Man Keller's kitchen.

All afternoon we slid. From atop the hill we could see the road leading toward Keller's property as well as the winding driveway. The way we figured it, we'd have more than enough warning that Keller was on his way home.

We were all pretty liquored up by the time the sun went down, numb in every possible way. It felt good. We were whooping it up when the first stars started to shine through the cloud coverage. Brooder was doing some sort of elaborate dance in the snow, and I was watching him as I almost always watched him, with both fascination and dread. Ray was on his way down for about the hundredth time. By the time we realized that the lights in the distance were headlights in the driveway, he'd already pushed off again, screaming something in his daddy's drunken French all the way down the hill. I turned to run in the opposite direction, over the back side of the hill. I was drunk but not stupid, and I knew it was my only chance. Brooder yanked my arm though, not letting me go, and made me watch what ensued.

Ray's feet hit the door, and the saucer flew up into the air just as the lights went on inside the house. He scrambled to his feet, but being both knee-deep in snow and drunk as a skunk, his attempts at escape were futile. He was able, however, to grab the saucer just as Old Man Keller swung open the back door and raised his shotgun. And as Keller fired, Ray ran, using the saucer like a shield, scurrying up the icy path our sliding had made. We heard the shot hit the metal and then everything was quiet all around us. It was snowing, big girly sorts of snowflakes—the kind you wish for on Christmas morning. Ray had fallen to the ground, and was lying underneath the saucer just a few feet away from where we had been crouching. I watched Old Man Keller, apparently satisfied, shoot his rifle into the air one more time and then close the door.

I knocked on the saucer, the echo of my bare knuckles on metal louder than I'd intended. Ray moaned underneath. Brooder lifted it off Ray and helped him get up. We all walked silently back down the hill, and in the dim glow of the one streetlight that illuminated the cemetery's entrance, we examined the sled. There were three holes, still hot, right in the middle where the shot had nearly gone through the metal. We marveled at it, and I shook Ray's hand, frankly in dumb wonder at his being alive. Ray whooped, and I echoed his joy and relief. Brooder, however, remained silent, ushering us quickly into his truck, peeling out of the cemetery and heading straight for Keller's house. At the foot of Keller's driveway, he cut the truck's lights and rolled quietly up the drive.

"Jesus Christ," I said. "What are you doing?"

But Brooder only opened the truck door, grabbed his shotgun from the rack in the back of his truck, and started walking toward Keller's barn. Ray and I sat stunned in the cab of the truck. The liquor was wearing off, and so was the blissful numbness.

"What's he doin'?" Ray asked, trying, as I was, to make out Brooder's shape in the darkness.

The shot rang out loud, but not as loud as the squeals of Keller's new baby pig. Several more shots went off, this time from Keller's gun, as Brooder ran back toward us. No one said a word when he got back in the truck, or during the entire drive back into town. There wasn't room for conversation. And I couldn't get that awful sound out of my ears for weeks.

Brooder enlisted in the army not long after that. He shaved off his wild man mustache and beard, went to Betsy's father for his first flat-top. I figure now he probably knew he wasn't likely going to graduate, and I knew, after that night, he was capable of terrible things. Maybe he did too.

Sometime that winter, I decided to go to college. Despite the escapades of our fumbling triumvirate, I was a straight A student. But my academic ambitions had little to do with getting an education and everything to do with Betsy Parker. When I finally accepted that she was really planning to leave me behind, the choice was clear. I gave in to my mother's pleas to become a matriculated student at her alma mater; with her legacy and my good grades, I was almost guaranteed admittance. Besides which, Middlebury was only about thirty miles from Castleton State College, where Betsy Parker would soon be a bona fide coed.

I never told Betsy what happened that night at Old Man Keller's. I was too ashamed. She understood people, and she'd been right about Brooder.

Eulogy

Because of the train wreck, Brooder's suicide, which would normally have had the town abuzz, occurred without much fanfare. Normally, it would have provided the old men and women who roosted at Rosco's Diner by the train station each morning with hours of speculation as to Brooder's motive for (and mode of) killing himself. But because a train derailed leaving forty people dead (well, thirty-nine), there was little time to discuss whether Brooder had caught his wife, Brenda, sleeping with Martin Hayward, the dentist, and how he'd managed to pull the trigger on his shotgun with the other end of it in his mouth. Brooder's death was relegated to the second to last page of the newspaper, in a short obituary with a spelling error as sad and violent as his death itself.

> Tony (Brooder) Kinsella, 34, passed away on Saturday, September 25, 1980. Born January 1, 1946, in Two Rivers, he was the grandson of Anthony and Sophia Kinsella. Tony attended Two Rivers High School from 1961 to 1964, leaving school to join the United States Army. A decorated combat soldier, he served four years in Vietnam and returned to Vermont in 1968. Tony is survived by wife, Brenda Hopkins, and son, Roger. He was a loving grandson, husband and father. A fearless and loyal fiend.

The funeral was to be held at St. Elizabeth's on Tuesday morning. In the chaos of the accident, Lenny was too busy to reject my request to duck out for an hour to attend the services. He was on the phone with the National Transportation Safety Board, and he brushed me away like a fly when, after several attempts at talking to him, I slipped him a note.

Inside the church, I found my way to a pew near the back and watched as the few guests filed in. Brooder's grandparents were long gone. His wife, Brenda, was from Florida—a girl he met when he went looking for his mother, the mermaid, in '68 after he got back from Vietnam. She was working at Weeki Wachee when he found her, starring in their "Underwater Dream Girls" show. It took him three years, but somehow he convinced her to marry him and move to Two Rivers. Only Brooder could persuade someone, especially someone as good-looking as Brenda, that she'd be better off living with him in the backwoods of Vermont than in sunny Florida. I didn't know her well. I'd only seen her from a distance before: at the grocery store, the post office. The last time I'd seen her was a few years before, when she and Brooder were walking across the street, pushing a baby in a stroller. Today, she entered the church alone, followed by a boy who could only be Brooder's son. It took my breath away. He was probably only about four years old, but he looked just like his father. The intensity of his expression did not belong to a child; his eyes, downcast, and scowl belonged to my old friend. They sat in the first row, Brenda genuflecting before sliding into the pew. Her hair was the color of sunshine.

Ray Gauthier, like me, had parted ways with Brooder twelve years ago, so I was pretty surprised to see the Gauthier clan enter the church. Ray and his wife, Rosemary, and their son, J.P., followed behind Ray's parents and six sisters. The air smelled sweet after they passed. Ray's head was lowered in what I suppose was something between respect and shame. He looked up only once and, catching my eye, nodded and then quickly lowered his gaze again. My chest was hot; it was suddenly hard to breathe.

The ceremony was brief, solemn. There couldn't have been more than thirty people in the church. No one offered a eulogy, and only Brenda cried. There was no reception in the church basement afterward, no dry sandwiches and bitter coffee. The attendees offered rushed condolences to Brenda and then moved together out of the church, a whispering swarm. I was familiar with this buzz, this threatening hum. *Had it coming . . . good for nothing . . . lunatic. If he didn't do it himself, somebody else sure . . .* Watching Brenda's small shoulders trembling with grief, I felt the momentary impulse to go to her, to tell her that, no matter what anyone said, Brooder had been a good friend. A loyal friend.

In the window next to me, bright autumn sunlight shone through a stained glass Jesus who had just been condemned. Pontius Pilate was pointing at Him in accusation, Jesus' face sadly defiant. I waited until everyone had left the church, avoiding looking at anyone, especially Ray and his family, and then I escaped out into the cold fall day.

I should have gone straight back to work. Orders were backed up, shipments had been delayed, people, including Lenny, were angry. But I couldn't get that buzz out of my ears. And so instead of returning to work, I got on my bicycle and pedaled down the steep hill away from St. Elizabeth's, through town, and then out toward the river. I didn't stop until my legs as well as my chest were burning. It was cold but bright in the woods, fallen red and gold leaves an autumnal pyre. When I got to the place where the two rivers meet, I threw my bike down to the ground, knelt on the cold damp earth, and wept.

1968: Fall

When Brooder comes out of the trailer, the man is following him, carrying a pair of jumper cables. Harper watches as they walk toward Brooder's truck. The man seems smaller than Harper remembered. Thinner. For a moment there is doubt. Just the slightest uncertainty. But when the man turns toward them, Harper is sure again. Anger rises up into his shoulders. It spreads to his jaw; he feels his teeth grinding.

The moon is swollen now, rising impossibly bright and orange over the horizon. Harper has never seen anything so ominous, or so beautiful. It is nearly as bright as the sun, casting strange shadows as Brooder pops the hood.

Ray turns the key, revving the engine. Harper feels like he is watching this from somewhere far away, a Ferris wheel view, as if he were watching these events unfold from the moon itself. Ray shifts the car into first gear and steps on the gas. Gravel and grass crush underneath the slow tires. He pulls the car up next to Brooder's truck and rolls down the window. "Find some cables?" Ray asks.

"Yeah," Brooder says, and then, nodding at the man, "mind hooking these up? I've got a flashlight in the car."

Harper is aware suddenly of a hangnail that he has been gnawing on. His finger is sore, the pain deep and sharp, yet he can't resist pulling at it with his teeth. Harper swallows loudly, wipes sweat away from his forehead with the back of his wrist.

As the man leans under Brooder's hood, Harper watches his back, studies the curve of his shoulders. The slope of his neck, the angles of his elbows. But when Brooder comes out of the car, Harper's eyes are drawn away from the man to the object in Brooder's hand.

Harper studies the tire iron with the same mathematical curiosity. He considers the perfect perpendicular metal bars, Brooder's hand grasping the point of intersection. But when Brooder stands behind the man and raises the tire iron over his head, the geometry shifts. Against the harvest moon, everything changes. Harper looks away from the weapon to the shadow cast beneath, and sees on the ground below a giant, elongated cross.

THREE

Freedom School

My father had a friend from college who worked for Honeywell—making electronics, including computers. When he told my father about a top secret work-in-progress, a "Kitchen Computer," designed to help busy housewives store and retrieve recipes, my father became obsessed. Apparently, this home computer would come fully equipped with a cutting board, so that the woman of the house could chop vegetables while reading a recipe from the computer screen. He rubbed his hands together, in his gleeful, mad-scientist way as he described it to me. *You can't tell your mother*, he said, conspiratorially. *It's an anniversary gift.* (In May they would be married twenty years.) The Honeywell version would eventually sell for just over $10,000, and so my father, ever industrious and frugal, disappeared into the basement the winter of '63, like a hibernating bear, only to emerge the following spring giddy and triumphant.

But while my father was wintering in his subterranean laboratory, my mother was entertaining aspirations more lofty than his electronic cookbook could ever fulfill. Still incensed by the atrocity of the Alabama church bombing the previous fall, she decided to join a group of volunteers to teach in a "Freedom School" in Mississippi for the summer. As my father tinkered and programmed below us, my mother confided in me, "My friend Susan, from Middlebury, has gotten involved with the SNCC, the Student Non-Violence Coordinating Committee," she said, her eyes bright. She was at the kitchen table with paperwork spread before her. "They're recruiting volunteers to go to Mississippi to help register blacks to vote and to teach in special schools set up to give Negroes a place to learn how to read, write. *Music. French.* About their rights. About their history."

"You're *moving*?" I asked, dumbfounded.

"Not moving," she said, peering at me over the top of her glasses. In the last year or so she'd started wearing glasses to read. It had made me feel for the first time like she was getting old. "Just working, for the summer. You and your father can fend for yourselves, I'm sure."

Though my mother disappeared inside her study for hours, even days on end, she was a fixture in our house. Like the Windsor chimes that announced each quarter hour. The worn velvet couch. I tried to imagine her absence and it felt like stepping into a hole.

She would have to interview in Boston first, a formality, she said. Then in late June (*after* my graduation, she assured me) she would take a bus to Oxford, Ohio, where she would attend an orientation at the Western College for Women. From there, she would make her way to Palmer's Crossing, Mississippi, where she would start teaching just after the Fourth of July at the Priest Creek Baptist Church.

"At a church?" I asked in disbelief.

"That's where most of the schools have been set up. In the South, the churches are the hubs for the black communities."

"Where will you live?"

"There's a family," she said, "from the church. They have two children who will be attending the school. A grown son who is a minister. He will teach at the school as well."

"What does Dad think?" I asked.

"About the Freedom School?"

"About your leaving us," I said.

"I'm not *leaving* you. This is one summer," she said, exasperated. She removed her glasses then, and I could see how tired she was. "Can't you understand that I need to *do* something with my life? Something important? I'm forty-two years old, and what have I done?" Her face was red, like a child's about to cry. It embarrassed me.

I thought about Betsy's mother. About her soufflés and cupcakes and the snowman she built inside their kitchen. I thought about Betsy's face when she told me her mother was dead. I nodded. And then I remembered my father's grand surprise in the basement.

"I need this," she said softly.

On my parents' anniversary, while my mother was at the library, my father recruited me to help him move his homemade computer upstairs. It had to have weighed two hundred pounds. I tweaked my back as we turned the contraption on its side to get it through the narrow doorway.

"Hold on a second," I said, adjusting my arms to avoid further damage.

"Got it?"

"Yep."

Somehow we managed to get it into the living room and set it down. I flopped onto the couch and really looked at it for the first time. It was a monstrosity.

"So what can it do?" I asked.

My father grinned. "Let me show you."

He proceeded to explain that, like its commercial counterpart, it was designed to store recipes in an electronic format. That he had taken my mother's battered box of recipe cards and programmed the recipes into the computer.

"But here's the best part," he said, beaming. "The Honeywell will have a cutting board built in—so does this one." He gestured toward the wooden butcher block situated below the computer screen. "But the Honeywell won't have *this*." He reached for a door, a converted glove box, in the front of the console and pulled it down, revealing a full set of kitchen knives, all tucked tidily into another wooden block. "Or this!" he said, opening a cupboard door on the far side of the console that revealed a brand new set of pots hanging from a rotating lazy Susan.

"Wow, Dad," I said.

He stood back and admired his invention. He was sweating; there were beads of condensation on his glasses. "What do you think Mom will think? Will she like it?" he asked, running a hand over his thinning hair.

I looked at the computer because I couldn't look at him. It was a *cookbook*. A two-hundred-pound cookbook. "Sure, Dad."

"Twenty years," he said, shaking his head. "That's a good, long time."

I nodded.

He was quiet then, as he circled the console. He put his hands on his hips. My mother was leaving in three days for her interview in Boston. "I figure we can break it in for her this summer, while she's gone. Work some of the bugs out."

My mother's eyes were huge when she came into the living room that afternoon. She was carrying an armload of books, which she set down on the coffee table without looking away from the machine. "What is *this*?" she asked softly.

As my father explained it to her, dizzily demonstrating how my grandmother's recipe for clam chowder could be conjured in only moments with the careful manipulation of a series of buttons and switches, my mother watched him. He had even brought an onion in from the kitchen, which he chopped into smithereens using the knives and the cutting board. When he had completed his demonstration, he stood back and looked proudly at the computer, and then anxiously at my mother.

I was standing in the doorway of the kitchen, eating a sandwich. I could barely swallow.

"Happy anniversary!" he said.

My mother's eyes were rimmed red. She removed her glasses and rubbed them with one weary hand. After an excruciating silence, she said, "Thank you," and reached the other hand out for my father.

He took her hand, kissed her palm gently and then swept her up in his arms, hugging her tightly. Proud. Triumphant. "Onions getting to you?" He laughed, releasing her, holding her at arm's length, and wiping awkwardly at a tear.

"Sure," she said, smiling. "Onions."

Alteration

I gave Maggie my room. It didn't seem right to make Shelly share the first bedroom she'd ever had to herself, and I was sleeping so little, I figured I hardly needed my bed anyway. She arranged the few things she'd brought with her on the top of my dresser (which I emptied for her): a photo of herself and two other girls, leaning against a red Chevy Monte Carlo. There was a giant willow tree in the background, a gray house. A clothesline with white sheets. The girls were all wearing short shorts and halter tops, posing, puckering their lips. There was a small painted wooden box with a gold clasp and tiny padlock, a bleached sand dollar, and a pack of matches from some place called Joe's. I didn't look inside the box, but I did strike one match. Just one, and held it until the flame tickled the tip of my thumb.

All week, I tried my best to pretend that none of this was out of the ordinary, secretly hoping the problem would some- how take care of itself. I kept waiting for her father to show up at my doorstep and just take her home. At work when Henry said that Stan told him I'd hired some help for Shelly, I stut- tered but stuck to my story about my mother's college room- mate's daughter. And each night as I fought my futile battle against insomnia, I vowed that I would contact Maggie's fa- ther. When dawn broke each morning, I rolled off the couch, resolute in my decision to send her home, and then I'd make my way to the kitchen, where she had already fixed bacon and eggs, ironed my clothes, and packed Shelly's lunch. The smell of starch and freshly squeezed orange juice worked like some sort of magic antidote to my resolve, making all of my late night ruminations seem somehow ludicrous. It also didn't help that Shelly had fallen head over heels for Maggie. Several times I had to shoo her out of Maggie's room at night, where she sat cross-legged at the edge of the bed, chattering on and on as Maggie painted her nails or braided her hair. This was the true rub. Just when I felt confident in my decision to turn her in, to throw her back into the water so to speak, I'd see the joy in Shelly's face. This child-woman with confused eyes, this stranger, had something to offer Shelly that I simply didn't.

"Can I go to the fall dance at school on Friday?" Shelly asked.

We were eating dinner. Maggie had made homemade macaroni and cheese, fried chicken. Biscuits that melted buttery on my tongue. My fingers were slick with grease, my stomach grateful.

"Aren't you a little young for dances? We didn't have dances in school when I was a kid."

Shelly rolled her eyes and speared a pile of macaroni with her fork.

"In my town, we started having dances in the fifth grade," Maggie offered.

I had to bite my tongue to keep something mean-spirited from coming out, willing myself to look away from her belly, which seemed to be growing exponentially each day.

"Do you have a *date*?" I asked, chuckling a little without intending to.

"*Yes,*" Shelly said, exasperated.

I lost my grasp on the piece of chicken I was holding, and it flew onto the table. "I'm sorry, that's out of the question. You're twelve years old."

"Exactly," she said. "I'm not a baby."

"I didn't say you were a baby. I said you were *twelve*. How old is your 'date'?"

"He's thirteen," she said softly. "In the eighth grade."

"Yep. Sorry. Forget it. Out of the question."

"What if she goes to the dance *without* a date?" Maggie asked, spooning another helping of macaroni and cheese on my plate.

I glared at her.

"Please, please?" Shelly asked. "I'll call him right now and tell him I can't go with him. I'll let you listen. You can tell him yourself."

"What's his number?" Maggie asked excitedly. She stood up and went to the phone.

I felt duped. I hadn't wanted Shelly to go to the dance at all. Now here I was, backed into a corner.

"Sit down, Maggie. And Shelly, you listen," I said, realizing that I had never ever talked like this to her before. Like somebody with rules to enforce. Like the father of a twelve-year-old girl. "I don't like this, but I suppose I don't have much of a choice. I trust you. That's all I'm going to say. Please don't disappoint me." I felt like a fraud.

Maggie told me that she and Shelly would clean up, sent me to the living room to watch the news with a bowl of hot peach cobbler in one hand and a cold glass of milk in the other. In the kitchen, their whispers and giggles mixed with the tinkling of dishes and water, and I knew I'd only been politely dismissed.

The wreck had created all sorts of havoc not only in my personal life but at my job as well. In addition to my normal workload, I'd had to act as a human shield protecting Lenny from the media, the railroad, and the victims' families—fielding calls from newsmen and TV stations, negotiating my way

through the literal mountains of legal paperwork from the railroad, and intercepting angry phone calls from grieving family
members. I spent most of each day convinced that Maggie's father would be the next voice I heard on the other end of the
line. I figured that by now someone from her family must have
gathered that she didn't make it to Canada. The train wreck
had been on the *national* news. I knew that somebody would
be looking for her. Soon. And that I'd better be prepared to explain how a fifteen-year-old girl wound up living in my house,
pressing my clothes and taking care of a child only a few years
younger than herself. It wouldn't look good. I was sure of that.

As I rode my bike home the night of Shelly's dance, I for-
mulated exactly how I would broach the subject of Maggie's
impending departure (first with Maggie and then with Shelly).
I was exhausted, starving, my legs shaking from the ride as I
climbed the steps two at a time to our apartment. Inside, Maggie was not in the kitchen as she had been every other night
since the wreck. I could hear laughter coming from the end of
the hall though, and after unloading my stuff and kicking off
my work shoes, I went down the hallway and knocked softly
on my own bedroom door.

"Who is it?" Maggie asked.

"It's me," I said, mildly annoyed.

"Just a minute."

It was time. This was ridiculous. I'd made a huge mistake.

The door creaked open slowly, and Maggie emerged, shut-
ting the door quickly behind her.

"What's going on in there?" I asked.

"She's almost ready," Maggie said, pushing me gently back
down the hallway. "I made some chicken and dumplings
tonight. My auntie's recipe." She ushered me to the kitchen
table. I sat down, rubbing my temples.

"Listen, Maggie," I said. "About your staying here . . . it's
time we talk about . . ." I started.

"What do you think?" Shelly asked. She stood in the doorway, her hands hanging awkwardly at her sides. In the pale blue dress, she looked like a child again. A child playing dress-up. The dress was short, barely covering the tops of her skinny legs. She was wearing makeup, her eyes lined in the same blue as the dress. Her cheeks were flushed pink with rouge. "Maggie found this in your closet. She hemmed it up for me, 'cause it's not so much in style anymore. But it's pretty, don't you think?"

The dull pain in my temples became the sharp, blinding pain of a migraine. I was angry, *furious*, and before I could think about what I was doing, I was holding onto Maggie's shoulders, shaking her hard. "What makes you think you had any right to touch that dress? Did you cut it? *Did you?*"

Underneath my fingers, Maggie's shoulders trembled violently.

Shelly screamed, "Stop, Daddy! What are you doing? You'll hurt her!"

And then everything went numb. The searing pain behind my eyes was replaced by a thick and familiar humming. I shook my head, as if I could shake that awful droning from my ears. I stepped back, still gripping her small shoulders tightly, and forced myself to look into her mismatched eyes, which, despite their differences in hue, were both filled with terror.

"Please don't hurt me," she cried.

And shaking, I let go.

Maybe Tonight

I asked Betsy to go to the prom with me in the same casual way I might have asked her what the capital of Montana was. I had to pretend like I didn't care one way or another and that this was just the polite thing for a friend to do when another friend's date canceled at the last minute—which is exactly what had happened to Betsy. In March of our senior year, Peter Heinrich had asked her to the prom, jumping the gun by more than a bit, I thought, and to my dismay, Betsy had agreed. But Heinie, who was as fickle as he was hasty, changed his mind in May, leaving Betsy stranded with only three weeks before the big day. This fortuitous rejection was exactly what I'd been hoping for, especially since I'd failed to have any sort of backup plan.

I asked her right after she beat me at our tenth straight game of badminton one Saturday afternoon. My father had suspended a net between two trees in our front yard, engaging my mother in a nightly match. My mother had played competitive badminton in college and had been bugging him to set up a net for years. With her impending departure, he gave in to a lot of her requests: badminton tournaments at dusk, freshly baked croissants with dinner every night, which they ate on a blanket outside. You'd have thought she had a terminal disease the way he gave in to her whims. Mint juleps and midnight bike rides.

Betsy was slapping a mosquito that had landed on her thigh.

"Why not?" she said with a shrug after I managed to get the question out. "Not like I have plans."

"Great." I nodded, slapping a bug that had slowly been draining the blood out of my neck. Cool as a cucumber.

We had never spoken about what happened at the Heights during the storm after Betsy's mother's suicide, but there wasn't a single day that passed that I didn't revisit that afternoon in my mind. I replayed it over and over again, like a favorite song. Every moment memorized: each excruciating and thrilling detail. I still didn't understand it, but that didn't matter. The mere fact of what had passed between us was enough to sustain me. I was waiting, just waiting for the next time, and I hoped it wouldn't take another tragedy to make it happen.

Meanwhile, Betsy Parker had been on exactly five dates since her father allowed her to start dating boys. She recalled all of the details to me, spinning the nights into what she thought were funny anecdotes about bumbling boys who tried to shove their hands up her shirt or who got so drunk at the drive-in that she wound up having to drive them home. Each story was agonizing, but I listened. I always, always listened, because I knew that if I didn't pass judgment, didn't let her know how much each of these stories killed me, then she would continue to tell me everything. I hoped that my receptiveness would keep her from keeping her secrets to herself.

I had only a few of my own stories to share with her. There was one double date with Ray and his girlfriend, Rosemary, who brought along her best friend. The girl's breath had smelled like mothballs, and she'd been so shy we barely said three words to one another all night. I'd also taken out a girl from my Physics lab who talked about Paul McCartney all night. And, most recently, was one miserable night spent with a girl Brooder insisted I take out. She pulled her bra out from underneath her shirt not five minutes after she got in the DeSoto, and panted like a hot dog in my ear for almost an hour, as I fumbled around with her breasts. I tried, I did. But I didn't want these girls. I wanted Betsy.

I knew it wasn't a real date, but still, I wanted to do things right. I rented a tuxedo from Moore & Johnson's in St. Johnsbury; it had a white jacket and bow tie, black pants. After I brought it home, I tried it on a dozen times trying to decide whether I looked handsome or idiotic. It seemed there was a fine line when it came to tuxedos. Hanna convinced Betsy that they should go to Boston to find a dress, despite Betsy's insistence that she could find something in town. If Mrs. Parker were alive she would have sewn Betsy's dress herself, but Hanna was a novice seamstress compared to Mrs. Parker, and so she took Betsy to Filene's. Hanna was more excited about the prom than anybody I knew. She arranged for us to have dinner at the Oyster Shell, the only fancy restaurant in town. She also suggested I rent a limousine, but it would have cost me every dime I had. The DeSoto would have to do.

At dusk that night, it was still nearly eighty degrees and humid outside. Clouds hung low in the sky, motionless and thick. In my tuxedo, I felt wooden, like a breathing Charlie McCarthy, as I walked across our lawn to pick Betsy up.

Hanna answered the Parkers' door, beaming. She seemed to be dressed for a formal occasion herself, complete with high heels. I gripped the gardenia corsage, which had wilted in the short time it had traveled from our refrigerator to Betsy's house.

"How lovely," Hanna exclaimed, grabbing the corsage from me, and sniffing it deeply, though its smell was so powerful you only had to breathe the air around it to become nauseated. "Harper, you look so *handsome*. Betsy!"

Betsy came out of the downstairs bathroom then, wearing a dress the color of a robin's egg. It was an impossible blue. The blue of dreams. Her hair was half up, half down, curlers and bobby pins evidence that she had been working at this. Her efforts made my heart quicken.

"I don't know how to do this," she said, like an apology, but I wasn't sure if it was meant for me or for Hanna.

"Come here, sweetheart," Hanna offered, and sat Betsy down at the kitchen table, where she unpinned and unwound and sprayed and coiffed until Betsy looked like she'd stepped out of a beauty parlor. Hanna beamed.

"Where's Daddy?" Betsy asked.

"He's on his way home. Lots of appointments today. With the prom and everything."

I ran my hand over my own head, suddenly aware that my father had forgotten last month's haircut.

"Do I look stupid?" Betsy asked, twirling in front of me like a little girl playing dress-up.

I shook my head. Couldn't speak.

Betsy's father took a photo of us with Betsy's Brownie Starflash when he came home, just one. I felt my eyes close as the shutter clicked, the moment preserved forever this way, as if I were asleep. Only dreaming.

Ray and Rosemary were doubling with us. Ray lived out-side of town in a big crumbling farmhouse. When we pulled up the long driveway, I could see his sisters all milling about on the porch. With less than a year between each successive sister, I never could tell one apart from the next. They all had dirty blond hair and beady little eyes. Ray looked like them too; if he'd been a girl, he'd have blended right in.

The Gauthier sisters made a big fuss as Ray emerged onto the tilting porch wearing a tuxedo just like mine. His big ears reddened as he made it through the mob, their identical hands straightening and tugging and adjusting. His mother stood in the doorway, waving and hollering, "Allo, Arper. You boyz, don't you geet yourselves in de mischief."

Ray got in the backseat and sighed.

Rosemary Ludlow and Ray had been a couple since the sixth grade. Rosemary came from a large Catholic family as well. They'd met at church. She lived in town though, near the high school, in a two-bedroom apartment with her family of seven. She looked shy and embarrassed in her homemade dress when she saw Betsy's Boston-bought one.

"You look so pretty, Rosemary," Betsy said. "I always wished my mother would make my prom dress."

Rosemary smiled, a small, crooked-toothed smile. She touched her hair self-consciously and sat down next to Ray in the backseat.

I was sweating terribly inside that tuxedo. I think in the confusion of cufflinks and tying my tie and shining my shoes I'd forgotten to put on deodorant. The humidity wasn't helping the matter either. By the time we pulled up to the Oyster Shell, I was drenched. The restaurant was equipped with only one ceiling fan, which was nowhere near our table. I suffered through a shrimp cocktail, the uncompromising shell of a lobster, and a chocolate parfait before I excused myself and went to the bathroom, where I took off my coat to assess the damage. Fortunately, my undershirt had taken the brunt of my excessive perspiration. I tried my best to let things air out, splashing some cool water on the back of my neck. In the mirror, I stared at my mop of hair and thought, *You're going to lose her before you even get her.*

The Tuesday Inn had served as the prom site for thirty years. It was a rambling old hotel perched on the hill above the river, the front porch wrapping around it like an embrace. It was built as a resort hotel in the mid-1800s, but by the 1920s, the only "guests" were rum runners, and they rarely checked in for more than a few hours. It got the nickname "Madame Tuesday's" sometime in its less reputable days, and the name had stuck despite its having been converted from brothel back into hotel in the last several decades. By the time we got to Madame Tuesday's, I was sweating again, and this time I knew it had penetrated all my layers.

It had gotten darker but not cooler. Inside wasn't any better. The prom was well in progress by the time we arrived, and all those sweating bodies coupled with the absence of a single window in the ballroom made for a virtual steam bath. Betsy pleaded with me to join her on the dance floor, and I relented, dancing to two or three fast songs before asking for a moment of respite on the porch. I took her by the hand, and we made our way out of the crowded ballroom, through the lobby, and onto the porch.

"Why don't you take off your jacket?" she asked, starting to tug at my sleeve.

I yanked it back up onto my shoulder a little harder than I had intended to.

Betsy scowled. "It's *hot*," she said. "You must be drenched."

"*That's* why I'm not taking my jacket off," I said.

"Oh jeez, Louise," she said, rolling her eyes. "Like you're the first guy who ever sweated before. I've been to a few football games in my day. Guys are supposed to be sweaty. Stinky."

And so I peeled off my wet suit jacket, holding my arms out in defeat. Betsy laughed as I stood there like Jesus with my arms outstretched, waiting to be crucified. And then in a movement so quick and startling, she came close to me, leaning into my chest. I hesitated only a moment before I let my arms close around her. When they did, she looked up at me and smiled. "Not so bad," she said. And I wasn't sure if she meant the smell or the sweat or the embrace. Betsy smelled like lilacs.

We sat down in a pair of Adirondack chairs that faced the river. Betsy slipped off her shoes and put her feet up on the railing. Her toenails were painted pink, like little seashells.

"I can't believe school's almost done already. Are you looking forward to college?" she asked.

I shrugged.

"Oh, I almost forgot! I got something for you in Boston," she said, reaching for her purse. "While Hanna was taking a nap at the hotel, I went to the Museum of Fine Arts. It was *amazing*. They had this Paul Klee exhibit, you ever heard of him? One of those Bauhaus guys. Watercolors mostly. Tissue paper collages. Anyway, they were *so* beautiful. Oh, Harper, they were so beautiful it could make you cry. These tiny little worlds, perfect little worlds, made of paper. I didn't even make it to any other exhibits. And so I went to the gift shop to try to get you a print of one of the paintings. There was this one of a tree filled with houses, the background was this beautiful red. It made me think of you, our fort in the woods. But they didn't have a poster, and so I was looking and looking, and just when I was about to give up and go back to the hotel, all of a sudden I saw *this*."

She reached into her little purse and pulled out a postcard, edges curled. *The Tree of Houses*.

"It's different than seeing the real painting, but isn't it beautiful?"

She handed it to me, and I touched the little houses, the branches. I didn't have any words for her, for what this meant to me.

"We can see each other all the time, you know," she said, nodding. "There's a bus that runs between Middlebury and Castleton. On the weekends and stuff. And there's always Christmas. And summers."

It was too much. I didn't want to talk about taking a bus to see her. I didn't want to think about winter. Winters in Vermont were long enough already, even when you weren't waiting for anything but spring mud on the other side.

Below us the river rushed loudly, though it was too dark to see it.

"Betsy?" I started, not sure what I wanted to say, just overwhelmed with the moment. But before I could finish what I had started, Betsy reached for my hand. She wasn't looking at me but out toward the dark river.

"You're my best friend, Harper Montgomery."

I held onto her hand, overcome with both affection and sadness.

"We've still got the *whole* summer." She smiled, squeezing my hand. "And I have some big plans for us." I didn't know what she meant; I didn't care. I just wanted to kiss her. I was *leaning forward* to kiss her when Rosemary Ludlow came running out onto the porch, her hair wet and sticking to the sides of her face. "Betsy, you've got to get inside! They just called your name for the court."

"What?" Betsy asked.

"The royal court!" Rosemary said. "Jennifer Paquette and Jason Wesson are king and queen, but you and Howie Burke are duke and duchess."

"Holy shit," Betsy said, dropping her feet from the balcony and searching under my chair for her shoes. I found them and offered them to her.

"Hey, what do you know?" was all I could manage.

Inside I stood at the periphery of the crowd as Betsy ran to the makeshift stage, where she was crowned and bannered and flowered. I also stood at the edges as she slugged Howie in the shoulder, their old rivalry now like some sort of intimate private joke. Unbelievable. And then he kissed her on the cheek (*kissed her, kissed her*), and they joined the rest of the royal court dancing slowly to "Maybe Tonight." She smiled at Howie as he spun her dramatically, one hand on his shoulder, the other clinging to her crown. "Maybe Tonight" flowed softly into "Are You Lonesome Tonight," and they kept dancing. I tried to catch her eye, but she was so caught up in the music, so caught up in Howie Burke's arms, I might as well not have been there at all. It wasn't a date anyway, I reminded myself. Just friends, *best* friends. And finally, when it seemed the band might play forever without even the slightest pause, I went outside again, alone.

I was still sweating, though the air had gotten cooler. I sat in the chair that Betsy had been sitting in. I pulled out the postcard and thought about Betsy wandering through the museum, about Betsy seeing this painting and thinking of me. The river was even louder now, louder than the music, which thumped and hummed in the background. My head was pounding. I waited a long time out there on the porch for Betsy, but I was used to it by then; I'd been waiting for her almost my whole life.

When she finally emerged, she was with Rosemary and Ray. She was still wearing her crown, but her hair had come loose and was wet with sweat. I shoved the postcard in the pocket of my tux.

"My curfew's midnight," Rosemary said, frowning.

Ray draped his arm over her shoulder. "I'm ready. The music sucks."

"Is your royal highness finished dancing already?" I asked Betsy.

She looked at me quizzically, and I immediately felt bad.

We all piled quietly into the DeSoto. The windows of Madame Tuesday's glowed brightly in the darkness. I thought about all of the men driving home after their rendezvous with the ladies of Madame Tuesday's. I thought about Betsy in the blue dress, her golden shoulders. I was pissed at myself for not kissing her, pissed at Howie. Pissed, even, at Betsy. The music struggled through the thick air and into the quiet car. I grew dizzy watching as the lights swirled and then disappeared in the rearview mirror behind us. In the backseat, Ray and Rosemary giggled and groped, quietly, trying to be polite. Betsy rolled down the window, leaned her head out, letting the air dry her wet hair. I felt my stomach roil.

Before we made it back into town, I knew I was going to be sick. And despite every effort to keep the growing nausea at bay (breathing deeply, rolling the window down all the way), as soon as I pulled into Rosemary's parents' driveway, I knew I couldn't stop the inevitable. As Rosemary and Ray said their good-byes on the front stoop of her apartment, I felt a wave stronger than I could will away. I opened the door, leaned over and vomited. I felt Betsy's hand on my back, heard her voice swimming to me, "Harper? You okay? Were you *drinking*?" But her voice was distant and muted; she was already so far away.

I figure now it must have been a bad shrimp in the cocktail, but in that moment it felt like sadness pouring out of me. Just bitter sorrow. When we finally got to my house, Betsy asked if I needed her to come with me inside. I shook my head and motioned for her to go home. I gave her an awkward hug and said, "See you tomorrow." Then I ran across the lawn, forgetting all about the badminton net, which captured me like a fly in a spider's web. I untangled myself and rushed into the house to the bathroom, where I tucked the postcard into the mirror's frame and then continued to vomit until my eyes burned and my ribs ached. I thought about the last time I got really sick. My mother made peppermint tea and we sat together at the kitchen table until my stomach stopped churning. She put me to bed, tucked me in, and brought me saltines and ginger ale. But tonight my mother was at her interview in Boston, and my father was already asleep.

Comfort Food

Shelly didn't go to the dance. Instead she went into her room and would not come out. When I knocked on her door, she said softly, "Just leave me alone." Maggie was sitting on the couch, watching TV, her arms crossed against her chest. She wouldn't speak to me either. I didn't know what to do to make things right again. With Shelly *or* Maggie.

And despite the chicken and dumplings waiting in a steaming casserole dish at the table for me, I excused myself and went downstairs to the bowling alley, where I ordered a bowl of chili and a beer. It was Ladies Night again, and the place was filled with women.

"Hey, Harper!" Missy Knowles hollered, waving with her left arm. Her right arm was in a sling. Missy was a regular on Ladies Night; she belonged to one of the women's leagues. She was in my class in high school, but I hadn't known her until we moved in above the bowling alley. I liked Missy. She was plump and friendly. Funny.

She came over to my booth, where I was just finishing up my bowl of chili, and slid in across from me. "What happened to *you*?" I asked, motioning to her arm.

"Slipped on some orange juice," she said. "Seems Jessie couldn't take thirty seconds of her precious time to mop it up after she knocked her glass over. Busy girl, you know."

"Is it broken?"

"Nah, just a sprain. I told Jessie it's fractured in four places though. Figure I should get as much mileage as I can out of it."

"Is it working?"

"She cleaned out the fridge and did all the laundry this week." Missy chuckled. Her cheeks were flushed.

"You playing tonight?"

"I'm here for *team spirit*," she said, and gestured toward my beer. "And my *spirit's* just about run out."

"How about I buy us a pitcher?" I asked. It felt good to have someone to chat with. I hadn't had a normal adult conversation since the wreck.

When I came back to the booth, Missy said, "Where's Shelly at tonight? Over to the dance?"

"Upstairs," I said. "Pouting."

Missy nodded, sympathetic. She had three daughters, each just a year apart. The youngest, Jessie, was in Shelly's grade. We'd commiserated before.

We finished off the first pitcher and then a second one before I checked my watch. Missy was telling dirty jokes. I'd been laughing so hard tears were coming out of my eyes. "I should really go back upstairs," I said.

"You got some help, I hear," Missy said. "A girl to help out with Shelly?"

I thought about Maggie then, for the first time all night, remembered the argument we'd had.

"Yeah," I said. "But it's just a temporary thing."

"It's real good of you to take her in," Missy said. "A lot of people's hearts only got so much room for a girl like that. Especially around here," she whispered.

I remembered Maggie's shoulders like two unripe plums in my hands.

"I really have to get home," I said.

"And leave me all alone?" she asked, flirting a little. This was the inevitable outcome of two shared pitchers with Missy. She was one of the few women who still bothered with me. I could always count on Missy.

"You're not *alone*," I said. "Here comes Louise."

Missy's best friend, Louise, kissed me on the cheek as I stood up and then slid into my seat in the booth.

"Goodnight, *ladies*," I said with a smile.

"See you at the bake sale tomorrow?" Missy asked.

"Bake sale?"

"At the graded school. The fund-raiser for the families of the people in the wreck? I was pretty sure Shelly told Jessie she'd be there."

"Sure," I said. "Bake sale."

In the morning, I woke up wishing I hadn't had either the chili or the beer the night before. I was paying for both. I made my way to the kitchen, my head thick and my legs shaky.

Maggie and I sat across from each other at the kitchen table eating leftover dumplings drizzled with maple syrup in complete silence. Each time I glanced up from my plate, she looked down at hers. Shelly was still in her room.

"Listen," I said, wiping my mouth with a paper towel. "I'm sorry about last night. But you really shouldn't have gotten into my things."

"That was a mean thing, what you did," she said.

"I know."

"You coulda hurt me." Maggie's face was that of a child's, her bottom lip trembling.

I nodded, resisted the urge to reach out for her hand.

Maggie shook her head, sniffed, a fighter going back into the ring. She folded her paper towel daintily and set it on her plate. "It *was* kinda your fault anyway. Shelly didn't have nothin' nice to wear to the dance. You know that girl doesn't have a single dressy dress? I was only tryin' to make her feel pretty. That's important, you know. She's not a little girl anymore."

"Yes, she *is*," I said, setting my fork down.

"Maybe in your mind, but not in hers."

I nodded. Point taken.

Maggie offered me another dumpling. I shook my head, took a long sip of my coffee. "Maggie, we really need to discuss what to do next," I said. "I understand that you don't want to go to Canada. I'm assuming that your family has arranged for some sort of adoption or something . . . you're obviously too far along for . . ." I took a deep breath. "But, what I don't understand is why you want to stay *here*. I don't mean to sound disrespectful, but for someone like you, Two Rivers is hardly the place to *blend in*." I thought about Missy's comment. I thought about the stares we'd already gotten at church. On the street. "You've got the baby to think about."

Maggie closed her eyes for a minute, her jaw tightening. She opened them again and smiled. "Are you sayin' that I haven't been a good guest?"

"That's not at all what I'm saying," I said, exasperated.

"I mean, you've come home to a hot meal every night this week. Shelly's been to school on time every morning; she gets her homework done every night."

"It's been very helpful having you here," I said, speaking slowly, trying to remember that Maggie was still a child. I had to try to think like a child. Whatever her father had said to her, done to her, he was still her father. "Don't you miss your dad? I'm sure he misses you."

Maggie's face softened; her eyes were wet. "I don't miss nobody."

"What about the baby's father?" I asked quietly. "Does he know where you are?"

Maggie's face grew hard again. She stood up and cleared

the dishes off the table, setting them down hard on the counter. A knife dropped and rattled onto the linoleum.

"I made a raspberry pie for Shelly's bake sale," she said, turning on her heel. "Unless you're fixin' to make somethin' else?"

Orientation

M y mother left for Ohio the day after my graduation from
Two Rivers High School.

The graduation party was thrown by Carla Simmons's parents, who owned a whole bunch of land, which they offered up for the all-night event. Most attendees brought tents and sleeping bags. If my mother hadn't been leaving the next day, I probably would have drank myself silly and passed out under the stars too, but instead I spent the whole night feeling disconnected from the music and laughter and celebration. Betsy found me sitting in one of two adjacent tire swings, which were suspended from a single giant oak tree near the creek. She sat down in the other one, swinging quietly, and we barely spoke. Nothing to say, maybe. Or maybe too much.

Just after ten o'clock, I stood up, my legs all pins and needles. "I should head home."

"Will your mom be up still?" she asked.

"I don't know."

"She's so brave," Betsy said, leaning backward and swinging slow and low.

"How so?"

"It's *dangerous* down there. It's not like it is here. People like your mom, just wanting to help other people, they get treated like they're criminals or something."

"Hmm?"

"*Helping* colored people? That's worse to those bigots than actually being Negro."

I hadn't thought much beyond what it would be like for my father and me after my mother was gone. I certainly hadn't thought about her being in any sort of danger.

"She's just teaching. *Piano* lessons," I said. I imagined my mother sitting in her straight-backed way at a piano, little colored children all around her.

"I'm just saying that it takes courage to do what she's doing."

"I'll tell her you think so," I said, feeling defensive. I was a little angry still, about my mother leaving us. And about Betsy leaving me.

"Someday I'm going to do something like that," she said.

"What's that?" I asked.

"Something big. Something that will change the world."

I wanted to tell her that she already had: that her very existence made the world a brighter place. I wanted to tell her that when I was around her I barely remembered to breathe. Instead I hopped off the swing and said, "Anyway, I gotta go."

"You okay to drive?"

I nodded. "Wanna ride?" I asked.

"Nah," Betsy said. "I'll catch a ride home later."

"Howie going your way?" I asked. Howie Burke and Betsy Parker seemed to have completely reconciled following their respective coronations. At graduation Howie had put Betsy in a playful headlock and called her "Duchess." When I told Betsy I couldn't believe she could forgive him for what he'd done to her, what he'd said about her mother, she'd only shrugged saying, *We were kids then. And it's not like he wasn't telling the truth.*

"Did you see where I put my shoes?" she asked. She was always losing her shoes. We couldn't see anything in the dark. "Oh well," she said. "Coming?" And she started walking barefoot through the grass back to the house, which was filled with light and loud with music. She was wearing blue jeans, rolled up, a soft white sweater that glowed in the little bit of moonlight that burned through the heavy clouds. I walked behind her as she skipped ahead. Her hair had grown so long it was touching the waistband of her jeans. I wondered what it would feel like in my hands. Imagined the way it would feel on my skin. I wanted to catch her up in my arms, collapse with her, make love to her. I wanted to *keep* her.

"You leavin' already?" Ray asked. He and Rosemary were sitting on the porch steps.

Ray was wearing his mortarboard crookedly on his head. He'd started his job as a maintenance mechanic at the paper mill on Monday. Rosemary was going to go to cosmetology school. I envied them, their certain futures.

"Come over tomorrow?" Betsy said to me, sitting down next to Rosemary on the porch.

"Sure, after we drop my mom off."

"Wish her luck," she said.

I drove home, sober and feeling slightly melancholy though I couldn't pinpoint why. It seemed like this day had signaled the end to so many things—some of which I wasn't quite ready to see end yet.

When I got home, my mother was in the kitchen, sitting at the table with a glass of wine. My father had moved the kitchen table into a corner in order to make room for the computer, which sat ominously in the middle of the room.

"Where's Dad?" I asked.

"I sent him to bed."

"What are you doing up?"

"Can't sleep," she sighed. "Thought this might help." She gestured to the wine bottle, which was half empty. "Want some?"

"Nah," I said.

She poured a little more and then peered into her glass.

"I bet it's hot in Mississippi in the summertime," I said.

"So they say."

"Are you nervous?"

"Nervous?"

"About the summer?" I could count on one hand the number of nights my mother had spent away from this house. I tried to imagine her with a church family in Palmer's Crossing, Mississippi. I tried to picture her pale moon face staring out at a room full of colored kids. What would she say to them? And they to her? I thought about the people there who would hate her for what she was trying to do.

She looked at me, studying my face. It made me feel self-conscious. "Did you know that when I was pregnant with you, I almost lost you?"

I shook my head.

"I was only a few months along. Barely showing yet." She smiled. "Your father was down in the basement, working on *something*, and I was cleaning out the cupboards. You wouldn't believe the stuff that your grandmother left behind. There was barely room for our dishes when we moved in. So, anyway, I was trying to get everything cleaned out. They call that the nesting instinct, though I've never much believed in that sort of thing. We had this step stool, but I still couldn't reach the top shelf. I figured I could just pull the drawers out, use them like steps. Like a ladder. Well, I should have known how stupid that was. Especially with my being pregnant, but I had my heart set on getting that junk cleared out, so I climbed up. And just as I was reaching up for a mason jar filled with bobby pins or some such thing, my ankle twisted and down I went. The next thing I knew, I was having terrible pains," she said.

She'd never told me this story before.

"I'd also knocked the wind out of myself, and so I couldn't make a sound to let your father know that I'd fallen. Luckily, I must have made a big enough thud when I fell that he heard it and came rushing upstairs. Back then, the closest hospital was in St. Johnsbury, so he was driving like a maniac to get me to the hospital, and I remember lying in the backseat *praying*. Like I used to when I was a little girl. The whole way to the hospital, I was bargaining with a God I didn't even believe in anymore to keep you safe. But what I mostly remember is thinking about what would happen if I *did* lose you. I hadn't wanted to have children, you see. . . ."

"Mom," I said.

"I'm sure you knew that already. You're a bright kid. You know you weren't exactly part of the plan back then. But that afternoon, I had three hours of sitting in the emergency room to think about what would happen if you *weren't* born. And even though I was scared out of my mind to be a mother—I *wanted* you. I wanted so badly to have you."

I picked up the bottle of wine and studied the label.

"You see, the things that terrify us—the things that scare us—are sometimes the best things *for* us. If not for you, I would probably have gone on to do all the things I planned to do. Moved home to Boston, gotten a job with the symphony, all that. But that would have been an easy life. Being a *mother*. Taking that leap of faith, that was the real thing. That, for me anyway, was taking a chance. And now I can't imagine having done anything else." She smiled and reached for my hand. "I'm so proud of you. Graduating from high school, in the wink of an eye. Off to college. I didn't do half as bad a job as I thought I would."

"So now your job is done?"

"Oh, I don't know about being done. But you're almost grown now. A man. A good, *kind* man." She squeezed my hand. "And now suddenly here is this opportunity. Of course I'm nervous. I'm *terrified*. But I have to do this. Not only for the people down there, but for myself."

"Betsy says that the white people down there will hate you," I said.

"It wouldn't be the first time someone hated me." She laughed and took a sip of wine. "Luckily, I never wanted to be belle of the ball."

I looked at the kitchen computer. "Dad won't know what to do without you here," I said.

"He'll be fine," she said. "Maybe now he can channel all that creative energy into something truly useful."

I smiled.

"You'll be home at the end of the summer?" I asked. "Before I leave for school?"

"I'll be home when my work is done," she said. "And I hope to be done by the end of the summer."

I wanted to tell her how much I would miss her, but I only managed to say, "Okay."

The day that my mother arrived at the Western College for Women in Oxford, Ohio, for orientation, three civil rights activists working for Project Freedom disappeared in Mississippi. We heard about this on the news, and my father sat pale and stunned on the couch for nearly an hour afterward. I knew then what the mothers and fathers of my classmates who had been sent to Vietnam must be feeling: a distant sort of terror, palpable but removed, like trying to touch someone's face through a window. There was only the TV screen between us and the horror of what had likely happened to those three kids, to what could very well happen to my mother.

I left my father on the couch and wandered around the house, feeling lost. Usually the door to my mother's study was closed all but a crack, revealing just a sliver of her frizzy hair, a glimpse of her peering over the top of her glasses, a flash of gray from her ratty old sweater. But today, the door was wide

open. I had never set foot inside that room, not that I could remember anyway. Even as a child, I never trespassed. I imagined
it though, dreamed a dark, quiet place—a tiny lamp on her
desk providing the only illumination. Everything, in my imagined version of this room, glowed an amber color and smelled
the musty smell of books. But now, on this early June evening,
sunlight streamed through the bay window, blinding me as I
opened the door. Her desk, which I knew was large, wooden,
and heavy, was not as large as I dreamed it, and it was not clut-
tered but completely tidy. There were books, of course, but
they were not in the disarray I had assumed they would be. In
fact, they were alphabetized, fitting snugly into the floor to
ceiling shelves along one wall behind her desk. There were no
stacks on the floor, no scattered papers, no calico cat purring
softly atop a pile of paperbacks. (I knew we did not have a cat,
but still, this is what I imagined.) The one lamp on her desk
was not amber glass but a simple banker's lamp—brass with a
green shade, the kind you find at public libraries. There was
not only an unexpected orderliness to this room but an *ordi-
nariness*. I felt the suspicions I'd been having suddenly con-
firmed; I didn't know my mother at all.

But just as I was about to leave, I noticed the familiar gray
sweater, the heavy cabled cardigan she almost always wore both
inside and outside this house, hanging on the back of the door.
I suppose I could have seen it as a good sign: that she would
soon be back, that there had been no real reason to take it along
for such a brief journey. But instead I knew that what it really
meant was that my mother, this mother of unexpected order
and efficiency, might believe that things were disposable. And
suddenly her absence was even more complete, as if I'd found
her very skin there. Shed. Molting one life for another. Only
the cast off husk remaining.

Missing

Eight of the eleven missing bodies had been found. The victims' families came to retrieve their loved ones' remains. They arranged for burials. They left white painted crosses at the place by the river where the train derailed. Most of the families came and went quietly. A few banged on the door of my office demanding to speak to the person responsible for the accident after they had exhausted every other ear that would listen. I offered them water, a place to sit. I listened to each of them, allowed them their anger. I rarely bothered with the canned explanations I'd been coached to provide by the railroad representative. The NTSB was still investigating, but they believed that the derailment was likely due to a fracture in the rail. The break was small enough to go undetected during routine inspections and maintenance, but under the passing train it simply split. It was an accident. Simple as that. But I knew this was not what they wanted to hear. In a true accident, no one is at fault. What these people, in their tremendous grief, wanted—needed—was to have someone to blame. I could understand this.

The families of the victims whose bodies had *not* been found (the twenty-five-year-old father of four from North Carolina, the eighty-year-old woman from Georgia) came as well. Both of them wanted to visit the place where it happened. And because the representative sent by the railroad was unfamiliar with the area and wouldn't have been able to find his way through the woods, I took them.

The widow of the missing man arrived at my office door with four children in tow. Though I suggested that I show her the way to the river, she insisted she could find it if I gave her directions. But as the children started to follow behind her, the baby clinging to her hip, I said, "You can leave them here. I don't mind."

She looked at me suspiciously, and then sighed, *"Thank you."* She lowered the baby to the floor and accepted my scribbled map. She placed the remaining three children in chairs facing my desk, shook a finger at them, warning, "Don't y'all tear nothin' up." And then to me, "I'll be back real quick. Promise."

"Please take as long as you need," I said. "They'll be fine."

When she came back just a half hour later, her eyes were rimmed red, her makeup smeared. She grabbed a tissue from a box on my desk and smiled at the children, who had, despite her request, left my office in shambles. The youngest had found contentment sorting through the crumpled papers in my wastebasket, but the others were climbers.

"Come on, y'all," she said, peeling the biggest one off the windowsill and gathering the littlest one in her arms. The other two clung to her legs. She said quietly, "I'm so sorry, sir. Thank you."

I knew that she'd likely had only enough time to get to the river and turn back around. Not nearly enough time to actually grieve. "Did you have enough time, ma'am?"

She looked at me confused, eyes filling again, and said, "He was *twenty-five years old.*"

When the old man whose wife had been on her way to visit her sister in Montreal came to the station, he accepted my offer to take him on the trek south from the station to the river. We walked slowly side by side through the woods; he had a cane, and his breathing was labored. When we got to the site of the crash, there was little evidence of the wreckage remaining, only the flowers. The crosses.

"Here?" he asked, gesturing toward the river with his cane. I nodded.

He walked toward the water's edge, and for just a minute I worried that he might accidentally fall in.

"How long were you married, sir?" I asked.

"Sixty-five years," he said without looking back at me.

"That's a lifetime."

"A lifetime and a half."

When it was clear that he wasn't in danger of falling in, I sat down on a moss-covered stump and watched him.

He knelt down next to the river, cupped his hands, and drank a handful of the cold water.

Then he reached into his pocket and pulled out an envelope. Without saying a word, he pressed the letter to his mouth and then rested it gently in the water. It was chilly out, and a shiver passed through my body. The current quickly grabbed the envelope from his hands and carried it downstream. The pale paper dipped and bobbed, and then disappeared around a bend in the river.

After a while, I helped him stand back up.

"Okay," he said. "Time to go home."

Freedom Summer

The summer of 1964 was the shortest summer in all of my memory, each day like a grain of sand, slipping through my fingers despite every attempt to hold on. From the moment I tossed my cap up into the blue sky on graduation day, time seemed to accelerate. Because Brooder was gone, shipped off to Vietnam by then, and Ray was working full-time at the mill, it was just Betsy and I again. But the lazy days of summers past were an anomaly to what I now knew to be true. Summer was fleeting, and Betsy Parker was as evanescent as summer. Before autumn arrived, before we parted for our separate futures, I knew I had to do something. *Say something.* I was running out of time. There was urgency to every minute of that summer. I must have been the most desperate man alive.

There was a Dylan song on the radio that summer, though it wasn't very popular, not part of the usual play list. If it had been, I probably would have quickly grown bored with it. But I only heard it maybe once a week or so, sometimes just catching the tail end as I got in the car and turned on the radio. Betsy loved it too, but because it wasn't on the Top 40, I couldn't find the forty-five anywhere. I wanted to surprise her with it. Wrap it in gold tissue for her. But instead, it became a running challenge, to catch it on the radio—to take the DeSoto out for long drives, suffering through "Chapel of Love" and "My Guy" in the hopes that those first few notes would take us by surprise. I thought of it as *our* song; it captured all that wild desperation I was feeling. All my crazy hope. One afternoon in July when it had easily been a week since the disk jockey had played the song, Betsy showed up at my house looking listless.

I had a part-time job that summer, mowing the sloping lawns between the tombstones at the cemetery. I'd gotten a scholarship to cover my tuition at Middlebury, and so I didn't need to work much that summer, just enough to save some extra cash for school. (I hadn't managed to save much though; I'd spent all of my graduation money and my first two paychecks on a brand new 35 mm camera, which I planned to give to Betsy for her birthday at the end of the summer.) I made my own hours, usually Monday and Thursday afternoons, when traffic through the cemetery was at a minimum. It was a Monday, and I was putting the mower into the trunk of the DeSoto when Betsy arrived.

"Let's go swimming," she said. "It's too hot."

"Okay," I said. No one was waiting for me at the cemetery.

Betsy and I usually went swimming in the river. There was a good spot not far from Paul and Hanna's. We'd swim all afternoon and then Hanna would make us dinner, hang our suits and towels out on her clothesline. Not too many kids knew about the spot, so we almost always had it to ourselves. But today as I started to turn down the road that would take us there, Betsy grabbed the wheel. "Let's go to Gormlaith."

Lake Gormlaith is up in the Northeast Kingdom, near Quimby and the Canadian border. It was mostly tourists up there this time of year, lots of rented camps. It's a beautiful lake though. There's a small island in the middle, and legend is the lake has no bottom. It was about a forty-minute drive; Betsy was quiet but restless. She rolled the windows down and leaned her head out, letting her hair get tangled in the wind.

After about twenty minutes, she sighed and said, "I can't wait to get out of here. I'm so tired of this place. There's nothing to do."

"What do you mean?" I asked.

"Ugh. Don't you get sick of this? Church, pastures, cows. River. Church, pastures, cows. River."

It was true. The small towns and hamlets were like loosely strung beads, between which was nothing but green pastures and so many cows. But I loved this repetition, this pastoral rosary. It was predictable.

"Where would you *like* to be?" I asked.

"I don't know," she said, leaning back into the car. "Anywhere but here, I guess."

"Hmm."

"You mad?"

"Nah."

"You're *mad*," she said.

"No I'm not," I said, feeling mad.

"Sure you are. I know you, Harper." She laughed knowingly and rolled the window down again.

"You don't know me," I said, a lot more loudly than I intended.

She turned toward me, her smile fading into a frown. "Where would *you* like to be then?"

"What do you mean?"

"I mean, when you grow up. When you realize that there's nothing here but small towns and small minds and cow shit. A whole lot of cow shit."

I sat silently, staring at the dirt road that curled like a gritty ribbon in front of us. I gripped the wheel tightly and reached to turn on the radio so that I wouldn't have to speak. I didn't know how to tell her that I didn't really care where I was, as long as she was there too. And so we drove for a while longer, not talking, until we were so deep in the woods that the DeSoto no longer had any radio reception.

"I only meant that I'm bored," Betsy said, touching my right hand. "Don't you ever get bored with all of this?"

"Sure," I lied. I wasn't ever bored as long as Betsy was around.

"Uncle Paul's got a camp up here. There's no running water, but there's electricity, and if you want to stop at Hudson's, we can get some hot dogs to make for dinner later," she offered, like an apology. "Marshmallows and Hershey's for s'mores?"

We spent the afternoon swimming at the boat access area of the lake, a rocky beach with a small grassy shore. The water was warm on the surface from the sun, but colder in the depths. My legs were numb as I crawled out of the water and onto the grass. Betsy had spread out two towels. She was lying on her stomach, fast asleep. I lay down next to her on the other towel, moving her hair out of her face so that I could see her better. She smiled in her sleep. I could have stayed there until the sun went down. I had never felt so content. God, I adored her.

I knew I had to do something, say something. I'd been carrying the words around in my head, at the tip of my tongue for so long now, they were no different than song lyrics to a favorite song anymore. While Betsy slept, I reached over her and quietly grabbed a pen and scrap of paper from her beach bag. I checked to make sure she was still asleep, and started to write down all of the things I'd been wanting to say. Couldn't say. It was like a relief, a release, but it also felt dangerous: the simple union of ink and paper making everything I'd been feeling and thinking concrete. In the world. I felt anxious. Exposed.

I thought about tearing the paper up, shoving it into a pocket and tossing it onto the fire later. But there, on the back of an old envelope, was my entire heart. How could I deny that? Destroy that? And so I left Betsy on the grass asleep, folded the envelope into a tight square, and put it between my teeth. I jumped into the water and swam all the way out to the island. It had to have been a quarter mile away, and by the time I got there my body was tired. I crawled through some heavy brush and spit the piece of paper out. Close to the shore was a big shady tree, where I sat and reread all those words. When they started to blur together, I folded the paper back up into a tiny square and stuffed it into the hollow of the tree. Then I jumped back in the water.

My body was shaking with exhaustion as I pulled myself out of the lake again at the access area and stood, dripping wet, next to Betsy. She woke up, disoriented and groggy. "Harper! I'm burned to a crisp! Why didn't you wake me up?" Her shoulders were bright red with sunburn.

"I'm sorry," I said. "Here." I handed her my T-shirt, which she gingerly pulled over her bathing suit.

"Let's get inside," she said.

We made a feast of hot dogs and potato salad and a few beers I'd stolen from our fridge, and ate on the porch of her uncle's hunting shack, sitting in a couple of ratty overstuffed chairs. Later, when the sun melted into the water, we stoked the fire and toasted marshmallows. Betsy's kept catching on fire. "You can't let it get too close," I said, meticulously turning mine, keeping it a safe distance from the flame until it was golden. "Here," I said, and sandwiched it with chocolate between graham crackers. A pile of charred marshmallows at her feet, Betsy sighed and said, "What would I do without you, Harper?"

If I'd been smart, I would have kissed her then. I would have reached to wipe the bit of melted chocolate that had touched the tip of her perfect nose and then kissed it off instead. But that moment, like every single moment of that summer, was gone before it had a chance to live.

She must have sensed that something was bothering me. That I was dying inside.

"What do you really want, Harper?" she asked softly.

"What?" I asked, sure now that she'd figured me out.

"Do you *really* want this?"

"What?" I asked again.

She picked a marshmallow up off the ground, blew on it, and studied it. "I'm never going to make perfect marshmallows." She smiled, shaking her head. "I'll *always* burn the marshmallows. I'm not patient. I'm not careful. Around me, things catch on fire. Things get ruined."

"No," I said. Reaching for the marshmallow. It was charred. Covered with dirt and grass.

"I'm contrary. I'm restless. I'm never happy. I'm a big messy mess."

I looked at her, at my beautiful Betsy. At her wild hair and big eyes. Then I looked at the dirty marshmallow in my hand. "I do. Want this," I managed. Then I popped the marshmallow in my mouth, the blackened skin gritty between my teeth. But the inside was still warm, sweet. I knew then that she would taste like this: that on my tongue, she would have this same warmth, this same sweetness.

"You're nuts," she said. "Certifiable. And I should know."

We drove home just after ten o'clock, and right as we were reaching the Heights, our song came on the radio.

"Pull over!!! Pull over!!!" Betsy squealed.

I pulled the car over, lurching to a crooked stop. Betsy turned up the radio and threw open the door. She came around to my side of the car and used both hands to pull open the heavy door. "Come on! Dance with me!"

"Nah," I said, shaking my head.

"Come *on*."

And then I was out of the car, and she was scrambling up onto the hood of the DeSoto. She reached for my hand and motioned for me to join her. I shook my head again, stubborn, and she yanked my arm. Hard. *"It's almost over."*

Betsy meant the song, but it meant so much more, so I joined her on the hood of the DeSoto. And then Betsy Parker was, finally, in my arms. We danced until the song ended, but I held on. I held on, careful of her sunburned shoulders. I held on, trying to figure out how to say the words I'd been reciting in my head like a prayer. I held on, silent, smelling the sweet soapy smell of her hair, until finally she whispered breathlessly, I thought, though it could have just been my imagination, *Soon.*

Forgiveness

A week after the dance, Shelly still wasn't speaking to me in anything but grumbles. I stood outside her door, attempting to coax her out, first with words and then with bribes. I brought home the things she loved: éclairs, maple candies, a brand new pair of tennis shoes. It was pathetic, this groveling, but I didn't know what else to do. And nothing worked; she just wouldn't take the bait. The éclairs grew stale in the fridge, the candies melted on the windowsill. The sneakers sat wrapped in tissue inside their box on the kitchen table. By Friday morning, I'd basically given up. I figured she couldn't keep this up forever. I found myself grateful for Maggie's company. At least she was still talking to me.

"I mended that rag you been wearing to work," Maggie said, handing me my favorite work shirt, which I'd worn threadbare at the elbows.

"Looks like you ain't been shopping in a while," she said.

Hanna had always brought things back for me when she went shopping for Paul. I made her give me the receipts and wrote her checks to cover what she'd spent. I had enough clothes in my closet to get me through a workweek. I ignored the loose buttons and torn seams.

"You didn't have to do that," I said, taking the shirt from her.

"*Somebody* did," she said with a smile. "I'll stop by that shop next to the drugstore. They got men's clothes, right?"

"Ledoux's," I said. "I can go."

"But you *won't* go," she said. "So I will."

When I got home from work on Thursday night, there were two piles of clothes on the table. One pile was for me, and one was for Shelly. Somehow, with the small amount of money I'd given her, she'd managed to get me three new button-down shirts, a pair of jeans and some new socks. In Shelly's pile were some shirts, a pair of jeans and a pale pink dress.

Maggie was sitting with her bare feet up on a chair, a washcloth across her forehead.

"You feeling okay?" I asked.

"Yeah, I just get real light-headed sometimes. If I can get my feet up quick enough then I don't faint."

"Is that normal?" I asked.

"I don't need to see no doctor, if that's what you're worried about."

I flinched. I *was* worried. Partly about her, and partly about how on earth I might *explain* her to Dr. Owens, the town's only baby doctor.

"I read in a book that it's from havin' low blood pressure. Book said eatin' something salty's supposed to help."

I went to the cupboard and started looking through the shelves. Maggie had rearranged everything: canned goods, dry goods, spices. The half-empty boxes of stale cereal had been removed. The almost-empty bottles of vinegar and sticky jars of molasses had been replaced with brand new ones and were lined up in neat little rows. She'd replaced the crummy shelving paper with new flowered yellow lining.

"How about some Jiffy Pop?" I asked, pulling the popcorn out by the metal handle.

It had been ages since I'd made Jiffy Pop. I actually recalled setting off the smoke alarm in Hanna's kitchen the last time.

(I'd burned most of the kernels, and the rest had remained un-popped and stuck to the bottom of the aluminum pan.) "Al-righty then," I said, and peeled off the cardboard top, reading the directions as I turned the burner on.

Maggie stayed in her reclined position at the table, her eyes closed.

"Where's Shelly?" I asked.

"Over to Hanna and Paul's. She's got a paper on Abraham Lincoln or something, and Hanna said she'd help her out," Maggie said. "I told her to be home in time for supper."

I stood at the stove, waiting for something to pop.

"Whatcha got it on, *low*?"

"No," I said. "It's on *medium.*"

"Oh, that burner don't work at all," Maggie said, opening her eyes. She put her washcloth down on the table and stood up. She gripped the edge of the table.

"I got it," I said. "Sit down."

I moved the popcorn to the back burner and turned it on. Shortly it was popping, the aluminum foil was ballooning, and I was elated. I even managed to pull it off the heat in time. "Ouch," I said, burning my fingers on the hot tin foil and steam. I poured the popcorn into a bowl and set it down in front of Maggie. "Wait!" I said as she reached in for a handful. I grabbed the saltshaker and shook it vigorously over the bowl. "There."

Maggie grabbed a handful of popcorn and threw a piece up into the air. She opened her mouth and caught it on the tip of her tongue. I tried the same, and my first attempt landed on the floor. "Try again," she said, laughing.

I tried again, and the popcorn landed square on my tongue.

"You feel better yet?" I asked.

"World's stopped twirling at least," she said, and shoveled another handful of popcorn in her mouth.

Shelly opened the front door, and seeing us sitting at the

kitchen table eating popcorn, she threw her backpack down and slammed the door shut.

"C'mere, Shelly-girl. It's just like the movies," Maggie said. "Just without Matt Dillon."

"Who's that?" I asked.

Shelly rolled her eyes.

"You hungry, I hope," Maggie said, standing up. "I got some chili on the stove."

Shelly looked at me and scowled. "I already ate. Hanna made me supper," she said, her lips drawn tight. "She said I need to put some meat on my bones."

I ignored the obvious attempt to make me feel rotten and grabbed another handful of popcorn.

"Hanna says I'm welcome anytime. She even set up a bed for me in our old room. Said I could sleep over whenever I want."

Now I was pissed. I had made it clear to Hanna that we were doing fine. I felt undermined. Betrayed.

"Look what your daddy bought you today," Maggie said, handing Shelly the pink dress.

Shelly looked at the dress. "Probably won't fit," she said. "He doesn't even know my size."

Maggie peered at the tag and said, "Looks like he do."

Shelly shrugged.

"Want some popcorn, honey?" I asked.

"I said I already *ate*," she said angrily.

"You shouldn't talk to your daddy that way," Maggie said sternly. The change in her tone of voice took me by surprise. Shelly's mouth gaped open, her eyes wide.

"It's okay," I said, feeling sorry for Shelly. "She's just . . ."

"She's *bein'* rude," Maggie said to me. And then to Shelly, "You're *bein'* rude. He's your daddy. I ever talk to my daddy like that I be laid across his knee. That's the truth. One time I sassed him in front of some church friends, and I couldn't sit down for a whole week."

The idea of Maggie getting a spanking seemed ludicrous. I kept forgetting how little distance was between her childhood and now. Only about four or five months.

"I've got homework," Shelly said, picked up her backpack, and started for her room. But then, as if she'd had second thoughts, she grabbed the dress off the table and ran down the hallway, slamming her door behind her.

Maggie smiled at me.

"Thanks," I said.

She tossed a piece of popcorn up into the air, and realizing it was for me, I opened my mouth and waited for it to land, salty and warm, on my outstretched tongue.

Heat Lightning

In August, in the season of wild blueberries and fireflies, Jeffrey Norris died in Vietnam. He was the first of our classmates to be killed. And after his body was flown home, I mowed the lawn around his new grave, thinking that the last time I'd seen him had been at graduation, and he'd used white medical tape to spell out USA on his mortarboard.

It was maybe a week later that I saw his mother sit down on the floor, in the middle of the post office, and weep when she received what must have been a posthumous letter from Jeffrey. It was embarrassing, this public display of grief. I was waiting in line to send my mother a package of items she had requested. Despite her earlier plans, she had decided to stay on in Mississippi through the fall. She'd asked for her Swiss Army knife, a piece of beach glass she had found on Nantucket when she was a little girl, and a check for $200. My father had packaged the objects up for her and carefully penned the address on the box. But he sent me to the post office, blaming a busy schedule. He missed her. We both did.

The post office was hot, one whirring fan spinning overhead, making shadows on the linoleum floor. When Mrs. Norris crumbled, after Larry Knowles (Missy's father, the postmaster) handed her the parchment airmail letter, it only looked as though she'd fallen. Someone offered her a hand, as you would to someone who had slipped. But when she refused his help, and a small moan grew in her throat and escaped through the painted O of her mouth, filling the post office lobby with the animal sounds of her sorrow, the post office patrons, including myself, looked at the floor, at the large numbered clock on the wall, at anything but Mrs. Norris, legs splayed out in front of her like a child, as she grieved.

In one week, I was to leave for Middlebury, and I hadn't packed a single thing. Betsy's room was filled with neatly labeled cardboard boxes. She was buzzing with excitement, positively antsy. I, on the other hand, was a sentimental fool, eighteen years old going on eighty. Every afternoon in the final weeks of summer, I insisted that we visit one old haunt or another: Vanilla Cokes and Orange Crushes at the Rexall, car rides to the Heights, bike rides to the river. Betsy humored my premature nostalgia primarily because our little outings made time go more quickly; she could barely wait to leave. Her excitement about the future mixed with my longing for the past (*for her, for her*) finally made me so melancholy I could barely stand it anymore. At the post office that day, when Jeffrey Norris's mother sat down and cried on the floor, I wanted to join her. I wanted to throw myself to the ground next to her and cry like a baby.

By the time it was time to actually go, I'd resigned myself to four years of desperate unhappiness. I saw the school year ahead as something to endure before I could return to my life in Two Rivers the following summer: three seasons of misery to suffer through. I packed reluctantly, and on the day before I was to leave, I only wanted to be with Betsy. I only wanted the last hours and minutes to decelerate, to freeze. I pictured the day as a photograph, a frozen image of the last day I would truly be happy.

Despite Betsy's pleas to go on an adventure (drive to Canada, go to the granite quarries in Montpelier, go try to get into bars in Burlington), we ended up spending the day swimming. It was so hot and muggy, there was little else to offer relief from the heat, and I didn't want to spend the day driving. It was the most ordinary of days. And, because of its import (in my mind at least) the most *extra*ordinary. It took every bit of my energy not to call Betsy's attention to the significance of the smallest things (the muddy bottom of the river, the slant of sun through leaves, the frogs that joined us as we cooled off on the cool, wet rocks). By the time the sun fell, heat lightning was lighting up the sky in intermittent pink flashes of light. Lightning without thunder, a storm without rain. It made me anxious, unsettled. Betsy's anxiety was also palpable.

"Why won't it *rain*?" she asked, as we threw our towels around our necks and got on our bicycles to make our way back home. I had the new camera in my backpack, waiting for the right time to give it to her. As we rode through the woods, I could feel it banging against my back. (It was heavy, an Argus C-33; they called it the "Brick" because of its shape and heft.)

The rushing air against our wet skin was the only relief from the heat. I rode behind Betsy, as I always did, as she chose the path that would lead us out of the forest. My eyes stung with river water as I watched the familiar way she navigated both branches and brush, her bare feet callused and pedaling furiously. I paid no attention to where we were going; I was preoccupied with the dimples on either side of her spine, just above the waistband of her cutoffs. I only realized that we weren't headed home when my legs began to strain with the incline. We had plans to listen to records at my house, as I finished my packing.

"Where are we going?" I asked.

"To watch the lightning," she said.

Betsy surprised me with her sudden fearlessness. Normally, she would have wanted to be anywhere but out in the open like this.

Just as the sun was starting to go down, we arrived at the top of a large hill. Though the view wasn't as spectacular as

from the Heights, you could still see down on most of Two
Rivers. Lightning streaked the sky, which was also brilliant
with a setting sun. Betsy laid her bike down and stood with
her hands on her hips, surveying the scene before us.

"Oh my God," she said.

I nodded, behind her, where she couldn't see me. If she
had, she would have seen an eighteen-year-old boy so sick in
love (with his hometown, with his life, with this girl in cutoffs
before him) that the idea that this moment, like all the other
moments before them, would soon be gone was almost unbearable. But she didn't turn around; instead she faced the sunset and the exploding atmosphere, feet planted firmly on the
ground and hair tangled from the ride.

I thought about the camera, but just as I was reaching into
my backpack to retrieve it, Betsy flinched, just the slightest bit,
slapping at the raindrop as if it were a mosquito. And then the
rain was coming down in hard, cold slivers and Betsy had turned
to me with that familiar look of terror.

"Come with me," I said, reaching for her hand and pulling
her down the other side of the hill where I could see a dilapi-
dated barn in the distance. We ran across a pasture that was
endlessly green and soft. Betsy could run fast, especially when
in danger, and I was breathless when we reached the barn,
which was, indeed, an abandoned structure. Shelter.

Inside, Betsy laughed, shaking her wet hair like a dog. It
sprayed me, and the cool water felt good. "Phew!" she said.

The barn smelled heavily of hay and rain, a wet sweet
smell. The roof was leaking in so many places, we had to search
for a dry place to stand. There were some rusty farm tools
hung on the wall, hammers, sickles: a rustic museum. Outside,
the sun was rapidly setting, and I wasn't sure how we would
find our way back to our bikes, never mind find our way home,
once the sun was gone. But inside that warm wooden barn
with the rain pounding against the roof and the impossible vi-

olet of heat lightning illuminating the fields beyond the barn outside, I didn't care if we never found our way home again.

"I have something for you," I said.

"Hmm?" she asked, distracted by the sky.

I pulled the camera out and offered it to her. "It's not the best one, but it takes good pictures. I don't know much about photography, but the salesman said this is a good starter. It has four lenses. You can use regular thirty-five millimeter film. . . ."

"Harper," she said, tentatively taking the camera from me. "This is too much. This is . . ."

"If you want to exchange it, it won't hurt my feelings."

"Is there film in it?" she asked, turning the camera over and over in her hands.

"Uh-huh," I said.

"We have to take pictures of this," she said. She held the camera up to her eye and fiddled with the lens. She clicked several times, rushing from one dry place to the next, peering out at the fracturing sky. After a while, she stopped shooting and came back to me. It was getting dark outside. She sat down on a wooden sawhorse, facing the open barn door, and set the camera down next to her. She pulled her hair behind her head and then over one shoulder, wringing out the rain. She sighed and stared out at the sight before us. "It's a beautiful world, Harper Montgomery."

I nodded again.

"I might not notice that sometimes, if it weren't for you."

I smiled.

She turned around to face me, but it had grown darker, and the brilliance of the sky behind her made it impossible to see the details of her face. I had them memorized though, so I imagined her smiling at me. I knew the way her lips curled a bit at the edges, the two faint lines at the corners of her eyes.

"Are you going to come sit with me or not?" she asked.

"Sure," I said, and ambled as coolly as I could toward her. I sat down and we faced the last remnants of the orange skyline together. Another hot pink flash of light, and she took my hand.

"Tomorrow's just another day," she said. "Just another beautiful day."

I couldn't have disagreed more, but I returned the squeeze.

The sun quickly and completely disappeared, but I didn't let go of Betsy's hand. The rain kept coming, thunder kept cracking, and lightning kept flashing. At least between the fireflies and the lightning, there were moments of extreme clarity, sometimes one after another. And each time the sky filled with light, I could see Betsy's face. Single seconds to study her and speculate what she might be thinking. Finally, I summoned up courage I didn't know I had and asked softly, "Do *you* want this?"

Betsy was so quiet, I wasn't quite sure she'd heard me. Wasn't sure I'd spoken at all.

"Yes," she said, finally, and in the next flash of light I saw that her eyes were wet.

And because I wasn't sure when the next flash would come, or if it would come at all, and because I had left everything to the last minute (as I always left everything to the last minute), and because I felt fearless and hopeless, exhausted and exhilarated, I turned to Betsy Parker, framed her face with my hands, and kissed her. And kissed her.

Our clothes were wet, stuck to our skin and difficult to peel off. I struggled with my shirt, my jeans, my shoes and socks. Betsy slithered out of her shorts and T-shirt and stood in front of me in only her panties and her bra. The skin of her stomach trembled. I went to her, wrapped my arms around her, and the second my skin touched her skin, I could barely stand it. I held her face in my hands and kissed her lips, her eyelids, her forehead. The top of her scalp. Her throat. I buried my face in her neck and kissed the skin there until my skin and her skin were hot. I wanted to disappear into her, into that incredible heat.

"Stop," she said, pushing me back gently, and I felt my heart sink.

I backed away, hard and ridiculous. Panting.

"Take a picture?" she said. "Of me?"

"Really?"

She nodded, reached for the camera, and handed it to me. She stepped in front of the open door, the rough wood with peeling paint making a sort of agrestic frame for her silhouette. She unhooked her bra and it fell to the floor. She bent over and wriggled out of her panties. When she stood up again she was naked, her body luminous in each flash of light. I watched this through the viewfinder. I listened to the shutter click. I made myself breathe.

"It's too dark, isn't it?" she asked softly. "It won't come out."

"It doesn't matter," I said.

"What if we forget?" she asked, desperate. "What if you forget?"

I shook my head. "We won't. *I* won't. I promise."

As we lowered our bodies to the hard floor, I thought about a lot of things. I thought about Betsy's body, pressed against mine. I thought about those dimples I'd never noticed before, feeling them with my hands as I explored her back. The rise of her behind. The slope of her thighs. I thought about the rain on the roof and the rain that was dripping down through the roof onto my shoulders. I thought about leaving, about not wanting any of this to end. And I also thought about Jeffrey Norris, writing a letter that didn't show up until after he was already dead. I didn't want to be gone before Betsy Parker knew how I felt about her. I didn't want her to read it in a letter when it was already too late. And so I whispered, "I love you." Just a simple comma at the end of first one kiss, and then the next. I must have told her a hundred times, until, at last I had disappeared inside her, and there was no longer any need for words.

The Montrealer

It had been two weeks since the wreck, and with every day that went by, fewer and fewer relatives of the victims came to the station. The excitement and novelty of the wreck had also worn off, and things were slowly getting back to normal at the station. The anxiety I'd been carrying with me to work every day like an extra lunch bucket had even started to ease up, because with each passing day it seemed that Margaret Jones's father either didn't know or, more likely, didn't care that his little girl was missing. But just as I'd let some of that fear go (the heart-thumping worry of every phone call, the way I almost jumped out of my skin every time someone knocked on the freight office door), I'd think about Shelly and what I would do if I knew she'd been on a train that crashed into a river. There had to be more to the story than Maggie was letting on, and despite wanting to believe her (wanting it to be this simple), I knew I probably should do some sleuthing of my own. Just to make sure. Maggie had lied to me already about her name, about her mother, and no matter how good she was at mending my shirts and minding my daughter, I couldn't just let things go on much longer without knowing the whole story.

Even though I spent most of my time in the freight office, I was still fairly familiar with the passenger lines. The Crescent ran from New Orleans to Washington, D.C., making stops in

Mississippi, Alabama, Georgia and North Carolina along the way. If Maggie had, indeed, been coming from Alabama, she would have taken the Crescent from Tuscaloosa to Washington, D.C., where she would have caught the Montrealer to get to Canada. The Montrealer, the train that derailed, was the only passenger train that stopped in Two Rivers.

Because of the accident, it was easy to get passenger information. Everybody wanted to be the hero, to be able to offer up something related to the crash. Just mentioning that I worked at the Two Rivers station opened up all sorts of doors, making me privy to information I shouldn't have been able to get my hands on otherwise. It only took one phone call to the ticket office at Union Station in D.C. to find out exactly where Margaret Jones had come from and where she was headed.

"Yep. Here she is. *Margaret Jones*. Picked up the Crescent in Tuscaloosa, Alabama. Transferred here. Montrealer headed to Two Rivers, Vermont."

"Yep, that's where the train derailed," I said, nodding. "But where was she supposed to get off? Cantic? Montreal?"

"I already told you," the ticket agent said. "Her ticket didn't take her to the end of the line, only as far as Two Rivers."

"Here?"

"Yes, sir, that was her destination."

Heat rose from my gut to my shoulders, spreading down my arms and up into my face. I hung up the phone and gripped the edge of the desk. *Here?* Why on earth had she come here? What about her aunt in Canada? I struggled to come up with a logical reason why a pregnant black girl from Tuscaloosa would get on a train headed to Two Rivers, Vermont, but there was no reason that made sense. None that I could handle anyway, none that wouldn't change the world as I knew it. I needed to get home, talk to Maggie.

When I looked up from my desk, Lenny was standing in my doorway.

"Montgomery, the toilet's clogged up again," he said. He was holding a dripping plunger, which he pointed at me accusingly. "Take a crap this morning?"

"Jesus," I said, standing up, reeling. The plunger was dripping sewage onto my blotter. Between the filthy water on my desk and the fact that I'd been holding my breath since I hung up the phone, I thought I might pass out. "I've got to go home."

"You sick? *Knew* it was you," he said, shaking the plunger again. "Come to work with the shits, and break the goddamn toilet."

I stumbled past him and out of the station. It was just five o'clock, but it was already getting dark. The sky was pink, streaked with orange. I raced home, as if I could beat the inevitable descent of darkness.

I ran all the way up the stairs to our apartment, but once outside my door, I could barely unlock it; my hands were shaking so hard. Out of breath, I stood panting in the kitchen. The apartment was empty. There was a note on the kitchen table, propped up in the fruit bowl. Her round cursive was like a child's: "Gone out for pizza. Be back by 8. Love, Maggie and Shelly."

Luigi's was just down the street; I thought for a minute about going there, about grabbing Maggie by the scruff of her neck and dragging her back. Instead, I threw off my work clothes and jumped in the shower. I scrubbed my legs and arms and hands, hard. As the hot water pelted my head and body I tried to imagine the anger, the fear, the sense of dread washing off me. There had to be a simple explanation for why Maggie had come here. The alternative was unthinkable.

On the roof, my skin raw but clean, I sat down and waited. The streetlights were dim, Depot Street cloaked in a thick haze. With the green glow of the pool, the entire town could have been under water. I half expected that if I opened my mouth I might breathe water instead of air. I thought about what I would say to Maggie, rehearsed my questions, my confrontation, the way an actor might memorize his lines. I had to be careful. I had to be smart. I couldn't afford to lose it. Not this time; there was too much at stake.

I could almost see the pizza place from this vantage point. I expected I'd see the girls as they walked home, but when Maggie rounded the corner, she was alone. She was carrying a pizza box, walking slowly up the street, stopping every now and then to look at the shop windows. I could hear her singing, something soft and sweet. She did that sometimes in the kitchen too.

My heart started to race. Where was Shelly? My hands were slick with sweat. And then finally, I saw her. She was walking with a boy. I struggled to make out his face; he wasn't anyone I recognized. When he threw his arm over her shoulder, I almost leapt down off the roof. Instead, I crawled toward the window and into the shadows to get a better view. Shelly and the boy were laughing. When he pulled her into him, I saw her look up toward the apartment, and I pressed my back against the wall. And then he kissed her. It was clumsy and quick, but still, I felt both angry and paralyzed. All of the stress I'd been feeling about Maggie was suddenly diverted, *derailed*. Somehow I managed to make my legs move me toward the open window and back into the house.

And then I heard Maggie open the door.

She handed me the pizza box, and I took it from her. "I got you a whole one, half pepperoni, half cheese. I didn't know what y'all liked."

"Where's Shelly?" I asked.

"She's just walkin' home with one of her friends. I was feelin' tired, so I came on home early. It's not even seven yet. She'll be home before eight."

I opened the pizza box and sweet smelling steam wafted up

into my face. *Stay calm.* I took out a piece of pizza, shaking my fingers after the hot greasy cheese burned them. "Shit," I said.

"Gotta watch out. I knew somebody who got a third-degree burn from a pizza once," Maggie said with a laugh.

"So your *aunt*," I said. "She's in Montreal?"

"Yeah?" she said, cocking her head at me.

"Because we got a phone call at the station today from a woman, a woman from Montreal, Canada, and she was looking for her niece. She said she was supposed to be on the Montrealer, the one that crashed into the river." I hadn't thought this through. Who did I think I was kidding?

Maggie scowled, sat down across from me and started to take off her shoes.

"She said she was really upset, that she wanted to come right down and look for her herself. Since, *technically,* her niece is still missing." I kept talking, worried about what would happen if I stopped.

Maggie waited a long time before she spoke. She turned her shoes in her hands, looking at the soles, at the heels.

"That sure is interestin'," Maggie said, setting the shoes down on the floor, putting her feet up on the chair next to me. "Boy, my feet hurt these days. Would you mind giving them a little rub?"

Because I was already in too deep, I reached for her tiny little foot. Maggie closed her eyes as I worked at the knots in her feet. I pressed my thumb into her arch, watched her back stiffen.

"There wasn't anybody waiting for you in Canada," I said. "Your ticket only went as far as Two Rivers." I let go of her foot and swallowed hard. "And I want to know what it is that you want from me."

Maggie didn't say anything. She leaned her head back, eyes closed, rolling her neck like she was just trying to get a crick out.

I held onto her foot, aware of every small bone.

After a while, when the silence was almost excruciating, she opened her eyes, looked square at me and said, "I got raped."

I let go of her foot as if I'd been burned.

"Nobody knows. They all think I went and got myself knocked up the usual way. And so now nobody wants nothin' to do with me anymore. Not my auntie, not even my daddy. I ain't got nobody in the world except for a big brother I never met. I came here looking for him."

1968: Fall

This is the way a body falls. It is not the slow, gentle collapse you'd expect. No quiet yielding. No gentle acquiescence.

The man resists. After the first strike, his limbs flail madly and he stumbles about as if he were only drunk. He lunges toward Brooder, who raises the weapon over his head again and strikes a second time.

Harper feels the sour taste of whatever it was he last managed to eat rising into his throat. Burning. He stares at his hands, which are gripping the dashboard of Ray's car.

"Jesus Christ," Ray says. "What the fuck?"

Harper squeezes his eyes shut, pretending that he is watching a movie. That what he sees through the windshield is only a projection, only vivid pictures on a screen. The drive-in movie theater. A Technicolor nightmare.

Ray rolls down the window and leans his head out. "Hey, man, that's enough!"

And then Brooder is staring back at them, as if he has completely forgotten they are there. He is both looking at them and past them. Entirely lucid but, at the same time, completely absent.

Harper's back tenses as Brooder raises his arm one more time, and the man circles him, swaying dumbly.

With this strike, the man goes down. The descent is both fast and loud. The body yields, but the ground beneath him does not. Harper presses his hands against his ears, anticipating the moans of the very earth as it catches him.

FOUR

Inside the House of Me

Without Betsy, I became a sleepwalker: my feet moving me from one place to the next while my mind was always elsewhere. (*Back in Two Rivers. Back inside that barn, lightning illuminating her in erratic and beautiful flashes.*) For the first month at Middlebury, I wandered the green expanse of campus, somnambulant. Oblivious. I had enrolled in five classes that fall: Ancient Philosophy, English Literature, Calculus, European History and French. In my "free" time, I audited an Art History seminar and a Poetry writing class. I figured that I might be able to fill my brain so that there wasn't any room left for Betsy Parker. But no matter how hard I tried, she occupied every corner, every crevice. I was dreaming her still, even when I was wide awake.

My roommate at Middlebury chain-smoked Chesterfield cigarettes and spoke fluent Latin. His name was Alfred ("Freddy") Van Horn III; he came from a long line of Van Horns who had made their money in the publishing industry. *Magazines.* His grandfather, Freddy the First, was the publisher of a certain gentleman's magazine that I recognized as the ones Betsy had introduced me to all those years ago. "Titties," Freddy explained over our first pint of beer at a pub on the outskirts of campus. "Titties and ass. *Ad nauseum.*" Freddy knew that I was only biding my time at college, that despite my apparent academic zeal, school was really just a distraction from the real obsession of my life. He'd seen the photos I kept tucked into the corners of my mirror, between the pages of my books, and in most of my drawers. Betsy Parker was everywhere. Freddy's attempts at diversion were tireless and admirable. He knew a lot of girls, and he was always bringing them by in the hopes that one of them might cause me to relinquish my devotion to Betsy Parker. There were short girls, tall girls, happy girls and melancholy girls. Good girls and bad girls. But the one thing they all shared was a fascination with Freddy Van Horn. He was like Brooder with a private school education. He had the charisma of a politician without any of the political aspirations. But he was also an academic savant, managing always to get good grades despite his lax study habits. There was something *easy* about Freddy Van Horn. Something I suppose that came with affluence and good fortune. He never had to work very hard for anything, and so he never perceived the world to be a difficult place. While I felt tortured by it, he saw the world at Middlebury as something created to serve him and his desires.

"What are her stats?" Freddy asked, peering over my shoulder at a photo of Betsy's face, which was marking my place in *Othello*. I could barely concentrate. It was almost Homecoming weekend, and Betsy was coming to stay for three whole days.

"Stats?"

"Hips, waist. Bust?" He outlined the shape of a woman with his hands, and in the invisible trail his gestures made, I imagined Betsy's body.

"Go away," I said.

"When does she get here?"

"After I get out of Calculus. I've got to get into town by three o'clock. Can I borrow the Vespa?" Underclassmen weren't allowed to have cars on campus, but Freddy had an Italian scooter that he had shipped from Italy the last time he was in Rome and upon the back of which I had ridden several times during his kidnapping attempts.

"But of course. Don't go crashing it into a tree now though."

"I won't. I promise."

"Is she staying at Battell?"

"Yeh," I said. "She's bunking with another girl coming in from Dartmouth."

"Wonderful! I know a way to smuggle her out pretty easily."

I rolled my eyes and picked up my books.

I drove the Vespa cautiously into town. I had hoped that some of Freddy's worldliness might rub off on me—that arriving to pick her up on a scooter instead of in the old DeSoto might prove to her that I had something exciting to offer now that I was a college man. I also imagined how it would feel to have her pressed against my back as we rode through the corridors of autumn foliage back to campus. But the Vespa wasn't as easy to drive as it was to ride, and when I arrived at the bus station, I slipped getting off and felt the terrible sensation of a burning hot exhaust pipe touching the exposed part of my ankle. I stifled a scream, grabbed my leg and pitched face forward toward the ground. I scrambled to my feet as quickly as I could, picked up the scooter, and glanced quickly around to see who, if anyone, had witnessed this ridiculous display. I limped into the bus station, my ankle stinging something fierce, and went straight to the men's room, where I splashed cold water over the welt. Back at the station, I nursed my wound the best I could, sitting on a hard bench near the restrooms, pressing a handful of shredded ice I'd grabbed from the café against my blistered skin.

"Holy crap," her voice said. I looked up and saw a pair of knees. Then two peachy-colored thighs. As I lifted my head, I didn't recognize the legs (thinner than I remembered) or the dress, a gray wool thing that would have been dowdy had it not been for its length, which barely reached the top of those glorious thighs. Betsy was also wearing makeup: lots of black mascara and a thin coat of white lipstick. Her hair was in two low pigtails on either side of her head. She had cut it, probably about a foot from what I could tell. I felt my heart sink.

"You cut your hair," I said.

"What *happened*?"

I glanced quickly down at my leg. The burn was bad. Purplish black. Oozing. Betsy squatted down next to me, and the skirt rose higher up her legs. She touched the skin near the wound, and even the slightest touch of her fingertips against my skin stung.

"Oh God, I can smell it," she said, covering her nose and mouth with the back of her arm. She stood up, and so did I.

"I'm fine," I said. I didn't want to talk about it anymore.

"How did you *do* that?"

"Jesus, what happened to *hello*?" I stepped back as if I were studying a painting or a sculpture. Betsy smiled broadly and then blushed, clearly aware that she didn't look at all like the girl I'd known only a month before. She leaned into my arms, suddenly shy, and hugged me. At least she still smelled like Betsy. Soapy. Lustre-Creme shampoo and lilacs.

When I showed her the Vespa, she shook her head.

"It's safe. Just don't touch the exhaust pipe. That's how I got burned. Here," I said, offering her help getting on.

"My skirt," she said.

We stood looking hopelessly at the Vespa. I kept thinking about her legs. "Take my sweater," I said. "You can tie it around your waist." I pulled the sweater I was wearing over my head, the air crackling with static. I patted down my hair, hoping it wasn't standing straight up on end. It had gotten much longer without my father's monthly cut.

"You need a haircut," Betsy said.

I got on the scooter and Betsy got on carefully behind me. I could feel her legs pressing against my legs as I pulled away. And then we were rushing through the autumn afternoon, and I realized I hadn't felt so alive since I'd left Two Rivers. The crush of leaves, the impossible scent of fall, and Betsy's chest pressed against my back with only her dress and a thin cotton Oxford between us.

"Is this it?" Betsy asked. Her breath was hot in my ear.

I nodded and leaned the Vespa into the curve, suddenly an expert driver. When we pulled up in front of my dormitory, I felt cool. And when Betsy Parker in her minidress and pigtails got off behind me, I hoped that Freddy was watching out the window. We walked across campus together to get Betsy checked into the girls' dorm where she would be staying. Betsy reached for my hand about halfway there and held onto it. I never realized how very small her hands were. When we got to Battell, I opened up my hand slowly, as if I were holding a bird or butterfly on the verge of escape inside. And suddenly overwhelmed by the architecture of her small bones, the incredible complexity and beauty of each digit, I lifted her hand up to my face, pressing it into my cheek. And then, embarrassed, I kissed her hand as if that's what I intended to do all along.

That night I had planned to take Betsy into town again for dinner and a movie.

Freddy feigned snoring. "Bo-o-oring."

It was, indeed, a mundane sort of thing to do with a girl I'd loved my entire life.

"Take her to Burlington," Freddy said. "Get drunk. Go skinny-dipping in the creek. Jesus. Dinner and a movie. Who *are* you, goddamned Archie Andrews?"

Freddy insisted on coming along with me to pick her up. I resisted at first, not wanting to share even a moment of this night, but finally his incessant pleading got the better of me, and I told him he could come along if he promised to leave us alone afterward. Plus his excitement at meeting the object of my affection was infectious, and I wanted to show her off.

Freddy and I waited for her in the lobby of the girls' dorm. The housemother rang her, and within minutes she materialized at the top of the stairs. The sight of her brought a lump to my throat.

"*Rare avis,*" Freddy whispered, as she descended the stairs. "What a rare little birdie."

She had changed from her woolen shift into a black pencil skirt and soft white sweater. She had also loosened her hair from the pigtails. I'd almost forgotten how dark her hair was, the blue-black stillness of it. Like water at night.

"You must be Freddy," she said, thrusting her hand toward him. It seemed to catch him off-guard, rendering him (for the first time since I'd met him) speechless.

"*Enchantée,*" he said, taking her hand and kissing it dramatically.

Betsy smiled. "*Moi aussi,*" she said, curtsying. And then to me, "I'm taking French at school. My roommate and I might study abroad junior year. Paris."

The lump in my throat felt like a hard candy. Stuck and suffocating. "Well then, our reservation's for seven," I said.

He kept staring at her.

"Bye, Freddy. See you later."

"Sure thing, old fellow," he said. "See you back at the room. Let me know if you need *assistance.*"

At the restaurant, Betsy said, "Your friend Freddy's nice."

"Hmph," I said. I was thinking about France.

"How's your leg?"

"Fine. I'll go to the infirmary on Tuesday." The truth was that each step sent pain shooting out from the wound in all directions. "So you're going to Paris?"

"Oh, I don't know. I'm doing really well in French though.

My professor says my pronunciation is good for a first-year student."

"Hmph," I said again.

The waiter brought us a basket of bread and a silver bowl of ice with little pads of butter on top.

"This place is *fancy*, Harper," Betsy whispered.

"I suppose," I said.

But despite the restaurant and its fresh flowers and linen tablecloths, its extensive array of flatware and silver candelabras, something felt spoiled about the night. All I could think of was Betsy going to Paris. About how on earth I would survive a whole year without her. Hell, I'd barely made it through the past month.

"I'm not very hungry," I said as I studied the menu.

"Oh, *I* am," Betsy said. "I've only had a cup of coffee and a bag of peanuts today."

"No wonder you're so skinny," I said.

Betsy blinked hard. She was wearing false eyelashes and thick black eyeliner, which framed her eyes in a way that made them both startling and pretty.

The waiter came with two menus, the size of newspapers, and I hid behind mine.

"Why are you being so mean to me?" she asked softly.

"I'm not," I said, feeling terrible. I lowered the menu but couldn't look her in the eyes. "I'm sorry. It's just, I'm just . . ."

"What?"

"You're so different," I said. "Wearing perfume. Makeup. It's just weird."

"I'm a *girl*," she said. Her voice was trembling. "And I thought this was a *date*."

I felt like a total shit. "I'm sorry," I said, desperate to backpedal. To rewind. To start over.

She looked toward our waiter, who was busy with another table, and said, "Can we *leave*?"

"Now?" I asked.

She nodded, reaching across the table and grabbing my hands. She leaned toward me and whispered, "I want to be alone with you."

I nodded and stood up, almost knocking my chair over backward. "Let's go."

Freddy had extended the loan on his Vespa, and as soon as we got on and headed into the night, I'd realized he'd been right about the dinner and movie idea. Betsy was no Betty. Hell, she wasn't even a Veronica. I drove us across the stone bridge that traversed Otter Creek and stopped. We both got off the scooter. Below us were the Otter Creek falls, an eighteen-foot cascade of crashing water.

"Wow," she said, peering over the bridge at the rushing falls below. When she climbed up onto the edge of the bridge to get a better look, I resisted the urge to pull her back to safety. She motioned for me, and I climbed up onto the ledge next to her. We sat there, our legs dangling over the rushing water. I couldn't even bear to look at her.

And maybe because I wasn't looking at her, the kiss startled me. But there she was, her eyes closed, her lips thick and soft and wet against mine. The water crashed below us, violent and loud. When I closed my own eyes, we could have been at home, at the river. She reached quickly, pushing her hand under my shirt. It was cold, and my stomach flinched involuntarily as she touched me. But by the time she started fiddling with the button of my khakis, her skin was warm. Her fingers were hot as they wriggled downward and touched me. I gasped, suddenly vertiginous, reeling with both desire and fear. Unbearable happiness and an intense need to get down off this ledge.

"We can't do this out here," I said, fearing my words lost in the noise of water below us.

But she must have heard, because she took her hand out of my trousers, and I jumped down off the wall, helping her down after me. "There's an old mill. It's abandoned," I said, leaving the Vespa where it was, and pulling her by the hand toward the stone building with its crumbling walls and shattered glass windows. We crawled through one of the open doorways and once inside we ran, clinging to each other with both fear and excitement, through the industrial innards of the building, navigating the labyrinth of ductwork and plumbing, the rusted guts of neglected equipment. When we reached a small dark room, Betsy ran to the one window, which faced the falls, and leaned out, bent at the waist, her feet lifting off the ground for one terrifying minute.

"Do you miss home?" I asked. What I meant was, *Do you miss me?*

"*Je* suis *chez moi,*" she said, lowering herself again and coming to me.

"I am the house of me?" I asked. I had never had my mother's affinity for languages. I spent most of the time I should have been studying my French lessons daydreaming about Betsy.

She smacked my shoulder. "No, not *I am the house of me,* you idiot. *Je* suis *chez moi.* I *am* home."

"What does that mean?" I asked.

Betsy grabbed me by the shoulders, like she was trying to shake some sense into me. "When I'm with you, I *am* home. Coming here, being with you. *This* is home."

Something about this admonishment, this wonderful reprimand, made me fevered. I tore at Betsy's clothes until she was naked. And her body, the splendid expanse of skin and hair and breath, looked even more human, more like nature itself, in this wasted place. Her skin was softer than grass, gentler than breeze, even as we banged our backs and elbows and knees against the concrete floor. Even as my wounded calf scraped against the exposed metal of a broken pipe.

We would both be bruised the next day. Scratched and battered, but it didn't matter. Because we were home, if only for the night. *Home.* And outside the falls kept crashing and crashing and crashing.

Ray

I dreamed about him. All night I tossed and turned on the couch, going in and out of sleep. In and out of those woods. In and out of that night. When I woke up in the morning, I swore I could smell pine in my hair; I half-expected to find it stuck with pitch. When I washed my face, there were scratches across my face and hands, as if I'd gotten tangled up in thick brush.

In the glaring light of the bathroom, I stared at my reflection. There were bruised half-moons under my eyes, which were bloodshot and teary. Her brother. *Her brother.* Was there any possible way that that man could have been her brother? I wracked my brain, trying to do the math. He was maybe twenty at the time; he would have to have been so much older than Maggie—at least sixteen or seventeen years. And how would she have found me? How could she possibly have known to come here? How could she have known about that night, about those woods? About me standing at the edge of that river? It was ridiculous. Only the thumping heart beneath the floorboards: just my own conscience, my guilt, my fear. And when I finally made it into the kitchen, Maggie didn't say a word about our conversation the night before, as if it had, indeed, never happened at all.

"You like ham and eggs?" she asked.

I nodded. I wanted to say something to her about what she'd told me about the baby's father. I had been so stunned when she said she was looking for her brother that I couldn't focus on anything else. I had excused myself, disappeared into the bathroom, where I stood in the hot shower until my skin ached from the heat. By the time I came out again, she had gone to bed. But now, watching her flipping thick pink slabs of ham in the frying pan, her tiny feet bare on my kitchen floor, I was overwhelmed by the idea of someone hurting her. She was a child, a little girl. The violence of that baby's conception made my eyes sting.

"Maggie," I said.

She didn't look at me.

"Don't you worry yourself over it," she said, turning around. She was smiling, but the corners of her mouth were trembling with the effort. "Folks do bad things. I known that for a long time now."

For one panicky moment, I thought this was an accusation. *She knew, she knew.*

Maggie turned back to the stove and cracked an egg against the cast iron skillet. "Besides, most folks ain't bad at all," she said. "Most everybody got love in their hearts. I got love in mine. And this baby gonna have lots of love in his too. Don't matter *how* he got here."

I wanted to go to her, to hold her. I wanted to tell her everything would be okay, that I'd make sure that nothing like that happened to her again. But I didn't know how. And still, if she wasn't looking for him, who was she looking for? Why was she here? And so I sat quietly, my heart and brain reeling, and filled my mouth with the salty ham and eggs, swallowed the orange juice she'd squeezed by hand so that I wouldn't have to say anything.

It was Saturday, but I told Maggie and Shelly that I had to

go into the station to catch up on some work that I'd put off because of the wreck. After breakfast, Maggie said she was feeling tired and went to her room to nap. Shelly's Abraham Lincoln paper was due on Monday; she said she was going to the library.

"Can I go to Luigi's after I'm done?" Shelly asked.

"I don't want you seeing that boy again," I said.

"What boy?" she asked, looking down at her open textbook.

"You know what boy. And if I find out that you did, you will not leave this apartment. Ever." Even as I said it, I knew it sounded ridiculous.

I got on my bike and pedaled slowly out of town, noticing for the first time that the leaves had started to turn. It startled me. I never missed the change from summer to fall. I had no idea how I could have been so oblivious to something so pervasive, but here it was: a thousand shades of red and gold. Like some sort of spontaneous combustion had occurred.

I didn't know whether or not I'd be able to go through with it until I was halfway there. Even when I rode up the dirt drive to the house, I could barely believe I was making this journey. It had been twelve years since I'd come up this path. Knocked on this door.

Rosemary stood behind the screen door, wide-eyed. "Harper," she said, startled as much as I was by my arrival.

"Hi."

"Come in," she said. "It's nippy out there." She ushered me into the kitchen, which was warm and messy. The last time I'd been there, their son was a baby still. Now he was a year ahead of Shelly in school. Rosemary, on the other hand, hadn't changed much at all. Other than a few wiry gray hairs springing from her ponytail, she looked exactly the same as she always had.

"You want some coffee?" she asked. "Cider?"

"Actually, could I just get some water?" My throat was dry from the ride.

"Sure, sure," she said, going to the sink. She reached for a glass and turned toward me before turning on the water. "Saw you at the funeral," she said.

I nodded, my throat going from dry to swollen. When she handed me the glass I took a long swallow, hoping it was only thirst rendering me mute.

"Ray at work?" I managed.

"He's up to his sister's. He'll be here any minute."

I sat down at the kitchen table, the table where Betsy and I had played cards with Ray and Rosemary a zillion times. I traced the cracked Formica with my fingernail.

"Brenda seems to be handling it okay," Rosemary said. "It's going to be hard, though, taking care of Roger on her own. At least she's got Brooder's disability checks to count on. Plus I think she does hair at Bobbi's shop. I don't know. We don't know her too well."

I glanced toward the door when I heard a car pull up the drive. I both wanted Ray to interrupt this awful conversation and dreaded what I would do when he did. I took another swallow of water when I heard him coming up the steps.

"Hey, whose bike is that outside?" Ray asked before the door was even all the way open. "Harper."

Ray reached his hand out to me before I had time to think. He was good like that, making uncomfortable situations comfortable. I stood up, shook his hand. It was such a formal gesture. I would sooner have curtsied than shaken Ray's hand.

"How are you?" Ray asked, peeling off his denim jacket.

"I'm good," I said, nodding my head a little too emphatically.

Rosemary handed Ray a Coke from the fridge, taking his

coat from him and draping it over her arm. "I'll leave you boys alone to catch up," she said, as if it had only been weeks since we'd last spoken. She smiled and disappeared into the other room.

I followed Ray out onto the screened porch, accepted the seat he offered me.

"Sorry I didn't get a chance to talk to you at the funeral," he said. "I heard you moved out of Paul and Hanna's place? Folks are sayin' you got a girl stayin' with you to help out with Shelly?"

"Ray, we've got to talk," I said. My pulse was beating hard in my temples and neck.

"Sure," Ray said, forcing a smile. He popped the top on his soda can, and it hissed.

I looked out the window at the thick foliage surrounding their property. I squinted my eyes, and all of the individual leaves (orange, gold and red) became one fiery blur. "I think somebody knows something," I said, careful.

"Whatcha mean?" he asked, glancing toward the open door to the house.

"About that night."

Ray stood up and walked to the door, closing it gently. He sat back down in his chair and stared at his hands.

"I know it sounds crazy, it's been twelve years, for Christ's sake. Nobody was there. But all of a sudden this girl shows up on my doorstep. She says she's on her way to Canada, and then I find out that her ticket was only to Two Rivers."

"That don't mean nothin'," Ray said, shaking his head. He lowered his voice then. "Just cause she's *colored* . . ."

"She says she's looking for her brother, Ray," I said.

Ray set the can down on the windowsill and put his head in his hands. It was peculiar to see Ray, now grown, using the same gestures he had as a kid.

"I'm a good man," he said, looking up at me, as if he had to convince not only me but himself as well. "I ain't never done nothin' to nobody."

"I know," I said. "I know that."

Ray and I spent the morning walking all along his property.

"Deer season's comin' right up," he said. "Last year I got a nine-point buck. Over two hundred thirty pounds. We're just now running out of venison in the freezer. J.P.'s gonna be fourteen come March," he said. "He's a good hunter. Can fend for himself out here."

I nodded and followed behind him.

"Last summer I bought up thirty more acres from my neighbor. I own this," he said, holding his arms out. "Far as the eye can see anyway."

I looked out at the glorious land, the pastures and woods. I thought of my own small apartment, our few belongings. I owned nothing. I had nothing to lose—except for Shelly. Except for every dream I had for her. For us.

After a while, we came to the creek, where Ray bent down and washed his hands.

"Ray, I don't know what to do," I said.

A look of panic crossed his face. He stood up, wiped his hands on his pants. "You don't even know who this girl is," he said matter-of-factly. "You're just bein' paranoid."

"Ray, what other explanation is there? Why *else* would she be here?"

Ray stood up. He was still so short, just up to my chin. He started walking again, looking out across his land, his hands shoved in his pockets. "For a long time, I thought he was coming back. Of course, I know that don't make no sense. My head knew that anyway. But still, I'd be out here, in the middle of *nowhere*, and I'd catch something in the corner of my eye and swear that it was him. Hiding in the trees. In the bushes. I'd hear his voice, only it was just the wind. It nearly drove me crazy. I think that's what got to Brooder. I won't let it happen to me. You and me, we were there," he said. "But Brooder was the one that done it. It was always Brooder."

"I guess," I said.

"You got to listen," he said. "This girl shows up, says she's lookin' for her brother. Maybe she hasn't even *got* a brother. You said she's been lyin' to you about just about everything. Why not this too?"

I nodded, wanting desperately to believe.

"All you got to do is get her on a train headed back down to where she came from. That's it," Ray said, kicking a rock with his steel-toed boot. "End of story."

But as we made our way back to the house, and twilight settled over those autumn hills, we both knew that there was no real end to this story.

1968: Fall

In the back of Brooder's pickup truck, the man is slumped over like a harvest dummy. Just a flannel shirt and pair of jeans stuffed with straw. Not a real man. Ray and Harper are following behind with only the fog lights illuminating this scarecrow in the truck bed. There is a chill in the air, and though Harper can no longer feel his hands, he rolls down the window.

"Where's Brooder going?" Ray asks.

Harper shakes his head.

"He's bound to come to soon. He'll probably jump."

Harper leans his head into the wind, which stings his face like a slap.

"He's just gonna scare him, right?" Ray asks. "That's what he said."

Harper thinks about opening the door, about jumping, about throwing himself out of the moving car. He wonders what the pavement would feel like as it kissed his skin. He tries to imagine the way his bones would feel as they shattered. He puts his hand on the handle and pushes his thumb, testing.

And then, as the pavement turns to dirt and Ray's car bounces into first one and then another rut made by the recent rains, Harper hears what he thinks at first is a baby's cry. It is piercing, strange. His head begins to ache and he hits the lock on the door.

The man is awake, sitting up and staring him in the face. Crying like an infant, or a wounded animal, into the night.

The New England Bell

We were going to run away. For real this time. By the end of our freshman year, when spring finally came with all of its requisite sunshine and mud, we both knew we couldn't take it anymore. The weeks between Betsy's visits were unbearable: the days liquid, slow and thick. And even when she *was* with me, I could barely enjoy her company; I was so fixated on her impending and inevitable departure. We clung to each other, desperate and mournful. You'd have thought one of us was dying, the way we held on.

It was Betsy's idea to drop out. "School's pointless. It's all pointless. I want to be with you. In the world. Doing things. *Living.*"

I nodded, emphatic, though truthfully, I didn't mind school much. It was being away from Betsy that wounded me. I could have been anywhere with her, as long as we were together.

"I'm tired of the projectors. The slides. It's ridiculous. Art shouldn't be studied. It should be felt. Experienced." Betsy was beaming. "Come with me?"

The plan was to go back to Two Rivers for the summer. We would both work, save our money, and then buy two one-way tickets to Barcelona. It was cheaper to fly into Spain than France, and we would get a Eurail Pass, ride the trains. Hitchhike if we needed to. The idea was thrilling, but abstract. When

I lay in my narrow bed at night, my whole body aching for Betsy, Paris came to me in tissue paper fragments, a busted kaleidoscope: the stained glass windows of Notre Dame, the smell of espresso, red wine, and the dizzying vertigo of the Eiffel Tower. It was like assembling the fragments of someone else's dream. So while Betsy counted the days until our European adventure would commence, I was content to imagine summer at home again.

It had been a difficult winter. Having sex on campus was punishable by expulsion, and finding love off campus was similarly impossible. (The hotels and motels in town were complicit in the college's aim to promote celibacy among Middlebury's students.) Terrified of being kicked out of school, I had only allowed Freddy to help Betsy gain entrance to my room two times. He snuck her in through a first-floor window both times without incident. However, getting her back out proved to be a more difficult and risky project. After leaving my room one late afternoon in February, Betsy was caught tiptoeing down the back stairs by a junior fellow. Luckily, he didn't know Betsy and bought the story that she'd only gotten lost, that she'd wandered into the dorm to get out of the cold. After that near-miss, I gave up, relinquishing any chance of romantic entanglement beyond our desperate groping at the movie theater in town. I couldn't wait to be back in Two Rivers, where it didn't seem like the entire world was trying to keep me from getting laid. Now that Betsy and I were lovers, Two Rivers became more than just our old stomping grounds. Suddenly, it was a place of tremendous romantic and sexual potential: every meadow, every wooded area, every remote and pastoral place of my childhood now a possible site for amorous rendezvous. When I thought about summer, I imagined my father busy in his workshop, my mother busy in her study, and Betsy and I free to make love wherever we pleased.

Of course, my mother was still in Mississippi, had been

there almost a year now. This was a fact that I knew to be true, but still had not quite connected with yet. Because I was away, when I thought of home, I still pictured her there. Perhaps if I had been in Two Rivers, I would have felt her absence more intensely, but as it was, I received a weekly postcard from her, which was much more frequent than any correspondence I had with my father, and it made her feel close. She never said so, but in my mind, she would be home by the time I finished up the school year. When the postcard arrived saying that she'd decided to stay on through another summer, I should have known the bottom was about to fall out. Then we got the phone call from Hanna, and it did.

Betsy's father had been giving Jack Miller, the high school principal, a straight razor shave before the Memorial Day parade when Principal Miller suddenly screamed out, leaping to his feet, bleeding from a six-inch gash in his cheek. At first, Mr. Parker (like Mrs. Norris at the post office) seemed to have simply fallen. However, when he did not stand up, and could not speak, he was quickly rushed to the hospital, where the doctors said that he had had a massive stroke.

Betsy was visiting me that weekend. We were sitting in two Adirondack chairs on the grassy lawn behind Battell, reading a *Fodor's Guide to Paris,* drinking ice tea when Miss Katy, the housemother, came rushing outside, her face flushed. "Betsy, honey, there's a phone call for you. From home. It seems it's an emergency, so you best come quick."

Hanna tried to explain to Betsy about what had caused the episode, as well as the doctors' prognosis, but Betsy only shook her head, blinking hard against the tears that were filling her eyes, and handed the phone to me. Miss Katy enveloped Betsy in her arms, and rocked her back and forth until I hung up.

Because the stroke affected the right side of Mr. Parker's body, he was completely unable to use his right hand, which meant that his bowling days, as well as his barbering days, were over. He wanted to keep the shop open, however, and he asked Betsy to help him run the business that summer, just until he could find someone to take over. She agreed, and we continued to plan our trip for the fall. He would be better by September, she said, he had to.

Orange Crush and sad eyes. This was Betsy Parker at nineteen. Every morning Betsy made her father breakfast, helped him get dressed, cleaned the house and then left him propped up in front of the TV with everything he would need for the day. Then she got on her bicycle and rode to the shop, which she opened, promptly, at 9:00 A.M. She thought at first that she might be able to get the necessary bookkeeping and other miscellaneous duties done by lunch, leaving Knight Rogers and the two other barbers to manage things until closing. But when I came to pick her up, sweaty still from mowing the nearly two-acre span of the cemetery, she was more often than not still sweeping mountains of hair up off the floor, washing out sinks, tidying the supplies—not having had even a moment to devote to the books. She worked late every night, and our romantic escapades were limited to frantic groping and making out in the alley behind the barbershop. So much for meadows and pastures.

And though I knew better, I felt cheated out of my summer. *Our* summer. As each day went by that Betsy was consumed with the upkeep of her father's barbershop and the upkeep of their home and the upkeep of her father's health, I found myself feeling more and more bitter. It was terrible, and I'm ashamed to admit it even now, but Mr. Parker's illness exasperated me, as if he'd gotten sick to spite me. In my darkest moments, I thought about how much easier things would have been if he hadn't lived through the stroke. And so when Betsy showed up at the cemetery, her face red and streaked with tears, a small, awful part of me felt joyous at the prospect that I would have her back. That she would belong to me again. But

Mr. Parker hadn't died, he'd just had another stroke, a terrible one this time, one that had rendered him unable to walk.

"He's so sick, Harper," Betsy said.

"He'll be okay," I said. We sat down together on the grass in front of a crumbling granite tombstone. "By fall?"

"We can't go," Betsy said softly. "To Europe."

Though Paris had been distant in my thoughts, unreal and hazy, it's what I'd been looking forward to since our summer plans had fizzled. This felt like a blow to the stomach.

"Harper, I don't even think I can go back to school."

"What about Paul and Hanna? Can't they take him in?" I asked.

Betsy shook her head. Hanna had always blamed Mr. Parker for her sister's suicide, though she never said so in so many words.

I wanted to tell her I wouldn't go back to school either. That I'd come help her: that I'd take care of her. That none of it mattered as long as we were together. But before I had a chance, she started crying.

"I'll never get out of here," she said, her eyes wild. "I had my chance. And now it's gone. I feel *trapped*, Harper. He trapped my mother, and now he's trapped me too." Her hand flew to her mouth as if she couldn't believe the words that had escaped.

"Betsy," I said, reaching for her, but she shook her head. And then she was running, winding her way through the gravestones toward the small stone chapel at the edge of the cemetery.

I went after her, slowly at first, unsure if I should follow her at all. When she disappeared into the chapel, I stopped. I leaned against a tree near the entrance and waited. When she didn't come out, I knocked softly before opening the door.

Inside, it was cool and dark. It smelled like pine. Like musty wood. Sunlight streamed through the dusty windows in narrow beams. She was sitting on a pew in the front of the building. "Betsy?"

"I don't feel God in here," she said.

I went to her and sat down next to her. "No?"

"I thought I might, but I don't. Do you?"

I looked around, at the raw wooden pews, at the crucifix. I closed my eyes and listened to Betsy's breath, which stuttered and caught like a child who has cried too long. I didn't know what God felt like, but I figured it was something like this. "I don't know," I said. I studied her face, noticing for the first time some new tiny lines at the corners of her eyes. And because I loved her more than anything in the world (more than the river, more than autumn leaves, more than fireworks on the Fourth of July), I blurted out, "I'll finish school and then I can get a great job somewhere else. Anywhere you want. And we'll go there. Europe. Paris. We'll get someone to take care of your father. A nurse, somebody . . ."

Betsy turned to me and looked hard at me. Then she squeezed my hand until my bones ached. *"Promise me,"* she said.

And because I loved her more than endless pastures and thick woods and sunshine, because I loved her more than snow, I whispered, "Promise."

Autumn was agony. By September, when Betsy and I should have been on our way to Paris, Mr. Parker was so ill he could barely get out of bed. Betsy had taken on almost all of the responsibilities of the barbershop, leaving her very little time or energy to make the bus ride to Middlebury on the weekends. My course load was heavy; going home to visit was impossible, and so Betsy and I were forced to carry on our love affair via the New England Bell. There was one pay phone in my dormitory, in the hallway on the first floor. The fall of my sophomore year I was known as "Phone Man." I was a fixture in that hallway, sitting for hours on end with my back against the wall, the phone balanced between my ear and shoulder, talking to Betsy.

I lived for the phone calls: for those hours when Betsy and I were still apart but miraculously connected, our voices winding around each other despite the distance between us. She had a way of talking to me on the phone that she never did in person. In many ways, our conversations were more intimate than when we were face to face, as if, deprived of each other's hands, we were forced to touch each other with our words. We talked until our throats were raw. Until there was nothing left to say, and then we simply listened to each other breathe. Sometimes I fell asleep out there on the hard floor of the hallway, the phone still cradled between my ear and my chin. I'd wake up, and her voice would come to me, "Go to bed, Harper. You were snoring."

But relying on her voice alone, without her eyes, without her hands, was also dangerous. It was too easy to misinterpret a sigh, a laugh. A silence that lasted too long. When Betsy called to tell me that she and Howie Burke had spent the afternoon at his grandmother's farm picking apples, I was studying for a Statistics midterm. (In light of our new plans, I had chosen Economics as a major and English literature as a minor. The major was meant to secure lucrative employment, while the minor was intended to ensure my sanity.) And though I was already sitting, when she described the sunset that colored the whole sky orange and purple, I felt like I was falling. There was a weakness somewhere in my joints, a sort of collapsing.

"It was incredible," Betsy said. "Just as it was getting dark, one of the mares went into labor. Howie's grandfather let us in near her stall, and I got to watch the foal being born. I should have taken pictures, but the camera was in the car and I didn't want to miss anything. I've never seen anything like it before. Have you?"

"Nope," I said, gripping the edges of my textbook, feeling completely untethered.

"Howie's seen about a zillion babies being born—calves and kittens and puppies," she sighed.

"Wow."

"I *know*. Did you know that something like twenty-five percent of mares die when they foal?"

"Twenty-five percent," I said, staring hard at my Statistics book.

"Something like that."

"How was the apple picking?" As I asked, I pictured Betsy climbing the ladder, her golden knees bending, her long thin arms reaching for the fruit.

"Nice," she said.

Nice. One breathy word, and I could almost see her plucking the apple out from the depths of the tree. She might have studied it, inspecting it for imperfections, or she might have been less cautious, yes, she certainly would have been less cautious. She wouldn't have looked at it at all; she would have just brought it to her parted lips and bitten. Below her, Howie Burke would have been holding the ladder steady, looking up at those amazing legs.

"How's your dad? Who took care of the shop?" I asked, feeling hurt and nasty, wanting only to get Betsy out of the apple orchard of my mind. Somewhere away from Howie Burke and his grandparents' fruit trees.

"He's okay," she said, and I felt my grip on the phone loosen. "Howie and I brought him a bushel of apples." And now, because I just had to ask, Howie Burke, captain of the cross country running team, the leader of the Glee Club, Duke of the goddamn prom, was following Betsy down that long hallway to the kitchen, where Mrs. Parker used to make lemon bars and cocoa for *me*. I could smell the apples, feel the autumn breeze coming in through the window.

"We made a pie," she said softly. Apologetically, I thought.

And now, Betsy and Howie were laughing in that kitchen: Betsy elbow-deep in flour and sugar and butter, Howie rolling the dough, sleeves pushed up to reveal the thin muscular arms of a runner, veins rising to the surface like thick rivers.

"Great," I said. "That's just great."

"You sound mad," Betsy said.

"Mad?"

"Yeah. Like I did something wrong."

"Hmph."

"Don't 'hmph' me, Harper," she said.

"I was thinking about coming home next weekend," I said.

"I thought you had midterms coming up."

I did. It was all I'd been talking about for weeks. I gripped the phone tighter. "You and Howie have plans already? You can tell me, you know."

She was quiet for a long time. Too long.

God, I hated myself. "Well, I guess I've got my answer," I said.

I knew I had to see her. If I didn't, I would lose my mind. I must have been a fool to think that conversation alone could sustain us. I needed to see her, touch her, hold her. I was lying on my bed, trying to figure out how I could possibly manage to get to Two Rivers without flunking my midterms when Eddie Lieberman knocked on my door. "Hey, Phone Man, phone's for you. *Again*," he said. I figured it was Betsy, and I was relieved. I could make up for being such an ass on the phone. I would tell her I was coming home.

"Harper?" my father said. My father almost never called me at school.

"I'm not sure how to tell you this, exactly, but your mother . . . she's in the hospital."

"What?"

"I don't have a lot of the details, but apparently there was some sort of conflict at the school. The police were called, and there were some arrests. I couldn't get much information from the hospital. I'm still waiting to hear back, but from what I can gather she's been beaten up really badly."

"*Beaten up?*" I asked.

"By the police," he said. "They say she was resisting arrest."

"*What?*"

"She's got a broken jaw. Broken ribs. A concussion." There was a strange tremble in his throat I'd never heard before.

I felt like the wind had been knocked out of me. "We have to go get her," I said.

"We can't," he said. "She's in police custody."

My father was in the basement when I arrived. I walked down the creaky wooden steps, lowering my head to avoid hitting it against the overhang. The first thing I noticed was the kitchen computer in the corner by the hot water heater. I have no idea how he managed to get it down there by himself. Seeing it there made me feel sorry for him.

"Hi, Dad," I said.

He looked up from something he was soldering. His eyes hidden behind a pair of safety goggles, which he wore over his glasses. He had on a canvas apron, like a butcher, and his hair was disheveled. He raised the goggles up on top of his head and smiled at me weakly. "Hi there."

"What are you making?"

His eyes lit up. "Why don't you come up and see?" Suddenly he was taking the stairs two at a time. We both ducked our heads as we reached the top of the stairs. I followed him down the hallway to my mother's study. The door was wide open, something I still had not grown accustomed to. Inside, everything had been rearranged. The desk was now in the bay window. The bookshelves had been moved to the far wall. And where her desk used to be was an elaborate machine.

"It's a printing press," he said. "This way she can continue with her newsletter from home. I've got a deal with the mill for paper. The only thing we need to worry about is the ink and the distribution." In the light, I could see that my father's hands were stained blue. His face was also smudged with indigo.

"This is amazing, Dad," I said. "This is the best yet."

That night I spoke on the phone to my mother for the first time in months. She was at the hospital, where she was going to be held until the following Monday morning when she would be arraigned. Because her jaw was broken, she could say little more than a warbled, "I'm okay." From her coworker who had been at the school when the "conflict" took place, I learned that the SNCC ("Snick") had a volunteer lawyer who had managed to get the others who were arrested out of jail. But the charge against my mother was battery. He hoped to be able to plea down to a lesser charge.

"Jesus Christ," I said. "When is she coming home?"

"If all goes well, by the end of the week we should know whether or not the prosecution will accept the plea."

The world felt tipped somehow, the same but skewed. The fact that my mother, a woman who puttered around in house slippers and a ratty sweater, glasses slipping and hair frazzled, was being accused of battering a police officer was so ludicrous, so inane, it made everything else I knew to be true seem somehow precarious. I felt like I couldn't trust anything anymore.

Needless to say, I had forgotten almost completely about Howie Burke by then. I realized as I hung up the phone with my mother that I was so distracted I'd even forgotten about Betsy. She had no idea I was home. But just as I was getting ready to go over to her house, I looked out my bedroom window and saw Howie's car coming down the street. He drove a 1963 convertible Galaxie 500. His father owned the only car dealership in Two Rivers. My own father had bought at least two of our family's vehicles from Mr. Burke. Though I'd have known the car anywhere, I was still in disbelief when it pulled into the Parkers' driveway, and Howie threw open the door, running around the car to open the passenger door for Betsy.

From my window, with the pair of binoculars I won in the seventh-grade science fair (for a wind machine my father both devised and expertly constructed), I had a vivid and unobstructed view of Betsy's house. Through my ill-gotten binoculars, I watched Howie open the screen door of the Parkers' house, holding it open as Betsy unlocked the front door. I watched the flickering lights of the TV through the filmy curtains of the living room, and Betsy and Howie's silhouettes moving behind them. I imagined Betsy's father asleep in front of the TV. My hands were sweaty, but I was afraid that if I put down the binoculars, I might miss something terrible. A light went on in the kitchen, and then a light went on in Betsy's room.

Focusing in on her canopied bed (on the place where she lay her head at night), I felt ashamed of myself; I had promised Betsy a long time ago never to use the binoculars to spy on her. I'd thought about it, of course, but up until now, I'd kept my promise. Tonight I studied every inch of Betsy's room: from the photos on her bureau to the books on the shelf over her bed, to the clothes that lay in dirty heaps on the floor. Everything was as I remembered it, save for a couple of new records (*Rubber Soul* and a live Joan Baez album) and a red sweater I'd never seen before. It looked small and soft. I thought about how it would look hugging Betsy's chest. I wondered if she'd worn it apple picking.

Howie sat down on the edge of the bed, watching Betsy, who was thumbing through her records. He lay back, resting his head on her pillow, and I felt like I was crawling out of my skin. I watched Betsy select a Bob Dylan album from the pile

(Bob Dylan of all things), watched her as she lowered it onto the spindle, could almost hear the record drop, and the needle lift. When I closed my eyes, I saw Betsy dancing on the hood of the DeSoto. Felt her in my arms. When I opened my eyes, Howie Burke was sitting up again, patting his hand on the bed, beckoning her to join him, and I was bounding down the stairs and out the door.

I didn't ring the Parkers' doorbell. I didn't even knock. I just threw open the front door and made my way down the hallway to Betsy's room. I only had to see the back of Howie's head leaning tilted and purposeful toward Betsy's surprised face, to know that what I was about to do was justified.

I had never punched anyone in my entire life. I wasn't even sure how to go about it. But rage has a way of informing a body, and despite my lack of pugilistic expertise, my fingers curled into an effective fist, which struck Howie square in the jaw before I had time to think. Howie stumbled backward and looked at me from the foot of Betsy's bed. Betsy stood stunned at his side. And I stood similarly stunned, my hand and head completely numb.

"I think you better leave," Betsy said, her voice breathy and calm.

"I'm sorry," I stumbled, shaking my hand as the numbness was suddenly replaced by excruciating pain.

"Not you, you idiot," she said to me. *"You."* She looked at Howie, who still looked bewildered.

Howie moved quietly toward the open door, rubbing at his jaw.

"Well, that was genius," she said after he was gone.

I sat down on her bed, where Howie and she had been only moments before. I was pretty sure my thumb was broken.

"You know I can fend for myself, you jealous bastard," she said.

"You were going to kiss him," I said, with disbelief.

"*No. He* was going to kiss *me*. And I was going to crack him one myself. What the hell are you doing here? You used the binoculars, didn't you?"

The heat of my broken thumb spread up my arm, across my shoulder, up my neck and into my ears.

She probably would have thrown me out next, but somehow I managed to explain everything to her (about my mother, about the kitchen computer gathering dust in the basement, about the midterm I was now pretty sure I would fail) in a way that made my insanity a reasonable defense.

"If you do anything that stupid again, we're done," she said, even as she held my wounded hand in her own. "The *last* thing I need is some sort of keeper."

She held me then, so close I could feel her heart beating through her shirt. And even though she had said otherwise, I knew she needed me. That she was glad I'd done what I did.

When my mother finally came home the following week, the first thing I noticed was that she was softer. Whatever she'd been eating in Mississippi had caused her to lose the familiar sharp angles of collarbone and ribs. When she hugged me at the train station, it felt like I was being held by a stranger. She hadn't held me that tightly since I was a little kid. I was overwhelmed with relief. I hadn't realized how much I missed her.

My thumb was broken in two places, and my mother was unable to speak because of the wires binding her broken jaw. We were a pair of walking wounded. But she was *home*, and I was home, and, for the time being, I knew that was all that really mattered.

Home

The weekend ticket agent was a semiretired guy who was hard of hearing. "Round-trip you say?" he asked, leaning close and turning his ear to the glass that separated us. I could see the white hairs curling inside his ear.

"*One-way,*" I said for the third time. "Two Rivers to Tuscaloosa."

And I put the ticket in my pocket, just in case Ray was right and it might, indeed, be as easy as this.

I went to my office, thinking I should really try to get some work done. Luckily Lenny didn't come in on the weekends, and I was spared his incessant interruptions, but by lunchtime, I knew I couldn't get anything else done until I had something to eat.

Rosco's was open, and busy. I had to wait ten minutes to even get a single seat at the greasy counter. I sat down next to a couple of guys who I knew worked in the yard. I nodded at them, and they ignored me. I picked up a menu and studied it. When the waitress finally got to me, I ordered a half-pound burger and a Coke.

"Hear 'bout that man over to Hardwick? The one 'at got shot?" the guy next to me asked.

"Ayuh," the other one answered.

"That's what you get." He nodded, taking a swig of his

noon beer. "Can't just go to sleep in somebody's barn. That James fellow just protectin' his property." He looked at me as the ketchup bottle I had been holding suddenly spilled ketchup all over my fries. He kept looking at me as if he were speaking to me instead of his buddy. "Course the bleeding hearts are all sayin' it's 'cause he was a black." He lowered his voice then and hissed, "Truth is, nigger was *trespassin'*."

My plate was covered in ketchup, a bloodbath. My appetite was gone. I reached into my pocket and pulled out my wallet. I counted out what I owed and a dollar more. I put the money down and looked at the man who was sitting next to me. He'd picked up a newspaper and was reading. I wanted to say something but couldn't, for the life of me, figure out what.

On the ride home from the station, I mulled over everything Ray had said. Every fear *I* had. As the sun sank behind the trees, filtering bright and relentless through the leaves, which were now in their full autumnal glory, I pedaled furiously, my mind reeling. Why did Maggie get on that train? If she were here simply to escape from her past, I'd do like Ray said and send her home. *End of story.* But it couldn't be that simple. Two Rivers is just a speck of dust on a map. Just a speck of dust on a speck of dust. Why on earth would she come *here*? She said she was looking for her brother, but if that were true, she certainly wasn't looking very hard. She had to know something. Something about that night. And if she was here because of that, because of twelve years of silence, then the story would end another way entirely. As I rode home, the sky turned violet and quiet, and the only sound was the hush of wind in my ears and the shrillness of my own fear.

I decided to look for Shelly at Luigi's before I went home and was forced to deal with Maggie. The restaurant smelled strongly of yeast and spices. I didn't see her right away, but then, as I made my way toward the back of the room, I saw her crammed into a booth with three other kids: another girl and two boys. I stopped before they could see me. Shelly was laughing, whispering and giggling into one of the boy's ears, and something took a hold of me.

"Shelly, it's time to go home," I said, marching up to the booth.

"Dad." She laughed, but her eyes were scared as they darted from me to the boy.

"Now," I said, and reached for her arm, pulling her out of the booth. I held on to her elbow as we made our way toward the front door.

Outside, Shelly waited until we'd turned the corner to Depot Street before she shook her arm out of my grasp. "Why did you do that? You're so embarrassing!"

"I told you, you were not to see that boy again."

It was dark now, and the streetlights flickered on, illuminating us.

"I hate you!" Shelly screamed, and started to run down the street, her sneakers slapping the pavement as she fled. She was fast, the fastest kid in her whole class as a matter of fact. I was out of breath by the time I caught up with her. She was sitting on the curb in front of the A & P, her head in her hands. I sat down next to her, close but careful not to touch her. Tears were running down her cheeks. I resisted the impulse to wipe them away. She smelled like the Heaven Scent perfume Hanna bought for her from Avon every year at Christmas.

"Why did you *do* that?" she asked.

But I didn't *know* why I'd done what I did. I couldn't explain it even now except that I felt, like I always felt, like a man holding onto a slippery rope, dangling over an awful precipice. So much of my life, it seemed, was spent just trying to hold on.

"Shelly, honey, I'm sorry," I started.

"I wasn't doing anything wrong. I was at the stupid library all day, on a *Saturday*, and I just went out for pizza with my friends. You treat me like I'm a baby. Like I'm still six."

I looked down the street toward our apartment building. The light was on in my window. I thought about Maggie, about the possibility that my time was up. I knew there was no such thing as forgetting. Maybe there was no such thing as forgiveness either.

When I turned back to Shelly, she said softly, her bottom lip trembling, "I want to go back to Hanna's house."

"What?" I asked. I breathed deeply, looked away from her.

"Hanna and Paul's. I want to go *home*."

I threw up my hands. "Fine. Go to Hanna's."

Shelly's eyes welled up. She looked at me with disbelief.

"Well, she obviously is better at this than I am," I said. "*She* thinks so. *You* think so. *Everybody* thinks so."

Tears started to run down Shelly's cheeks. I felt terrible. When I took her hand, it was cold. A soft breeze blew; the smell of Shelly's perfume was the smell of her childhood. A childhood that was fleeting, disappearing. I breathed her in, inhaled her. After a while, I felt the small but certain squeeze of her hand.

"Let's just go home," she said, defeated.

Back at the apartment, Maggie was still in her room. I asked Shelly to go in and check on her.

"She doesn't feel good," Shelly said as she closed the bedroom door behind her. "I told her I could make her some soup, but she doesn't want it."

"Has she got the flu?"

"I don't know. She just said she didn't feel good."

"I'm sure she'll be fine," I said.

"*You* hungry?" she asked.

"Yeah." I nodded.

I went to the cupboard, but Shelly pushed me away. "I'll do it. Just sit down."

I obeyed, sitting down at the kitchen table, as she busied herself at the stove. She still wouldn't look at me. "Did you get your paper finished?" I asked.

She nodded, pointing to the table. There, next to her books, was her essay, complete with a yellow construction paper cover. A silhouette of Lincoln's profile in black. "May I?" I asked.

She shrugged her shoulders. "I guess."

I picked it up and opened it, reading the first few sentences and then scanning the rest. It was riddled with spelling errors. None of the paragraphs were indented. There were no topic sentences. No thesis. What on earth were they teaching her at school? Hanna had always helped her with her schoolwork. I stepped in for long division, but that's where my tutoring had ended. I couldn't remember reading a single paper she'd written before; it made me feel like a rotten dad.

Shelly ladled the Chicken and Stars soup, heavy on the stars, into two bowls and set them down at the table. She handed me a spoon. "I worked really hard," she said.

My heart sank. "It's a good start, honey, but I think we should maybe go over it a little bit more before you hand it in. Can we do that tonight?"

Shelly shrugged and slurped from her soup bowl. "Daddy?" she said.

"Yeah?"

"I don't really want to go back to Hanna's. I was just saying that to be mean."

I looked at her, at the sorrow in her eyes. "I know," I said. "And I didn't mean to embarrass you."

As we ate dinner, it almost felt the way it used to. The weeks before the wreck, before Maggie, felt distant and unreal now. And watching Shelly sip the broth from her bowl, I imagined for a minute what it would be like to have my old life back. If only I could start over, I'd do everything different. I'd be involved. Pay attention. Hell, I'd be *Father of the Year*. I'd quit my stupid job, move us someplace new. Someplace where the schools were more concerned with education than basketball games and bake sales. Where people didn't say "nigger" in public (or private for that matter). Where we could get a fresh start. Where my past, our past, wasn't lurking around every corner. But the truth was that the train wasn't the only thing that derailed that day. My whole life had as well, and now I was pretty sure there *was* no going back. And the fear that had been gripping me by the shoulders all day suddenly turned into a tremendous sadness. The idea of losing this (this old table, the pale yellow wallpapered kitchen, the lulling sounds of the bowling alley beneath us) filled me with regret. And the idea of losing Shelly was unbearable. "It's time for Maggie to go home. To her family," I said.

Shelly looked up at me. "You can't!"

I was like a bull in a china shop tonight, smashing everything in my reckless path. "She needs to be with the people who love her," I pleaded.

"*I* love her, Dad," Shelly said loudly, her eyes filled with tears.

"Her baby will be coming soon," I said. "She can't exactly have the baby *here*."

Shelly took the paper napkin she had laid in her lap, wiped her eyes and was all business again. She looked at me and clenched her jaw. "Daddy, tell me about the night I was born," she said.

I shook my head. "Honey, that has nothing to do with Maggie. That was something else entirely. . . ."

"It was *exactly* the same," she said, her jaw set. *Here* was

Betsy, right here in this determination of tiny bones. "You had a baby, and you were all alone. The only difference is that Paul and Hanna took you in."

"We're not her family," I said.

"*Tell me,*" she said, "about the night I was born."

1968: Fall

*W*hen Brooder pulls his truck off the main road, Ray follows behind him down the old logging road. In the back of the truck,
the man has slumped over again, making Harper wonder if he only
imagined the cries. The orange moon has risen and is so bright it could
rival the sun. It makes Harper feel exposed. He looks behind them, at
the road disappearing, wondering who might be out there watching. He
runs his hand through his hair over and over again, trying to smooth
down a stubborn cowlick. A nervous habit. A tick.

"He's going to the junction," Ray says. "Where the rivers meet."

Harper remembers standing knee-deep in cold water, casting out
into the rushing current. He remembers the smell of coffee and dirt in
the can where he kept the night crawlers he plucked from the ground
before dawn. He remembers the prick of the hook, the sharp sting and
the blood. He remembers Betsy peering into his empty bucket.

"She's really dead?" Harper asks then, as if Ray could make it
untrue by simply denying it.

He looks at Ray, at the Sox baseball cap pulled down over his
ears. He's worn it everyday since Ted Williams's final home run in
1960. The brim is worn, the insignia faded. It is familiar. Comforting.
Harper looks at his friend, eyes wide and scared, and he waits for him
to take everything away. To tell him that she's not dead at all, that it
has all been a misunderstanding. A terrible dream.

But Ray just holds on to the steering wheel and stares straight
ahead. "He's just gonna scare him. That's what he said."

Freedom Press

Though she couldn't smile or even really speak (her jaw was still wired shut), my mother beamed when my father showed her the makeshift printing press he had set up in her office. She clapped her hands together and threw her arms around his neck in a way that reminded me of an adolescent girl instead of a forty-three-year-old woman. My father seemed suddenly bashful, pleased as punch with himself. It had taken two decades, but he'd finally used his talents to make her truly happy.

By the summer after my sophomore year at Middlebury, the *Freedom Press Monthly* was in full operation with a circulation of about a thousand. When I arrived home for summer vacation, there was an electricity in our house that I had never felt before. It was infectious. Each morning my mother woke before dawn, the smell of coffee infiltrating my dreams. By the time I managed to drag myself out of bed, she would have been up for hours already and would read her works-in-progress aloud to me as I ate breakfast.

" 'While Klan activity in the South is often overt, the Ku Klux Klan may be New England's best kept dirty little secret. Because despite the Klan's subversion, it is experiencing a frightening resurgence in the northern states.' "

"The *Klan*?" I interrupted.

She put her fingers to her lips. "Shhh. Listen. 'The history of the Klan in Vermont, for example, might be surprising to those who currently live there. A state that is known for its tolerance and political progressiveness has also served as a hotbed for Klan activity throughout history. Presenting itself to these communities as an organization resolute on promoting family and patriotism and religion, in the early part of this century the Klan quickly gained followers. By the 1920s, over 14,000 Vermonters had paid the $10 initiation fee to the organization.' "

"Ma, that was forty years ago."

"Last summer someone set a cross on fire at the home of a Negro family in Rutland."

"Wow," I said.

"It's not something people around here want to talk about. It's festering just under the surface. I want to open it up. Make people look at their neighbors. Look at themselves."

But while my mother's motives were obviously admirable, it just didn't seem relevant to me. There were still no black families living in Two Rivers. I was pretty certain the family in Rutland might have been the only one in the entire state. The handful of black kids at Middlebury were athletes. They lived together, ate together, socialized together. My mother's passion seemed to rise up out of a place I couldn't understand.

As if sensing my detachment from the discussion, she said, "It's not just Negroes they hate, you know. It's French Canadians, it's Indians, it's *women*."

Three days after my mother's article hit the stands, someone set our mailbox on fire. Convinced that the two incidents were related, my mother asked my father and me to help her catch the culprit. We replaced the mailbox promptly, and as my mother pounded away a journalistic account of the episode as well as her speculations regarding those at fault, my father and I set the bait. We gathered literature my mother had accumulated from the SNCC. Left the mailbox door wide open, the article titles taunting a would-be racist. When more than two weeks had passed without further incident, even my mother seemed to believe that it had perhaps just been a fluke. Just teenagers raising hell, not a brood of hooded men. My mother's activist zeal didn't wane, but I was just so grateful to have her home, to be home again myself, that nothing could dampen my happiness.

I mowed the cemetery lawn two days a week and helped Betsy at the barbershop on my days off. I loved the smell of the shop, the antiseptic scent of aftershave and the soapy smell of shampoo. I took over the books for Betsy, who had always struggled with math, and she seemed grateful to be relieved from this particular duty. We closed up shop as soon as the last haircut or shave was finished, usually around six o'clock, and then we were free. With me home again and with Howie Burke out of the picture (shortly after his thwarted attempts with Betsy he'd enlisted in the army—a move I felt was rather extreme, but a blessing nonetheless), I thought that everything would return to normal. I figured that now Betsy and I could just slip back into our old lives. Like a comfortable shoe. A worn pair of jeans.

The previous summer we'd spent a lot of time with Ray and Rosemary, bowling, doubling at the drive-in. But they had gotten engaged this summer (an event expedited by Rosemary's pregnancy and Rosemary's father's proverbial shotgun, according to Ray). They didn't go out much; Rosemary was sick all of the time, and Ray was spent from his work at the mill. Besides, Betsy had no patience for our usual activities anymore. Bowling and drive-in movies, swimming and bike rides—nothing made her happy. She was edgy and impatient. Restless. Maybe it was because her daily life had become so mundane, but after she closed and locked the barbershop door each night, she seemed to need more excitement than she had before. It had always been exhilarating to be with Betsy, but sometimes she almost scared me now. I kept wondering when she'd go too far.

We broke into the first camp in early June.

Because of the blackflies, most of the summer camps on Lake Gormlaith were unoccupied until the Fourth of July. And the vacant cottages were easy to find: lights out, blinds pulled, boats stored away in sheds. The key to this one (and to every one after) was hanging from a hook behind a loose window shutter. The first night, I was terrified. I was sweating, wiping at my forehead long after it was clear no one was home. As Betsy raced from room to room, I stood in the dark kitchen waiting for her to get scared and go home. "Come here," she said from the upstairs. The walls on the summer homes weren't insulated, and even her whispers were loud. The floorboards creaked underneath her feet. I followed her voice up the stairs to an open room with exposed rafters and two beds with bare mattresses. She was standing at a cupboard on the wall, touching something inside. "Feel this," she said, reaching for my hand. "I bet a thousand people have slept on them." When I touched the sheets, carefully folded and put away for the winter, it didn't take long to understand what she had in mind.

We never stole anything, not even the sheets. But Betsy always made sure to strip the beds when we were done and put the sheets, soiled by our bodies (the dirt, the sweat, sometimes even the blood) in a laundry basket, which was almost always waiting, empty, in the bathroom. For those rustic camps that didn't have indoor plumbing, she would fold the sheets and put them in a brown paper bag by the door.

By early July, when the summer people started to arrive, we must have broken into twenty camps. Sometimes, Betsy took photos. The idea of the lives that had passed through these temporary homes thrilled her. She wanted to document these places that, once occupied, would evolve from this strange dormant state into a place of activity. Of life. "It's like a shell," she said. "And the summer people are like hermit crabs. They crawl inside, and suddenly it belongs to them. But just for a while; then they crawl away. And it's empty again." She took pictures of the pillows without pillowcases, blue and white ticking stained with circular drool stains. The empty drawers. The empty closets. The empty cupboards. She photographed the cobwebs. The dead flies on the windowsills.

On the Fourth of July not a single camp was empty, though we must have circled the lake twice looking for the telltale signs. Every window was filled with light. The boats were moored to the docks, which bobbed in the water in the moonlight. As I drove around the lake for the third time, Betsy started touching me. She knew I was incapable of driving while she was doing that. I was incapable of doing *anything* when she was doing that. "Stop," I said. "I'll drive us into the lake."

"There's the tree house," she said.

"We can't." I shook my head. The McInnes family owned the camp that had the tree house. We knew them because we borrowed their boat once to paddle out to the island. They were home tonight. I had seen Mr. McInnes and his wife, Gussy, sitting on their sunporch each time we'd driven past their camp. "They're home."

"But they're not in the tree house," she said.

I couldn't argue with that. Their only daughter was our age, too old for tree houses.

Betsy was halfway up the tree before I had even gotten out of the car. I'd had to wait for my body to return to its unexcited state, and she'd left me behind. She must have used her hair clip to jimmy the padlock, because by the time I'd climbed up, she was already inside.

"Oh, Harper," she said, looking around and smiling. "It's

just like that Paul Klee painting. The one of the tree full of houses." I'd kept the postcard she gave me in my underwear drawer at school, like a secret.

The tree house had four walls, a roof and windows. There were bunk beds but no mattresses. A small desk built into the wall. It was dark inside, but I could see the outline of her body as she undressed; the one window that faced the lake filled with color as the first of the Fourth of July explosions went off. Gormlaith was normally quiet, this holiday excepted. I was grateful for the noise, because as we began to move together, the tree moved with us, and I was sure that the beating of my heart was louder than any Roman candle or M80s. The McInnes's porch was about ten yards away, and all their windows were open.

"Do you have something?" Betsy asked, breathless, her lips grazing the skin of my torso.

I shook my head.

"Damn it," she said, rolling off me.

"Sorry. We can, we can do what we used to do . . . you know, I won't," I stumbled and stammered and pleaded. Since Rosemary got pregnant, Betsy had insisted on birth control. Where crossed fingers and prayer had worked before, now only rubbers would suffice.

"*No,*" she said.

"I'll be careful," I pleaded. "I promise."

She stood up and started to yank her clothes back on. "Harper, I don't want a baby. I don't ever, *ever* want a baby."

"Fine," I said, struggling awkwardly to get my pants back up.

"You'll thank me later," she said. "After the swelling goes down."

I knew I should have been grateful for her prudence, but something about her definitiveness on this matter made me

feel slighted. Like she'd just made up both of our minds. Forever.

We crawled down through the branches, careful not to
make any noise as we snuck across the McInnes's lawn to the
car, which, thanks to my flustered condition earlier, was parked
in a ditch. Fireworks detonated and then fell like rain over the
lake in showers of red and green and gold.

"Get something before tomorrow night," she whispered in
my ear when I dropped her off and moped back to my own
house, defeated and more than a little hurt.

Inside, my mother was printing the latest edition of the
newsletter, the whir and clack of the press in the other room
drowning out the sound of the TV, which my father and I
parked ourselves in front of immediately after reheating me
some dinner. He had made spaghetti, heavy on the garlic. The
whole house reeked of it. It was too loud to watch TV so I
mouthed, "I'm going to bed," to my father and then went to
my room to sulk and hopefully sleep.

With the clack-clacking of the printing press as my lullaby,
I quickly fell into a deep slumber, the kind where you don't
move, rendering one or both arms completely numb. It was in
this paralyzed state that I found myself when I woke and saw
my mother coming through my bedroom door. She rushed to
my bed and pulled back the sheets, yanking at my useless arm.
"Harper, get up! Get out of bed. There's a fire!!"

"What?"

"Fire!" she screamed. "They're trying to burn the house
down."

Within minutes the town's only fire truck had arrived, and
everyone in the neighborhood was standing on our front yard
watching our house burn. My father was sitting dumbly on the
grass, Indian style, as if this were only a Boy Scout campfire.
My mother was standing in the middle of our street in her

nightgown, wringing her ink-stained hands, looking up and down the street. "Someone needs to call the police!"

"What happened?" I asked my father.

"I must have left the burner on. I don't remember." He shook his head sadly.

I went to my mother then, who was still standing in the middle of the road. "Mom, Dad said it must have been the burner. On the stove."

Her mind was somewhere else. A sprinkling of ash landed on her bare shoulders, and it could have been snow.

"No," she said, shaking her head. "They found me." She was frantic, pacing.

Betsy came running from across the street and reached for me. "Oh my God," she said. I put my arm around her, and we watched the house fall in on itself.

Suddenly the front windows, the windows to my mother's office, blew out, glass shattering and littering the front yard. The flames reflected in the glass, a thousand tiny fires in the broken shards. The smell of hot ink was nauseating and thick. It was then that I saw what my mother must have already known would be there. At first, it could have been ash instead of paint, but when the fire grew, lighting up the sky as bright as any sun, the words scrawled in black paint on our driveway were unmistakable: *NIGGERLOVER*.

Mermaid

On Sunday morning, Maggie said she was feeling better, and so she and Shelly went to church. After they left, I went to visit Brooder's widow.

I found her address in the phone book, but I didn't call first. They lived in town as well, just down the street from the bowling alley, in an apartment above the Laundromat. When I opened the main door to her building, I was greeted with a blast of hot, soapy smelling air. At her door, I knocked quickly, before I had time to change my mind.

"Brenda?" I asked.

She stood in the doorway, clutching her robe with one hand. She was strikingly pretty, even without makeup. But she looked tired; beneath her long-lashed black eyes were dark circles. Her skin was the color of sunshine though; she was a Florida girl after all. Her hair was tousled, on top of her head in a messy ponytail. I felt like an intruder.

"Can I help you?" she asked.

"I'm a friend of Brooder's. Of *Tony's*," I said.

"And?"

"And I just wanted to offer my condolences." I hadn't thought much further than this.

"Thank you," she said, and started to close the door.

"Is it Daddy?" a little boy asked, and I saw her wince. And then between her legs was Brooder's son, scowling at me.

"He doesn't understand," Brenda said, shaking her head.

"Listen, can I just come in for a minute?" I asked. "I just wanted to talk for a minute."

Brenda looked at me suspiciously and then opened the door.

Inside the fresh laundry smell persisted, creating a feeling of cleanliness even amidst the filth. I could tell that Brenda was embarrassed by the state of her home.

"I'm sorry, things have sort of fallen apart since Tony . . ." she said, scrambling to pick up a pair of dirty socks, a glass of curdled milk.

"Oh no, no," I said. "It's fine. I understand."

"You're a high school friend?" she asked.

I nodded.

"Most of his high school friends sort of fell by the wayside after he came home from the war. At least that's what Tony said. Hey, do you mind if I throw something more respectable on?"

"Not at all," I said. "Please."

Brenda disappeared into a room off the living room, leaving me with the little boy, who had parked himself on the couch and was watching me.

"Who are *you*?" he asked.

"My name is Harper. I was a friend of your daddy's."

"My daddy don't have no friends."

"Now, I'm sure that's not true," I said.

Roger got off the couch and grabbed the cushion. He picked it up and put it on the floor. There were cigarette butts, bottle caps and silverware where the cushion had been.

"Wanna play Swamp?"

"Sure," I said.

"Daddy and I always play Swamp. You have to shoot the alligators or else they'll eat your legs off."

"Okay," I said, glancing quickly at the bedroom door. No sign of Brenda.

"Your feet can't touch the water. You have to stay on the rocks. These are the rocks." Roger pointed to a variety of objects that were strewn on the floor: a pizza box, a crumpled up T-shirt, a stack of bills. He got down off the couch and jumped from one to the next, like stepping stones.

"There's one!" he screamed, pointing at a cat that had slithered into the room from the kitchen. He cocked his gun and aimed. The cat licked its paw and slithered away.

"Now you," he said.

Thankfully Brenda emerged from the other room before I had to kill any imaginary alligators. She was dressed in jeans and a low-cut blouse. Her hair was loose, and she smelled perfumed. "Now, what's your name again?" she asked.

"Harper Montgomery," I said.

"Oh! It's nice to meet you." She nodded, smiled.

I felt something then that I hadn't felt in a long time, a sort of warmth rising up through my legs, spreading into my lap. I wanted to stand up from the couch, to thank her for her hospitality, and then leave, but I was stiff as a brick, and mortified. I coughed, sniffed, tried to will it away. *What was I doing there anyway?* I wanted answers to questions that she certainly didn't have. Brooder was gone now.

"You're the only one to come by, you know," she said.

"Really?" I asked.

She cocked her head, looked at me as if she were trying to figure something out. "You want some coffee?"

"Sure," I said, relieved to find that my problem seemed to have resolved itself.

"All I got's decaf."

"Decaf's fine," I said.

She went into the kitchen and I stood up, looking around at the place where Brooder had lived for the last several years.

There was a fake fireplace along one wall: the cardboard kind they sell at the hardware store around Christmas. Above it was a bunch of framed photos. Most of them were of Roger as a baby. I recognized the snarled brow. There were a couple of Brooder and Brenda. One of the whole family standing in front of Cinderella's Castle at Disney World. There was also a professional photo of Brenda in her mermaid costume, posing on a pier. She looked happy. Sexy.

"This you?" I asked.

She leaned her head into the living room. "Sure is, before I traded in my tail for these." She smiled, lifting her pant leg to reveal one magnificent expanse of leg.

"That's a big sacrifice. For Brooder?"

"Yep," she said.

"Will you go back now?" I asked. "To Florida?"

"Can't ever go back." She laughed. "Like the fairy tale. I'm just a regular girl now."

I smiled.

"Coffee's ready," she said.

Roger sat with us at the kitchen table, slamming a plastic hammer over and over again on a pile of plastic dinosaurs. Dinosaurs littered the linoleum under our feet.

"No banging, honey," Brenda said.

I sipped my coffee, and Roger kept banging.

"Tony was the one who disciplined him. He always said I was too easy on him."

"I've got a daughter. I'm raising her by myself too. It's hard. I never seem to do the right thing. Her mother," I started, but then wondered why I was telling her this. What Betsy had to do with this beautiful woman, *Brooder's wife*. I stopped. "I lost my wife too."

Brenda's eyes went soft.

In some pathetic effort to get back to the subject, I said, "Brooder, I mean Tony, and I grew up together. He and Ray

Gauthier and I. The three stooges." I chuckled. I wanted her to know that I was more than a casual acquaintance. For some reason, I suddenly really wanted her to trust me.

"Tony didn't have a lot of friends," she said. "People were afraid of him. The scars, you know."

I thought about Brooder's face. I could only remember it in fragments now, in flickers of orange light. Nose, lips, chin. Scars like rivers underneath his skin.

"It's nice to meet somebody who knew him before," she said softly. "This whole town thinks he's just a lunatic that finally got what he deserved."

I nodded, took another long pull on my coffee.

"Can I show you something?" she asked. She looked at me hard, again as if she were sizing me up.

"Sure," I said.

"Okay." She nodded and smiled. When she leaned over to push away from the table, her blouse opened a little, revealing the golden skin at the top of her breasts. I blinked hard, feeling guilty.

She disappeared into the back room again and came out with a piece of notebook paper.

"This is the closest thing I have to a note," she said, unfolding the yellow piece of lined paper and pressing it onto the table.

On it was what looked, at first, like a grocery list. But as I glanced quickly over the items (*coonskin cap, Schwinn 10 speed, $24.00 cash, small sack of weed*), it clearly was neither suicide note or grocery list.

"May I?" I asked, and Brenda handed me the sheet of paper.

Jenny Noyes. Lisa Grimes. Nancy Lessard. These were all girls from high school. Girls Brooder had dated. *Six packets cherry Kool-Aid, silver lighter, one pack Chesterfields, dental floss, rations and boots—size 13.*

I looked at Brenda, confused. She shrugged her shoulders. "That's stuff that would have been in his pack, during the war."

"*19" TV, Martin D-21 acoustic guitar, father's cuff links,*" I read aloud.

"Our apartment got broken into a while back. That's what they took."

I read the remaining two items to myself: *1958 Chevy pickup. Betsy Parker.*

These were the stolen things, each item on the list something that had been taken from him. This was his ledger of everything he'd lost at someone else's hands.

Things Spared

We lost almost everything in the fire.

The next morning, as steam rose off the ground where our home used to be, Betsy and I made our way through the wreckage. In the first thick white light of dawn, there was dew on the grass, and the air was dense with late summer humidity. The blackened skeleton of our house was similarly damp, soaked by the firefighters' attempts to put out the fire. We waded through this strange river, holding hands, afraid to touch anything.

The smell after a house fire is simultaneously familiar and alien. It might initially seem innocuous: just the scent of burned wood. The smell following a bonfire. A campfire. *Extinguished.* But beyond this was something more pervasive and disconcerting—like the feeling that lingers after a nightmare: the recollection of terror, sharp at first and then fading. Even the few artifacts we were able to salvage from the wreckage retained this scent. It was as if everything we owned carried the memory of the fire. For years, even the smallest of items could conjure that night again if I held them close enough to my face to smell.

There was no logic to those things that were spared. While my mother's library of books perished, a copy of *TV Guide* lay unharmed next to where our sofa used to be. My mother's clothes were turned into a pile of ash, but my father's ties remained untouched. We gathered what we could recognize, bent over and searching as if we were only berry picking. My Red Sox baseball cap, an embroidered handkerchief, a pair of blue jeans, rivets still hot. Jewelry melted, tools melted, silverware melted. We were careful not to burn our fingers on the glowing embers.

We stood at the edge of the foundation and looked down into the basement, where my father's workshop was covered in a blanket of gray ash and shattered glass.

"Jesus," I said.

And Betsy wept.

After the fire, my mother feared for her life. But despite the neighbors' initial outpouring of sympathy (casseroles and blankets and bags of used clothes), it was clear that most people in Two Rivers believed that, while the fire was a tragedy, my mother's radical behavior was somehow to blame. Because the neighbors who had donated pillows and towels still smelling of mothballs were the same neighbors who would not look her in the eye when she asked for help posting WANTED signs to catch the arsonist. Voices hushed when she entered any of the shops in whose windows she asked to post a copy of the missive left in our driveway.

By the end of the summer, it was clear that the town just wanted to forget what had happened, and even the police seemed to have no interest in capturing the criminal who had stolen everything from us. My parents had been staying at a motel, and I'd been sleeping on Betsy's couch. A week after I returned to school, my parents loaded up a rented truck and left, moving into an apartment just outside of Boston. My father was hired by Sappi Fine Paper, and my mother took a job as a music teacher at her old elementary school. My mother smiled broadly as they drove away, the window rolled down and her hair loose around her face.

"A fresh start," my father said when I asked him what he thought about leaving.

I still had two years of college left, an eternity. Betsy pleaded with me to draw it out as long as possible. Maybe fail a class or two. The longer I stayed in school, the longer I could avoid making a decision about what to do when I graduated and went from being safe to being 1-A, *registered and ready for service.* Betsy had started her own antiwar campaign in Two Rivers, though her legion was, so far, pretty small: a few girls from our high school class, a hippie couple with twin babies who had just moved to Two Rivers from New York. For the most part, Two Rivers was a town of patriots. Boys were still enlisting, lured equally by their allegiance to the flag and the potential for heroism. Three boys from our high school had died in Vietnam by then. Brooder was there. Howie Burke was there too. And Middlebury (which required all of its male students to serve in the Army ROTC program for at least two years) seemed to be directly violating the unwritten law that college was supposed to protect boys like us. It infuriated Betsy. It infuriated Freddy too, though he had a plan, as he always did.

Freddy came from money, a lot of money. His father could easily have paid a psychiatrist to "diagnose" Freddy with any number of mental illnesses. I'd heard all sorts of stories about Middlebury alums found unfit to serve by reason of insanity. You'd think school was an asylum what for all the psychotics and schizophrenics in our midst. But despite the power Freddy's father had, he was a former military man himself. Army. A decorated veteran of WWII. And he was more proud of his military history than he was of his millions. On the few occasions when he visited Freddy at school, he'd shaken my hand so hard it had nearly brought me to my knees. He was the kind of man who would grab you in a headlock rather than embrace you in a hug. He'd insisted that Freddy stay in

ROTC so that he could graduate and immediately become an officer.

My own parents had been pleading with me to declare myself a conscientious objector. My mother knew people from the Society of Friends who could assist, but for some reason, I had a hard time bringing myself to go to the Friends meetings, which were held at the Unitarian Universalist Church in Burlington. I went to an informational meeting once, ate their sugary doughnuts, listened to their arguments for pacifism and peace. But even though by that time I was growing more and more opposed to the war (standing with a burning candle at more than one of Betsy's midnight vigils), I felt like a hypocrite. Other than the few visits I'd made to Mass with Ray, I had very little experience with God. Using religion to get out of going to war seemed underhanded.

Freddy lamented our predicament on a daily basis, particularly as he trudged off to his various ROTC activities. His lack of athletic prowess might have gone unnoticed had it not been for these required exercises. Freddy was good at faking most things, but athleticism was not one of them. He was a heavy smoker; even at twenty years old his voice was raspy with it. Girls thought it was sexy or else he probably would have quit.

"If I were you, I'd go to Nova Scotia," he said. "Either that or shoot my foot off," Freddy said on my birthday as we sat eating cake and smoking cigarettes in our room. While he had been doing endless sit-ups, I'd been reading Dante's *Inferno*. He'd had cheesecake mailed to our dorm from a favorite deli in New York City, and we were going at it with forks without even taking the thing out of the box. It was the most delicious cake I'd ever tasted. The autumn sunset outside made the room glow orange. Smoke hung low in the room, and even as the sun set, we didn't turn on the lights.

"Either Canada or amputation? Is there a Latin phrase for that?" I laughed, scooping up a huge fork full of cheesecake.

"Me duce tutus eris," he whispered. "Under my leadership you will be safe."

Freddy showed me photos of Nova Scotia he had torn from books and guides in the library's travel section. Though defacing books of any sort was a sacrilege as far as I was concerned, there was something so enticing about the pictures of fishing villages and cliffs and lighthouses, I quickly forgave him his vandalism. Over the course of our junior year, Freddy worked quietly, planting the seed. The wall where he had hung the first photo, of a lighthouse perched at the end of a rocky peninsula, became a collage of stolen images designed to entice: coves and waterfalls and a rocky shore. It reminded me of Maine. He knew me so well. He knew I was picturing Betsy there, sitting on the edge of a rock with wind in her hair.

By the spring of 1967, I'd become so disenchanted by my precarious future, I wasn't sure I'd even bother returning to college in the fall. It seemed pointless with Betsy at home and the absolute lack of control I now seemed to have over my future. I felt like staying at school was just putting off the inevitable, and so I returned to Two Rivers for summer vacation and asked Betsy Parker to go to Nova Scotia with me.

It was early June, and we had just visited Rosemary and Ray and their new baby, J.P. They were living in a house on Rosemary's folks' property. It only had one bedroom, but they didn't seem to mind. I felt a pang of something like longing, watching them in the kitchen together, this brand new family: Rosemary at the stove balancing the baby in one arm, Ray kissing the top of the baby's head and then his wife's. I wanted this. I couldn't *believe* how much I wanted this.

After the baby had gone to sleep, Rosemary served us heaping portions of *tourtière* (pork pie). We played Hearts until long after midnight when Rosemary yawned and excused herself for bed. Ray convinced Betsy and I to stay, and we sat out on the porch drinking (beer for Betsy and me, Coke for

Ray, who stopped drinking after the baby came) and talking softly so as not to wake Rosemary and J.P.

"You know Brooder's comin' home," Ray said.

"He is?" I asked. It felt like ages since I'd last seen Brooder. A little part of me thrilled at the prospect of his homecoming.

"He got hurt," Ray said.

"How bad?" I asked.

"Real bad. Bad enough to get a Purple Heart."

"What happened?" Betsy asked.

"He got burned, saving his buddy from a fire. Some bass-ackwards village somewhere. That's what I hear anyway."

"Where is he now?"

"First he got sent to Japan. Now he's at an army medical center in Texas. He's supposed to be sent home soon though. Maybe by the end of the summer." Ray said he'd heard the burns were mostly on his face and his hands. That the fire was set by Brooder's own platoon; a whole village of people went up in flames.

At around four A.M., Betsy and I got in the car. "You want to go home?" I asked. Since my parents had moved, Betsy's father agreed to let me sleep on his couch until the first of July. I had three weeks left, and no real plan other than the vague idea of whisking Betsy off to Nova Scotia with me.

"No," Betsy said. "Let's drive."

I had little more to go on than the images imprinted on my brain (of snowcapped mountains and stone houses) and Freddy's maps. When I packed up for summer vacation, he took the maps down off our wall and folded them carefully before handing them to me. I'd studied them, traced the coastal edges with my fingers, examining the inch of paper water separating the U.S. and this imagined haven.

We drove all the way to Gormlaith, and by the time we pulled up in front of Betsy's favorite cottage, the one with the stained glass windows and red wooden swing, I was sober now, and my nerves were raw. I opened the glove box where I'd been keeping the maps. I hadn't thought any of this out, not in any real way.

"See, we just drive to Bar Harbor and take the Blue Nose to Yarmouth," I said. "We tell them it's a day trip. Just seeing the sights. It's as easy as that. We can have our things sent later."

Outside the sun was rising. I was delirious from staying up all night. My head was spinning, my heart heavy with thoughts of Brooder. I smiled and touched Betsy's hair, tucking a piece behind her ear. "It's supposed to be beautiful there. We can get a little place near the water."

She leaned into my touch, closed her eyes as if she were imagining it herself.

"I'll catch fish," I said.

The cottage was dark. Still deserted. "Let's just go inside." She shook her head and laughed, starting to open the car door.

"I'm not joking."

"What about school?" she asked. "You still have another year. The war could be over by the time you get out."

"The war's not going to be over in a year. I'll graduate and get drafted."

"There are other ways," Betsy said, still smiling.

My skin prickled. "Sure, I could join the reserves or the National Guard. Would you like that? For me to support this? Or, better yet, I could join the coast guard, then I'd not only be supporting the *war*, but I'll also be *gone* for five years. Is that what you want?" I felt like my entire world had been narrowed down to a short list of possible futures. None of them even remotely resembled the life I'd envisioned when I arrived on campus three years before.

"You know we can't leave," Betsy said, looking up at me, her smile sad and nervous.

"Sure we can," I argued, but even as I said it, I knew we couldn't.

"Harper."

"Why not?" I asked, knowing perfectly well why not. Her father would die without her here. She *was* trapped. We were both trapped.

My chest hurt. Every muscle in my body was flexed. Lately I'd felt like I was constantly bracing myself for a blow. I was pissed at her father, pissed at LBJ and his cronies, pissed at a world that always, always seemed to be conspiring to keep Betsy and me apart.

"Do you understand what will happen to me if I stay?" I asked, my whole body trembling.

"You can finish college and go to graduate school. It'll be okay." Betsy nodded her head, reached for my hand.

"Betsy, there are a *half a million* troops over there. What makes me so special? Why should I be spared?"

Betsy's eyes were brimming with tears. "Don't yell at me."

"All you've ever talked about your whole life is getting out of here," I said, aware, even as I said it, that I was being ridiculous. Cruel.

"Stop it." Betsy's face looked pained.

"And now here I'm telling you we can go. We can really go. And we can be together. Make a *life*," I said, reaching for Betsy's chin and making her look at me.

Betsy looked out the window at the cottage, which we had broken into more times than I could count. In the mornings, when the sun came up inside this house, it patterned our bodies with pink and orange and violet light.

"We can't keep borrowing other people's lives. Trespassing. Playing house. It's time for us to make our own life. Be grown-ups."

"Who says?" she asked, her jaw set hard.

"You're so worried you're going to wind up like your mother," I said, so angry and miserable now I could barely stand it. "But I think you're crazier than she ever was."

I knew I'd gone too far, but still Betsy's slap startled me. The left-hand side of my face stung. "Take me home," she said.

Betsy didn't speak to me all the way back to Two Rivers. When I pulled up in front of her house, she looked at me hard and then got out, walking quickly up her sidewalk to the front door. She didn't turn around; she just opened the door and disappeared inside.

Head buzzing, I made a U-turn and parked the car in our old driveway, forgetting for a moment that I couldn't just go home. I looked at the plot of land where our house used to be. The people my father had sold it to had put up a chain-link fence. According to my father, the new owners planned to build a house using this same foundation. Despite the devastation to the rest of the house, the substructure was unharmed. I got out of the car and went to the fence, climbing over easily and standing at the edge of the concrete basement below.

Everything was gone now. My entire childhood had been reduced to a hole in the ground. I wanted to hit something. I wanted to scream. I wanted to throw myself into that awful cement grave like a tragic widower. But instead I stood at the edge and concentrated on my breath. It was June, and the air was redolent with the smell of lilacs. The lilac bush in our backyard was in full bloom. Petals had fallen and covered the basement floor like a layer of pale purple snow.

I got back into my car, jaw clenched tight, and headed first to St. Johnsbury and then east. It's only about 250 miles from St. Johnsbury to Bar Harbor, but you can't go very fast, because Route 2 goes through just about every small town along the way. I stopped for lunch somewhere near Farmington, a little diner attached to a lady's house. I was the only patron, and the woman who ran the place seemed grateful to have me there. I ordered clam chowder, toast and a cup of coffee. The chowder was thick, the coffee thicker. She brought me a slab of raspberry pie smoth-

ered in vanilla ice cream. By the time I got back on the road I
was full and exhausted. I hadn't slept for over thirty hours. As I
drove through a sea of birch trees, my mind started playing tricks
on me. The birches with their white bark became tall white
monuments. As I drove, I felt like I was back at the cemetery,
navigating my way through the headstones with the lawn mower.
I gripped the steering wheel, trying to stay awake, thinking
about the bodies buried beneath me. I was delirious, hallucinating tombstones. By the time I got to Bar Harbor, I knew I
had to get some sleep.

I found some run-down cottages on Frenchman's Bay,
about ten of them in a perfect row, all of them overlooking the
water. The woman at the main house insisted on giving me a
tour, gesturing grandly to the grungy kitchenette inside and
the rusted barbeque outside. "Ever been to Bah Hahba befo-
ah? How long you stayin'?"

I offered some half-baked story about sightseeing, about
hiking in Acadia National Park, thinking only of climbing into
bed and falling asleep. Finally she left me, waddling back to her
own cabin, and I went to bed without even bothering to take
off my shoes.

I awoke at dusk, completely disoriented. I drew back the
heavy curtains to reveal a twilit sky and so much water. The
chowder and pie were the only things I'd had to eat all day.
There were still raspberry seeds stuck in my teeth, but I was
weak with hunger. I hadn't brought a change of clothes, but I
knew I had a long-sleeved shirt in the car. I went out to the
DeSoto and grabbed it. The neon light hanging in the main
house's window blinked NO VACANCY in flashes of red light,
but none of the other cabins appeared to be occupied. I
walked up the gravel walkway to the main house and went inside. The woman who had rented me the cabin was sitting behind the counter, knitting and watching TV.

"Full house tonight?" I asked, gesturing toward the sign.

"Sign's broke," she said. "Not so great fah bizness."

"Why don't you turn it off?" I asked.

"Not *my* bizness."

"Mine either, I guess." I laughed. "There a good place to get dinner around here?"

"Sure, lots of places on Main Street. Any one of 'em's as good as the next."

I found a pub with outdoor seating near the pier and ordered myself a real downeast feast: fish chowder, boiled lobster with steamers and mussels, French fries, cole slaw, homemade biscuits and, because nobody asked for ID, a bottle of red wine. I dipped most everything with butter and was dripping in it by the time I pulled the last bit of meat out of my lobster's claw. I drank the whole bottle of wine myself too and felt pleasantly relaxed for the first time in months. It was chilly outside with the wind coming off the water, but the wine made me happy and warm. I asked the waiter if there was a good place to go get a drink around here.

"There's the Quonset hut, but it's pretty dead 'till after the Fourth of July. Probably not much going on in town. You might want to drive up to Ellsworth. Go to Jasper's or the Hilltop Lounge."

"How far's that?" I asked.

" 'Bout twenty miles, I'd say."

"Thanks," I said. I didn't want to drive even another mile, so I found the Quonset hut. The place was quiet, except for a handful of pretty girls and a couple of local boys playing pool. There was no band tonight, just music coming from the jukebox. I bellied up to the bar and ordered a bourbon and soda from the bartender. She couldn't have been more than eighteen, blond curly hair pulled into a ponytail and blue eyes like the Neptune marbles Brooder and I used to collect. I watched her for a while, washing dishes, replenishing the condiment tray with cherries and lemons and limes.

"Pretty quiet this time of year?" I asked.

"Ayuh," she said without turning around. The scent of lemons was strong.

"What do you know about Nova Scotia?" I asked, feeling cavalier and a little drunk.

She turned around then and looked at me sadly. Her eyes were startling, even in the smoky half-light of the bar.

"I mean, what's it like this time of year? I was thinking about a day trip. Take the ferry over tomorrow."

She turned back to the cutting board and grabbed a lime from a box on the counter. "It's cold," she said. "Lot like here. Windy. Better bring a coat."

I nodded, though her back was still to me. I left the bar and put a quarter on the pool table. I watched the game they had going and then dropped my coin in the slot to release the balls when it was my turn. I played and lost in a matter of minutes. I shook my opponent's hand and returned to my roost at the bar.

"That was quick," the bartender said.

I shrugged my shoulders. "You got some matches?" I asked.

She tossed me a pack of matches and I lit a cigarette to give my hands something to do.

"Shouldn't smoke," she said. "It'll give you cancer."

"That's the least of my worries," I said. A little too dramatically, I thought.

"Want another drink?" she asked.

"Why not?"

She poured me a fresh cocktail and cleared away my old glass, washing it in the sink. I dug around in my pocket for a couple of dollars to pay her. She must have heard me rustling around because she said, "S'on me."

"Thanks," I said. I'd never had a girl buy me a drink before. I wasn't sure what it meant, but after a few sips I didn't really care.

I stayed until after she had put all the chairs up on the tables (except for mine) and after she'd swept up the cigarette butts and peanut shells that littered the dirt floor.

"I'm closing up," she said after a while.

"Okay," I said. "Thanks for the drink."

The girl nodded and then turned out the lights behind the bar.

I made my way to the front door. "Can I walk you home?" I offered.

She looked at me suspiciously.

"I've got a girl," I said, partly to let her know I didn't have any ulterior motives, and partly to remind myself, though I wasn't even sure if that was true anymore.

Whatever my motives were, it seemed to ease her mind. Her shoulders relaxed for the first time all night, and she smiled. "I don't feel like going home yet," she said. "You got a car?"

We walked back to the cabins and I cleared the junk out of my front seat to make room for her. "Where do you want to go?" I asked.

"I don't care. Just let me roll the window down so I can get some fresh air. I can still smell the smoke in my hair." She undid her ponytail, releasing a cascade of curls down her back. I felt my heart quicken in a dangerous way. And for a terrifying half-moment, I thought that maybe I'd been mistaken. Maybe there wasn't just one single future awaiting me. Perhaps there were many, many possible lives I might live. Maybe I'd gotten it all wrong.

And then the girl said, "Tell me about your girlfriend. And about why you're really here."

We drove up Cadillac Mountain with the windows rolled down, and I told her everything. I told her about Betsy at twelve, sipping on an Orange Crush by the barber pole, about the way she could climb a tree just as good as any boy. I told her about the way Betsy was afraid of thunder and about the time, in the barn, as heat lightning illuminated the sky. I told her about the fire that lit up our house like a jack-o'-lantern and about the hole in the ground that remained. I told her about Two Rivers (gave her all of the colors of autumn and spring). I told her about snow, about rain, and about the sound of the train. And then I told her about the dreams I'd been having lately, the ones I'd been too afraid to say out loud. The ones where I was on my belly, crawling through the jungle. About the snakes that slithered from my dreams into my waking, how I woke up sometimes convinced I was being strangled.

"Tell me about Nova Scotia," I said.

"My brother's over there," the girl (her name was Nancy) said.

"Canada?" I asked.

"Vietnam."

My whole back tensed.

"Nobody's heard from him in three weeks."

I didn't know what to say, and so I didn't say anything. For the first time in hours I kept my mouth shut. When she looked at me, she seemed to need something, though she must have known I had nothing to offer. No words anyway. And so I just reached for her hand.

We sat in the car until the sky started to fill with light. I think I must have slept a little. I know she did. But she never let go of my hand.

"Did you know this is the very first place in the United States that you can see the sun rise?" she asked sleepily, rolling her head against the headrest to look at me.

"Really?" I asked. "Then we're the first people in the whole country to see this sunrise?"

She smiled and nodded.

"Good morning, then," I said.

"Good morning."

The sun rose over the water. But even from here land was impossible to see. Nova Scotia was as far away as Vietnam. As much of a dream.

We drove back down the mountain, through the pines, the sun glowing warmly around us. I pulled into the driveway of her parents' house and got out of the car to open her door to let her out. "Nice meeting you, Harper," she said, and politely shook my hand.

"You too," I said.

She hugged me then, awkwardly. *"Go home,"* she whispered into my ear. "While you still can."

Later I fell asleep on Sand Beach, on a towel I stole from the cabin. The whole beach was made of crushed seashells; when I awoke they had pressed a crazy pattern into my skin. My face was red and pocked when I stared at my reflection in the rearview mirror as I pulled out of the cabin's driveway. They faded as I drove, away from the shore, past the giant Paul Bunyon statue in Bangor, and through the birches. And by the time I got home, I could still feel where the shells had imprinted my skin, but the marks were long gone.

Betsy must have known I would be back. She was sitting on her front porch when I pulled up. And without saying a word she forgave me, holding me until I finally stopped crying.

Ticket

I carried the train ticket in my pocket all weekend, and all day at work on Monday I thought about how I might go about offering it to Maggie that evening. I'd arranged for her to catch the Montrealer back down to Washington, D.C., and then transfer to the Crescent, which would deposit her in Tuscaloosa. Of course, it was up to her. There were dozens of stops along the way. A dozen other places she could debark. I would give her some money, enough to get by for a little while. The rest was her decision. I assumed she would accept the ticket, and tried not to think about what would happen if she refused. By early afternoon, I felt a sense of calm resolve. Even Lenny's idiocy couldn't dampen my spirit.

"You catch SNL this weekend?" he asked, standing in the doorway of my office, picking his teeth. He smelled vaguely of whatever he'd had for lunch. Something with garlic. There were traces of whatever it was on his tie, which hung crookedly down his barrel chest.

I shook my head.

"That Belushi's a fucking riot," he said. He flicked his toothpick into my trash and picked up a ruler off my desk. He started flailing his arms about, swinging the ruler wildly, just missing my head. *"Hi—ahhhhh."* He squinted his eyes. "That samurai shit's a fucking riot."

"Is there a reason you're here?" I asked.

Lenny stopped his routine. "You mean *here*, on *earth*?"

"Yes," I said, and couldn't help but smile. "That's *exactly* what I meant."

I rode my bike home leisurely that night, stopping to pick up some apples that had fallen to the ground. The first ones I found were just crab apples, hard and sour, but not much further down the road I knew there was a Macintosh grove. I kept one for the ride, and filled the leather bag strapped to the back of my bicycle seat with the rest. The apple was hard and tart. Perfect.

At home I spilled the bag of apples into a colander and offered one to Maggie. She eyed it suspiciously. "This like Snow White?"

"Hmm?"

"The poison apple? Evil witch? Glass coffin? Damn, you raisin' a little girl and you don't know about Snow White?"

"I just . . ." I said, my good mood instantly deflated.

She picked up one of the biggest apples in the pile and took a bite. "You got some lemon and cinnamon, I'll make us a pie."

Maggie made tuna casserole for dinner. String beans. Apple pie. Shelly was especially talkative, chattering away about school.

"And then Mrs. LaCroix makes Jason Stimpson stand in the corner with gum on his nose! But the funniest thing was . . . " Shelly was shoveling the pie in, talking with her mouth full.

"Close your mouth when you chew, honey," I said.

She closed her mouth and chewed, rolling her eyes impatiently as she labored to swallow. "The funniest thing *was* . . . his fly was unzipped! You know, XYZPDQ?"

"Did you hand in your report?" I asked.

"Uh-huh," Shelly said. She and I had spent most of Sunday rewriting the Lincoln report. Maggie just kept bringing food and drink to the table where we were working, and after only a few hours Shelly seemed to have grasped the concept of the five-paragraph essay. I had piled up carrot sticks, balancing saltines on top to demonstrate the idea of supporting sentences.

"So, he's got gum on his nose, and the barn door's open . . ."

"Shelly."

"Something's wrong," Maggie said, setting her knife and fork down.

"What?" I asked. "Are the apples bad?"

"With the baby. Something's wrong with the baby."

"What's the matter?" I asked.

"I don't know," Maggie said. She pushed away from the table and hung her head down. When she looked up again, she was bent over, clutching her stomach. "My belly ain't never felt like this before. It feels like, it feels . . . oh lordy, it's like cramps. Like my monthlies are comin'." She stood up, still holding her stomach as if it were something about to fall.

Embarrassed for her and for myself, I stood up. But once standing I wasn't sure what to do. I started clearing away the dishes from the table to keep my hands busy.

"I think I need to use the restroom," she said, and ran down the hall.

After the bathroom door slammed shut, Shelly said, "She needs a doctor. A baby doctor."

She reached for the phone book in a stack of junk on the kitchen counter and started thumbing through the yellow pages: a ridiculous task since there was exactly one baby doctor in all of Two Rivers: Dr. Owens, who had delivered both me *and* Shelly (as well as almost everyone else in Two Rivers). The only babies he hadn't delivered were the ones born in the backseats of cars on the way to the hospital.

"Wait a minute," I said. "Let's just see what Maggie wants to do."

When Maggie didn't come out of the bathroom, I thought about asking Shelly to go in after her, but Shelly (as far as I knew) hadn't even started her period yet, and I didn't want to scare her. However, the prospect of checking on Maggie myself seemed both inappropriate and terrifying. And so I gave her a few more minutes and then I went down the hall to the bathroom door and knocked softly.

"You okay?" I asked. It was dark in the hallway, only a sliver of light under the bathroom door. I could hear her shuffling across the bathroom floor. The sound of the faucet running.

"Just a minute," she said. She sounded breathless.

I was about to knock again when she opened the door. Her face was twisted, the whites of her eyes shot red. "I'm bleedin'," she said, quiet and scared. "I got to get to a hospital. Quick."

"Last time I tried to start it up, it wouldn't turn over," Mrs. Marigold said, digging through a basket full of junk for the keys to my Bug. I had given them to her when she started watching Shelly. She looked at me suspiciously, maybe still a little mad that she had been usurped by a fifteen-year-old.

"Thank you," I said. "It's sort of an emergency."

"Shelly okay?" she asked, worried.

"Yes, she's fine."

"Is it that colored girl?"

I nodded.

"What's the matter with her? Something with the baby?"

And because I didn't know how I was going to explain anything to anyone, because panic was growing like an electrical storm, buzzing in my head and shoulders, I said, "She's bleeding."

"How far along is she?"

"I don't know, maybe four, five months?"

"Bring her over here," she said. "I'll take a peek at her. You may still have to take her to the hospital, but I'll be able to tell if it's something to worry about or not." She paused then. "Save you a trip to the doctor."

I sent Maggie over to Mrs. Marigold's and returned to my apartment, where Shelly was pacing back and forth in the kitchen. The whole kitchen smelled like apple pie. Vanilla ice cream was melting on all three of our abandoned plates.

"Will the baby be okay?" Shelly asked.

"I'm sure everything's going to be fine," I said, though I truly had no idea.

"What if Maggie *dies*?" she asked, her voice breaking.

"Shelly, honey," I said. "Come here." I motioned for her to come to me. She leaned into me, and my arms closed around her. I could feel her chest heaving against mine, her heart beating against mine. "I won't let anything happen to Maggie."

After about twenty minutes, Mrs. Marigold knocked on the door. She was alone.

"Can I talk to you?" she asked.

"Sure, come on in. Shell, hon, can you give me a few minutes to talk to Mrs. Marigold alone?" I asked. She was sitting at the table, pushing the soggy pie around her plate.

"Why? She's okay, isn't she? Is the baby okay?" Shelly looked panicked.

"She's fine, honey. She's just getting some rest," Mrs. Marigold said. "Promise."

Shelly reluctantly left us and went to her room. I waited until I heard the door close before I spoke. "Does she need to see a doctor?"

Mrs. Marigold shook her head. "She's fine. The bleeding was just hemorrhoids. Real common. I gave her some witch hazel. That should help. And the cramping is just Braxton Hicks contractions."

"Contractions?"

"Just practice ones. Also real, real common."

I sighed, louder than I had intended. The relief more intense than I expected.

"Then she's okay?"

"She's fine. But listen, there's something you should probably know. She's a bit further along than you thought."

"Excuse me?"

"Mr. Montgomery, she's about seven months along already. She's only got a couple of months to go. And I don't mean no offense, but it hardly looks like you're ready." She gestured vaguely toward the living room. "If I've done my math right, we're looking at a Christmas baby here."

Official Hair Styles for Boys and Men

Christmas in Boston was not the same. In the little two-bedroom house my parents had bought in Cambridge, I was given the sofa to sleep on. (The second bedroom was devoted to the operations of the *Freedom Press*.) My family tried to carry on its few traditions despite the change of venue, but nothing about it felt quite right. And trying to sleep on an old burlap couch, one my father had saved from certain euthanasia at a local thrift store, I felt displaced.

Usually on the night before Christmas, my father would cook a pot of oyster stew. As a kid, I was more fond of the salty hexagon-shaped crackers served with it than I was of the stew (which always tasted a little too fishy and gritty with sand to me). As I got older, I acquired an affection, if not a taste for it, and insisted that my father make it every year for the holiday. We were the only people on our street, and quite possibly in all of Two Rivers, to wait until Christmas Eve to set up our tree, but what was probably just the product of my mother's procrastination became a beloved tradition in our household. As my father cussed and struggled to get lights strung, my mother and I would drink eggnog. Then we would hang our assortment of mismatched ornaments to Handel's *Messiah* as our neighbors went off to midnight Mass.

In Boston, my parents had already put up a small aluminum tree, barely bigger than a potted plant. We ordered Chinese take-out on Christmas Eve and sat in front of the TV eating Lo Mein as we discussed school and my future plans.

"Have you been going to the Friends meetings?" my mother asked, waving her chopsticks at me in a way I considered to be vaguely threatening.

"A few," I said. I had, indeed, returned to the Unitarian Universalist Church where the Friends meetings were held on a couple of occasions that fall, but I was actually more engrossed by the UU literature I found in the church vestibule than I was by the discussions of war. I even attended one sermon given by a diminutive Buddhist monk entitled "Without Autumn: Transience and Impermanence." He wore an iridescent orange robe and could barely see over the podium, as he discussed the notion that acceptance of change is an integral step in achieving enlightenment. When the service was over, he moved slowly through the congregation to the back of the church, his robe billowing behind him dramatically like a falling leaf. When I walked out of the church that crisp afternoon I felt relaxed for the first time in ages. Back at school, I walked for hours in the woods, listening to the leaves under my feet. Maybe this is God, I thought. Just the crush of leaves.

What I didn't know was that while I was wandering in the woods that day, contemplating the impermanence of things, Betsy was in the hippie couple's VW bus on her way back from Washington, D.C., where she'd nearly been arrested during the March on the Pentagon after spitting on a U.S. Marshal's shoes. Instead of hauling her off to jail, he'd simply hit her legs with his club over and over again until she collapsed and her friend was able to carry her away. He also took her camera and smashed it to pieces. Betsy called me late on Sunday night, weeping.

"God, Betsy, why didn't you tell me you were going?"

"I didn't want you to worry," she said. "I knew you wouldn't want me to go."

"Jesus, Betsy. I don't get this. Look what happened to my mother. I couldn't stand it if anything happened to you. If I lost you."

Betsy's voice changed. "It's not always just about *you*, Harper. God, can't you for once look past your own nose? I *care* about this. This war is wrong. We shouldn't be there. I went to D.C. because of all the *other* mothers. The Vietnamese mothers whose babies are being slaughtered. The soldiers' mothers whose sons are being murdered."

I didn't know what to say, and so I didn't say anything.

After several awful moments of silence, Betsy softened. "I'm sorry. I know I should have told you."

I did understand her need to protect me, though; I was protecting her as well. I'd been keeping a secret too, a secret I knew would worry her, anger her. What I didn't tell Betsy, or my parents for that matter, was that after graduation I planned to join the Reserves. I knew it was a terrible compromise. Cowardly. But I also knew that if I wasn't willing to exile myself from everything I knew and loved, from *Betsy*, I had only a few options. She was right. I couldn't see beyond the tip of my own nose. But the truth was, it was just a matter of time before I had to make a choice. Some friends of mine in the class ahead of me at Middlebury had received their draft notices within days after graduation ceremonies. I might have been shortsighted, but I wasn't deluded. I had found out exactly what I would need to do to join the Reserves, and what that would really mean for me. For us. Of all the options, it seemed the most reasonable. The most rational.

And, in the meanwhile, I tried to accept the impermanence of things. I even thought I'd been doing pretty well (with my parents' move, with the resignation of my favorite professor at Middlebury, even with the Lo Mein) until my father yawned and said he was going to hit the sack early.

On Christmas Eve we *always* stayed up until midnight. And just as my mother's Windsor chimes rang out, my father would make a big show of going to get the Yule log (which was actually nothing special, just the biggest piece of wood on the wood pile), and my mother would ceremonially disappear into their bedroom. A few minutes later, she would come out with a handful of splinters from the previous year's log, which she kept in a shoe box under her bed. Then she would light the fire, using the splinters as kindling. This tradition, one my mother pilfered from her distant European ancestors, was meant to keep the home safe from fire and other demons. I hadn't thought about the irony of this, one of my mother's few but beloved customs, until this moment. I felt suddenly wrecked with nostalgia.

"Good night," she said, reaching for my father. He went to where she was sitting with her knees curled under her in an overstuffed armchair. They looked at each other in a way that made me blush and then kissed each other in a way that made me squirm with embarrassment. Boston seemed to have rekindled something in my parents—something I thought had been extinguished with my birth.

"Good night," he said to her, winking (winking!), and then to me, "night."

"What about the *log*?" I asked, sounding like a whiny child but unable to stop.

"We don't have a fireplace," my father said, removing his glasses and rubbing his eyes.

"Oh." I glanced around the room as if a chimney and mantel could appear at will.

"Were you warm enough last night?" my mother asked, concerned. "We can turn the thermostat up. Your father keeps it at sixty-five. I've told him that's too cold."

"I'm fine," I said. How could I have not noticed that this house did not have a hearth? Its absence seemed ludicrous.

I spent the rest of the night tossing and turning on the thrift store couch. I got up to get myself some water and cracked my toe against the coffee table. I grabbed my foot, silently cussing, afraid to wake my parents, whose bedroom was also on the first floor. Instead of making a second attempt, I lay down again, defeated, and let my heart beat in painful rhythms from my head down to my toe.

I took a bus from Boston to Two Rivers right after Christmas. I planned to spend the rest of my holiday break with Betsy. Her father had agreed to let me stay at their house as long as I slept on the couch and kept the woodstove stoked throughout the night. Getting up and putting wood on the fire was a small price to pay to be close to Betsy again.

Betsy's father spent most of his time in a rented hospital bed now, which Betsy had set up in the dining room. She had single-handedly dismantled the elaborate mahogany table her mother had once used to entertain and put it away in the garage. This allowed her father, who now used a wheelchair, to easily navigate from his bed to the kitchen and downstairs bathroom. It also gave him a perfect view of the living room, where I was supposed to spend my nights. Fortunately, her father was a sleep-talker, and I had become quite skilled at determining the exact moment at which he had fallen into a sleep deep enough that the sound of my sneaking upstairs to Betsy's room would not disturb him.

It usually took a half an hour or so after he turned out the lights, but eventually he'd begin mumbling. The first few times I heard him, it sounded like nonsense. But after a few nights, I realized that it was only garbled because the stroke had paralyzed half of his mouth. If you listened closely, you could hear him singing. *Beatles* songs. It was as if the music that had poured out of Betsy's room in the years before had somehow become a part of her father's subconscious. And these nightly serenades were my signal that I could safely make the long trek up the stairs to Betsy's room.

The first night that I spent with Betsy, I noticed right away that something was different about her. After Mr. Parker started humming the first few bars of "Paperback Writer," and I made my way up the stairs to her door, she pulled me into her room and quietly started to undress me. She seemed to be scrutinizing me, studying me with her fingers, as if she were memorizing every inch of my skin. It made me nervous. She didn't smile, or tickle me, or whisper silly things in my ear. She unbuttoned my shirt quietly, tracing a line down the center of my body, and when I started to speak, she pressed her finger to my lips. When we crawled under the covers of her childhood bed, she clung to me in a way she never had before. Even after I felt the familiar shudder that seemed to ripple through her body like an electric current, she held on. Even as the light in her room began to change, from absolute darkness to the glow of early dawn, she wouldn't let go.

"I've got to get downstairs before your dad wakes up," I whispered. I was lying on my side, and she was pressed against my back.

"Not yet," she whispered back, and then slowly lifted her arm, which had enclosed me for hours. I could feel her eyelashes, wet flutters against my skin.

Every year there was a big New Year's Eve black-tie party thrown at Madame Tuesday's. There was typically some sort of band brought in from out of town, and the whole place was decked out. At midnight, from the second-story balcony, a giant pinecone made from a bunch of small pinecones was lowered in Two Rivers's version of Times Square's ball drop. It was *the* social function of the season. Neither Betsy nor I had ever attended the event before. In high school, we usually spent New Year's Eve shivering around a bonfire at an outdoor party. But this year, Betsy insisted that we go. She had gotten tickets, bought a new dress. I rented a tuxedo from Moore & Johnson's again, vowing that this would be the very last time. I felt awkward and uncomfortable. I dressed in the downstairs bathroom, and came out when I couldn't get my bow tie tied straight.

"God, you need a haircut," Betsy said, shaking her head.

My hair was well past my shoulders now (more a result of my laziness when it came to grooming than any sort of radical fashion or political statement).

"Come on," she said, pulling me by the hand. "Let's run down to the shop real quick."

"Can't you just trim it up here?"

"I haven't got any good scissors or clippers here," she said.

It was snowing like crazy outside. The sun was just starting to set, and the streetlights on Depot Street illuminated the falling snow in a way that made me feel more merry than I had so far during the holidays.

"Stop," I said, as Betsy trudged toward the barbershop, single-minded and purposeful in her floor-length evening dress and winter boots.

"What?" she asked, unable to hide the irritation in her voice.

"Look," I said, motioning toward the sky. "Look at the snow."

She sighed and stood with me on the steps of the shop, looking toward the black sky as snow fell down around us. I reached for her hand, pulled off her mitten, and stroked her fingers.

"You need a haircut," she said again, blinking hard when a large snowflake landed on her eyelid.

Inside the cold barbershop, I sat down in one of the barber chairs. Betsy made me get up and take off my jacket and then she carefully secured an apron around my neck. She turned me to face the mirror and started to cut.

"Just clean it up a bit," I said. "I want to keep it long, but maybe just get it out of my eyes."

She didn't answer. But in the mirror I could see her nod as she worked. I could also see the poster hanging on the opposite wall, the one that had hung there since we were kids, OFFICIAL HAIR STYLES FOR BOYS AND MEN, the one with the black and white drawings that illustrated a variety of haircuts: *butch, crew cut, flat top, flat top with fender, brush back, forward brush, professional, ivy league, businessmen's.* Below this was a guide to acceptable haircuts for the various branches of the military.

Betsy saw me studying them. "I guess I should be grateful," she said. I could feel the cold touch of her scissors on my ears as they expertly snipped and clipped. I listened to the click-clack of their blades.

"Why's that?"

"This war, this *fucking* war, at least it's keeping me in business."

Since the March on the Pentagon, Betsy's antiwar sentiments had become less idealistic and more anguished. She grew red in the face whenever she talked about the war. At night, when we watched the news, she wrung her hands together. Muttered and fumed. I had no idea how I would tell her about my decision to join the Reserves.

"Hold *still*," she said, putting her hands on my ears and steadying my head. We watched each other in the mirror.

I was too afraid to speak.

"I just want it to be perfect," she said softly.

"What's that?"

"*Tonight,*" she said, exasperated. "Everything."

At Madame Tuesday's, we danced to every song, even though the band ended up being just four high school boys playing mostly Beach Boys covers. But even when my feet started to hurt, Betsy kept pulling me out onto the dance floor. She was manic, beautiful. She danced so hard during the fast songs, she collapsed into me during the slow ones. It was hard not to get caught up in her fervor. If it hadn't felt so desperate, so urgent, it would have been sort of sexy. She was sweating, delirious when the MC announced that it was nearing midnight, and asked everyone to put on their coats and go outside to watch the pinecone drop.

Betsy shook her head when I offered to get her coat. "The cold air will feel good," she said, smiling and wiping her brow with the back of her wrist. She pulled me by the hand through the front doors. It couldn't have been more than ten degrees out. My feet, inside a pair of thin socks and rented shoes, were numb within minutes. Betsy's hair was plastered with sweat to her neck and cheeks. I pulled at a strand that ran across her face to her mouth and tucked it behind her ear. There must have been a hundred people in the crowd, counting down as the pinecone glittered above us. She smiled weakly at me, let me enclose her in my arms, and we stood like this, anxiously waiting for midnight to come.

"Ten, nine, eight," Betsy whispered in my ear. "Seven, six, five, four, three, two, one."

When she kissed me, she tasted like the ocean. Salty from sweat. Salty from tears. She trembled in my arms, not with the cold but with something that seemed to be wracking her whole body. And in that single moment, as 1967 became 1968, I felt terror for the first time. It passed from her into me, infected me.

We stood there embracing long after everyone had returned inside the building. After the band started to play "Auld Lang Syne." After I could no longer feel where my arms ended and her body began.

Betsy noticed him first.

"Harper, someone's watching us," she said, without pulling away. Her breath was hot against my cold skin.

"Where?"

"Over there, by that car."

In the parking lot, I could see a dark figure leaning against a car, the orange glow of a cigarette and the white trail of smoke rising into the dark sky. I pulled away from Betsy and raised my arm up in a ridiculous wave. "Hello!"

Betsy grabbed my arm as the figure dropped the cigarette and started moving toward us. As the porch lights began to illuminate his face, I thought I was hallucinating. This was the monster who lived in my closet as a child, the disfigured demon who invaded my dreams.

"Great party," he said as he came closer.

Familiar. And real. Betsy squeezed my hand. He was fully illuminated then. When he took off his hat, I tried not to gasp. And because I couldn't speak, instead I reached to shake his hand and leaned into him, patting his back in an awkward embrace. "Brooder."

"Montgomery," he said.

I pulled away and looked at him, knowing that I *had* to look at him. That I owed him this.

"Pretty fucked up, huh?" He laughed, jutting his chin out, turning his face right, then left. Half of his face looked like melted wax, one eyelid drooping, one side of his nose and mouth pulled downward toward his chin. The skin was puckered and purple: the scars on his neck disappearing into his collar. But the other half of his face was exactly as I remembered it, untouched. "Ruined my pretty face." He laughed again and slapped me on the back. I laughed awkwardly, but Betsy said nothing.

"Welcome home," I said.

"Quite the party they're throwing for me," he said, motioning toward Madame Tuesday's. "Nothing like a hero's welcome. Must've known it was my birthday."

That night, Betsy disappeared quietly into her room, leaving me with her father downstairs. He had waited up, afraid that we'd wrecked the car in the snowstorm that was in full force by the time we left the party. He was eating a bowl of graham crackers soaked in milk, a nightly ritual.

"How was the party?" he asked, his speech slow and labored.

"Fine," I said. "Cold night though."

"Thanks for getting her home safe." He nodded and set his bowl aside. At least Betsy's father still saw me as the hero I once imagined myself to be. She hadn't told him what happened in Washington, and I was grateful. I knew he would have blamed me. He trusted me to take care of her, since he couldn't. I almost felt guilty later, after he'd gone to bed, when he started singing the opening bars of "She Loves You," and I made my way slowly up the stairs.

Betsy was already naked when I crawled into the bed. It startled me, to feel all of that skin so suddenly. She pulled at my clothes, and I took them off as fast as I could. She pulled me against her, pressing every square inch of that glorious skin against mine. She didn't speak. And she moved quickly, touching me in the places, and in the ways, she knew I was powerless to resist. And then she put me inside her and pressed harder against my body until there could not have been a single molecule of air between us. She didn't make any moves to open the drawer where she kept the condoms I'd bought just for Christmas break (red and green ones that I thought might contribute to a festive ambiance). But when I tried to speak, to remind her, to protest, there wasn't even enough room between our bodies for words. Not for a single one.

Home Remedy

Shelly fell asleep waiting for Maggie to come back from Mrs. Marigold's. I found her in the living room, sprawled out unconscious on the couch. Her hair was tangled, covering most of her face. I thought for a moment about lifting her up, carrying her to her room like I used to when she was little. My arms would remember how to cradle her. But she wasn't little anymore. One long, skinny leg was stretched out, resting on an armrest. The other was dangling to the floor. *When did this happen?* Her hands were like water spiders, her fingers thin and long. Besides, she looked peaceful like this: her lips making a bow, her eyelashes dark against the tops of her cheeks.

After she was born, when they sent her home from the hospital with me, I spent exactly one night alone with her before I went to Hanna for help. That night, I remember the sky outside our small rented house was the color of plums. Starless. Afraid that too much light would wake her, I sat perched at the edge of my bed, in complete darkness, as she slept like a new kitten in a cardboard banana box at my feet. Every few minutes I bent over her, pressing my palm across the tiny expanse of her chest, terrified that she'd stopped breathing. I remember the house was so cold. The rain that had been incessant for nearly a month had suddenly stopped, and was replaced with a dry and bitter chill. I dressed her in the warmest newborn pajamas I could find from the bags Betsy had piled in the closet. And then I swaddled her in not one, but three receiving blankets. I kept the hat I'd been given for her at the hospital pulled down over her ears. There was little of her exposed except for her tiny squinty eyes and cold, red nose. But while sleep was impossible for me, Shelly's slumber was remarkable. She woke only once (and I thrilled at the cries, at the company). I brought her with me to the kitchen, sat the box on the kitchen table, and heated the bottle as the nurses at the hospital had instructed me. But only moments after her lips closed around the nipple, she fell asleep again, leaving me alone.

"It's not right for her to be sleeping in a box, you know," Hanna said when I arrived at their house just before dawn, carrying her cardboard bed like a fragile basket of eggs.

I didn't argue. I only handed her the box and said, "Hanna, I don't know what to do." It was so cold, my words were like wispy white ghosts lingering in the air between us after I spoke.

And Shelly was right. Hanna *did* save my life that morning. It couldn't have been more than twenty degrees, but after Hanna brought Shelly inside, she stood in that doorway in her nightclothes, hugging me, holding onto me until my legs stopped trembling enough for me to climb the three steps to their house. She took me in. She took us in. Without a single hesitation.

"How are you feeling?" I whispered to Maggie when she came back.

"I'm okay," she said. A rosy color bloomed beneath the coffee color of her face. She was still wrapped in a blanket Mrs. Marigold had loaned her. It reminded me of when I used to give Shelly baths, wrapping her up in an oversized towel to keep the chill out.

"Want some pie?" I asked.

She nodded and sat down at the kitchen table. I cut two

slices from the tin on top of the stove and smothered them both with ice cream. The pie was still warm.

"She told me those pains you have been feeling are normal," I said, nodding like some awful bobblehead doll.

She nodded too.

I looked down at my fork, at the chipped yard sale plate beneath my pie.

"Shelly sleepin' already?" she asked brightly.

"Uh-huh."

Maggie yawned.

"You should hit the hay too," I said.

"Sorry about all the fuss," Maggie apologized.

"Shelly was really worried about you," I said. "We were both worried about you."

"Y'all worry too much," she said, putting the blanket back up over her shoulders.

I thought about the train ticket still in my coat pocket. I tried to imagine bringing Maggie to the station, the way she might look standing on the platform, holding her suitcase. It was nearly impossible now.

She looked at me, willed me to look into those crazy eyes. "Mrs. Marigold *did* say that travel by train wouldn't be wise. Not with the baby coming so soon, and me havin' practice contractions already. It'd be a long, bumpy ride home; it could even make the baby come early."

I swallowed hard, the ice cream freezing my throat. "What makes you think I was planning to put you on a train?"

"Maybe that train ticket in your pocket?"

"What were you doing going through my pockets?" I asked, feeling both angry and guilty.

"I was emptying your *pockets* so I could bring that nasty old coat of yours to the cleaners. You know it smells like somebody up and died in it."

Now I just felt embarrassed.

"We've got a pretty serious situation on our hands then," I said. "If you can't go anywhere until after the baby comes, I think we need to figure out exactly what your plans are."

Maggie didn't argue. Instead she nodded. Emphatic and certain. "I already thought it out," she said.

"That's great."

Shelly stirred in the other room. I glanced toward the living room nervously.

"I suppose you wanna know what I'm fixin' to do. With the baby?" she whispered conspiratorially.

"Sure," I said.

Maggie wrapped the blanket tightly around her, only her face poking out. A slow grin broadened into a smile. "I'm gonna give it to you."

Valentine

Betsy surprised me for Valentine's Day by coming out to visit me at school. With the full load of classes I needed to graduate, I hadn't expected to be able to see her until spring break in March. But as I was trudging through a small storm to the library, wool scarf pulled up to shield my face from a bitter wind, her voice called out, as soft as snow, "Hey! Montgomery!"

The whole campus was blanketed in a fresh coat of white; in the distance she was only a blurry crimson spot, like a fuzzy drop of blood against all of that white. But as she approached, and her face began to come into focus, I felt my heart quicken. It was a Wednesday, the middle of the week, and there she was: smack dab in the middle of the quad wearing a dark red coat, carrying her suitcase.

"Suppose Miss Katy will let me sneak into an empty room?" she asked, hugging me.

"Maybe if we bring her some chocolates."

"Let's go get some chocolates then, and some coffee. I didn't sleep a wink on the bus."

"What time did you leave Two Rivers?" I asked, pulling my sleeve up to check my watch. It was only eight o'clock.

"*Early*. It was still dark out."

"Who's watching the shop?"

"I asked Hanna to check in today. I can only stay tonight, and then I've got to get back."

"Where do you want to go for coffee?"

"Anywhere that's warm."

I was hungry. On Wednesdays I didn't have class until the afternoon. I usually skipped breakfast and studied all morning at the library, continuing to study over a tuna sandwich at the dining hall on campus. We settled into a booth at Lockwoods (the students all called it "Lockjaws"), and I ordered steak and eggs, hash browns, toast and juice. Betsy asked for toast and coffee.

"Aren't you hungry?" I asked.

She shook her head.

"So what do you wanna do tonight? If I'd known you were coming I'd have planned something. All of the nice places to eat are probably booked up already."

Betsy shook her head again and accepted her plate of toast from the waitress. Betsy looked at the toast and then said, "Oh, please, can I get this dry? I'm so sorry," and handed the plate back to the waitress. "Actually, if you could just bring me a glass of juice."

"You okay?" I asked. Betsy was never the kind to send back food at a restaurant. I'd seen her eat a steak that was still bleeding when she'd ordered it well-done, runny eggs when she'd requested them over-hard, salads with bleu cheese dressing when she'd asked for Italian. She was easy like that. "You look like you've lost weight," I said.

She shook her head again, looking a little green. She forced a smile. "Thanks."

When she set the cup of coffee down and looked out the window, I became suddenly overwhelmed by the possibility of something terrible. What if Betsy was sick? What if she had come to tell me that something was wrong with her? She was pale, thin; she couldn't eat. But rather than just asking her, I kept trying to get her to eat—as if a fork full of my hash browns dripping in ketchup could solve all her problems.

"I don't want it, Harper!" she said angrily, as I slipped a piece of steak from my fork onto her plate. Betsy sipped on her coffee, looked out the window.

"Want some muffin?" I tried again.

"No!"

"You look awful," I said. "You're too skinny. You're pale."

"Jesus Christ," Betsy sighed, looked me square in the face and threw her hands up. "I meant to tell you later. Make it special. But you had to be such an ass."

I looked at her, bewildered.

"I'm *pregnant,* you stupid idiot."

"What?"

"A *baby.* We're going to have a baby."

I could feel the blood draining from my face.

"Have some water," she offered, pushing a glass toward me.

I shook my head. "We can't have a baby," I said. "We're not even married."

"You don't have to be married to have a baby."

"I mean . . . you don't want this . . . you always said . . ." I looked at her, all of that blood that had rushed out of my face now pulsing somewhere around my chest.

Betsy picked up the glass of water and drank deeply from it. She reached across the table and took both of my hands. "I want *you,*" she said.

"You have me. You'll always have me." None of this made sense. My heart was thumping hard against my ribs.

"Don't you understand?" she cried, pulling my hands to her face, kissing them, her tears spilling onto my knuckles. "You're *Three-A* now. A father. You can't get drafted."

That afternoon we persuaded Katy to let Betsy bunk in with a freshman girl whose roommate had failed out after first semester. I wanted to go somewhere, be with her, let all of this settle in. But despite Betsy's news, I still had a midterm in the morning, so Freddy offered to take her to a matinee while I studied. I spent the next three hours hunched over my books at my desk thinking about the baby growing inside Betsy's belly. "It's already this big," she had said, picking up a handful of snow and rolling it into a tiny snowball that I carried in my bare hands all the way back to the dorm, until my fingers were numb and the snow had melted. As I tried to study for my Macroeconomics exam, I thought instead about that little life growing inside Betsy and about the enormity of its impact.

After the matinee, Freddy helped sneak Betsy into our room. I think he must have bribed the house director because there was actually very little secrecy or sneaking involved. Freddy just showed up with her on his arm and presented her to me like a gift. In that red coat, she looked exactly like a girl-sized Valentine.

We lay side by side on my twin bed in absolute darkness. (Despite Freddy's assurances that there was nothing to fear, I still insisted we pull the shades and turn out the lights.) It was so dark I couldn't even see her face.

"Betsy, are you sure this is what you want?" I asked softly.

But she didn't answer; her shallow breaths had slowed and deepened. And I thought about that time we tried to run away to Maine, about her incredible resolve. Her fearlessness. As she slept I let my fingers explore the place where our baby was growing. I must have drifted off like this, fingers pressed against her stomach, because when I woke up, her hand was covering my hand. And instead of allowing panic about my impending fatherhood or guilt about Betsy's tremendous sacrifice seep into this moment, I just let an irresistible and overwhelming sense of relief wash over me like rain.

★   ★   ★

We agreed to keep the baby a secret. And I carried that little snowball with me through the winter: on my way to and from class, in the shower, in the dining hall, in the library. No one at school, except for Freddy, knew that by October I would be a father.

I don't know how I made it through that final semester. I was swamped with schoolwork, but I took the bus back to Two Rivers every weekend, terrified of missing something. I read on the bus, in a free barber chair as Betsy worked, and on the Parkers' couch for hours after both Betsy and her father had fallen asleep. By the time I got back to campus on Sunday night, I was so exhausted I collapsed into bed before the sun had even set. But my exhaustion couldn't begin to compare with what Betsy was going through.

Keeping the secret was relatively easy for me; I just kept my mouth shut. But for Betsy, who was vomiting almost hourly and so sleepy she once fell asleep midsentence on the phone with a Lucky Tiger salesman, explaining her behavior took a great deal more creativity. She told her father that she was just tired from working so much. She told her patrons she was tired from taking care of her father. At home, she was able to keep the visits to the toilet a secret by using the upstairs bathroom. But at the barbershop she started sneaking out to the alley when one of her regulars raised an eyebrow when she excused herself for the third time while giving him a simple shave. (The smell of Barbasol, unfortunately, was one of the great offenders.) And the alley certainly couldn't have helped matters: the barbershop was right next door to Athena's Diner. The combination of smells (of shaving cream and fried eggs) must have made the alley something akin to hell for Betsy.

She didn't go to a doctor—couldn't go to the doctor. Her family physician would never have been able to keep it to himself, and Dr. Owens, the only baby doctor in town, got his hair cut at her daddy's shop. Word would get back to Mr. Parker. She figured it would be best to wait until after I was done with school and had procured at least some form of employment before she sprung the news on her father. So, in the meantime, Betsy relied on Rosemary's wisdom. Rosemary told her to drink peppermint tea and ginger ale. To eat water crackers. And to nap whenever she got the chance. She gave her pamphlets she had received from Dr. Owens, which Betsy studied with the same intensity as I studied my Monetary Theory and Policy texts. Each weekend she offered me another fruit analogy: *plum, peach, orange, grapefruit*. By the time spring arrived, she was hiding a small honeydew.

"So, Montgomery, do you plan to marry that girl?" Freddy asked one day in late March.

It was the first day the sun had shone in months. It was still only forty or so degrees, but everyone had come outside to welcome the sunshine, removing their coats to reveal a sea of white arms. Freddy and I were sitting on the steps to the library, drinking coffee, trying to study. Freddy had given up, closed his books and leaned back with his hands behind his head, basking in the small warmth offered by the sun.

I couldn't tell him that while Betsy Parker was willing to have my child, I was highly doubtful that she was ready to become my wife. It was something I knew would sound ridiculous if I tried to explain it, and so I said, "Just waiting for the right moment, I guess."

"*Cadit quaestio.*" Freddy smirked.

"What does *that* mean?" I asked.

But he only shrugged his shoulders. Over the last year, Freddy had become more and more cryptic. Since my decision not to emigrate to Nova Scotia, I'd felt like a failed protégé.

"I'll ask her," I said, aware that I was being scolded. "When the time is right."

Freddy leaned back against the steps and closed his eyes.

"I *will.*"

What he didn't know was that I had scoured the pawn-shops for a ring that might somehow represent my tremendous gratitude. (I knew I could never find or afford a ring that would adequately signify my love.) I had rehearsed the speech I would deliver to her father. I had even practiced how I might broach the subject with Betsy, though this part of my ruminations always left me in a cold sweat. I knew that I had to ask her; hell, I'd imagined asking her this single question almost my whole life. And so I bought a bus ticket to Two Rivers for the first weekend in April, and spent all of my savings on a ring that I hoped might ask the question for me.

On Monday I felt optimistic, excited even, on Tuesday my optimism and excitement had devolved into a sort of blind determination, and by Wednesday I was ready to call the whole thing off. I was spinning the ring across my International Trade textbook at my desk when Freddy came into the room. He was in his ROTC uniform, sweaty and breathless. "They shot King," he said.

"What?"

"Martin Luther King. Some sniper got him coming out of his hotel room."

The ring spun across the page and dropped to the floor. It rolled under the bed, a jingle-jangle and then silence.

There was no answer at my parents' house all afternoon. I parked myself in the hallway next to the pay phone, redialing every fifteen minutes. The anxiety I'd been feeling about the impending proposal was edged out by the much larger worry about my mother. When night fell and there was still no answer, I reluctantly returned to my room. I turned on the radio and listened to the reports regarding the chaos that was erupting in the streets all over the country. Outside my window, all was quiet; the sun was gone, the promise of spring broken, as snow started to fall, softly at first and then with a sort of frenetic quality. I'm not sure how I managed to sleep, but I did, for a couple of hours, leaping to my feet when the phone rang out like a shot.

My mother had printed up a special edition of the *Freedom Press* almost immediately after the bullets riddled King's body. The headline read DREAM TURNS NIGHTMARE. Below this was a candid photo of Martin Luther King Jr. holding his infant son, both of them smiling.

She was out on her usual delivery route, the back of her station wagon filled with bundled copies of the paper. She made this trek monthly, leaving the *Freedom Press* in coffee shops and beauty parlors and schools all over the city. There wasn't a single neighborhood she neglected: from Cambridge to Little Italy. Brookline to Dorchester. But on April 4, when she drove down Blue Hill Avenue, the street was on fire, and the last thing the residents of Roxbury wanted to see was a crazy-haired white lady driving a Buick through a riot. When they swarmed her car, rocking it like a cradle in their arms, she didn't scream in protest or try to explain. She simply waited. When a dark-faced man ordered her to roll down the window, screamed obscenities at her, and spit in her face, she only smiled and closed her eyes. And when they smashed the windows and glass fell all around her, she quietly accepted the punishment she must have felt we *all* deserved. This is what I imagined anyway, as my father tried to explain. The beating she suffered this time might have been endurable had she been younger, stronger, a *man*. But she wasn't, and after only an hour in the Harvard Medical Center emergency room, she went into a coma and then quickly died. My father arrived after she was already gone.

After I hung up the phone, Freddy found me sitting on the floor speechless and trembling. He offered me his hand, pulled me up, and then guided me back down the dark corridor to our room. He made a pot of coffee on a contraband hotplate and made me sit down on the edge of my bed and tell him what happened. And as I spoke, as I tried to articulate the smell after the fire, the smell that still permeated my dreams, as well as the sound of my father's voice like shattered glass on the other end of that line—as I tried to explain the recollection of my mother's hands stroking my hair after a childhood nightmare, the memory of her wading into a pond to capture pollywogs in a jar for me, the image of her trying to teach my father how to do a cartwheel in the backyard, I knew that the sadness I felt was already yielding to something more powerful than grief. A child was growing inside Betsy's womb, but something terrible was growing inside me. I had never felt anger like this before; it was an anger as cold and as deep as a bottomless lake.

1968: Fall

*B*rooder *drives until the logging road abruptly ends. The smell of pine is so strong, so antiseptic, it reminds Harper of the science lab on campus. Of formaldehyde. When he squeezes his eyes shut, he imagines steel trays. The rigid bodies of frogs and pigs and cats. He had no stomach for that. He has no stomach for this.*

Brooder stops the truck and cuts the lights. Ray follows behind him and does the same. Inside the car, the air is quiet and cold. The dash lights dim as Ray cuts the engine. Ray's hands are shaking now. Harper watches him try to light a cigarette, each match going out in his unsteady hands.

"Shit," he mutters, trying again.

When he succeeds, and the paper crackles orange and hot, Harper is grateful for the smell of smoke. He reaches for Ray's cigarette and takes a long, hard drag. He lets the smoke fill his lungs and tries to imagine his chest expanding. His body growing. He is so constricted now, compressed, he fears he might snap. Or crack. Like ice. Or glass.

It is dark here, in the woods. Now the moon casts only an orange glow, distant and strangled by trees.

The sound of the man's body hitting the ground makes Ray jump, dropping the cigarette in his lap. And then there is only the antiseptic scent of the pines, the smell of burnt denim, and the stink of flesh.

FIVE

Home Brew

My father was sitting at the kitchen table when Betsy and I entered the house in Cambridge. It was hot in the kitchen, the windows all closed tight despite the warm spring day. The table was strewn with copies of the *Freedom Press*, most of them torn, all of them wet, the ink running onto his hands. My father looked deflated, a withered balloon sunken in on itself. His eyes drooped behind his glasses, which were also smudged with ink.

When he stood up from his chair, Betsy rushed to him, throwing her arms around him. She cried into his chest, and he awkwardly stroked her hair. Watching him in his clumsy attempts to comfort her made me feel embarrassed, as if I were witnessing a private moment I wasn't meant to see. Betsy must have sensed my discomfort, because she pulled away after only a few moments.

"Well," she said, wiping at her tears.

"Well," my father said, forcing a smile. "You must be hungry after the drive? Thirsty? Would you two like some root beer?" He gestured toward a crate sitting in the corner by the refrigerator. "It's been brewing for nearly a month. The first batch was a disaster. Blew up and ruined a whole batch of your mother's papers."

"These?" I asked, pointing to the pile on the table.

"What?" he asked, looking confused. "Oh, no." He sat back down at the table, looking sadly at the bleeding newspapers. He rubbed the top of his head, smoothing his hair down nervously. "These were all over the street." He sat down and picked up one paper, futilely pressing it flat. "I went there, to Roxbury, to get the car. To see where it happened. To try to figure out . . . and the whole street was littered with them. It was like there had been a parade."

Betsy's hand flew to her mouth when a startled gasp escaped.

"Every month since we came here. Every single month, she drove to that neighborhood and dropped off the papers. She knew the names of every shop owner, every clerk, every person who lived on that street."

"Who was it?" I asked.

My father shook his head.

Betsy sat down next to him at the table. "What have they said? The people she knew there? Has anyone called?"

My father shook his head first and then nodded, reaching for a *Boston Globe*, which was sitting on top of one of the piles of paper. He thumbed through the pages until he got to what he was looking for. " 'The community leaders of Roxbury express their disappointment and remorse for the damage incurred to property during the riots,' " he read.

"Who was it?" I repeated. I wanted a name. I wanted to give features to the dark shadow faces I saw every time I closed my eyes. I wanted eyes, flecked with yellow. I wanted noses and lips, hair and teeth. I wanted the sounds of their voices and the smell of their breath.

"I'm sorry, did you say you did or didn't want a root beer?" my father asked again, standing up and grabbing two bottles from the box on the floor. He set them down on the table and then sat down again. When neither one of us accepted, my father looked at us, defeated. Sunlight streamed through the window, catching in the brown glass of the two unopened bottles on the table.

I was hot.

Betsy reached for his hands and took them in hers. "Maybe they don't know all of what happened. I'm sure if they knew, someone would do something."

My father looked down then and studied Betsy's hands. He turned them over and over in his own, examining them—the same way I'd seen him study a circuit board, the insides of a clock.

"She hated to drive," he said. He looked up at me. "Remember that, Harper?"

I nodded, though I was still imagining those strange, dark faces pressed against the windshield of the station wagon.

"When I met her," he said. "The very first time I met her, she was walking along Route 125, walking from campus all the way into town. There was a blizzard. I pulled up next to her and offered her a ride. It must have been thirty degrees below zero with the windchill."

I'd never heard this story before. At least I couldn't *remember* hearing it before. Something about that, about the fact that I'd rarely considered the moment that my parents met, made me feel tremendously sad. I'd somehow assumed that they had always known each other. I'd never had the slightest notion of them as anything but the two people who lived inside the walls of our home. Their separate histories had never really occurred, or mattered, to me before.

"She was giving piano lessons then, to help pay for school, and one of her students—a little boy, maybe six, seven—his father lost his job, couldn't afford to send him anymore. But he had a great deal of talent you see—she could always see that, the potential in people. But his father wouldn't accept charity. Told him that he had to quit. And so once a week she walked into town and met him, in secret, at his elementary school, where she gave him lessons."

"Did she accept the ride?" Betsy asked.

He smiled sadly. "No." He laughed. "Said she needed fresh air."

I was suddenly so hot I felt like I might burst into flames. I ripped off my sweater and unbuttoned the top button of my shirt. I reached for the bottle of root beer and popped the lid. It bubbled and ran down onto my hands. I held it to my lips and tipped the bottle back, but instead of refreshment, the warm bitter liquid burned my throat.

"When are the services?" Betsy asked my father softly.

"She didn't want anything like that," he said. "She wanted to be cremated. No funeral."

"Maybe we could invite people to come here. I could make hors d'oeuvres. Sandwiches. Punch. Just something small. For her friends."

"Good idea." My father nodded.

My whole body felt like it was about to ignite. "Sandwiches?" I said. "Fucking punch? Jesus Christ. She didn't die in her sleep. She was *murdered*. By those *people*. Those ungrateful bastards."

Betsy stood up and reached for my elbow. I yanked my arm away, and she shrunk away from me as if she'd been burned.

"Somebody has to *do* something." I looked at the bottle in my hand, at the brown glass. I watched my grip tighten around the bottle, the veins on the back of my hand rising to the surface. My father stood, bewildered, running his hands through his hair over and over.

"Goddamn it, Dad, why don't you do something?" I yelled, and threw the bottle at the refrigerator. It shattered against the door, shards scattered across the linoleum. I stared hard at my father's sad face. *"For once?"*

Samurai

At work I couldn't concentrate on anything. In the freight office, the one place where I had always been able to focus, I felt suddenly scatterbrained. I had always thrived on the order of numbers, their predictability and reason, but suddenly the numbers seemed to mock me: so tidy and certain, while my own life was in such utter disarray. On top of my own inability to concentrate, the representative from the railroad had left, and Lenny was at my door every five minutes with a new question.

"You filed that report on the Bloom family?" he asked, his boorish frame filling my doorway.

I looked up from a sea of paperwork. "What?"

"The Bloom fam-i-ly," he said, enunciating every syllable as if he were speaking to a child.

"Yes," I said, irritated.

"You had lunch yet?" he asked ten minutes later.

I had made the mistake of joining him for lunch one day early on in his tenure, and ever since he considered me his lunch buddy. Most days I brought my own lunch to avoid having to sit across from him at Rosco's as he chewed with his mouth open and gossiped about everyone who came in and out of the diner. He was a transplant, but he still had dirt on just about everyone in Two Rivers.

"No," I said. "I need to get these orders processed."

"Come on, Montgomery. Everybody's got to eat."

"I said, I'm busy."

"Fine," he said, gruff and pissed off.

While he was gone, I struggled to focus long enough to complete even the smallest tasks. I couldn't stop thinking about Maggie, the sweet earnestness of her face. Her awful naiveté. My own. I hadn't been able to look her in the eyes since we'd had the conversation about the baby.

I looked through the phone book for adoption agencies. The closest one was in Burlington. I scratched the number on a piece of paper and then crossed it out. She was a minor. I was pretty certain that this small detail would likely be accompanied by some fairly enormous legal ramifications. I had no power of attorney, no custody. Besides, she claimed she was here because she didn't *want* to give the baby up for adoption. I flipped through the worn phonebook and looked for a list of teen counselors. Again, the closest was in Burlington. I scribbled a couple of names and numbers and then crumpled the piece of paper up. I couldn't imagine a counselor making any headway with Maggie. Or vice versa. Frustrated, I chucked the whole book in the trash can.

When Lenny came back an hour later smelling of meat and a lunch hour cocktail, I couldn't take it anymore.

"You got the number for Bellows Falls?" he asked, picking at his teeth with his pinky nail.

"Jesus Christ, Lenny," I said. "I'm trying to get some work done here."

"Well, excuuuuse me," he said. This was the fifth time he'd performed this nails-on-a-chalkboard impersonation today.

I stood up from my desk and waited for him to leave. When he didn't budge from the doorway, I went to where he was standing and started to close the door.

He put his foot in the way and said, "People over to Rosco's are saying you got yourself a new girl." His breath stunk of onions. Liver. Vodka.

"Get out of my office," I said.

Lenny lifted one meaty finger then and pointed into my chest, pushing me back into the room. "Little half-breed with a nice sweet apple of an ass," he hissed.

"I said get the fuck out of my office," I said, catching my breath.

"Hear she's only fifteen years old too. Not much older than your own girl. A guy could go to jail for that. Especially if you're that baby's daddy."

My fist made contact with Lenny's face before I knew what I was doing. The sound the blow made was loud enough to send a few people running down the hallway toward my office. And the broken bones in my thumb that had healed so many years ago were suddenly shattered again. Just like that.

Lilacs

We got married at the Unitarian Universalist Church the day after graduation. I didn't invite my father, but I told Betsy she should ask her own to come. She just shook her head and sighed. "I hate that whole daddy giving away his daughter thing," she said. *"Please."*

"Are you sure?" I asked, because I could see she didn't believe it even as she said it.

"Yeah, no need for all that mushy crap."

"What about Hanna and Paul?"

"Let's keep it small," she said.

Here is Betsy on our wedding day: pale dress, black hair, lilacs. We held hands throughout the ten-minute ceremony. She looked me directly in the eyes, barely blinking, during both the sermon and the vows. It was as if she wanted me to know that she was certain of this. And that she had no regrets. I was grateful for her clear-eyed tenacity. For the scent of lilacs.

I had told my father about the baby after the guests at my mother's makeshift memorial had all left, and we were cleaning up the dirty plates from the living room. Betsy was resting in my parents' room. I had barely spoken to my father since I'd smashed his root beer against the refrigerator. I wasn't ready to apologize.

"Betsy's pregnant," I said.

My father was clutching a balled up napkin, staring at a serving tray of sandwich meats. I studied his face, looking for something that might reveal his disappointment or anger or joy. And just as the waiting became almost intolerable, he asked, his voice cracking a bit, "A baby?"

I nodded.

My father opened his mouth, as if he were going to say something, and then closed it again. Changed his mind. "Betsy's a good egg," he said finally. Then he thrust out his hand, and it took me a moment to realize that he was trying to shake it. My father and I had never shaken hands. "She's a lot like your mother," he said.

I was still angry with him, though when I accepted the handshake, my anger quickly gave way to pity. I was embarrassed by the lack of strength in his grip. In that terrible moment, I felt his passivity, his weakness. And I realized that it would take so very little to crush him, to shatter the small bones of his hands. In an instant, I became aware that my father's life meant nothing now that my mother was gone. It made me pity him, and it made me despise him. I didn't want to wind up like him.

Betsy padded down the stairs, still rubbing her eyes. "Did you tell him?" she asked.

I proposed in the car on the way home, after we stopped to get some gas.

"Betsy?" I said. She was unwrapping a candy bar. Her nausea had abated in the last couple of weeks and had been replaced with an insatiable sweet tooth. The glove box was filled with candy bars.

"Uh-huh?" she asked, tearing at the wrapper with her teeth.

"I should have done this earlier . . . I know, but I didn't know how . . . and now, with everything with Mom . . . I'm sorry . . ." Heart pounding in my chest, I reached into my coat pocket and pulled out the ring. There was some pocket lint clinging to the solitary diamond. I felt embarrassed as I held it out to her.

She looked at the ring and then up at me, chewing slowly on her Three Musketeers. And I waited.

"You have to ask me," she whispered.

"Oh." I nodded. "Right. Betsy, will you marry me?"

She took the ring and blew on it, the little piece of lint disappearing with her breath, and then she put the ring on her finger. "Yes," she said.

Yes. The only word that mattered in the world anymore.

When she kissed me, she tasted like chocolate.

We picked lilacs from the bushes behind the church before the ceremony. Betsy wound them through her hair, the pale purple in striking contrast to her dark tresses. Though she didn't come to the ceremony, Hanna had made the dress. The skinny straps were a little too long, and the chest a bit roomy, but it had ample room for the belly that was starting to swell underneath even the loosest clothes.

"Ready?" she'd asked as we walked into the church, squeezing my hand.

I wanted to tell her I'd been ready for this moment my whole life. Instead I said, "Why not?"

Miss Katy prepared finger sandwiches, cake and ice tea, and my friends from school and some of the girls Betsy had gotten to know from the girls' dorm joined us on the back lawn of Battell.

"Look at you, Montgomery, all grown up," Freddy said, rubbing his hand across the top of my head in a way reserved for playground bullies and older brothers.

"When do you take off?" I asked.

Freddy's father had arranged for Freddy to spend a couple of days in New York with his family before he shipped off to Vietnam.

"Tomorrow I'm going to New York. Maybe catch a show. See the city." He flailed his arms out dramatically. "Then I'm off to exotic Saigon. I hear the weather is quite nice this time of year."

"Are you worried?" I asked.

"Hell, not as worried as you should be. Vietnam ain't got nothin' on fatherhood."

As we were leaving, Freddy kissed Betsy's hand, bowing to her. She played along, batting her eyelashes and blushing. Then, her eyes filled with tears, and she threw her arms around him, pressing her face into his chest. I was suddenly overwhelmed with the possibility that we might never see Freddy again.

"Be safe," I said, and firmly shook his hand.

We spent the night at the Middlebury Inn in town. After four years of sneaking around campus, having sex anywhere we could, something about clean white sheets and pillows felt illicit.

Navigating Betsy's new body proved both challenging and scary. I was so afraid of hurting her, of hurting the baby, I found myself hesitant where I'd always been sort of reckless. The new swell of her breasts was both provocative and intimidating. I was drawn to them but too afraid to touch them. It was a terrible paralysis. More than once, Betsy picked up my hands and placed them where both of us wanted them. It was like having a free trip around the world and being too afraid to get on the plane.

We stayed awake that night, neither of us able to sleep. I suspect Betsy was uncomfortable; she was a stomach sleeper, and with her growing belly, this position was now impossible. I, on the other hand, was stricken with a bout of insomnia. I was torn up inside, elated and forlorn all at once. Everything

I'd ever wanted was right here, but I couldn't help feeling the same way I felt the one time I cheated on a test. Like this was stolen somehow. Like I didn't really deserve it. And in the morning, when dawn finally came and the bright spring sunlight fell across our bodies, something about the lilacs that found their way from her hair onto those clean white sheets made me feel sad. Wilted already, and curling in on themselves. The heady scent of lilacs faded, replaced with a sort of small sorrow.

And two days after our wedding, before we had even returned to Two Rivers, Betsy's father passed away.

We rented a little two-bedroom bungalow near the river that summer. Hanna made polka-dot curtains for the kitchen windows. Betsy planted flowers, and I painted the nursery a pale yellow. I framed Betsy's best photos (many of them of the empty cottages on Gormlaith) and hung them in every room. The house was small; the garage sale furniture we collected barely fit into the awkward tiny spaces. The plumbing was cranky and the hot water never quite got hot enough, but at night, as we slept with the windows wide open, trying to stay cool, we could hear the river. Behind the house was a rambling backyard. It tumbled a good hundred yards away from the house before it met the river. We put a couple of lawn chairs back there, a plastic kiddy pool, and a picnic table. I hung a tire swing from the oak tree. It didn't matter that the house was cramped, that the roof leaked, because there was *this*.

Betsy put the Parkers' house up for sale. She wanted to start fresh, she said. Start over. She also accepted Knight Rogers's offer to buy the barbershop. Knight had worked for Betsy's father since he opened the shop twenty-five years before. Selling the barbershop was hard for Betsy. But though she never once complained about taking care of the shop (or of her father for that matter), now that these burdens were lifted from her shoulders, there was a new sort of calm about her. There was a certain stillness about everything that summer. We didn't talk about the future, about what we would do after the baby was born. It was too soon, I think. We were on the edge of something huge, but for now, everything was easy. Every day felt like one, long breezy sigh.

I took the job at the freight office not long after the wedding. The station was close enough to our house to walk, which, at twenty-two seemed like a pretty good reason to take a job. Besides, I knew it wouldn't be forever. What I hadn't told Betsy was that I'd been applying for jobs in Portland. I'd also gotten applications to the University of Southern Maine for her, found scholarships she was eligible for. I wanted to surprise her. Now that her father was gone, and nothing was keeping her here except for me, I wanted to give her everything she'd wanted. She never said so, but I knew she still felt trapped in Two Rivers. And I also knew that my getting a job somewhere else would be the key to unlock the cage.

Each morning, I left before Betsy awoke, kissing her on her forehead and then her stomach as she lay sleeping, and then I walked along the tracks to the station. When I got home at night, she was usually in the backyard sitting with her feet soaking in the swimming pool, a pitcher of lemonade and a pile of books on the table next to her. We'd sit out there, listening to the river, chatting about our respective days until the sun went down. I'd grill hamburgers on the barbeque, make a salad from some of the things growing in our little raised-bed garden. Betsy had taught herself both how to garden and bake bread, and almost every night, she'd bring some delicious smelling steamy loaf to our outdoor table.

Sometimes Ray and Rosemary would come with their baby, and we'd play cards outside as J.P. toddled about the yard. I watched Betsy watching the baby, watched as she cradled her own belly with one hand. She'd started wearing loose skirts,

Indian print dresses, when nothing else would fit. When I remember Betsy those last few months before Shelly was born, I recollect the softness of cotton. The colors of India. The little bells that jingled on the bottom of her skirts when she walked. I remember the sway of her new round hips beneath the fabric as she and Rosemary walked alongside J.P. near the water.

Brooder visited sometimes too, usually arriving just as we were about to eat. After Brooder's accident, Betsy's heart opened up to let him in. On those nights, she always ushered him through the house to the backyard, where she would set an extra plate for him. Pour him a glass of something cold. Sometimes, he'd come by before I got home, and I'd find them in the backyard looking at the garden or just talking. Their new friendship mystified me.

"What do you two talk about?" I asked Betsy one day.

"I don't know."

"Well, you must talk about something."

"We talk about books sometimes." She shrugged. "Brooder likes mysteries."

"Brooder can read?" I asked, smirking.

She rolled her eyes and then continued, "He brings his guitar. He's been writing songs lately. They're just beautiful. He's a real poet."

I laughed despite myself. Brooder had never struck me as much of a wordsmith.

She nodded and said, "I've asked him to play at the protest next month."

The annual county fair was coming up, and Betsy had organized a peaceful protest in front of the Army recruiting tent. I was worried about it; the recruiting exhibit was usually right next to the beer tent. Military guys and drunks and antiwar activists seemed like a potentially dangerous combination to me. What I wanted to say was that I was worried about the protest. She didn't know Brooder like I did; she didn't know that he sometimes would take things too far. That for Brooder the term *peaceful protest* was an oxymoron. What I did say was, "I think he's got a crush on you."

"Don't be ridiculous," she said.

"I'm just saying you shouldn't encourage him. He's not right in the head. Not since he got back," I said.

"You'd be messed up too if you'd seen *half* of what he's seen."

My shoulders tensed.

She threw up her hands in defeat. "Listen, he just needs a friend, and so do I," she said. "I enjoy his company."

"Fine," I said. "Have fun with your *friend*."

I went inside to sulk, leaving her alone in the backyard. The kitchen smelled of rye bread. I sat down at the table and started thumbing through the mail that was sitting in a heap. Betsy never bothered with the mail, leaving it for me to sift through. Near the bottom of the pile was a postcard. It looked like it had weathered some pretty serious storms to reach us. The photo was scratched, and the ink was blurred. Below the picture it said, "Lighthouse at Peggy's Cove, Halifax County, Nova Scotia." And on the back, in messy handwriting it said simply, "*Docendo Discimus*. By teaching, we learn."

Freddy. I forgot all about the argument with Betsy. I flew out into the backyard, where she was kneeling in the dirt. She was barefoot, and the pink soles of her feet were dirty. When she wiped her forehead, she left the faintest trail of soil on her cheek.

"Look!" I said, thrusting the postcard at her.

She set down her trowel and took the postcard in both hands. "What does it mean?"

"It's from *Freddy*."

Betsy's eyes welled up and she smiled at me. "Canada?"

I nodded, squatted down and hugged her. She smelled like bread and earth.

"I'm sorry about earlier," I said. "It's not about Brooder. I'm just worried about you. I don't want anything to happen to you. To the baby."

She nodded, as if she'd been scolded. I didn't like the way that made me feel.

"What are you planting?" I asked.

"Bulbs," she said. "They won't come up until spring though. Daffodils," she said. "Irises." Her hair was in a braid over her shoulder. There were wisps of hair around her face. I watched the gentle curve of her neck as she contemplated the arrangement of the bulbs.

"I really am sorry," I said. "I know this is important to you. I'm proud of everything you're doing."

"It's *okay*." She nodded, turning to me and reaching for my hand.

And for a moment, I thought about telling her that a woman from the University of Southern Maine had called me at work that morning. It had only been a brief interview over the phone, nothing definitive, but she did seem enthusiastic. It was a job in the university's business office. Starting January 1. A good salary, full benefits, and free tuition for spouses. I thought about telling her that I'd been calling on some rentals on the harbor in Portland, that we might finally get to Maine. But instead I just held onto her, as she stroked my thumb, the one that I'd broken smashing Howie Burke in the face. Instead of telling her, I closed my eyes and thought of daffodils. Irises.

That night Betsy and I made love. Gingerly. I kept thinking about how precarious everything was: our little life, the one we'd made in this house by the river. It was like a miniature world inside a snow globe. Perfect. Delicate. The job in Maine would change everything.

Afterward, when she had fallen asleep, I pressed myself against her, wanting every inch of my body to touch every inch of hers. I laced my arm across her belly and pressed my palm against her skin until the baby acknowledged me with a gentle kick.

I couldn't sleep, so I untangled myself from Betsy and went to the nursery. We didn't have a crib yet, not even a dresser; I was waiting for my next paycheck to buy the bigger items we would need for the baby. The only piece of furniture in the room was Betsy's father's rocking chair. It was late July, the air muggy and hot. I opened the window as quietly as I could to let some air in. With the window open all of the sounds of summer filled this quiet room: crickets, bullfrogs, the river. Mother Nature's cacophonous symphony. I peered out into the darkness. There were no street lamps here, only the sliver of moon illuminating the yard, intermittent flashes of fireflies. I sat down in the rocking chair near the window and closed my eyes. Here it was. Everything I'd ever wanted.

Broken

Outside the station, I managed to get on my bicycle only to find that I couldn't ride it because of my hand. Still pissed by everything Lenny had said, and more pissed that I'd lost my temper over it, I got off the bike and when it fell to the ground I gave it a good kick. It didn't take much; the front wheel bent, and the fractured spokes punctured the tire. I gave it another kick, and the crossbar crumbled. I gave it one last kick for good measure, and the handlebars twisted from a U into a sort of misshapen W. Winded from the assaults on both my boss and my bicycle, I huffed and puffed to the main road, where I stuck up my one good thumb, hoping to hitch a ride to the hospital.

I must have walked two miles before a car passed. I had made a makeshift sling out of my work shirt, but it kept slipping. The pain in my thumb was excruciating. I was kicking gravel and cussing out loud by the time Rene pulled up next to me in his truck. It was chilly outside, but I had worked up quite a sweat. My hair was stuck to my head, and I could feel perspiration soaking under my arms.

"What happened to *you*?" he asked, pulling up next to me.

I shrugged.

"Who at de other end o' dat fist?"

"Lenny," I said.

Rene threw his head back and started laughing. "Glad somebody did it. I'da mind to myself a few times."

I felt a smile creeping up on me.

"Well, get in da truck, Mr. Rocky Balboa," he said, reaching to open the door for me.

"You sure you have time?" I asked. The closest hospital was in St. Johnsbury, which was more than a thirty-minute drive from here.

"No problem," he said. "I'm off Tuesdays."

Rene was one of the few car knockers who were consistently friendly to me and the other guys who worked inside the station. Most of the yard workers stayed to themselves. He and I worked different shifts, but we ran into each other every now and then. I hadn't seen him since he'd shown me the way to the wreck.

"You can drop me off here," I said when we pulled up to the emergency room entrance at the hospital in St. Johnsbury. "I'll find a ride home."

"I'll wait right here for ya; dey got a cafeteria where I can get something to eat. I done spent lots of time at dis hospital," he said. I seemed to remember someone telling me once that he'd lost a child a few years back, a toddler who had run out into the road.

The emergency room was empty except for a woman who kept running to the restroom, where I could hear her vomiting. Her husband was with her, and during one of her trips he said, explained, as if he had to, "Food poisoning. She just *had* to order the clams."

I was frustrated that it was taking so long, when there didn't appear to be anyone there besides the bad seafood victim and me. Finally, the woman was called in and a few minutes later the nurse beckoned me in as well.

Three nurses, one doctor, and an X-ray later, I went back out into the waiting room with a brand new plaster cast and a prescription for some painkillers. I had hoped Rene decided to head back to Two Rivers without me, but he was still there, fast asleep in an orange plastic chair.

"Hey," I said, gently prodding his arm with my good hand.

Rene's eyes shot open, wide and startled. "It broke?"

I nodded and held out my hand for him to see. I could feel my heart beating in my hand, the rhythmic pain strangely soothing. An odd music

"Thanks," I said, as he pulled up next to my apartment building. "I owe you one."

I got out, careful not to bump my bum hand on anything. After I shut the door and was walking to the sidewalk, Rene rolled down the passenger side window and leaned out. "Hey, before I forget agin . . . I mean to ask you something."

"What's that?" I asked, turning to the car.

"The day of da wreck, dat girl, dat colored girl. Did she find you?"

"What do you mean, did she *find* me?" I asked. The pulsing in my hand intensified. I held my arm tightly into my waist.

"Strangest ting," he said. "She com'd up to me, soakin' wet, asking if I know somebody named Montgomery. Dat worked for da railroad. Course, I know she means you. She ask if I know where you live. She had a piece of paper, wid your name on it." Rene paused, adjusting his visor to block out the sun. "She said she needed to go to your house, that she come looking for you."

My arm throbbed. My head. My chest.

"And I told her, *You don need to go to his house. He right over dere underneath dat big tree.*"

Midway

It began to rain in August and did not stop until September. The river swelled with the initial deluge and then spilled over, flooding the entire village. Depot Street became an extension of the river; the culverts were so blocked with leaves and debris, the rain had nowhere to go but through town. Our little backyard became a sort of marshy bog. If you tried to walk across the grass, you'd sink in to your ankles. The hole in our roof turned into a dozen holes. We had little tin pots placed all over the house to catch the steady drips. Walking through any room in our house required a series of quick steps and dodges. There was almost no place to go to stay dry. Betsy was still afraid of storms, and it was a month of storms. She spent a lot of time sitting in the car in the driveway, waiting out the lightning, convinced our little house would get struck one of these days. That it was only a matter of time, and she didn't want to be inside when it hit.

The county fair was postponed for the first time in Two Rivers's history, and the whole town was in an uproar. The fair was a tradition, the official end to the summer. Without the fair, summer might go on endlessly. And so might the rain, it seemed.

Because the fair had been postponed, all of Betsy's plans for the protest were put on hold. Brooder still came by in the afternoons, but the rain forced them inside. Most days I'd come home after work and find them sitting at the kitchen table, stuffing envelopes or making fliers. "Hey, Montgomery," Brooder would say. He'd taken to saluting me, a gesture I found both silly and disconcerting. I answered with a nod. Betsy always had something warm on the stove top: lentil soup, minestrone, beef stew. She made decadent desserts: cheesecake, chocolate mousse cake, bread pudding. The three of us ate together most nights and then Brooder would head back home.

Betsy was so big now she couldn't see her feet anymore. The baby pushed and rolled, making waves underneath her skin. I watched her, fascinated. Spoke to the baby by pressing my lips to her belly button. Betsy had a blouse she loved to wear then. It was purple, thin cotton with embroidery and tiny little mirrors sewn into the fabric. When I lay my head on her stomach to listen for the baby, I could see our whole world reflected in them.

"What is she telling you today?" Betsy asked. She was convinced that the baby was a girl.

"That it's going to stop raining soon."

A drop of water plunked into the pot at the foot of our bed.

"That she won't come out until it stops," I said.

"Smart girl. I wouldn't either." Betsy smiled.

But August came and went, and still, it rained. Children returned to school in a daily parade of shiny yellow slickers and rubber boots past our house to the bus stop. I walked to work each day (leaving Betsy the car in case of lightning), my hood pulled tightly over my head. I'd given up on my umbrella after only a couple of weeks. It was a short walk to the station, which was always warm and dry inside.

Finally, in late September, the rain began to lessen. It didn't cease exactly, but the storms became less frequent, less severe. Signs went up announcing that the county fair would, indeed,

be held. Come hell or high water. And all of Two Rivers rejoiced, Betsy most of all.

The fairgrounds were flooded, but the midway moved in
anyway, erecting roller coasters, haunted houses, a Tilt-a-
Whirl. This deviation, this marvelous delay, seemed to have the
entire town buzzing with anticipation. And on opening day,
the sun miraculously appeared.

I got the call from the University of Southern Maine offering me the job in Portland just as I was leaving work early
to meet Betsy to help out with the protest.

"We'd love to have you," the woman said. "Please let us
know as soon as possible."

I clutched the phone feeling like I might burst. "Thank
you, thank you," I said. "I just need to talk to my wife."

I raced home, the sun warm on my face for the first time
in over a month, rehearsing exactly how I would tell Betsy. I
could barely wait to see the expression on her face, but I
wanted to do it right. I wanted it to be special. I'd have to wait
until after the protest. I didn't want anything to spoil this moment, to steal this wonderful thunder.

Since high school, Ray and Rosemary, Betsy and I would
go to the fair on opening day. We'd wander around the midway, Ray and I slamming hammers, shooting clowns full of
water, and tossing baseballs onto the tops of milk bottles in an
attempt to win stuffed poodles or bears for the girls. Chivalry
and bravado at its finest. We'd ride the Himalaya and the
Cobra, leaving Rosemary (who got motion sickness even on
the carousel) to watch from behind the chain-link fence. Later
we'd get French fries doused in malt vinegar, fried dough dripping in maple syrup, and go to the grandstand to watch the
Demolition Derby.

The protest was supposed to start at dusk. Betsy had
planned on a candlelight vigil. Her friend Sara was going to

read the names of all of the soldiers from Vermont who had
died in the war, and Brooder was going to play guitar and sing
some of his songs. We decided to go early, hang out for a while
before the protest. Brooder came with us, and we met Ray and
Rosemary at the 4-H exhibits. In the children's petting barn,
Brooder teased a turkey with a long piece of straw, and Betsy
and I watched a mother sow and her baby curled into each
other in the corner of their pen. Smiling. Betsy squeezed my
hand, ran her hand across her stomach. I thought about Old
Man Keller's pig, about Brooder's shotgun. It still raised the
hair on the back of my neck. Rosemary had pushed J.P.'s
stroller close to a pen with a few goats and a lamb inside. A
goat stuck his nose through the fence to see J.P., who squealed,
startling the pigs from their slumber. We bought homemade
maple ice cream, which we ate as we watched the cows line up
for the cavalcade. Brooder popped the last of his cone in his
mouth and said, "Let's hit the rides!"

Everyone in town knew what happened to Brooder, but it
didn't stop the stares. While half of his face was completely
normal, the other half was distorted. Like looking into a fun
house mirror. People gawked.

"That was so rude," Betsy whispered after one woman
gasped and pointed at Brooder as if he were one of the freaks
escaped from the sideshows.

Brooder, who was fully aware of the extra attention he was
getting, did not let it go unchecked. "Beautiful, isn't it?" he
asked the lady loudly.

"I don't know what you . . ." the woman stuttered.

"This weather we're having, beautiful, isn't it?" He laughed
loudly.

The woman scurried away.

Instead of winning stuffed animals or goldfish for our girls,
Ray spent almost ten dollars playing Skee-Ball before he won

a stuffed giraffe, which he gave to J.P. And the pink teddy bear I won fishing plastic rings out of a pool was just the right size for a baby. We played Bingo at the Bingo tent, watched J.P. ride around and around in a miniature fire engine, and got corn on the cob and hot dogs smothered in mustard and sauerkraut at the Grange booth. By the time we finished eating, it was beginning to get dark. The sky was starting to feel heavy again. Swollen.

"We're gonna take J.P. home," Rosemary said. He had fallen asleep in the stroller. His mouth was ringed in pink—though it was impossible to tell whether it was from the cotton candy he'd had or the cherry snowcone he'd nursed until it melted. "Good luck with the protest. Stay out of trouble," Rosemary said, shaking her finger and smiling at Brooder.

"Yes, ma'am," he said.

After they left, Brooder smacked my arm. "How about a few spins on the Himalaya?"

"Don't we need to get over to the recruiting tent?" I asked Betsy.

"Go!" Betsy said. "You guys can meet me there in a minute. I have to find Sara anyway; she's got the candles and paper plates."

"I'll come with you," I said to Betsy.

"Pussy," Brooder said.

"Jesus," I said.

Brooder crossed his arms.

"*Fine,*" I said. "We'll ride the Himalaya."

Brooder and I walked silently across the midway, which was littered with a day's worth of carnival debris, past the carousel and Ferris wheel, past the carnies trying to convince us to put our money down on the impossible carnival games. I noticed that Brooder walked faster now, like someone was following him. Even with my long strides, it was hard to keep up. At the Himalaya, Brooder said, "Let's rock 'n roll!" Music was thump-

ing, the air vibrating with it. We had to wait for the ride to stop
and everybody who was already on it to get off. When it was
our turn, the guy running the ride opened up the entrance
gate to let us in. He was tall, broad, and his skin was the blue
black of a night sky. I felt my back tense despite myself.

Brooder ran up the metal ramp to the first cart, which was
painted to look like a sleigh. He leapt in, pulling me in after
him, and lowered the bar across our laps. After everyone else
had boarded the ride, the carny locked up the gate and went
into the glass booth where the controls were. I watched him.
And I thought about my mother. I couldn't help it. I wondered
what she must have thought as they attacked her. I wondered if
she felt angry. If she fought back. I thought about his hands,
and I thought about the hands of the men who killed my
mother.

The music was loud, rolling under our seats. Brooder
pulled off his baseball cap, swung it up over his head and
hooted. Inside the glass booth, the carny leaned into a microphone and said in a slow, low voice, "Hold on, folks, y'all are in
for the ride of your life."

As we got off the ride, I cracked my neck to first one side,
then the next, waiting for my equilibrium to return before I
followed Brooder back down the metal ramp to the exit. The
carny was waiting at the exit gate for us.

"Y'all have a good night," he said, opening up the metal
gate. I made myself look at him and nodded. His eyes were
large, soft. He had a dimple in his cheek—he was probably my
age, younger, but he had a face like a kid.

"Yeah, you too," I said.

I looked around, the lights leaving trails when I turned my
head. I looked back at the ride, watched the Himalaya guy
usher in the next group of riders. I watched him run a white
handkerchief across his forehead, stuff it in his back pocket.

"We should get back to Betsy," I said.

"It bother you?" Brooder asked. For a minute I thought he meant the carny. But how could he know that I felt wound up like a spring?

"What's that?" I asked.

"Me and Betsy. Hanging out, this protest shit? 'Cause you know, I'd never . . ." he said.

"Oh, no," I said, shaking my head. "It's cool. It's fine. You guys are *friends*. I respect that." I wanted to get out of this conversation quickly. I looked toward the recruiting tent. I could see a bunch of hippie kids hanging around. A few old guys watching from the beer tent.

Betsy was handing out candles. "How was it?" she asked.

"Fucking fast!" Brooder hooted.

"Shhh," Betsy said, and Brooder looked at her meekly. "Sara's got your guitar," she said.

Brooder shoved his hands in his pockets and walked over to Sara, who had his guitar case slung over her shoulder.

"Hi," I said.

"Hi." She smiled, her face glowing in the neon lights coming from the grandstand. I hadn't seen her this happy in a long time. She kissed me quickly and then handed me a candle. "I gotta go speak," she said. "I'll meet you right back here after."

"We are here tonight because our government believes that it is okay to send off children to war. *Boys* off to war. Most of them are not even twenty years old. *I* am here tonight, because I do not believe in the murder of children." Betsy stood on the milk crate podium, her hair loose around her shoulders. She cradled her belly with her hand and held the bullhorn in the other. In that moment, even with the distant sounds of the rides and the girlie shows, with the cheering of the crowd, with the revving engines and smashing cars in the Demolition

Derby, I could only hear Betsy, her voice strong and clear, un-wavering as she continued. "Ralph Waldo Emerson once said, 'The real and lasting victories are those of peace, and not of war.' "

My heart swelled.

When the cheering subsided, Sara took the bullhorn from Betsy and helped her down off the milk crate. Brooder started to strum softly on the guitar, and Sara read the list of names. Afterward, for a moment, there was a sort of quiet.

When Brooder began to sing the songs he had written, I knew right away that the songs weren't just for peace. They were for Betsy. Every single one was a love song. They were beautiful. It *was* poetry. As Betsy made her way back to me, I wanted to hold her. To rock her in my arms. To feel our baby beneath her skin. I loved her more than anything in that moment. More than life. It seemed to me for the first time that someone understood how I felt about Betsy. Brooder smiled at me and kept singing.

"I love you," I said to Betsy, but before she had time to answer, a voice hollered out from the beer tent, "hey, man, what happened to your face?" Brooder stopped singing, peered out into the crowd.

After a minute, he started strumming again. Picking up where he'd left off.

"I said, what happened to your face, hippie freak?" The voice was louder this time. I scanned the crowd, but couldn't see where it had come from.

Brooder set the guitar down, stood up.

"Oh shit," Betsy said, pulling away from me. Before I had a chance to stop her, she was moving back through the crowd toward Brooder.

Beyond the grandstand, cars revved their engines, and the loudspeaker boomed and reverberated.

"I'll tell you what happened to my fucking face!" Brooder hollered, throwing his shoulders back. Puffing up his chest.

Betsy had reached him and was tugging on his arm. I started to push my way through the crowd to get to her. By the time I got to her, Brooder had climbed up on the milk crate and was ripping off his jacket. And then he yanked his T-shirt over his head. The floodlight from the grandstand illuminated him like a spotlight. His torso was riddled with a series of red welts, skin rippled and twisted and scarred.

"Fucking Charlie! That's what happened to my fucking face! You asshole. I *fought* your fucking war."

"Please," Betsy said, reaching for him; she was crying now. "Jesus," I said.

But then Brooder was charging into the crowd, which parted for him like water. He suddenly had the guy by his shirt collar. The crowd circled around them, spectators at a cock fight. I braced myself for the first blow, and then there it was: the awful crack of bone against bone. Brooder's hair was flying madly; spit and blood splattered everywhere. I'd seen Brooder get into fights before, but never like this. He was like an animal. A wild, rabid animal.

I watched in horror and disbelief as Betsy pulled away from me and went to him, screaming, "Stop it!"

Brooder seemed oblivious to what was happening, oblivious even to her. He was dancing around the circle with his fists raised, like a boxer. Like he was in for the fight of his life. Betsy grabbed at his shirt, as if she could simply pull him away.

"Betsy!" I said, pushing my way through the crowd. I knew I had to get her out of there before something terrible happened. I reached for her hand, and I half-expected she would pull away from me, intent as she was on stopping the fight. But when I touched her, she looked at me, stunned as if I'd woken her from sleep. Then she looked down at her stomach, cradled it with one hand, and closed her eyes. I put my arm around her, enveloping her, and steered her, the best I could, out of the mess. Once we were away from the crowd, she collapsed into my arms, crying big, awful sobs.

Brooder threw one more punch, and the guy went from staggering to falling. Brooder spit a mouthful of blood onto the guy's shirt and shook his hair out of his eyes. "I fought your fucking war," he hissed again, and then he disappeared into the crowd.

"Let's just leave," Betsy said, defeated, wiping her nose with the back of her hand.

The first few drops of rain were cold, unexpected.

"Oh, Jesus, I thought this was *over*," Betsy said. When thunder rumbled, she grabbed my hand. We ran, as quickly as we could with Betsy's awkward gait, to the exit and into the parking lot. It took a few minutes before we found the DeSoto among the hundreds and hundreds of cars, and lightning streaked across the sky just as I was opening the passenger door. Inside the car, rain pelted at the glass, and Betsy wept.

"We'll be home in a few minutes," I said. The fairgrounds were only a few miles away from our house.

"No." She shook her head. "Not until the storm is over."

I made my way through the rain, climbing into that unrelenting sky until we got to the top of the Heights. The heater blew warm air into the car, but Betsy shivered.

"You want a blanket? I've got one in the back," I said.

Betsy shook her head. She leaned her head back and closed her eyes. She was quiet for a long time.

"We did the right thing," she said quietly.

"What?"

"The baby. This is the right thing. I truly, truly believe that." Betsy put her face in her hands. Her shoulders trembled. I could hear her trying not to cry. Everything inside me ached.

And then I remembered. In all the commotion, I had completely forgotten about the job. I had to tell her about the university, about Maine.

"You know, after the baby comes . . ." I started.

Thunder cracked.

"I'm scared," Betsy said.

"It's okay," I said. "I'm here."

Betsy looked at me, desperate and sad. "Turn the headlights out? Let's just watch the storm."

Acts of Contrition

"You okay dere?" Rene asked, leaning out of the window as I stood on the street below my apartment. "Maybe you best go lie down."

I nodded.

"Dat Demerol, it knock you right out."

I nodded again, still unable to speak.

After Rene pulled away, I stood staring down Depot Street. When I looked up at one of the windows of my apartment that faced the street, I could see Maggie's silhouette moving behind the kitchen curtains. I blinked hard and started walking in the opposite direction. I stopped when I got to the Laundromat, stood for several minutes just breathing the clean smell of detergent and bleach before I went in.

In the hallway outside Brenda's apartment, the hum of the washers and dryers below was almost pacifying.

"Come in," she said. "You look like you've seen a ghost."

Once inside, I didn't know what to say. Why I was there. What to do. Brenda motioned for me to sit at the kitchen table. "Let me get you something to drink." She handed me a bottle of beer and furrowed her brow as she sat down across from me.

"What?" I asked, suddenly self-conscious.

"You need a haircut. It's the *eighties*, you know. You and Tony, both of you, caught in some sort of time warp."

Before I knew it, she had me leaning over her sink as she used the spray nozzle to wash my hair. The warm water felt good on my neck. I watched the soap swirl down the rusty drain. Her fingers pressed into my scalp, making my skin tingle. Come alive. She threw a towel over my head, and left me to dry it myself.

"Sit down here. You mind if your shirt gets some hair on it?" she asked.

I looked down at my shirt and shook my head. She draped the towel I'd used to dry my hair over my shoulders and disappeared into the living room. She came back out with a velvet-lined case, a shining pair of sheers lying inside as if it were a casket.

"Where's Roger?" I asked.

"He's with his nonna," she said. "Tony's aunt. I usually work at Bobbi's shop in the mornings and then pick him up after I've had a chance to run some errands."

"I'm sorry," I said. "Am I keeping you from something?"

"Nah. I was just gonna run to the post office. Mail some bills."

"I haven't had a haircut in over a year. . . . I can wait another day or so. . . ."

"Shh."

The hair fell all around me, curling dark and wet on the floor. Her fingers kept touching the sides of my face, my neck.

"What happened to your hand?" she asked.

I shook my head.

"Did somebody's face get in the way?"

I smiled, but it felt like something inside me was fragmenting. Fracturing.

"There," she said, holding up a plastic-handled mirror to my face. I barely recognized myself. "You like?"

"How much do I owe you?"

"Forget about it," she said and smiled. "I don't charge my friends."

I smiled back at her; the thought of us being friends seemed like a strange idea. I wondered what Brooder would think of me sitting in his kitchen now. I reached for the beer, which had grown a little warm, and took a deep pull. We were quiet for a while, just sitting and drinking.

"Tell me about your wife," she said softly. "About Betsy."

Brooder had obviously told her more about me than she'd let on before.

I shrugged. "There's not much to tell. She died twelve years ago. We have a little girl."

"Do you still miss her?" she asked.

I wanted to be able to tell her *no*, to tell her that the gash Betsy's death made grew narrower and narrower with each passing year, but I couldn't. The wound was in a spot that couldn't heal, aggravated by even the simplest things, torn open again and again. Brenda wanted me to tell her that she wouldn't always feel the sharp sting of Brooder's death, but, as far as I knew, it would always hurt.

"I'm afraid that I won't be able to raise Roger on my own," she said. "Thank God for Tony's aunt. I don't know what I'd do without her." She was playing with the wedding band on her finger, spinning it around and around with her thumb.

"Betsy's family helped me out, *helps* me out too," I said. "But you'd be amazed how capable you are. How much you can do by yourself."

"Sounds to me like we've got a lot in common," she said. "You and me."

I smiled and swallowed another swig. She kept opening bottles of beer, and I kept drinking them. Every one of them made everything that was happening seem further and further away. Remote. Just a story I heard once. And Brenda's edges softened with each drink. She was so pretty. Her hair was loose today, and hanging down over her shoulders. She looked like summertime.

"It's nice to talk to someone who knew Brooder. *Before*. When I met him, when he came to Florida looking for his mom, he was like that. Normal, you know. Even with the mess the war had made of his face, he was still sort of charming. He wrote me songs, on his guitar. It was, I don't know, sort of romantic. And he was so generous. He'd give you the shirt off his back, the *skin* off his back if you asked." She chuckled, and then her smile faded into a sort of grimace. "But almost as soon as I got back here with him, he started to . . . change." She looked out the window.

"He didn't . . ."

"What?" she asked, her eyes wide.

"He didn't ever hurt you?" I stopped. It was none of my business.

She shook her head, turned back to me. "No. He wasn't right, in the head. But it wasn't like that. And it wasn't all bad. I would have turned around and gone back home if it had been *all* bad. He was a good father. And a mostly good husband. Plus, he needed me. He had so much shame inside. So much anger and shame."

"About Vietnam?" I asked.

She looked at me, hard.

I lowered my head.

She reached across the table and grabbed my hand before I could reach for my bottle. "He adored her, you know. Your Betsy. She was his best friend."

I lifted my head up, willed myself to focus on her eyes. On her face. Everything was collapsing now. She squeezed my good hand.

"I know," she said. "About that night. I know what happened. *Why* it happened."

I felt my insides growing hot. The warm beer buzz became molten sobriety. And before I could speak, I was crying. As if all that heat inside me had run out of room and was coming out in hot tears.

She got up and came to me. She kneeled next to my chair and leaned into me, resting her head in my lap. I could feel the warmth of her face through my jeans. I stroked her hair, traced the outline of her face. I touched her lips with my finger, felt the soft, wet place where they parted. I pressed my palm against her cheek then, and she lifted her head, looked at me with sad eyes. And then she was kissing me: my hair, my forehead, my throat. I closed my eyes. When she reached my mouth, I kissed her back softly. Quietly. Both of our lips were salty with tears.

"I'm sorry," she said, pulling away. Embarrassed.

"No," I said. "I'm sorry. It's okay." And it was okay, because for the first time in twelve years I felt like someone was inside *with* me, staring out from the same hollow place. And so I told her what I'd never told a soul before.

"I thought Brooder was just going to scare him," I said. "I really thought he was just going to teach him a lesson. He said that if we didn't do it then nobody would, that by the time the cops got to him he'd already be gone. But I let him do it. I didn't stop him. It's my fault."

She wrapped her arms around my waist, leaned her head against my chest, and whispered, "It *wasn't* your fault. It was a terrible thing, but you didn't do anything wrong. He told me that. He did."

The Heights

It sounded like a tremendous crack of thunder, but then I felt my face hitting the steering wheel, my neck snapping forward and back. Something had hit us from behind. But as I turned around to see what had happened, the DeSoto pitched forward, and we began to fall. Everything went black and starry for a moment. For hours? Another crack, crack, and when I came to again, I was staring at a thousand shards of broken glass.

Here is Betsy in repose: she was lying on her back, halfway in the car, her long legs stretched, golden and thin still. Her back was arched, her belly rising up, a small mountain, her arms over her head, which was thrown back, her neck exposed. Her hair hung to the ground, the edges dipping in the dewy grass. I touched her leg first—grabbing tightly onto the delicate bones of her knee, cradling the kneecap in my palm. As my head began to throb and my vision became blurred with what must have been my own blood, I felt something like a fire starting to catch—a heat in my legs, my calves burning. I looked away from Betsy only long enough to verify that I wasn't actually on fire. I watched my hand moving toward the swell of her stomach, my fingers trembling (like the first time I touched her, like every time I touched her), crawling across the exposed skin of her stomach. I rose to my knees and was crawling across her body, shielding her. *Too late, too late.* I grabbed handfuls of her hair and tried to pull her back into the car, grasping onto her hair, pulling. I enclosed her, enveloped her. Made a fortress out of my own body, but it was too late.

I could feel the baby moving under her skin, the rolling and jabbing, an insistent reminder: *I am here. I am here.* I pressed my cheek to her throat, listening for the sound of blood rushing, imagining it like the river. I buried my face in her neck, buried my hands in her hair.

There was a pair of bright lights glaring in through the back window from above. Confused, I opened the driver's side door and crawled out of the car. I was looking up at the lookout where we had been parked. The DeSoto was about thirty feet down the embankment, stopped in its descent by a large plateau of rock and grass.

I stood and shielded my eyes from the bright glare of the headlights, and when I did I saw the man standing there, staring down at us. At first he looked only like the shadow of a man, like a paper cutout. A silhouette. But when he stepped away from the car, peering down at us through the crumpled guardrails, the headlights illuminated everything. I saw his face.

"Hey, please help us!" I said. "My wife is pregnant! She's hurt!"

The man looked down into the darkness, as if trying to place where the voice was coming from. In the bright headlights I could see him. That boyish face, the wide deer eyes and the dimple like a comma in his cheek.

"Please!" I screamed. "She's dying!"

But instead of scrambling down the cliff to help me, the man froze. He held up his hands, his palms pink, his long fingers spread open wide in a strange gesture of surrender, and then he was running. I could hear his feet on the damp grass, see his shadow body running away through the bushes and rocks. I could see the handkerchief in his back pocket, a flash of terrible white receding in the distance.

And then I was back inside the car, lifting Betsy up in my arms. Cradling her, I climbed the slippery embankment, mud and rocks making every step difficult. The man's car was still at the top of the lookout, the lights still on. But the man was gone.

I looked into the car to see if he'd left the keys in the ignition, but they were also gone. I kicked the tire, the bumper, and buried my face in Betsy's hair, weeping. And then I made my way to the middle of the road, still holding Betsy in my arms, where I stood in the rain until we were both drenched. Finally, a car came. I don't remember much after that except that when the woman driving the car asked me if she was breathing, I couldn't speak.

I stood next to the hospital bed where she lay; my pants weighed down with water, the cuffs making muddy puddles around my feet on the clean white floor, and wished only for the quick blink of her eyelashes, the minute movement that would make all of this untrue. But she was gone. She'd been gone since they pulled the baby out of her.

The rain had soaked my hair, my clothes, my shoes. Even my chest was heavy with it. It took so much effort to move down the corridor where I knew Paul and Hanna were waiting. It was like one of those terrible dreams where your legs won't work. Paralysis. Quicksand. Fighting a powerful current. Because waiting at the end of the hall was this: Hanna, standing, weeping, and Paul, sitting on the bench, hunched over, his head in his hands.

Later that night, the nurse took the baby from the incubator. "At least we were able to save the baby," she said, handing her to me like some sort of consolation prize. But I only wanted Betsy. At that moment, if I could have traded one for the other, I would have.

"Sit down," the nurse said, motioning to the rocking chair. "I'll leave you two alone."

I sat down, and peered into the baby's tiny face, and knew then that no matter how hard I tried I would always fail her.

The car that hit us, that killed Betsy, was a 1968 Thunderbird. Cherry red. It belonged to Jimmy Burke, Howie Burke's father. Howie was on his way home from Vietnam, and the Thunderbird was going to be his coming-home gift. Mr. Burke had taken it out for opening night at the fairgrounds. He and his wife took their younger son to the fair that night, parked the car in the fairgrounds parking lot. But when the boy threw up after too much cotton candy and a few too many spins on the Tilt-o-Whirl, and they decided to go home, they couldn't find the car anywhere. The police figured it had to have been someone from out of town, someone with the midway, who decided to take it out for a joy ride. Nobody in Two Rivers would have stolen a car from Jimmy Burke.

At the hospital, I told the police I wasn't sure if I had seen the person driving Howie's car: that he was only a silhouette, running away. I mentioned something about his handkerchief. Something about the midway, the lights. I knew they'd want to talk to me again. I was delirious when we spoke; my head thick with grief and glass. Shattered.

The baby couldn't come home with me yet. She was jaundiced, her skin the color of an unripe peach. And so the next morning in the half-light of dawn, I returned to our house by the river alone, and found Brooder sitting on my front steps.

"Who did it?" he asked.

I looked down at my feet.

"Who?" he asked.

I looked at him, saw that he too was fragmenting. I almost

reached out to touch him, but I knew it would have been like touching the edge of a broken glass.

"I think it was the guy running the Himalaya," I said.

"That dirty nigger?" Brooder asked, standing up, his face red. Angry.

My chest heaved. I knew that what I said next would change my life. But the rage was already inside me; it was born when my mother was killed, its roots growing deep and sinuous. Now it had broken through the surface and was growing into something I no longer understood.

"Yeah," I said. "It was him. I saw his face."

1968: Fall

*B*rooder drags the man across the ground by his arms, which are tied together with one of his own bootlaces. The man is barefoot now, his clothing and hair covered in wet leaves. Ray and I watch him from the car. After a while Brooder looks back at us and motions for us to follow.

Ray says, "Where is he taking him?"

"I don't know," I say.

"We should get out," Ray says. "We gotta make sure he doesn't do anything crazy."

I open the car door, am aware of the creaking of metal, the crush of leaves underfoot. Ray follows, and then we are running. When we get to the place where the two rivers meet, we find Brooder and the man.

He is awake now, and pleading. "Don't kill me," he says.

Brooder is silent. The man is on his knees, his hands tied together in front of him. In another circumstance, he might look as if he were only praying. Genuflecting to the harvest moon. But Brooder is standing behind him on a rock, his shotgun aimed toward the thick tangle of trees beyond the river.

"There are more of them out there," Brooder says quietly. He gestures with his chin toward the deep woods. "Just because we've captured this one doesn't mean we're safe."

"Come on," Ray says. "Let him go."

"Shh," Brooder says. "Listen."

I close my eyes. I listen. But beyond the buzzing in my brain, the chattering of my teeth, it is quiet here.

"I didn't mean to hurt nobody. . . ." the man says, his whole body is shivering in the cold. "It was an accident."

Brooder turns toward the man, aims the gun at his head.

Ray grabs my arm. "Let's go."

Brooder frowns. "Already? The ride's just about to start."

"Please," the man says, and looks at Ray and me. "Please, help me."

I squeeze my eyes shut. On the back of my eyelids, I see Betsy, on a late summer afternoon, picking blackberries. She is bending over to examine a berry on a bush in the backyard. I had watched her that day; she didn't know I was there. She pricked her thumb on a bramble, and wounded, she stuck her thumb in her mouth and sucked it before returning to her task. And I knew then that there was nothing more perfect than that moment, of Betsy with sun in her hair, plucking a ripe berry and putting it to her tongue.

When I open my eyes, the man is looking right at me.

"You coming or not?" Ray asks.

I stand still, cannot speak.

I hear Ray turning away, running back to where we left the car. I hear the car start. The slow rolling backward through the dark woods.

Brooder pulls the hammer back.

I move toward Brooder to stop him, but I know that it is already too late.

"You better back away," Brooder says, turning the gun on me. I hold my hands up, starting to back up slowly. Brooder hisses, "This ain't got nothing to do with you anymore."

I stumble on a rock.

"You know how to swim?" Brooder asks the man.

He shakes his head. He is weeping now.

Without lowering the gun, Brooder kicks the man in the chest hard with his boot. The man falls backward into the river. He is strug-

gling against the current. He looks at me again, reaches out his teth-ered hands for help.

"Please," he pleads.

And for a moment, I begin to reach for him. I know that without my help, the river might carry him away. That Brooder might just squeeze the trigger. But just as I am about to grab hold, to save him, I think of Betsy again. And it's too late. It's too late; I can't think of anything but blackberries in summertime.

"Go home," Brooder says, turning the gun on me again.

So I leave Brooder standing on the rock, watching the man hanging onto a fallen tree branch that straddles the two rivers. I back away, back through the woods, backward through the night. And I imagine that if I walk far enough, I will arrive again at the moment Betsy asked me to turn out the headlights.

Edges

I left Brenda's apartment at dusk, sober and tired, my throat swollen with grief. My hands still smelled of her; I cupped them to my face and breathed her in. The whole world felt heavy. It was cold, and the clouds were thick. Blue. The streetlights were late coming on, evening an unanticipated visitor. As I walked past the barbershop, the jewelry store, the drugstore, downtown Two Rivers felt foreign to me now. I climbed the stairs to my apartment slowly, my feet no longer able to recollect the height of each riser. The smell of old wallpaper in the hallway was stronger than I remembered, the echo of my footsteps on the floor more hollow. Before I opened the door, I ran my hand across my new haircut. Felt the end-of-the-day beginnings of a beard on my face. I probably looked like hell.

Inside Shelly was sitting at the kitchen table with her books spread out before her. "Hi, Daddy," she said, without looking up.

"Hi, honey," I said. My throat constricted even tighter. I wanted to go to her, to hold on to her. I wanted to be able to pick her up in my arms and bury my face in the soft skin of her neck. I wanted to apologize, for everything that came before her and everything that was likely to happen now. I sat down next to her at the table and picked up one of her books. It was an English textbook. A grammar book filled with diagrammed sentences. A jumble of words. I absently thumbed through the pages.

"What happened to your arm?" she asked, looking up from her work.

I shook my head, swallowed hard. "I made a mistake."

"Is it broken?" she asked.

"I'm fine." I smiled, looking at her hand holding her pencil. The eraser was gone, the wood was riddled with tiny teeth marks.

"You shouldn't do that," I said, pointing to the pencil. "It's got lead in it."

"Can I sign your cast?"

"Sure," I said, and she reached for a highlighter. I gently set my arm on the table, and she pulled the cap off with her teeth. She signed her name in pink, and then reached for the yellow to make a flower. She squinted, concentrating hard on her work. She held the pen in her fist, like a child still.

I noticed then that she had curled her hair, two angels' wings on either side of her face. "I like your hair," I said.

"Thanks." She smiled and kept drawing. "I like yours too."

I could have stayed like this forever. I willed the moment to last. Wished for a garden to grow in this plaster. But then Shelly snapped the cap back on the pen and sat back to check her work. "You like?"

I looked at her name there, surrounded by yellow flowers, and nodded. "Where's Maggie?" I asked, her name catching in my throat like a burr.

"She's in the bathtub. She'll probably be a while; she brought in a book."

I nodded. "Get back to work," I said. "I've got to go find something."

I went to my bedroom, feeling like I was trespassing. Once inside, I closed and locked the door. The bed was neatly made, and the whole room smelled of fresh linens. Maggie's suitcase was tucked neatly under the bed, and her few things were still arranged on top of my dresser. I picked up the sand dollar and held it in my hand. I rubbed my finger against the gritty striker on the pack of matches. I picked up the photo of Maggie and her girlfriends, peered into the distance, looking for him.

Like Ray, I saw him everywhere. He lived in the corners of my eyes, hiding just out of sight. In the periphery of things. I was ready now. Ready for him to come out from behind the trees, the buildings. He'd been watching me through the spaces between the cars in passing trains for too long. "Come out," I whispered. But the harder I looked at the picture, the more absent he became.

In the other room, I could hear Maggie in the bathtub. The sloshing of water.

The little wooden box was sitting in the center of the bureau still. The flimsy gold clasp broke easily when I pinched the soft metal between my fingers, and I slipped off the tiny padlock. As I opened the lid, a ballerina sprung up and began to pirouette to music box music. It startled me, and I looked quickly at the door. The mechanism finally wound down, and the ballerina stopped dancing. I heard the water start to drain from the tub, the sound of Maggie's wet feet on the bathroom tile.

Inside the box were trinkets: a ladybug stickpin with green-jeweled eyes, a rusty barrette, a tiger's-eye marble. There were broken necklaces, a cigarette, three wads of Bazooka. And in the little drawer in the bottom was a photo and what looked like a worn piece of glass. As Maggie's wet hand struggled to open the locked door, I pulled out the photo with trembling fingers.

It was a color photo with scalloped edges. The date stamped along the side said "May 1965." The photo was of a woman sitting on a sofa, holding an infant. To the right was a man sitting on the arm of the sofa, peering down at the baby. I stared at the man's face for a long time, at his dark skin, at his black eyes. I was trying so hard to see him, but it was like trying to examine the sun. And blinded, I didn't notice the woman and the child. I didn't even see the pale-skinned woman, her hair piled on top of her head in two frizzy braids. I didn't see my mother's face, looking down at the newborn child who even then had one blue, and one black eye.

SIX

Exactor Extractor

After Betsy died, I kept in touch with my father mostly be cause of Shelly. Over the years, we'd take the train to visit him in Boston a couple of times a year. The last time we visited, she was nine years old, and he had just been diagnosed with bone cancer. She adored him—and he her. But after that visit, I knew we wouldn't ever go back.

Shelly had a loose tooth. Usually, Shelly couldn't sit still the whole way. I'd give her a dollar, and while I slept or read, she'd go to the snack car for barbeque chips and chocolate milk. This time she sat in her seat the whole time, peering at the tooth in a pocket mirror.

My father had retired not long after my mother was killed, and he had converted her office/printing press into a workshop. Whenever we visited, he and Shelly would almost always spend the entire time working on some invention or another. Over time, the inventions had become less and less practical, and the ones he created with Shelly were pure whimsy. Once they made a clock that played "The Star-Spangled Banner" every hour on the hour. She assisted him installing a doorbell that asked, "Who is it?" and helped him make a device that simultaneously watered the flowers in his window box and cleaned the windows above it. Shelly appreciated his passion for innovation like neither my mother nor I ever did.

When we got off the train, I was surprised to see my father standing on the platform, waiting for us. Though he'd just found out he was sick, I had prepared myself for the worst. He looked the same as he had the last time I saw him, the only dif-ference being the cane he was carrying. "It's also a litter stick," he said, pulling a lever on the handle, which released a sharp rod at the bottom of the cane. "Try it!" he said, and Shelly dropped the bloody napkin she'd been using to work on her tooth. He aimed the stick over the napkin and speared it.

Shelly squealed with delight.

"I've got a loose tooth," she said. "Wanna touch it?"

"Sure," he said, smiling and bending down to examine her mouth. He reached his finger in and gently wiggled. "We may need to come up with a little something to help that tooth on its way," he said.

Shelly's eyes opened wide.

"An extractor," he said with a nod.

"Will it hurt?"

"Of course not, it will be very gentle. An exactor extractor of the most delicate kind."

At the house, I watched my father pretend that nothing was wrong, that he wasn't in any pain. If I hadn't spoken to the doctor myself, I would have thought it was all a big mistake. He had asked me to come to get his finances in order before he had the final draft of his will drawn up. He said it was only a precaution, just in case. He set me up with all of his papers at the kitchen table, where I struggled to make sense of his wretched bookkeeping and filing.

He and Shelly disappeared into the workshop, my father coming out only to make lunch. He made tuna sandwiches and picked two apples as big as grapefruits from the tree in his backyard before disappearing inside the workshop again.

As I struggled to make sense of the mess, I came across a file of bank statements. The account was in Hattiesburg,

Mississippi. I assumed, at first, that it was something my mother had established while she was living there. However, as I went over the figures, I realized that no money had ever been withdrawn from the account. It was a savings account with exactly one deposit made every month starting in 1965, with the most recent deposit made just that month. Both of my parents' names were on the account, but so was a Reverend Lawrence Jones's.

When my father emerged from the workshop, his face looked pained. "I need some water," he said. Hunched over at the sink, he held his back, rubbing his fingers into his spine. "It's not so bad in the mornings," he said. "It's the afternoons that get me. Later in the day."

"Who is Lawrence Jones?" I asked.

My father set his glass of water down and looked out the window over the sink. "He's the oldest son of the couple your mother stayed with in Mississippi. The preacher?"

I remembered my mother mentioning him in some of her postcards. He had built a library for the school. She taught him how to play the piano, and, in exchange, he taught her how to cook. "Why do you have an account with his name on it?" I asked. "An account with over thirteen thousand dollars in it?"

"We send money to help out the family. Just seventy-five a month. It's nothing really." His hands trembled as he drank some more water. "Your mother, she felt *indebted*. They took care of her. This is her way of taking care of them."

"But they've never taken a dime out of it," I said. "They must not need it that much."

My father turned to face me, smiled sadly. "There's a little girl. She's twelve. Maybe they're saving it for her to go to college."

"*Or*," I said, "maybe they don't feel right accepting charity from somebody who's dead."

My father massaged his temples with his thumb and middle finger. "Let it go, Harper."

"Dad, that's a lot of money. And I don't want to sound un-grateful, but it doesn't appear that you've set up any sort of trust fund for *Shelly*."

"I said let it rest," my father said.

"Christ, Dad. Mom just gave and gave and gave. She gave two years of her life to them, to their *cause*. And for what, Dad?"

"You don't understand," he said, shaking his head. "It's complicated."

"What's complicated? She was *killed*," I said. I couldn't stop. Every inch of my body was aching. "*Murdered*. By the people she loved more than her own fucking family."

I felt the slap, but it took several seconds before it regis-tered that my father had struck me. I caught my breath.

"Harper," he said, his face twisted.

Shelly opened the workshop door and stood, triumphant, in the doorway, holding out her apple, the bloody tooth stick-ing out of its flesh. "I didn't need the exactor extractor!"

Later, as we got on the train to go home, my father kissed the top of Shelly's head, and wiped at his eyes. He hugged me, and whispered in my ear, "This was important to your mother. Can you understand *that*?"

"No," I said. "I'm sorry. I just can't."

Last Wishes

I opened the bedroom door and let Maggie in.

"What y'all done locked yourself in my room for?" she asked. "I mean, I know it's your house, and everythin', but . . ." she started, and then she saw the photo in my hand.

I looked at Maggie, standing in Shelly's old purple bathrobe in the doorway, and then I looked at the photo of her in my mother's arms. My mother looked just like she did in my memory, but it was as if she had been cut and pasted there, into this odd scene. *May 1965.*

"Is that your father?" I asked, pointing to the man in the photo.

Maggie nodded.

"Lawrence Jones? The preacher?"

"Not anymore," she said. "He got runned out of the church after I was born." Maggie pulled the robe around her, tighter. She was small inside. "The whole town was angry— our neighbors, Daddy's friends, the police. After the cops beat her up, she didn't have no choice but to leave, and neither did we. Daddy decided we ought to go to Alabama, where nobody knowed us. Of course, I don't remember any of that. I was just a baby then." She leaned over the picture and traced her father's face with her finger.

"Why didn't you tell me?" I asked, the words prickly in my throat. *"Who you were?"*

Maggie sat down on the edge of the bed and lowered her head. Quiet. She played with the hem of the bathrobe, plucking a loose thread. Outside, the moon was bright. Full. When she finally looked up at me, her eyes were wide. "It was my daddy's best friend that raped me."

I sat down across from her on the window seat.

"When my daddy was gone one day, he com'd over, askin' for him. When I told him he weren't home, he com'd in anyway. Askin' me if I had somethin' for him to drink. So bein' polite, I offered him a pop, but he said he wanted whiskey. I remember thinkin' that was odd since it weren't even noon yet, but I found some whiskey in the cupboard and poured him a nice tall glass. He drank 'bout half of it, and next thing I know he's pulling at my shirt, playful like. I thought he was just teasin', so I laughed and kinda pulled away. But then he threw the rest of that whiskey in my face, and I knew he wasn't playin'."

I looked out the window, and then forced myself to look at her.

"He took me outside, to the back where we got this chicken coop. He takes me in there, I'm guessin' 'cause it's so loud nobody might hear me if I screamed. But I didn't scream." She shook her head. "I knew it wouldn't help nothin' anyway." She bit her lip and looked past me out the window. "He kept me in there for two hours. Two whole hours, and the chickens were flying around everywhere. And it smelled so terrible. I still can't get that stink out of my head."

She looked back at me again and smiled, threw her shoulders back. "Well, *anyway*, after everybody found out I was havin' a baby, like I *told you* . . . I knew I couldn't be stayin' there. My daddy already been through so much disgrace and all. Plus, I know he woulda blamed himself. He likes to think he be keepin' me safe, first movin' me away from Mississippi. Raisin' me up in the church. He's my *daddy*. He'd a wanted to die if he knew what really happened. So I let him think it was just a regular boy that I got with. That it was my fault. He wanted me to go to Baton Rouge, stay with my auntie until the baby was born and then give it up. But this baby ain't never done nothin' to nobody. It ain't his fault how he com'd to be. I knew I couldn't keep him, but I also couldn't dream of givin' him to a stranger. So I decided to come here. I did- n't tell nobody where I gone. I left a note for Daddy sayin' I gone to Mississippi with the baby's daddy. I knew he would- n't come lookin' for me there, an' if he did, he wouldn't find me."

"But why me?" I asked, my chest tight.

"Well, your daddy always been so kind to us, sending money even after she got killed. He sent me other stuff too, you know? Pictures of her, some of her special things." She reached over into the box and pulled out the piece of sea glass. "Her books and things she wrote. It was almost like I knew her, 'cause of him. So I wrote to him first, told him about the baby. I knew he wouldn't judge me, and I thought maybe I could go stay with him for a bit. But he sent me a letter back, sayin' he was real sick. He said he might not be around much longer, but he wanted me to know I had a brother and that he had a little girl too. That you was raising her all by yourself, up here in Vermont. He said you were a good man."

I put my face in my hands, my chest heaving. When I looked up, Maggie was softly stroking her belly.

"What made you think I'd take you in?" I asked.

Maggie shrugged again. "I don't know. I guess I took my chances. But when I found you sitting by the river, after the train wrecked, you looked like you were somebody with some pretty big sorrow. And I may not know much about babies, but I do know one thing. There ain't no way to be sad when you're holding a brand new baby in your arms."

I looked back down at the photo I'd been clutching in my hand. At my mother beaming at Maggie.

Bat in the Owl House

I took the train by myself to Boston. Outside my window, the leaves had peaked. By the following week, they would litter the roads and streets, but for now, they held on. Orange and gold. Purple and red. It felt like the train was rushing through a tunnel of fire. I brought only a small bag; I wouldn't be staying long. Brenda said she'd come over to help out with the girls while I was gone, but I wanted to get home as soon as I could.

I took a taxi from the train station to Cambridge, and the cabbie dropped me off down the street from my father's house in front of a deli. It was one of those paradoxical autumn days: blue sky, bright sun, but vividly cold. *Crisp*, that's what most people call it. But to me it just felt like obstinacy. Like a struggle. As if summer itself was refusing to let go of its hold. I put my sunglasses on against its stubborn glare, and tightened my scarf against the equally determined chill. I ordered a cup of coffee from the old man working behind the counter and took it to a bench in front of the shop, trying to warm myself from the inside out.

When I called my father to tell him I was coming, he didn't seem surprised. He only said, "Good, good. I hope you plan to bring that sweet granddaughter of mine."

I shook my head.

"Harper?" he asked when I still hadn't answered.

"Yeah?"

"Did she find you?" His voice sounded like bones rattling in a bag. "Margaret Jones?"

"Yes."

When the coffee had turned cold, I walked up the steps to my parents' house, aware of the warm sun, the chilly breeze. He opened the door before I had a chance to knock.

He was so thin, a sliver of himself. The cane had been replaced by a walker, which he maneuvered across the kitchen floor and then relinquished in favor of a seat at the kitchen table. His breathing was labored, his face and chest so thin. "Sit down," he said, motioning to the other chair.

I sat down across from him. The vinyl tablecloth was covered with crumbs. Papers.

"How's Shelly?" he asked, his lips cracking as he smiled.

"Good, good." I nodded.

"Work? The train wreck was all over the news. Even down here."

I reached for the saltshaker in the center of the table. A pink ceramic poodle, one of the few relics from the fire that had been spared. The peppershaker had not survived.

"Can I get you something? To drink? Eat? I don't keep much in the fridge these days."

"Dad?" I said.

"Yeah?"

I set the shaker down in front of him, took a deep breath. "Did she love him?"

My father picked the saltshaker up and held it in the palm of his hand. He turned it over and over, as if the answer to my question was inside. He set it down again and looked at me. He looked so old, so tired. The past three years could have been thirty. His milky eyes filled with tears. I felt my stomach tighten.

"You have to understand," he said softly. "It was bigger than that. More complicated."

"How?" I asked.

"Do you remember the owl house I built out back?" he asked.

I nodded. He had spent a whole weekend one summer building a house aimed at attracting the owl population of Two Rivers. But not long after the owl family arrived, a bat took up residence inside the owl house, and all of the owls left. The lone bat stayed in the owl house all summer; you could hear its wings flapping against the sides of the house. Finally, when my father realized the bat had no intention of leaving, and that the owls would not return until the bat was gone, he set out poison to get rid of it.

"His family took her in. He took her in. They worked *together*, doing the kind of work she was born to do. And he fell in love with her. Despite everything she was, *because of* everything she was." He winced and reached for his back. He rubbed it methodically, closing his eyes.

"Why did she come home then?" I asked. "Why didn't she just stay there?"

"Most folks don't want bats in the owl house." His voice was thin and weak.

"But she had a *baby*," I said. "How could she leave a baby behind?"

"They would have killed her if she'd stayed. They almost did. You know that."

"The fire," I said, remembering. NIGGERLOVER, scrawled across the pavement. "How did they find her?"

"The Klan had people everywhere then. Even in Two

Rivers. They weren't always dressed up in hoods and robes, you know. And word spread quickly. About where she'd gone."

"She couldn't go back," I said, for the first time feeling sadness for my mother. The grief she must have felt leaving her baby behind.

"She stayed in touch with him, but only to talk about the baby. She did that out of respect for me, I suppose, but I knew she would go back someday, to be with them, where she felt she belonged. And then she never got a chance."

"But after she came home, you both seemed so happy. Was *she* happy?"

He nodded. "Sometimes, there's room for more than one real love. I know it doesn't seem possible, couldn't seem possible to you after Betsy."

I thought about the way it felt when Brenda kissed me, that terrible combination of desire and remorse. A wave of sadness rolled under my skin.

"Most people find love where they can. Your mother found it here first, and then down there. It wasn't something she went looking for."

"Why did you take her back?" I asked. "Most people would think you were crazy."

"When she came home, it was like I got a second chance. And I made it my job to make up for all of the years I wasted trying to turn her into something she wasn't. I owed her that. But none of what happened was because she didn't love *us*. It wasn't that at all."

"She loved us?" I asked, suddenly a child again. This was the only question I really needed answered.

He nodded.

"She's my *sister*," I said. It was the first time I had said this. Felt this.

"Yes." He smiled. "She is."

★   ★   ★

I called the cab from my father's house, and he sat with me outside on the steps until it arrived. He lit a cigar, and the smoke smelled sweet.

"When did *you* start smoking?" I asked. He had always hated my mother's cigarettes.

"Last week." He smiled. "Josephine bought these for me. To celebrate." Josephine was the widow who lived next door. "I got a patent," he said.

"You *did*? For what?"

"The weather predictor," he said. "I finally got the bugs worked out. Only took me twenty-five years." He laughed, a big happy laugh, and it made me smile.

"What does it say today?" I asked.

"Looks like fall's almost over," he said. "It'll snow before long. But today, just sunshine."

The cabbie shook his head when we got to Blue Hill Avenue in Roxbury. We were parked in front of a whole block of vacant buildings. The storefront windows were broken. Only the painted signs remained. "I ain't droppin' you off here," he said.

"Isn't that your job?" I asked.

"Sorry, man. I can't be responsible for that." He shook his head again.

"Just tell me my fare and let me out," I said, irritated.

"How long you gonna be?"

"Why?"

"I'll turn off my meter and wait for you. If you don't plan on being gone too long."

"Go," I said, paying him, and then stepped out of the cab.

The cabbie pulled away slowly, and I started down the street. There was a vacant barbershop: a red, white and blue barber pole out front, rusted and immobile. I peered in the window of the shop, shielding my eyes from the sun's glare on the glass.

Inside, the barber chairs were prone, empty. I smiled when I saw the poster illustrating the official hairstyles for boys and men. I could almost smell the sweet familiar scent of Barbasol. Of soap and aftershave.

I pulled the napkin my father had scribbled on out of my pocket and walked to the place where my mother had parked her Buick that day. There was a dirt lot, a brick building covered with graffiti, a few cars parked on the street and trash everywhere. When I got to the corner, I sat down on the curb. I'm not sure what I expected, but it certainly wasn't this. There was nothing here to explain what had happened. No ghosts.

"Better get a move on there," someone behind me said, startling me. I felt something hard nudging me in the back.

"Excuse me?" I said, looking up.

A policeman was standing above me. A big man, with skin the color of paper. His billy club was still poking into me.

"I'm fine," I said.

"No loitering," he said. "Up."

"Jesus," I said as he lifted me by the elbows.

"You'd be smart to get yourself back to Harvard," he said.

"I said, '*I'm fine.*' "

The policeman put his billy club back into its holster and pretended to wash his hands. "No blood on these," he said, and then he walked back down the street.

I stood up and started walking down the sidewalk again. I felt my pace quicken, suddenly anxious. I thought about my mother delivering the *Freedom Press* to the barbers and jewelers and grocers that must have once occupied these empty spaces. I could almost picture her, bracelets jingling, heels clacking on the pavement. A big smile and the wave of her hand. I wondered if she ever felt afraid.

A few men were gathered on the corner, talking loudly and laughing. When I crossed the street, they hollered after me. "Hey, college boy!"

When I didn't respond, they shouted louder. It didn't seem to matter to anybody here that I was thirty-four years old and that I hadn't been on a college campus in over a decade. Thankfully, they returned to their conversation and I kept walking. I was moving pretty quickly when a small voice behind me said, "You lost?"

My heart quickened again, but when I turned around, it was only a child looking up at me. The whites of his eyes were bright against his dark skin. He was chewing gum, smacking it hard. He couldn't have been more than six or seven.

I shook my head.

"You ain't from here," he said.

This more than anything made me feel like I was an intruder. A bat in the owl house. "No." I shook my head and then, as if there were a way to explain, I started, "I used to know somebody . . ." But my voice trailed off.

"You give me a dollar and I'll walk you back to your car."

"What's with everyone wanting to be my escort today?" I laughed nervously, and then I reached into my pocket and grabbed a dollar. "I *will* give you a dollar if you tell me where I can find a church though."

The little boy grinned and grabbed the dollar out of my hand. He examined it as if checking to make sure it wasn't counterfeit. Then he pointed across the street to an old movie theater. The marquis said OUR LADY OF PERPETUAL SORROW, and the windows were boarded up. "Ain't no sermon today," he said.

"That's okay," I said.

"You sure you don't want me to walk you?" he asked.

"Will it cost me?"

"*Complimentary.*"

I smiled, and he skipped along next to me as I made my way to the church.

"Where do you live?" I asked him.

"Right here," he said. "My whole life."

"That's a good long time."

He nodded and cracked his gum.

"You like it here?"

He looked at me dumbly. "Roxbury's my home. Course I like it."

This, I understood.

"Malcolm X from here too."

"You don't say," I said.

When we got to the church, he said, "Now, I got business on the other side of town, but you should be okay as long as you don't take no alleys. And keep your head up."

I nodded, lifted my head. "No alleys." And then he was gone.

Inside Our Lady of Perpetual Sorrow, the concession area had been converted into a vestibule. I dropped two quarters in the slot of a wooden box and lit two candles. Then I went down the carpeted hallway to the converted theater. Inside, I sat in one of the rickety seats. The springs were shot, the upholstery threadbare. Where the screen used to be was a large wooden cross. A pulpit on the stage. I was alone here.

After a while, I knelt down on my knees, the cement floor cold and sticky. I rested my elbows on the back of the seat in front of me and clasped my hands together. I closed my eyes and said two prayers: one for Betsy, and one for my mother. And then, I said one for the man I left behind.

Night-blooming Cereus

After that night by the river, I waited. I waited for his body to be found, for somebody to discover him. I imagined someone stumbling upon his body, tangled in the bushes at the river's edge. I waited for his family to come looking for him. Demanding to know what had happened to their son. I waited for him to arrive, alive at my doorstep still wet with the river, looking for me. It was excruciating, this waiting. Every phone call, every knock on the door jarring me into a state of terror. Ray wouldn't speak to me, and Brooder took off for Florida, told people he was going to find his mother. I would have gone to the police but I didn't know how to explain what had happened. I felt like I was living at the edge of a terrible precipice, in a vicious wind with nothing but fragile branches to cling to.

And still, Betsy was gone. Grief rubbed my shoulders, ground its hard knuckles into the tendons of my neck, crippling me. My muscles ached with her absence.

After her funeral, I returned to work. We settled into a sort of routine at Paul and Hanna's. When I came home from the station, we had dinner at Paul and Hanna's table, and afterward, I showered and went to bed. But every time I closed my eyes I felt Betsy lying next to me: the heat of her body or her breath. I would awaken, fevered and tangled in sheets I had imagined were her legs. Shelly woke up every two or three hours, and I fed her a bottle, sitting in a stiff-backed chair in the midnight kitchen. Grief and regret pummeled me alternately, two angry bastards beating me as if I were only a bag of sand. I watched the windows. I listened to the unfamiliar sounds of the house (missing her, missing her), its breaths and moans, always certain that he was out there, somewhere, waiting for me.

But after about a month when no body was found, and no one even seemed to know he was missing, sometimes it felt as if I had only dreamed that night. During the day, when I was busy with the concrete details of my life (work, bills, the baby), the details of what had happened became abstract, a string of images and smells and sounds: *moon, trees, river*. During the day, it lay dormant. Asleep. But at night, as I sat rigid, holding a bottle while Shelly slept in my arms, these abstractions assembled themselves into a continuous waking nightmare, which was vivid and real.

There is a desert plant called the night-blooming cereus. During the day, the cactus resembles little more than a dead bush. But once a year, just as night falls, its heady-scented petals open, blooming into a glorious moon-colored flower. When dawn comes, the flower closes in on itself and dies. For me, the flower opened again and again. Each and every night: its fragrance almost unbearable, its white petals blinding.

And still, Betsy was gone. Sometimes, I heard someone cry out and it would take a moment before I realized it was my own voice. As if the grief were inside me as well, living in my throat, a caged animal tearing at my esophagus.

When the first anniversary of her death (and Shelly's first birthday) arrived, I had resigned myself to a sort of fugue state. I was alive, but living a kind of waking dream. Everything I'd known to be true didn't seem true anymore at all. Everything I had trusted had failed me. Everything I believed about myself was no longer relevant or real.

Hanna made cupcakes; they were yellow, I remember, decorated with daisies. It was just the four of us; my father was still working then and couldn't make the trip up from Boston. Though it was fall, it was still warm, and Hanna set the picnic table in the backyard with a daisy tablecloth, bowls filled with pretzels, and a pitcher of lemonade. She made potato salad and Paul grilled hamburgers. Hanna strung balloons in all of the trees and put Shelly on a blanket on the grass with some toys.

I was preoccupied with a loose railing on the back porch. As I rocked in the rocking chair, I kept noticing that it needed to be repaired or replaced. Normally things like that didn't bother me, but something about this rail, wobbly and crooked in a long row of perfectly vertical rails, was unnerving.

Hanna was stringing the branches with yellow crepe paper, and Paul was lighting the coals. Shelly was sitting happily on the blanket, and so I wandered to the shed and searched through Paul's tools for a hammer. Locating one underneath a pile of old lumber, I felt a surge of purpose. I went back out again to the yard.

Hanna was still teetering on a kitchen chair beneath the trees, yellow crepe paper ribboning out beneath her, and Paul was standing over the pile of hot coals. When I looked to the blanket, though, Shelly was gone. Panicked, I spun around, trying to catch sight of her. And then the possibility struck me hard in my stomach: the river.

I started to run down the slope of grass that led to the river's edge, but just as I was about to scream her name, I saw her, shiny purple birthday hat on her head, toddling toward the water. I ran to her, my feet barely touching the ground, and scooped her up in my arms. And as I carried her back to the yard, pressed against my chest, I felt a clarity I hadn't felt in over a year. As my heart slowed down again, and Shelly burst into tears, I kept holding her, rocking her, pressing her against me and apologizing, "I'm sorry, I'm so sorry."

Hanna never said anything. She offered me a glass of lemonade and fixed me a burger as I sat on the porch holding Shelly on my lap. And later, when the sun went down, and Shelly had fallen asleep in my lap, she came out onto the porch and nudged my shoulder gently. "You should get some sleep, hon." She smiled sadly. "It's been a long day."

That night I slept more soundly than I had in months, Shelly nestled against me, her breath milky sweet and warm against my neck, my hand feeling the rise and fall of her chest. And I wasn't sure who was keeping whom safe anymore.

Finding Snow

I didn't tell Shelly that Maggie was my sister. I couldn't find the words or the need. Not yet. Besides, as far as Shelly was concerned, Maggie was already family. And that's all that really mattered. But the baby, that was something else altogether.

Maggie and her father had both agreed to consent to the adoption. The baby's father would not have a say in the matter. Everything would be finalized within thirty-six hours after the baby was born. When Maggie told her father what had really happened, he wept. She comforted him quietly, and then she handed the phone to me. His voice was gentle, kind. He talked about Maggie, about how much he loved her, and he thanked me for taking care of her. He asked me if I thought I could do the same for her baby, and I agreed. We didn't talk about my mother. There would be time for that later, I imagined.

"You mean Maggie's baby will be my brother or sister?" Shelly asked.

"Brother," Maggie said. She insisted the baby was a boy, though she had nothing other than intuition to go on. She was sitting on the couch, knitting a blue blanket. Mrs. Marigold had taught her how to knit and given her some yarn. It was bumpy and messy but so soft. I had held it once, pressed it against my cheek.

"My *brother*?" Shelly asked.

I nodded.

"Okay," she said, shrugging. "But what about you? Why can't you stay *too*?"

Maggie had a way with Shelly, a way I both admired and envied. "I ain't done bein' a kid yet. I gotta get home and finish that up." She smiled at me. "My own daddy's waitin' on me."

Lenny happily accepted my resignation at the station. I gave him two months' notice, plenty of time to secure someone to fill my shoes. Even then he offered, "Why don't you collect on some of that vacation time you got coming to you? Leave a little sooner?" And so a few weeks later, I packed up the few things I kept in the freight office (a baby picture of Shelly, a snapshot of Betsy and me on our wedding day, a smooth stone Shelly painted with acrylics) and rode home on my damaged bicycle, balancing the box on the handlebars. As I pedaled away from the station, I loved the cold November wind in my face. Could almost taste winter on my outstretched tongue. I stopped by Bobbi's Beauty Parlor on the way home and asked Brenda if she'd like to join me for a cup of coffee. We sat together at Rosco's, ignoring the whispers and heads nodding knowingly around us. I liked the way she held her coffee mug with two hands. I liked that her eyes were always smiling, even when her mouth wasn't.

"Will it snow?" Maggie asked one afternoon when the sky was heavy and thick. "I ain't never seen snow."

"It might," I said. And then an idea hit me. "Let's go for a drive."

"Really? In the car?" Shelly asked. Shelly had ridden in the Bug only a handful of times.

"Get some hats and mittens. Find Maggie a coat."

Excited, Shelly ran to the closet, where she dragged out the box filled with all of our winter stuff.

Maggie was so much bigger now, uncomfortable in the backseat of the Bug as we drove across New Hampshire and into Maine. When she finally settled down and fell asleep, Shelly crawled into the front seat next to me. "Can you see the whole world from the top?" she asked.

"Almost." I laughed.

"Do you really think it will snow?" She looked out the window at the birches lining the road. "It's not snowing here."

"Maybe," I said. "No promises."

We got to the top of Cadillac Mountain just as the sun was starting to set. The granite boulders along the roadside glowed pink in the twilight. Maggie woke up when we stopped, sat up in the backseat, rubbing her eyes. "This is pretty," she said, leaning forward between the seats. "Is that the ocean?"

"That's it," I said.

"Can you turn the heat on, Daddy?" Shelly asked, shivering.

I pulled the button that opened up the vent, and hot air blasted onto my hands and face.

"Better?" I asked.

"Mmm-hmm." She smiled.

"Can I get out?" Maggie asked.

Shelly opened her door and leaned forward, giving Maggie just enough room to crawl out.

Maggie walked along the rocks, balancing somehow despite her misplaced center of gravity, peering out at the ocean. Despite every impulse to get out and reel her back in away from the edge, I stayed in the car, watching. She kept turning back to us, saying, "Look! Look!" For ten minutes, she just looked and pointed at the cold Atlantic below. And just as she was about to get back in the car, a few flakes of snow landed on the windshield, an answered prayer. She stopped and looked up at the sky, arms outstretched and mouth wide open. She was wearing one of Shelly's hats: it was a long striped stocking cap that had a big pom-pom at the end. It dangled nearly to the ground behind her. I'd given her a pair of Sorels somebody left at the station; they were giant on her small feet. The coat she borrowed was Shelly's old parka. It barely covered her now enormous belly. But still, there was nothing quite as beautiful as this. Snow falling softly, the sun setting, and almost the whole world below us.

On Monday I would start doing the books for Kinsey's, for the bowling alley. I'd lined up enough clients to make a living working at home until we figured out what to do next. I had some ideas then, vague notions of other places, possible new lives for the three of us. But for now, I had set up shop in the living room, next to the bassinet Maggie had picked out. On Monday, my new life would begin. There would be things to worry about, but right now, there was only this. My daughter. My *sister*. A baby. And snow. And I knew then that this was for-giveness. Right here.

EPILOGUE

Nativity

On Christmas Eve, we went to the train station so that Maggie could catch the Montrealer, which would start her on her way back home to Tuscaloosa. The baby had come a week earlier, surprising all of us except for Maggie, who insisted he wouldn't wait until Christmas.

Shelly was sitting next to me on the wooden bench on the platform outside the station, looking at the ground, as if she were only studying her shoes.

"You okay?" I asked. She nodded her head, but wouldn't look up. I put my free hand on top of hers, which was gripping the edge of the bench.

The air was cold, but not bitter.

"I sure ain't gonna miss this," Maggie said, gesturing to the ink-colored sky. She shivered. "Brrr. Is he warm enough?" she asked, leaning over the bundle in my other arm. She peered down into his face, rubbing her cheek against his nose and smiling. "His nose is cold."

When the conductor motioned for her to board the train (she was the only passenger getting on in Two Rivers), she picked up her suitcase and stepped back, looking at the three of us. Feeling awkward, I stood up, and she came to me, kissing my cheek. "I'll be coming to visit y'all by summertime. Y'all let me know when you're settled in your new place." I nodded.

Shelly lifted her head and wiped her eyes with the back of her wrist.

"You help your daddy," Maggie said, and kissed the top of Shelly's head.

She leaned in close to the baby again and whispered, "Bye, sweetness."

I looked at the infant nestled in the crook of my arm. She'd given him my mother's name, Wilder, followed by my own. *Wilder Montgomery.* He looked like Maggie, his skin like a smooth brown stone. But his eyes were mine, the ones I inherited from my mother, the still blue at the confluence of two rivers.

As the train hissed and rumbled and then slowly pulled away, Shelly's chest heaved with a pain I understood, a sorrow for something you had for a while and then had to let go. The sorrow of something lost: stolen or gone by its own free will, it didn't matter which. It all hurt the same.

"Ready?" I asked, putting my free arm around her shoulders.

She nodded and leaned into me, crying hard.

In the distance, the whistle blew loudly, and the baby startled in my arms. Quickly, I pressed him close. "It's okay," I said. "It's okay." We walked this way, the three of us pressed into each other, all the way back to the car.

It was past midnight by the time we got home, and snowing hard. Outside the door was a cardboard box. I brought it inside and opened it up at the kitchen table.

"What is it, Daddy?" Shelly asked, peering in.

There was a handwritten note on top. "Thought you could use these. Merry Christmas. XO, Brenda." Inside were stacks and stacks of tiny onesies and pants, little socks and tiny shoes and one puffy miniature snowsuit. Roger's baby clothes.

Shelly had insisted on hanging two stockings—one for her and one for the baby. She had also left a note for Santa with

her requests and two cookies, just
when she still believed. Just before
went to bed. After tucking her in, I to
my old room, where I lay him down
wrapped him like a gift.

My room was chilly, the windowpanes fra
like lace. He shivered as I powdered his bottom
diaper. Remarkably, after twelve years, my hands
how to fold and tuck and pin, and it made me think
ese paper folding. Origami cranes and frogs. I worked
pulling the soft cotton pajamas onto his tiny legs, puttin
little arms into the sleeves. And then I swaddled him in lay
of flannel receiving blankets until he was almost mummified.

Downstairs, the bowling alley was closed for the holiday,
and the apartment was strangely quiet without the crashing of
pins and the hollow echo of rolling balls. I turned out the
overhead light and watched snow falling in the bright white
beam of the streetlight outside my window. I lay down next to
him on the bed, my face close enough to his to hear the sound
of his breath. I put my arm across his chest and held him. And
even though—like Shelly—I knew better, it still was Christmas Eve, and because it was Christmas Eve, I let myself believe.
I thought about Mary, on the night her own son was born—
wondered what she must have felt like when she held him for
the first time. Because despite all the fanfare, she was really
only a parent, after all, just like me. And I bet she must have felt
pretty much exactly the way I did right now. Like I was holding the very world. Like the future itself was asleep in my arms.

like she
one
k Wilde
on the bea
med by frost, ice
changing his
emembered
of Japan-
quickly,
g his
ers

gelos, tangerines. *When I saw our future,*
nt, sweet, whole.

s in May. We loaded up the Bug with our few
...d said our few farewells: to the bowling league ladies, to
Mrs. Marigold, to Hanna and Paul. I said my own good-bye to the
trees, to the train tracks, to the leftover snow. To the mud, to the rain, to
the frost-edged grass on the side of the road. I said good-bye to Ray. To
Rosemary. To Brooder. And as we drove away, I waved quietly. To
Betsy. And to that night at the river.

Brenda's brother sold me the plot of land for a song. It was a
small, ten-acre orange grove just north of Tampa. It was already fully
staffed, and there was a house on the property, with three bedrooms
and a wraparound porch. When I pictured our new life, I saw myself
sitting out on that porch with Shelly, surveying the blue sky. I pictured
Wilder learning to walk among those trees. I thought about sunshine
and the sweet, sweet taste of oranges.

The grove was just about a half hour drive from Weeki Wachee
Springs, where Brenda had decided to return to her life as a mermaid.
By then, I had started to fall in love with her, the way you fall into
your own bed after a long trip. And, it seemed, she was falling in love
with me too. Even though we were both still broken and scared, when
I thought of tomorrow, I saw her there. Her rainbow tail, scales glis-

tening. For the worst fisherman ever, I'd somehow managed to catch myself a real big one.

But most importantly, the grove was just a day's drive from Maggie's house in Tuscaloosa. She planned to spend her summers with us, until she graduated from high school and decided what she wanted to do with her life. She told me she thought she might like to be a teacher, and I told her I thought that was a good idea.

Shelly fell asleep in the seat next to me before we even got out of Vermont, but Wilder was wide awake in his car seat in the back. As I drove, I checked on him in the rearview mirror every few minutes. Most of the time, he was just watching the world pass by in the window as he sucked his thumb or toes. But sometimes, I'd catch his eyes, and he'd be looking right at me. Those still, blue river eyes intent. Waiting for whatever was coming next. Trusting me to get him there safe.

TWO RIVERS

T. Greenwood

ABOUT THIS GUIDE

The following questions are intended to
enhance your group's reading of
TWO RIVERS.

Discussion Questions

1. At the beginning of the novel, Harper suggests that twelve years after the incident at the river he wants only to find forgiveness, to make amends for his involvement in the crime. Do you think that by the end of the novel he has done so? Why or why not? Is he forgiven? If so, by whom? Do *you*, the reader, forgive him?

2. Discuss the role that race plays in this novel. Is the crime against the carny racially motivated? Does what happened to Harper's mother factor into this decision? What are Brooder's motives?

3. Why do you think Harper agrees to take Maggie in? Is it a selfless act or a selfish act? How did Shelly factor into his decision?

4. What role does religion play in this novel? Do you think that Harper believes in God? Of what significance is the scene at the makeshift chapel in Roxbury?

5. *Two Rivers*, at its core, is a love story. Discuss the relationship between Harper and Betsy (both as children and as young adults). Does the tragedy of losing Betsy justify Harper's involvement in the scene at the river? Consider the blackberry imagery . . . both in the description of the carny's skin color and the memory he has of Betsy plucking a blackberry in summertime.

6. Discuss the mothers in this novel: Mrs. Parker, Helen Wilder, Betsy. How do each of them reject/redefine/

embrace motherhood? Are they victims of their times? Why or why not?

7. Discuss Betsy's pregnancy. What sacrifices do you think she makes to keep Harper from going to Vietnam? Did she have a choice? She blamed her father's stroke for trapping her in Two Rivers, so how do you think she feels after he died? Does she still feel trapped, now by her own pregnancy?

8. Is Harper a good father to Shelly? Will he be a good father to Wilder? Discuss his relationship with his own father.

9. In the end of the novel, Maggie suggests she might like to be a teacher when she grows up. What is it that she teaches Harper?

10. Why does Harper decide to leave Two Rivers? Could he and his new family have moved on without leaving? Where do you see his relationship with Brenda going, and do you think it could have gone there if they hadn't left Two Rivers?

11. What are some of the stronger images that stood out to you? How do they tie together Harper's past and present?

12. Discuss the effectiveness of the time period as a backdrop for Harper's story. How did the civil rights movement and the Vietnam War change his life and shape his views? Would you have made the same choices if you were in his situation at that time? Today?

13. All of the flashbacks to the fall of 1968 are in the third person point of view except for the last one, which is told

through Harper's first person account. What is the significance of this change?

14. Discuss the symbolism of the two rivers and their confluence.

For more insight from the author, visit:
www.kensingtonbooks.com/readinggroupguides